IGNITING IVY

samantha christy

Saint Augustine, FL 32092

Cover designed by Letitia Hasser | RBA Designs

Cover model photo by Reggie Deanching | RplusMphoto.com

Cover model – Blake Sevani

ISBN: 9781794243729

For the first responders.

Samantha Christy

IGNITING IVY

Samantha Christy

CHAPTER ONE

SEBASTIAN

"And your wife?" the guy on the other side of the counter asks me. He stretches his head to the side and looks behind me, then he checks his computer. "It says here the reservation is for Mr. *and* Mrs. Briggs."

I shake my head. "No. It's just me. That isn't a problem, is it?"

"No," he says. "We have several tours going up at once. We'll just add another solo rider to this one."

It's not the first time someone has asked about Brooke. It happened at the hotel when I checked in last night. I guess I should have changed the names on everything, but I didn't think it would be such a big deal.

"Step up on the scale, sir," the guy says. "They will seat you according to weight. Then you can head over there behind that wall to watch the safety video."

I laugh to myself thinking that just about every woman I know would take issue with this weighing rule. But then I see the lady at the counter next to me being weighed and I realize the only people who see the weight are the people behind the counter.

I go find a seat on one of the benches behind the wall. As we watch the video and are handed compact life vests that we buckle around our waists, I look around at the couples and families who are mostly excited to be here.

A few people look scared. Maybe they're afraid of heights.

One woman looks sad, which I find strange considering we're about to go on the excursion of a lifetime. It's said to be the best one on the island. I look around, waiting for her companion to join her, but nobody does. Maybe that's why she's sad.

"Please follow me." A woman escorts us outside and then directs each of us to stand on a number painted on the pavement where we're to wait to be called over one at a time.

I look at the big blue helicopter in awe. It's fantastic. We don't get to see many helicopters in the city.

I'm standing next to the sad woman. Her hair is blowing around from the wind being produced by the helicopter's blades. A strand gets caught in her mouth and I watch her get it out with a crook of her finger. She's beautiful. About my age. Petite. She catches me staring and gives me a weak smile. An obligatory smile. And that's when I notice a small smattering of freckles across her nose.

"Number two!" the person by the front door of the helicopter shouts for the second time.

I touch her shoulder. Her soft, tan, toned shoulder. "That's you," I say, nodding to the number she's standing on.

She walks over and gets helped into the helicopter. Then they call me over.

I'm seated in the front, next to the sad girl. We're in the two seats to the right of the pilot and there are four additional people sitting in the back.

"Enjoy your ride!" the helper shouts over the loud drone of the engine. "Aloha."

The pilot holds up a headset, indicating for us to put ours on. Then he gives us some instructions about speaking. Every two people have a small microphone to share, and if you want to talk, you have to press a button and hold it close to your mouth. Everyone on board will be able to hear what everyone says.

"While we wait our turn to leave, let's test the mics out," the pilot says. "I'm Dustin Holloway. I'm originally from Seattle, Washington, where I flew for the Coast Guard for twenty years. This is a tad less stressful."

We all laugh, but nobody can hear any laughter over the loud sound of the propeller.

"Let's have everyone introduce themselves and tell us where you're from and what brings you to the beautiful island of Kauai." He looks at me. "You can start, number one."

I hold up the mic to my mouth and press the button. "Hi, I'm Sebastian Briggs, but everybody calls me Bass. I'm from New York City and I'm" —I roll my eyes— "I'm technically on my honeymoon."

The woman next to me narrows her eyes at me and looks to the back where there are two other couples. She looks at me again, questioning me with her confused stare.

I shake my head. "Long story," I say to everyone who is listening.

I hand her the mic, her petite, soft fingers momentarily touching my longer, rough ones as she takes it from me.

"I'm Ivy Greene. I'm also from New York City. But, uh, we're not traveling together," she says, nodding to me.

"You going solo, too?" the pilot asks. "What brings you to the great State of Hawaii?"

She looks down at her hands and her eyes close for a brief second before she lifts the microphone to her mouth again. "Yeah. I'm going solo. I … I've just always wanted to see Hawaii, I guess."

She quickly hands the microphone back to me like she doesn't want to use it anymore.

"Small world," the pilot says. "How about the four of you in the back? You aren't from New York City too, are you?"

The four of them introduce themselves and then the pilot announces we're ready to take off.

I've never been in a helicopter before and from the seat I'm in, I imagine I will have the best view of all the passengers. I can see everything on this side of the helicopter, including what's under my feet as the floor is made of glass. I feel sorry for the people stuck in the middle. I assume they paid as much for their tickets as the rest of us but surely their experience won't be as spectacular.

I almost wish I could give my seat to the sad woman next to me. Ivy. What an unusual name. But it's pretty. And it suits her. Her hair is long and brown and parts of it are layered, and the ends of those layers curl up almost like vines of a plant climbing up her hair.

As the helicopter lifts off, Ivy grabs my knee and squeezes. When she realizes what she's done, she quickly removes her hand, her face turning three shades of red.

"Sorry," I think she says. But all I can see are her lips moving because I'm still holding the microphone. And all I can think about is that the hand of a stranger on my knee has made it feel like a bolt of lightning just shot through my body.

She grabs onto the sides of her seat instead of my leg. I want to tell her it's okay, that she can grab my leg if she wants. But I'd probably embarrass her since everyone on board would hear me.

The pilot gives us a history of Kauai, telling us it's the oldest Hawaiian island. He says hundreds of movies have been filmed here. He tells us everything from the history of the sugarcane plantations to the best places to eat.

I realize I'm only hearing about half of what the guy is telling us because for some reason, my mind is still on the hand that was momentarily on my leg. I'm being ridiculous. It's not like I'm some fifteen-year-old adolescent experiencing his first touch by a girl.

I try to regain my focus and force myself to listen to Dustin.

As we head off the coastline, he introduces us to the Na Pali Coast. It's breathtaking with crystal blue water meeting thin lines of brown sandy beaches in front of a backdrop of the greenest mountains I've ever seen.

Dustin explains that most of these beaches are only accessible by boat, and I wonder how much it would cost to rent one. I know I wouldn't be able to afford it, and it would be a waste to go alone, but damn—the pictures I've seen of this island don't do it justice. It really is paradise.

I look at everyone else to see if they are as awed as I am. When my eyes fall on Ivy, I see she is the most affected by the beauty of our surroundings. I follow a single tear as it makes its way down the right side of her face.

After the pilot doubles back to let those on the left side of the helicopter get an up-close view of the coast, we head inland, flying over the most picturesque landscape I've ever laid eyes on. There are so many waterfalls it looks like white hairs on a green background. There are hundreds of them.

When we come to the most impressive waterfall, Dustin hovers at a safe distance. "This is Manawaiopuna Falls, but you will all know it better as 'Jurassic Park Falls' from the movie."

For ten minutes, we fly in and out of valleys, admiring waterfall after waterfall.

When I take a peek at Ivy—*why do I keep peeking at her?*—I see she's got her own waterfall going on. Right down her face. I'm not talking about just *one* tear. She's downright crying. Ugly crying. Her body is shaking like she can't catch her breath. And to be honest, her reaction is taking *my* breath away.

"Are you okay, Ivy?" the pilot asks. "Do we need to head back?"

I hold out the microphone to her in case she wants to answer him. Her shaky hand takes it from me.

"I'm f-fine," she stutters into it.

"It is pretty breathtaking, isn't it?" he says. "Sometimes I forget that since I see it four or five times a day."

All Ivy can do is nod, more tears flowing out of her like she can't control it.

I feel compelled to reach out and grab her hand. Because I can clearly see that her tears are not tears of joy or awe. They are tears of pain. She looks to be in excruciating agony. It's hard for me to sit here and watch it. I help people. It's what I do. It's my job. At least that's what I keep telling myself as I resist the urge to comfort her.

If I talk to Ivy, the whole group will hear me. That's not fair to her. So I do the only thing I can. I sit back and look out the window, taking it all in, knowing this may be the only time I will ever get to come to Hawaii. Because guys like me—people in my profession—we don't normally get to take trips like this.

Dustin flies us over Waimea Canyon. And then he flies us down into it. He points out some popular lookouts and hiking trails. We see people standing on the edge of cliffs, waving at us as we fly by. I smile knowing I'll be one of those people in just a few days. Hiking the canyon wasn't on my official itinerary, but it's something I want to do. And it's free.

Thirty minutes later, after we've flown over a better part of the island, the pilot starts talking about flowers. The yellow hibiscus is the state flower. All his jabbering about flowers is the most boring part of the trip. Apparently, Ivy thinks so, too. Because she removes her headset, puts it in her lap, and closes her eyes until we land.

One by one, we are asked to exit the helicopter and are then escorted into a gift shop where we can buy T-shirts, souvenirs, and even a video of our entire flight.

While the other two couples stay and browse, Ivy and I head for the exit.

"Mahalo!" a worker says, opening the door so we can leave.

"Thank you," Ivy and I say simultaneously.

We silently make our way to the parking lot to find our cars. The lot is full of Jeeps—the rental car of choice on this island. I laugh as Ivy mistakenly tries to open the door of my rental, getting frustrated when her key doesn't work.

I come up behind her. "Maybe you should try these," I say, dangling my keys in front of her.

She looks down at her keys and then around at the other similar Jeeps.

"Sorry," she says, embarrassed. "They all look alike."

"Ivy?" I say, as she walks away.

I'm not even sure what I'm going to say to her. I just know I want to stop her from walking away.

She turns around and raises a brow.

"Since we're both here alone, maybe we could do some other things together."

"Uh, aren't you on your honeymoon?"

I laugh. "Technically."

"So where's your wife? Did she chicken out?"

"Yeah, she chickened out all right. She chickened out about nine months ago right before she was supposed to walk down the aisle."

Ivy's hand covers her mouth in surprise. "Oh, I'm so sorry, Sebastian."

"Bass," I say. "Or Briggs. Nobody calls me Sebastian."

"Okay. Well, I'm sorry, Bass. And I'm Ivy."

"I remember," I say, taking a few steps closer. "Is there a *Mr.* Greene?"

"No. It's just me."

"Well, we obviously have the same tastes," I say, motioning to the helicopter and then our identical Jeeps. "What do you say we have a few more adventures together? I have two tickets for just about every excursion on this island."

She ponders my question for a brief moment and then shakes her head. "I don't think so. But thank you."

"Are you leaving Hawaii soon?" I blurt out awkwardly.

She shakes her head again. "No. It was nice to meet you, Bass."

"You, too, Ivy. I hope you enjoy your stay on Kauai."

I hope you enjoy your stay on Kauai? Jesus, I sound like a travel commercial. Is that the best I could come up with?

She laughs sadly before waving and walking away.

As I watch her get into her white four-door Jeep and drive away, I'm left wondering what could possibly make a beautiful woman on a beautiful island so darned sad. And I find myself wishing I had the chance to find out.

CHAPTER TWO

IVY

I love walking along the beach. Especially at sunset. The beach here in Poipu isn't particularly long. Eventually, you run into black lava rock that is impassable. But it's long enough to get lost in thought. And sometimes it's long enough for me to forget.

I pass a point on the beach that juts out into the water and see a few seals catching the final rays of the hot sun. There is a woman, a volunteer named Erma, who I've gotten to know quite well over the past week. Erma gets called every time the seals are spotted sunbathing. She comes to the beach and cordons off the areas with rope so that onlookers don't bother the endangered seals.

Erma tells me these two particular seals have been coming for months. They've even been given names. Flip and Flop.

I stop for a few minutes to talk with her, letting her impart to me more knowledge of the monk seals that are so important to her and the State of Hawaii. I think Erma must be a hundred years old. Her skin is tan and weathered and has so many wrinkles it's almost hard to see the woman within. But she is happy coming out here to protect her 'babies.' She's content with her life.

I envy her.

A family comes over to admire Flip and Flop, and Erma excuses herself so she can go educate them. It's obvious she loves her work.

I continue down the beach, watching two small groups of surfers who are trying desperately to catch as many waves as possible before the sun goes beyond the horizon.

There is a man who works the surfboard stand at my resort. Every day when I walk by, he offers to teach me how to surf. And every day I tell him 'maybe tomorrow.' It's not that I don't want to learn. I think it might be fun. I just don't want to learn from *him*. He kind of creeps me out in a stalkerish kind of way.

I've thought about trying to find someone else to teach me. But like most of my other good intentions, I usually end up doing nothing. It takes all I have just to get through each day, and the idea of having fun actually makes me feel worse—guilty even.

It was hard enough to get the courage to go up in the helicopter today. It took me a week to work up to it. And it was every bit as wonderful as it was devastating. Just as I knew it would be.

And as hard as it was, it was a welcome change from my normal daily routine—which pretty much consists of walking the beach, eating, crying, napping, and then walking the beach again.

Only a handful of people are left on the sand at this hour. Families have packed up and headed back to their rooms to wash up for dinner. Most of those left are couples walking hand in hand, enjoying the magnificent colors of the sunset like I am. There is a woman walking her dog. There is a girl selling flowers. There is a man in the distance sitting on a lava rock, playing guitar.

When I get close enough to hear the guy play, I realize just how good he is. This guy isn't just strumming the strings—he can *play*. I'm in awe of the sounds coming from his acoustic guitar and

I find myself plopping down in the sand about twenty feet behind him just to get lost in his music.

Several other people stop and listen. One couple dances and then the man tries to give the guitar player some money, which he refuses. But he stops playing to have a conversation with the couple. When he stands up and turns around, I realize it's the guy from the helicopter this morning. Sebastian. Or Bass, as he prefers to be called.

He looks over at me and it's clear he's surprised to see me. He flashes me a brilliant smile and lifts his chin.

I stand up and give him a small wave before turning to walk away. Then it hits me—why would he be happy to see *me?* I'm embarrassed as I look around, certain he was smiling at someone else. But then he runs up alongside me, guitar in hand.

"Ivy," he says. He points to the resort we're standing in front of. "Are you staying here?"

I stop walking and wiggle my toes in the sand as I talk with him. "No. I'm down the beach a ways."

"Wow. Small world."

I nod to his guitar. "I heard you playing. You're very good. Do you play professionally?"

"I almost did," he says. "I even attended a music school for a few years before leaving to pursue my real dream."

"But you play so well. It's hard to believe you wouldn't want to do it as a career."

"I do love to play, but not as much as I love being a firefighter."

I cock my head to the side. "A firefighter in New York? You work for FDNY?"

He nods. "I do. You say it like you know someone else who does."

"My cousin did, but that was a long time ago. He quit to sell cars. He said it was too stressful."

"It can be pretty intense at times, but it's also very rewarding," he says. "So now that you know what I do, what's your profession, Ms. Greene?"

"I work for my parents. They own a chain of flower shops in the city."

"That sounds nice," he says, just as the girl selling flowers walks up to us. "And what timing."

"A flower for the lady?" the girl asks.

"Of course," Bass says, pulling out his wallet and handing the girl a few dollars.

"Bass." I touch his hand. "Thank you, but that's not necessary."

"I insist," he says with a warm smile.

"It's beautiful," I say, bringing the flower to my nose.

"Put it in your hair. Just over your ear," the girl says. She looks between Bass and me. "A flower on the right means you are single. One on the left means you're taken."

Of course I know this, being a florist, but I let her explain it anyway.

"Thank you," I say, putting the flower above my right ear.

I can see out of the corner of my eye that Bass is happy I put it behind my right ear. And although I'm still unsure of his intentions, I realize he is a welcome distraction.

The girl leaves just as the sun starts to get swallowed up by the sea. I'm mesmerized by the sight. I stand and watch the amazing beauty of it, happy and sad at the same time. Happy that I'm fulfilling a promise to do this very thing. Sad that the person I made the promise to is not here to witness it with me.

I hear the guitar again. It's soft and soothing and brilliant. Almost as if he has written a tune to go along with the setting sun.

"What song was that?" I ask when he finishes, just as the sun falls below the horizon.

He shrugs. "Something I made up just now when I was watching you watch the sunset."

I feel myself blush knowing I was the inspiration.

"You're very good."

"Thanks."

"Well, I'd better get back." I glance down at my bare feet. "It gets hard to navigate the beach after dark with all the lava rocks. It was nice to see you again, Bass."

"You too," he says. Then he studies me. "Ivy, I meant what I said earlier today. I have extra tickets for a lot of things. I'm here for two weeks and have no one to hang out with. Everyone else here is part of a family or a couple. I think we might possibly be the only two single people on Kauai. And we're about the same age. At least I think we are. I'm twenty-four."

"I'm twenty-four, too" I tell him.

"See? There you have it. And you walking down my beach is like the universe telling us we should hang out."

"*Your* beach?" I raise a brow at him.

"Okay, *our* beach," he says.

"I'm not sure that's such a good idea," I tell him.

"Why? Are you here with someone? You said there isn't a Mr. Greene. Is there a boyfriend? A fiancé?"

"No."

"Girlfriend?" he asks with a playful smirk.

I laugh. "No. No girlfriend *or* boyfriend."

"How long have you been on the island?" he asks.

"A week."

"And when do you leave?"

"On the twenty-ninth."

He looks surprised. "That's in four weeks, Ivy. You came here for over a *month?* All by yourself? Damn."

"I needed some time away."

He nods. "Bad breakup? Divorce maybe?"

I shake my head, averting my gaze.

"Well, whatever it is, I think we ran into each other for a reason. I'm going tubing tomorrow. Do you remember the pilot today telling us about the old sugarcane plantations that used to be here? Well, you can go tubing down the old irrigation ditches. You tube through caves and stuff. It actually sounds pretty fun."

"Yeah, I know all about it," I say, thinking back to last year when I learned all there was to learn about this island.

"But you don't want to do it?" he asks.

I shrug. I don't tell him it's one of the things I'm supposed to do. Just like the helicopter tour.

"Come on. It'll be fun," he says. "And educational."

"I'm sorry. I just can't," I say. "I should go."

I start to walk away, but he grabs my elbow and gently pulls me back toward him. He pulls me so close our chests almost touch. He puts his other hand on my shoulder. I close my eyes briefly in an attempt to shut down. To remind myself why I'm here. But I can't ignore the feeling of his hands on me. It's nice. It's demanding without making me feel controlled. It's confident without seeming arrogant. But most importantly, I realize that for a second, I could forget.

He doesn't let go as he stares into my eyes. I'm not sure what he's thinking, but I know what's going through *my* head. That he is the first man to touch me like this, to *stare* at me like this, since Eli. It's been what, nine years since a man other than Eli has had his hands on me? It's not that I haven't wanted it. It was just too complicated to try and be with anyone. And then, well, I was just too … numb.

Suddenly, a wave of grief overwhelms me, and I pull away.

He looks sad. He turns and picks up his guitar. "I tell you what, Ivy Greene. I'm going to come down here at ten o'clock in the morning. I'll wait right here by this rock until ten thirty. If you're not here by then, I'll go tubing without you. But I really hope you show up, because I have a feeling that behind those sad and mysterious eyes, there is a woman who needs to have an adventure." He reaches his hand out and I shake it. "Maybe she's even a woman I will write another song about. Either way, it's been a pleasure meeting you."

"You, too, Sebastian Briggs," I say, reluctantly pulling my hand out of his.

He laughs at me for using his full name. He smiles at me for remembering it.

As I walk away, I can feel him watching me. I want so desperately to turn around and look. But I don't. However, I do feel a smile creep up my face. And I realize it's not even a sad smile. It's a smile I haven't felt in at least a year. And it's damn welcome.

When I get to the point and see Erma packing up her rope, the seals having gone for the day, I finally turn around and look behind me. Bass is sitting on his rock, playing his guitar. And part of me wonders if he's writing a song about the girl he met today. The girl with the sad eyes.

And I think, for just a second, what would be the harm of getting lost in a fantasy for a while? After all, maybe a fantasy is exactly what I need—one that can bring me moments of peace.

CHAPTER THREE

SEBASTIAN

I sit on the large rock, feeling a bit battered and bruised after my second morning of surfing. It's not that I haven't surfed before, but the waves in Hawaii are far different from the waves in Jacksonville, Florida, where I grew up. But I'm beginning to get the hang of it again. Surfing is like riding a bike. There is a lot of muscle memory involved, and once your body figures out how to keep your balance, it becomes a lot easier. The hardest part most of the time is paddling out to the break point.

I check my watch and then peer down the beach. It's almost ten thirty. I decide to give her five more minutes just in case she's one of those people who is always late.

I rub my forehead. *Why am I obsessing over this?* I don't need a relationship right now. Especially with someone who seems so, I don't know, confused. But something about her is different. And I can't deny the instant connection I felt with her.

"Aloha, Mr. Briggs," a resort worker says. "No guitar today?"

I laugh and shake my head. I stayed out here for hours last night, playing guitar. Some of the workers heard me and came down to the beach after their shifts to listen. "Maybe later, Mr. ..."

"Tua," he says. "Call me Tua. You play very well."

"Thank you. Do you play?" I ask.

"I play the ukulele."

"Maybe we could make it a duet some night," I say.

He smiles. "I would like that."

"You could teach me some traditional Hawaiian songs."

"That I could. But now I must go back to work. And three is a crowd," he says, nodding over my shoulder.

I turn around to see Ivy standing behind me carrying a beach towel and a string bag. She holds up the bag. "I didn't know what to wear, so I brought a change of clothes."

I smile big. Then I realize what she's wearing, and I try not to outright ogle her. She's got on a sheer cover-up that barely hides the bright-blue bikini she's wearing underneath. And, Holy God, I know she'll have to remove the cover-up for our tubing adventure, and I wonder if I will even notice anything else on the tour.

I swallow and try to conjure up some words. "You were right to wear a bathing suit. You're sure to get wet. Uh, I mean, I'll get wet, too. Everyone on the tour will get wet." *Jesus Christ, why am I getting so damn tongue-tied?*

"I think we also need water shoes, but they'll provide those for us." I stand up and reach for her bag, slinging it over my shoulder. "I'm glad you came."

"I almost didn't," she admits.

"Why not?"

She shrugs, and I can see in her eyes that she doesn't want me to press her, so I don't. She's obviously here alone, in one of the most beautiful places on earth, for a reason. A reason she doesn't want to share with me.

"Come on," I say. "Let's go tubing."

We make our way to the parking garage underneath the resort I'm staying in. Ivy laughs when we walk through it. "How does anyone ever find their car?"

The spots are filled with dozens of Jeeps. When I find the right one, I point to the bright yellow window cling of a hula dancer on the rear window. "I may have tried to get in the wrong one myself yesterday, so I bought that at a souvenir shop."

She giggles, studying the silly sticker. "Good idea. Wish I'd thought of it. I'm always losing my car."

I open the door for her before getting in myself. "Do you go out a lot? Exploring the island or to restaurants? I could use some good recommendations for places to eat."

"I haven't been out much," she says, looking embarrassed. "I've been to the local market a few times. I have a full kitchen in my rental, so I've been cooking there."

"And the exploring?" I ask, putting on my sunglasses as I drive out of the parking garage.

She shakes her head. "The helicopter thing was the first time I did any of that. I do walk the beach a lot, though."

"You've been here a week and that was the first time you'd seen any of the island outside of our little strip of Poipu Beach?"

She nods, but again offers no explanation.

I wonder what would keep her holed up in her room for a week in a place like this. She must be dealing with some deep shit. I happen to have a few friends who went through some pretty terrible things. Things that kept them from fully living their lives for a lot of years. I think maybe Ivy is one of those people. Stuck in a rut she can't get out of. Maybe all she needs is a nudge. And I don't know why, but I feel compelled to be that nudge. More and more, I feel like meeting Ivy comes with some greater purpose.

My phone rings and I glance down and smile when I see who it is. "I hope you don't mind if I take this call," I say. "It's my best friend."

"Go ahead," Ivy says.

I put the call on speaker. "Hey, Penny. How's it going?"

"It's great to hear your voice, Bass. Have you found any hotties to surf with yet?"

Ivy snickers and covers her mouth.

"Aspen, I'm in my car and you're on speaker. And please don't make me sound like a player when I've got a woman sitting next to me."

Laughter dances through the phone. "Well, then you might want to warn me that I'm on speaker next time. Hello, woman sitting next to Bass, I'm Aspen Andrews."

"Uh, hello," Ivy says awkwardly. "I'm Ivy Greene."

"Ivy and I met yesterday on a helicopter. She's from New York City."

"That's fantastic!" Aspen squeals.

I can already hear in her voice that she's thinking this will be the one.

Aspen has been trying to set me up for months. Even though she lives in Kansas City now with her fiancé who plays professional baseball, she still picks out women for me by way of her friends back in New York.

"I won't keep you then," she says. "I just wanted to tell you the good news."

"Good news?"

"Sawyer and I picked a date."

"That's great, Penny. When is it?"

"January second. We wanted to be able to take a honeymoon before I had to be back for spring semester. And we've decided to get married back in New York City. It makes sense. It's where most of our friends are. Except Denver, and he's hoping to get an exception to leave Missouri. There's no way I'm getting married without him, so I'm fully prepared to cancel if he can't attend."

"I'll mark it on my calendar so I'm sure not to be on shift."

"You better not be on shift," she says. "You're my best man."

I sneak a look at Ivy, who has no choice but to listen to our conversation but is trying not to be obvious about it.

"You get to bring a plus-one, you know. I wonder who that will be."

I roll my eyes at her tenacity. "Goodbye, Penny. I'll talk to you soon."

"Bye, Bass. Bye, Ivy."

The phone goes dead.

"She seems nice," Ivy says. "And very direct."

"You are correct on both counts. She's the reason I'm in Hawaii by myself."

I glance at her to see the look of surprise on her face. "*She's* the one who left you at the altar? How is she your best friend then?"

My GPS tells me we're at our destination and I turn into the parking lot.

"She's not the one who left me at the altar. But she's the reason I got left there." I shake my head. "It's a long story, but right now, we're going tubing."

We check in at the booth in the warehouse. We sign a waiver and then get issued water shoes, gloves, and helmets with a light on top.

Ivy looks adorable in her helmet with her long hair cascading past her shoulders to just below her breasts. And those breasts, holy shit, now that she's removed her beach cover-up, I can see her tanned skin that is a contrast to the slivers of creamy-white flesh at the edges of her bikini top. She must do a lot of walking on the beach in that bikini.

I have to talk myself down before a full-on stiffy embarrasses me in front of our entire group.

We're loaded into a large van and proceed to follow two other vehicles through back roads to our starting point where we're given instructions by the guides who will go with us.

When we head down to the water, Ivy pushes me in front of her. "You go first," she says. "They said the water is cold."

I sit back into my tube, feeling the shock of the cool water, and then I watch Ivy do the same. As soon as her butt hits the water, goose bumps line her arms and her nipples pebble up. It's hard to get myself to look away. And she doesn't fail to notice my gawking. In fact, a hint of a smile crosses her face.

I've just made it my mission to make this woman smile. Because as beautiful as she is without one, I'll bet she could bring a man to his knees if she smiles at him.

I'll bet she could bring *me* to my knees. And it's refreshing to think that. Because even though I've tried dating over the past nine months, I've not felt this way about anyone. Not one girl has made my heart race and my shorts get tight. Not since Aspen. And it took me a long time to accept that we would never be together. I'm just glad we didn't let it ruin our friendship.

With Ivy, everything is different. I can't put my finger on it, but when I look into her eyes, I just know we were supposed to meet.

I start to drift away from Ivy and she reaches out to grab my hand. She pulls herself back over to me, but I don't release her. I realize we're holding hands through our gloves—the thick ones that ensure we don't cut ourselves on the sharp walls of the caves we're about to go through—but for some strange reason, that doesn't make it feel any less intimate. And the way she's looking at me, I know she's thinking the same thing.

The guide releases the rope that was keeping us from going forward and we start to drift down the narrow waterway that is heavily lined with all kinds of foliage, branches, and trees. We come to the first cave and are instructed to turn on our headlamps. The force of the water behind us has us rushing through the cave, bouncing our tubes off the cave walls like balls in a pinball machine.

It's dark, but I can hear laughter behind me. I hope it's Ivy. It sounds like Ivy. But she just doesn't seem to be the laughing type. I'm hoping to change that.

When we emerge from the cave, it's raining, and we've slowed to a crawl. Some of the people on the tour grumble about the rain, but not Ivy. She lets her head fall back against her tube then she opens her mouth and looks like a child who wants to catch the raindrops on her tongue.

I'm mesmerized just watching her.

Someone bumps into her from behind and her eyes fly open as she sits up. I could swear I see tears spilling out of her eyes. Then again, it could just be the rain.

We get separated in the next tunnel, and somehow, I end up in the front of the pack with Ivy in the rear. It's hard to control the tube, but I try my best to let people pass so I can ride alongside her. By the time we reach the fourth cave, she's caught up to me. And I'm glad, because in the middle of this cave, we are stopped and told to turn off our headlamps. It's pitch-black as our guide tells us a ghost story, one that has Ivy reaching for my hand once again.

I pull my hand away and remove my glove, putting my naked hand on her arm. She briefly pulls away from me and then places her bare hand into mine. And in the darkness, we hold hands. I wish I could see her face right now, but we're enveloped in total blackness. However, I'm not sure I need to see her face to know what she's feeling. The grip she has on my hand tells me everything I need to know. And when I caress her knuckles with my thumb and she gives my hand a squeeze, I smile. I smile in the dark because I know that little squeeze is the sign I was hoping for.

And I wonder if all this time, through all my heartache, Ivy Greene isn't just the woman I've been waiting for.

CHAPTER FOUR

IVY

As we pull back into the parking garage in Bass's Jeep, I think about our experience. It was everything I thought it would be and more. The glances. The bumping elbows. The hand holding. The lingering touches. Those are all things I didn't anticipate. Like the helicopter, the tubing excursion was another tough pill to swallow, knowing why I was there. But with Bass by my side, it wasn't quite as painful. And I realize that maybe this was more than just me using him to forget.

"Care to join me for lunch?" Bass asks as we get out of his car.

"I don't think so. But thank you so much for taking me tubing. It was a lot of fun."

He cocks his head to the side, studying me. "Was it? A few times you looked sad and I wondered if you even wanted to be there."

"I may not have wanted to be there, but I needed to be. And you made it fun. So, thank you."

I think any other man would ask me to explain. But he doesn't. He seems to get that I have something I don't want to talk about. He seems to get *me*. I see it every time he lets his eyes burn into mine.

He opens the car door again. "At least let me drive you home."

I pull my bag from the back seat. "That's okay. I like to walk along the beach. It's not far."

He walks me out of the parking garage and through the gardens that line the interior of his resort as we follow the path out to the beach.

"Which one is yours?" I ask, looking around at all the buildings.

He turns me around and points up to the fourth floor to a balcony overlooking the gardens and the pool. "That one."

I look over at the ocean and try to determine if he has a view of it.

"From my balcony you can just see a sliver of ocean through those trees over there. I'm sure my ex's parents paid an arm and a leg for the *ocean view*," he air quotes.

"Your ex's parents paid for this trip?" I ask, surprised.

"They did. And all the side trips, too. Hell if I'd be able to afford all this on a firefighter's salary."

I'm amused. "Sounds like there's a story there."

He laughs. "There is. How about I tell it to you over dinner? One of the workers here said I need to eat at a place called Kalapaki Joe's just down the way. It's a bar and grill that sounds right up my alley."

I think about it for a second, chewing on my lip as I stare at the water. It has been a nice change of pace to spend time with someone. It keeps me from going too deep in my head and getting lost there. That's why my parents sent me here after all, to find myself or something.

"I heard a few people talking about that restaurant when I was on the beach yesterday," I tell him.

"How about it? It's close. I could walk to your place and then we could walk to the restaurant from there."

"I guess I could do that."

"Six o'clock?"

I nod. "I'll meet you on the beach. My resort is the one with the red roofs."

"I think I know where it is. I walked right by there this morning."

"You like to go for walks on the beach?"

"I do," he says with a sly grin.

Maybe we have more in common than I thought. "Do you like flowers?" I ask.

"I do now, Ivy Greene."

I can't help my smile. I sling my bag over my shoulder and walk away. "See you at six, Sebastian Briggs."

His laughter trails behind me.

~ ~ ~

I try to take a nap, but all I can think about are those intense blue eyes of his. And his hands. They are so big that mine practically got lost in them. I'll bet he's a good firefighter. He's tall. And built. And protective.

I think about the only man I've ever been with and compare the two. Eli's hands are soft, like mine. Probably because he's a school teacher and doesn't need to use them to fight fires and save lives. And Eli's height is about average. Good-looking, yes, but not gorgeous like Bass. Bass is one of those guys they put on a firefighter calendar. He's probably *Mr. January*, or whatever.

I find myself getting all worked up just thinking about him, and before I know it, my hand is underneath my panties and I'm touching myself. I think of his eyes. His hands. His short, sexy hair. He's strong, that's for sure. He's the kind of man who can pick you up and carry you to bed. He's the kind of man who makes fantasies come true. And he's just down the beach. Alone. Asking *me* to dinner.

It's been so long since I've had the energy to even think about a man, let alone bring myself to orgasm over one. Yet, here I lie, rubbing myself harder and faster until I throw my head back on the pillow and call out his name.

Then, as I lie in silence, I'm overcome by enormous sadness. *How can I allow myself these moments?*

Immediately, I feel guilty. Guilty for feeling. Guilty for wanting. Guilty for living.

I shut my eyes and try to sleep it away. But I know I'm kidding myself. There is only one face I see when I dream.

~ ~ ~

His eyes take me in as he walks toward me. They start at the top of my head, stopping to appreciate the makeup I carefully applied, moving down to the cleavage my sundress reveals, and continuing to my tanned legs only to finish at my bare feet before he works his eyes back up to my face.

"Wow," he says. "You look fantastic."

I can't help my smile. I feel more thoroughly bedded after his perusal than I did hours ago when I made myself come. "Thank you."

He smiles back. "I knew you'd have a great smile."

I feel myself blush.

I had wanted to cancel and just hide away tonight. But his reaction gives me confidence that I made the right decision.

He nods to my shoes on the ground beside me. "Want me to carry those?"

"That's okay, you've got your own to carry. But thanks for asking."

If I've learned anything about Sebastian Briggs in the past twenty-four hours, it's that he's chivalrous. He opens doors for everyone. He's always concerned about others. He's very outgoing. He can hold a conversation with anyone. And he doesn't take no for an answer.

Okay, so maybe I know more about him than I thought I did. And I'm about to find out a whole lot more. He got left at the altar? That's got to hurt. I can't imagine. But he said it was nine months ago. I wonder why it took him so long to take this so-called honeymoon.

I wonder if he expects me to tell him *my* story. No way will that happen. The only people who know my story are the people who lived through it with me. It's still too hard for me to even *think* about my story, let alone say it out loud.

Because I do. Think about it. Every damn second of every damn day.

But then I turn and look at Bass and realize that for a moment today, when we were on the tubes in the dark tunnel, I wasn't thinking about my story. And on the beach last night when I watched him play guitar I wasn't thinking about it either.

So, no, I won't tell him my story. But I will use him to try and forget it. Not the whole thing, of course, because there are so many beautiful parts. Just the bad parts. The parts that rip my heart out and put it through a grinder.

"Nice day," he says, as we slowly make our way to the restaurant.

"It's always nice on Kauai. There hasn't been a bad day since I've been here."

"I thought Dustin, the pilot, said it rains more on this island than anywhere in the U.S."

"It does. But not always on the coast. And sometimes it will only rain for ten or fifteen minutes and then turn perfectly sunny again. Most of the rainfall occurs in the mountains. In fact, they had so much rainfall here last spring that they had to close off part of the island to traffic, which was difficult seeing as there is pretty much only one main road that goes around three-quarters of Kauai. I'm glad the road is open again. I might want to take a trip to the north side."

"You seem to know a lot about the island," he says.

"I do."

"Did you research it before coming?"

"You could say that."

I sense him staring at me as we walk. "You don't give much away, do you, Ivy Greene?"

I have the urge to smile when he uses my full name. But I can feel myself fighting it.

"Oh, look," I say, seeing a familiar face up ahead. "There's someone I want you to meet."

I introduce Bass to Erma and have her tell him all about the monk seals that like to sunbathe on the beach.

"I'm sorry you just missed them," I say as we bid Erma goodbye and continue on our way.

"Maybe we should come out earlier tomorrow and try to catch them."

My insides flip over at the thought of spending more time with him. "Yeah, maybe we should."

"Look at the waves breaking over those rocks," Bass says. He reaches into his pocket and pulls out his phone. Then he pulls me over next to him, turning our backs to the rocks.

He holds his phone at arm's length and snaps a couple of pictures. He looks at them, apparently unhappy with the way they turned out.

"Wait," he says, getting his phone ready to take a picture as he watches the next set of waves come in. "Wait. Here it comes. Ready? Okay, now."

We spin around, and he snaps the photo just as a wave breaks over the rocks behind us.

He shows me the picture. I stare at it far longer than one usually stares at selfies. I stare at it because what I see is most unusual.

I'm smiling.

"Can you send it to me? My family would love to see it."

I think that maybe seeing a picture like this—me smiling, and with a man—will get them off my back for a while. I'm so tired of the daily texts and phone calls. I swear, between Holly, Alder, and our parents, one of them is always calling or texting me. They call it being supportive. I call it suicide watch.

"Sure. Give me your number." Then he elbows me. "But I have to warn you that once I have it, I might just ask you out every night. I mean in a charming and not-at-all stalkerish way."

I laugh. *Oh, it feels so good to laugh.* Then I give him my number. Because in this moment I realize I want to see him every day. I want to see him every night. Because he numbs the pain. He's better than drinking. He's better than drugs. I should know. I've tried both over the past six months.

"There. Done," he says, sending me the photo. "Penny will freak when she sees it. She's been dying for a picture ever since we spoke on the phone earlier."

He points to a restaurant through the trees. "Look, here we are."

We go up the walk and are seated immediately by the back wall, which is all open-air windows overlooking some tennis courts, and beyond that, the ocean.

"Are all the restaurants like this?" I ask. "You know, open windows with a great view?"

He shrugs. "Don't know. But I think we should find out. I'll let you pick the place we go to tomorrow night."

"Is that so?" I say with a smirk.

"Yup." He waves his phone in the air. "I have your number now. You have to say yes, or I'll hunt you down and find you."

"But in a charming and not-at-all stalkerish way, right?" I joke.

The waitress comes by and takes our drink order. Then Bass shows me a text on his phone.

Penny: She's beautiful. You make a good couple. Tell her I said hello.

Bass taps around on his phone and shows me a picture. "She knows what you look like. It's only fair you know what she looks like."

She's very pretty. About my age. Brown hair. Slender. And she's standing next to a very attractive man. It must be her fiancé.

"She said her name is Aspen. But you call her Penny?"

"Yeah. We met when we were both freshmen at Juilliard."

She raises a brow. "You went to Juilliard? But you said you're a firefighter."

"I am. I dropped out of Juilliard after two years so I could focus on getting trained as an EMT, then as a paramedic, and finally as a firefighter."

"And Penny? Er … Aspen? Actually, what should I call her?"

"Most people call her Aspen. Her brother and I are the only ones who have nicknames for her. Well, and her parents, but they both passed away."

"That's horrible," I say.

"They died in a car accident shortly after she started at Juilliard."

"I can't imagine being without my parents."

"Me neither. They are pretty much the only family I have. I'm an only child. Do you have any siblings?" he asks, just as our drinks get delivered.

I take a sip, wondering just how much personal information I want to divulge. But talking about my siblings seems benign enough. "Two. Both older. Alder is thirty. He's married to Christina. They run the shop on Long Island. Then there's Holly. She's twenty-eight. I guess you could say she's my best friend. Holly and I run the shop in Brooklyn. Well, mostly she runs it. Especially lately. And my folks run the one in Manhattan."

"Alder? Holly? Ivy? Your parents really *are* into horticulture, aren't they? And a chain of flower stores. That's cool. What are they called?"

"The Greene Thumb," I tell him.

"Of course they are," he says, smiling. "I think I've seen your shop in Brooklyn before. Wasn't there a fire in the business next to yours a few months back? I vaguely remember having to cut through the wall to make sure it wasn't smoldering." He stares at me. "But I don't recall seeing you there. I definitely would have remembered you."

"I, uh … I haven't been working there much lately. But yeah, we had to repair a lot of drywall." I fidget with my menu. "So, you work at a firehouse in Brooklyn?"

"Engine Company 319."

"Are you ready to order?" the waitress asks.

We place our order and then a band begins playing Hawaiian music. It's lovely and we sit and listen. I welcome the break in conversation. It was starting to get a bit personal.

A few women get up from their tables and start dancing. I'm mesmerized. Their movements are soft and fluid and beautiful. And each dance tells a story to go along with the song that is being played.

One of the women sees me admiring them and she comes over and invites me to join them.

"Oh, no, I couldn't. I don't know how."

"I'll teach you," the short, stout, Hawaiian woman says.

"Uh … okay," I say, reluctantly following her over to where the band is playing.

I look at Bass with what I'm sure is terror in my eyes, but he just nods encouragingly. And for the next ten minutes, I'm all too aware of him staring at me as I fail miserably at learning how to dance in a way I've never danced before.

I must look ridiculous compared to the native women dancing next to me, but the moves they are teaching me are sensuous. And the way my body is moving makes me feel something I haven't felt in a long time. It makes me feel sexy.

And if Bass's heated stare is any indication, I'd say he thinks so too.

Suddenly, it's like a fire has sparked in my belly. One that was put out years ago. I wasn't sure it would ever be ignited again. This feels like more than just a moment I can use to forget. And as I stare at Bass across the room, I realize I'm not at all hungry for the food that's just been ordered. But at the same time, I'm a starving woman.

CHAPTER FIVE

SEBASTIAN

Dinner was torture. The whole time, all I could do was think about how Ivy looked dancing to the traditional Hawaiian music. The way she moved, it was damned sexy. And it made me want to write a song just so she could dance for me. In private.

On the way home from dinner, I reach out and grab her hand. She lets me. Together, we walk and watch the last of the day's die-hard surfers.

"I'd like to try that sometime," she says.

"Really? I could teach you. I'm no expert, but I grew up in Florida so I surfed a lot. I've taken a few lessons myself over the past two days, just to get back up to speed."

"There is a creepy guy at my resort who keeps asking if I want to learn how to surf. But the thought of his hands on me …"

I squeeze her hand. "But the thought of *my* hands on you—that's okay?"

She looks at me and I can't tell if she's blushing or not, but I'm pretty sure I have my answer.

We stop and watch the sun get swallowed up by the sea. The colors of the horizon are brilliant. Usually I like to be out here playing guitar at this time of day. The sunset is quite inspirational. But now, I think I've found a different kind of inspiration.

"Ivy, would you like to come back to my place for a drink?"

"No," she says, still looking out at the ocean.

I try not to be too disappointed. But after the day we've had together, it's hard not to be.

Then she squeezes my hand and nods behind us. "My place is closer."

Relief flows through me as a smile overtakes my face. I have the urge to pick her up and carry her, but I don't. I fear I've already scared her a little with comments of asking her out every night. But after what happened with Aspen and then Brooke, I promised myself I'd be truthful when it came to women. And it's true—I want to spend every day with Ivy. I can't even explain why I'm drawn to her. Maybe it's the fireman in me wanting to protect her from whatever is behind those sad eyes. Maybe it's the way she feels so much emotion when she sees a waterfall, or looks at a sunset, or when it rains. Maybe it's her intense beauty.

Whatever it is, I know we were meant to meet. And I plan on making the most of every minute we have together.

She leads me up to her rental. She's in a resort, just like I am. All the resorts on the beach are nice, but this one is a notch above the others. Every worker we pass seems to know her name and we are asked no less than three times if we need anything as we make our way through the grounds.

"Welcome back, Ms. Greene," a woman says as she holds the door to her building open. "Your bed has been turned down and the fruit you requested is on the counter." She hands Ivy a flower—one a woman might tuck behind her ear.

"Thank you, Leilani. Have a good night."

"Aloha, Ms. Greene. Enjoy your evening."

"That's the concierge," Ivy explains, as we get on the elevator.

"You have a concierge? Just for this building?" I ask with a raised brow. "I mean there is one at my resort, but she sits behind the desk in the main lobby and services *everyone*."

Ivy shrugs as the elevator doors open. We pass by two doors on the way to hers and I notice it takes a lot more steps to get from one door to the next than it does at my place. When she taps her key card to the magnetic lock and the door opens, I can see why.

The place is spectacular. It reminds me of the homes of a few of my friends. The friends who make millions of dollars a year playing professional baseball. I take a minute to look around at my opulent surroundings.

"Your family must sell a shitload of flowers," I say.

"We do. But it's just money, Bass. And money doesn't buy everything."

I watch her put the lone flower down on the counter. There is something dark and distant in her eyes. A sadness like I've never seen.

She sees me watching her and tries to paste a smile on her face. But it's not genuine.

"How about a glass of wine?" she asks, pointing to a bottle on the counter.

"Sure." I grab the bottle and go in search of a corkscrew while she gets some glasses from the cabinet.

"We can have a drink on the balcony," she says.

I pour each of us a glass and we walk over to the balcony doors, my jaw going slack when I see her view. It must be the best on Kauai. Her balcony wraps around a corner and she has an unobstructed view of both the ocean and the picturesque island.

We sit on the outdoor couch, sipping our wine as the stars become more and more visible in the sky.

"Why was Aspen the reason you got left at the altar?" Ivy asks out of the blue. "I mean, if you don't mind my asking. You did say you would tell me the story over dinner."

"I did, didn't I?"

She nods encouragingly.

I take a drink of wine and then a breath, hoping I won't be opening old wounds when I rehash the past for her.

"I was in love with her," I say.

"You were in love with Aspen?"

I nod. "You already know we met freshman year. We dated for a brief while, but we decided—well, *she* decided we were better as friends. So that's what we were. Friends. And we quickly became *best* friends. We spent every minute together. I helped her get through some bad times when her parents died. She made me not feel guilty about leaving Juilliard and following my dream. We became roommates a year after we met and lived together until she moved in with Sawyer."

"Sawyer?"

"That's her fiancé. Sawyer Mills. He plays professional baseball."

"Oh, right. He plays for the New York Nighthawks, right?"

"He used to, but now he plays for Kansas City."

"And you loved her the whole time?" she asks. "That must have been hard for you to watch her fall in love with someone else."

"You have no idea. But it was my own fault. I never told her how I felt. And I ended up doing some stupid things." I shake my head, remembering how idiotic I was. "I was jealous when Penny started having feelings for Sawyer, so I moved in with Brooke. She was an old friend from school who I knew had always liked me. Then when Penny and Sawyer got engaged, I went off the deep end and asked Brooke to marry me. I didn't really mean to. I was hurting because I knew for sure that Aspen and I would never be together. And I thought that maybe I was also losing my best friend."

Ivy puts her hand on mine. "I'm so sorry."

"It's fine. I'm fine now. But Brooke saw right through me and when it came down to it, she didn't want to be my second choice."

"Smart girl."

I laugh. "Yeah, she is. We still talk sometimes. It took me a while to contact her after she left me. But I needed to apologize. We're on good terms now. Friendly, but not exactly friends."

"And Aspen? Are you still in love with her?"

I take a drink of wine and think about her question. I've thought a lot about that very thing over the past nine months. And for the first time in almost five years, I know what the answer is.

"No, I'm not. I love her. I'll always love her, but like a friend. A sister. She's happy with Sawyer and I can honestly say I'm happy for them. It took me a while to get there, but I did."

"So, why wait nine months to take this trip? Did you wait until you were over her?"

"I had to wait until I had enough time off," I say. "I had just started my job a month before the wedding. For the past ten months, I've been taking on extra shifts and saving up my vacation so between my accrued time off and all the favors owed to me, I could take these two weeks."

"But what about the other ticket? Brooke was supposed to come with you? Why not just bring someone else?"

I shake my head. "There was no one to bring. Not that I haven't dated since Brooke. I have. But not anyone interesting enough to share Hawaii with." I lace my fingers with hers. "And now I'm glad I came alone."

"Tell me about Denver," she says. "The one Aspen said might not be able to leave Missouri for the wedding. I assume they are related—Denver and Aspen."

"They're twins."

"Oh, that's nice. Are they close?"

"Extremely. And it's killed her to watch him go through what he has. He was falsely convicted of a crime and now he's on probation and hasn't been able to leave the state for a long time."

"What was he convicted of?"

I shrug. "Some white-collar crime. Ponzi scheme or something. Aspen is one hundred percent sure he wasn't aware he was defrauding people. In fact, she gave him her inheritance to invest and lost it all in the process. Denver would have never taken her money. I met him a few times. Before he was arrested, he would fly up to New York so they could spend their birthdays together. Cool dude. He and I would jam sometimes. He likes guitar, too."

She puts her drink down and stands up. "Stay here. I have something I want to show you."

She goes inside and returns a minute later with a guitar. It's nothing special. Old and weathered for sure. But it brings a smile to my face.

I raise my brows in question.

"Don't flatter yourself, Sebastian Briggs. I didn't get this because of you. There is a second-hand shop next to the market. I was browsing through the shop last week and came across this, so I bought it."

"You play?" I ask excitedly.

She laughs. "Not much. I can strum a tune or two. Nothing like the way you can, though. I'm actually a bit embarrassed even to show it to you."

I hold out my hand. "Let me see it."

I spend the next few minutes tuning it. "It's not half bad," I tell her.

"Can you play something?" she asks.

"Of course."

I play the song I composed yesterday while I was watching her walk away from me on the beach. I finished it this afternoon.

"That was beautiful," she says when I'm done. "What song was that?"

"It's an original. I recently composed it."

"What's it called?"

"I call it *Greene Eyes,"* I say, looking deep into her chocolate brown ones, wondering if she understands the meaning.

Her skin flushes and her tongue darts out to wet her lips. We stare at each other until I put the guitar down and lean in for a kiss. When our lips touch, it's like nothing I've ever known. Her lips are soft. Delicate. Desperate.

I was worried she might not want to be with me. I was afraid I was scaring her away. But in this moment it seems all she wants to do is get closer. And when I deepen the kiss, she climbs onto my lap. She devours my mouth with such anguish I can almost feel her emotional pain. Part of me feels like she's doing this for the wrong reasons. But I don't care. I need her, and she needs me, and that's the only thing that matters right now.

I stand up, holding her in my arms as I do. She reaches out to open the door. I carry her through, not bothering to close it behind us because I love hearing the sound of the waves crashing against the beach.

I carry her into the bedroom and put her down on the bed. She quickly pulls away from me, rolling to the edge of the bed as if she just remembered something. She reaches over to put something into a drawer. A picture frame, I think. I didn't see what, or who, was in it. But undoubtedly, it's a clue as to why she's here.

"Kiss me again," she says when she rolls back over.

I crawl over her, hovering for a second so I can study the beauty of her lying beneath me. Then I lower my head to hers and taste her lips. They still taste like wine. She opens her mouth for me and I let my tongue explore hers again, this time more slowly and deliberately.

She claws at my back like she can't pull me close enough. Her hands are everywhere. They are on my arms, my ribs, my hair.

When I reach a hand between us and caress her breast through her clothing, she moans and I'm instantly hard as steel.

She untucks my shirt from my pants and pulls it up until I have no choice but to break our kiss and remove it. She works her hands under the waistband of my pants and boxer briefs and grabs the flesh of my ass. She arches her back as she pulls me into her.

"Take my dress off," she commands.

"With pleasure," I say, sitting up to straddle her as I hike her dress up and over her head.

"Those, too," she says, motioning to her bra and panties.

Jesus. I've never been with such a passionate and demanding partner. It's a huge turn on.

As soon as I've rid her of her undergarments, I remove everything else I'm still wearing. Then I take a moment to appreciate her body. Her creamy white breasts and pelvic area practically glow in contrast to the rest of her tanned body. My cock stands at full attention, knowing what's about to happen.

I'm about to climb up her body when she rises onto her elbows. "Please tell me you have a condom. I mean, I'm on the pill, but, well … you know."

"I get it. You don't know me from Adam. It's fine, I've got one."

In record time, I get my wallet out of my pants and retrieve it.

She narrows her eyes at me. "How long has that been in there?"

I laugh. "Long enough for you to think I'm a respectable guy, but not long enough for it to have expired."

Her lips turn up in a half smile. "Good. Put it on."

I motion to her naked body that I've barely even touched. "Don't you want me to—"

"Please," she says. "I need to feel you. I've never …"

She stops herself, looking like she might reveal something I'm not supposed to know.

"Whoa. Wait, you've never done this?" I ask, utterly surprised. The woman is twenty-four. And quite aggressive I might add.

"That's not what I was going to say. Of course I've done *this.*"

"What were you going to say?"

She raises a brow at me. "Do you want to talk, or do you want to have sex?"

"Right."

I put on the condom and climb up her body. I use my fingers to see if she's wet. I slide two of them easily inside her and then put my thumb on her clit.

She cries out, "Please, Sebastian!"

I've never liked the way my name sounded coming off someone's lips more than I do right now.

"Are you sure?" I ask, as my dick touches her entrance.

"I need this," she says, her eyes begging me along with her words.

I lean down and capture her mouth as I push myself inside her. Her tight walls feel so good around me. I pull out and push back in, each time going a little deeper. She grabs my ass, forcing me to hit the end of her. We both groan at the sensation.

"You feel so good," I tell her.

I increase the timing of my thrusts. She bucks her hips and squeezes me from inside. The sensation is almost too intense. It's all so much. The dancing, the guitar, the sunset, the beach. It's all a fantasy come to life and suddenly, she has become the woman of my dreams.

My balls tighten and I pull back and bite my lip, needing to wait for her. I reach a hand between us and pinch her nipple. Then I angle myself to the side and rub her clit as I continue to pump myself into her.

"Yes!" she shouts into the night. "Oh, God."

She spasms around me and I watch her face as her mouth falls open and her head lashes against the pillow beneath her.

I thrust one final time, my powerful orgasm rocking my body as I still inside her.

I collapse down onto her. "Jesus, Ivy. That was—"

"Fast?" she says.

I laugh, rolling to her side. "Hey, you were the one who wanted to speed things up. I promise you that next time, we're doing it *my* way. I'm going to take my time with you."

"Next time?" she asks.

"Yeah. Next time."

She lies back on the pillow, looking content. But not necessarily happy.

"Do you have any bottles of water in your fridge?" I ask.

"Yes."

"Stay here," I say, getting up to fetch them.

In the kitchen, I see the flower the concierge gave Ivy. I pick it up and bring it and the water back into the bedroom. I set the bottles on her nightstand and put the flower in her hair. I smile as I put it behind her left ear. The one that means she's taken.

She, on the other hand, doesn't smile at my gesture. She sits up with her back against the headboard and covers herself with the sheet. Then she takes the flower from her hair and holds it in her hands, studying it.

"Bass, I need you to understand something. I like you, I really do. But I don't want you to expect more than what we have here in Kauai."

I narrow my eyes at her. "The flower wasn't a marriage proposal, Ivy. I just thought that, well, since"—I wave my arm at the bed—"and we do both live in New York. I thought maybe we could, I don't know, date."

She shakes her head sadly. "I don't think so."

"You mean to tell me *'what happens in Vegas, stays in Vegas'?"* I ask.

"Yeah, something like that."

"Are you okay, Ivy? Did something happen to you?"

She shakes her head again. "I need this, Bass. Maybe more than you know. But when you leave in twelve days, that's when it ends. When I go back to New York, I'll be a different person. One who isn't capable of this. I know that makes me sound like a terrible person. One who will just be using you. And I guess I would be. But it's all I can offer. I guess you need to decide if you want to take it or leave it."

I think about what she's offering me. She's more beautiful than any woman I've ever seen and she's handing herself to me on a silver platter—no strings attached. It's every guy's fantasy. But then why does the thought of having her and then losing her eat me up inside?

I study her. I study the broken girl with the sad eyes and one thing comes to mind. Sawyer Mills. He was the same way with Aspen at first. Unwilling to let her in beyond the terms of their arrangement. And if he could get past his issues, maybe Ivy could get past hers. But Aspen had months to get him to open up. I have twelve days.

Ivy opens her bottle of water and takes a drink. She watches me as she puts the cap back on. "It's a lot to ask," she says. "And I'll understand if you say no. But tonight was fun. I enjoy spending time with you. So I hope you'll say yes."

"Under one condition," I say.

"What's that?"

"You do everything I'm going to do. You come with me on all my excursions and outings."

"You want me to give you the honeymoon you had planned?" she asks.

I laugh. "Well, we already consummated our relationship, so yeah."

"You drive a hard bargain, Sebastian Briggs."

"In the words of some naked girl I know, take it or leave it, Ivy Greene."

A small smile creeps up her face. "I guess I'll take it."

"Good," I say, taking her bottle of water, finishing it, and then placing it on the nightstand. Then I pull the sheet off her, yank her down so she's lying flat on her back, and work my way down her body. Right before I place my mouth between her legs, I tell her, "Because we're going to do this one *my* way."

CHAPTER SIX

IVY

I wake up surrounded by Bass. He's not here, he left last night. But I can still smell him on my pillow. I can still feel all the things he did to my body. It was like a dream. An escape. It was everything I never knew I needed and more.

He thought I was going to tell him I was a virgin. That I'd never had sex before. But what I was really going to say, what I almost said, was that I'd never felt like that before.

Sex with Eli was good. Even fun at times. But we were high school sweethearts. And having sex with someone at seventeen was awkward. We didn't know what the other wanted. We didn't know what *we* wanted. And even as we grew up, it never turned into anything like last night. It was always just … ordinary. Comfortable. Even after we broke up we sometimes used it to comfort one another.

I turn over in bed, noticing the flower Bass tried to put in my hair last night. It's a daisy, an unusual flower for a native Hawaiian to give a tourist, and I wonder if Leilani just ran out of all the other ones. I bring it to my nose, inhaling its earthy scent. Some people don't like the smell of them. I'm not some people.

I open the drawer in my nightstand and pull out the picture frame, running my finger across the face inside it.

"Maybe I'm not exactly going about this whole thing with Bass the right way, but I know you would want this for me," I say to it. "All you ever wanted was to see me happy. But how can I ever be happy again knowing you can't be? I'm trying hard to enjoy all the things we said we'd do together when we came here." A tear rolls down my cheek. "I should be doing these things with *you*, not him. God, I miss you so much, baby."

I place the picture back on the nightstand, knowing I'll probably have to hide it in the drawer again at some point. Because last night, I agreed to do whatever Bass wanted for the rest of his stay. And I'm willing to bet that includes a repeat of last night.

My body starts tingling just thinking about it.

There was nothing awkward or ordinary about it. Being with Bass was … passionate.

My phone rings and I look at the time, wondering what he has in store for me today. Without even looking at the name on the screen, I answer it.

"A tad eager, are we?" I ask with a smile.

"Eager for what, little sister?" Holly says.

I sit up in bed, pulling the covers protectively around my naked body as if she can see me.

"Holly."

"Oh my God!" she squeals. "You thought I was the guy in the picture, didn't you?"

"Oh, you saw that?"

"Are you kidding? Mom texted it to me as soon as she got it. I think we're all in shock. But, Ivy, we're so glad you've met someone."

"Don't get your panties in a twist, Hol. It's just casual. And I only sent it to Mom so you guys would quit bugging me all the time. I guess you drew the short straw today, huh?"

She scoffs into the phone. "There are no straws. We all care about you. We want to make sure you're okay."

"I'm okay," I say flatly.

"Are you?"

When I don't answer, she asks another question. "Tell me about him."

"There's not much to tell. He's on the island alone. I'm on the island alone. We're just keeping each other company."

"Have you shagged him yet?"

"Holly!"

"Oh, come on. Spill. Do you know how long I've waited to be able to talk to you about *your* sexual conquests? For years you've had to sit and listen to me talk about mine. And we both know that's a hell of a lot of listening." She giggles into the phone.

Unlike Alder and me, Holly has always been a free spirit. That's just a nice way of saying she's a bit slutty.

"I'm not giving you a play-by-play, Hol."

More squeals come through the phone. "So, you *did* sleep with him. Good for you, Ivy. Did he make you come? How many times? God, that man is seriously hot. He about made *me* come just from looking at his picture. How did you meet? Where's he from? How long is he staying? Are you seeing him again? Oh my God, is he lying in bed with you right now?"

I can't help but laugh at her inquisition.

Holly doesn't fail to notice. "And you're laughing? I think he must be a saint. Tell me everything."

I blow out a deep breath, deciding to tell her. She is, after all, more than just my sister. She's my best friend.

"If I tell you, you can't get all weird about it. Because it's no big deal."

"It's a *huge* deal, Ivy."

"Holly," I scold her.

"Fine. I promise not to make a big deal about it."

"We met two days ago on a helicopter ride. He asked me out then, but I said no. Then I ran into him on the beach. He's staying at a resort here in Poipu. He's a firefighter. He plays guitar. He's here for twelve more days. He's from New York, too. Oh, and he's on his honeymoon."

"He's *what?*" she screams through the phone, causing me to laugh again.

I spend the next ten minutes explaining, and by the time we hang up, I'm pretty sure *Holly* wants to date him. Heck, maybe she could. I could introduce them when we're back home.

Then something unfamiliar and unwelcome runs down my spine when I think about Holly with Bass.

I shake off the feeling and toss my phone onto the bed on my way to the shower.

Fifteen minutes later, as I'm towel-drying my hair, my phone pings with a text. I wonder which one of them is texting me. Mom, Dad, Alder, Christina? I'm sure Holly called all of them immediately after we hung up.

I pick up my phone and read the text.

Sebastian: Today's itinerary – meet at the beach after breakfast. Say, 10:00. Wear the blue bikini. I'm taking you surfing. Then after lunch, we're going hiking. Dinner will be at the place of your choosing.

It pings again.

Sebastian: Oh, and I had a great time last night, Ivy Greene.

I look at the time. It's only seven thirty. Even though I've been here for a week, it's hard to get over the six-hour time difference between here and New York and I find myself waking up very early. That's okay, though. Morning walks on the beach are one of the best parts of my day.

Me: See you at ten.

I pull on some shorts and a halter top and head out for my walk. I'm surprised when I see Erma out here so early. The seals don't usually come on the beach until the afternoon, but one of them is here.

"No rest for the weary?" I ask.

"I think she's hurt," Erma says. "I've placed a call to our marine veterinarian."

"That's awful. Where's the other one?" I ask. "Don't they always travel together?"

"Not always. This one probably got mobbed and came up here to recover."

"Mobbed?"

"It's what happens when a lot of males fight to breed with a female. She will often get hurt in the process."

I cover my gasp. "As in she was gang raped?"

Erma chuckles and touches my arm. "It's not as bad as it sounds, dear. It's how monk seals have behaved for millions of years. They don't form lasting relationships like humans do. Like you and that handsome boy of yours."

I raise my eyebrows at her. "We haven't formed a lasting relationship, Erma. We're just friends."

She eyes me like I'm full of shit. "Shame," she says. "You two make quite an attractive couple." She looks back at the seal and then at me again. "You know, Flip doesn't have any choices about how she lives her life. It's all pre-programmed in her genes. But that's the wonderful thing about humans. We have choices. And sometimes that one choice we make can define the rest of our lives. So think long and hard before you make yours."

People begin to encroach upon the seal, so Erma excuses herself to make sure they all stay behind the ropes she's placed around her.

I walk twice as long this morning, doubling back and re-tracing my route just to get the extra beach time. I think about what Erma said. Old people think they're so wise. They think they know everything because they have more life experience than we do. I think she's just spent too much time in the sun. Too much time watching people in love who walk the beach. Too much time seeing how happy people are here in paradise.

In paradise, she doesn't get to see the other side. The dark side. The side where people are taken away far too soon.

I look at the time and see it's nine thirty, so I head back up to get ready for my … date?

CHAPTER SEVEN

SEBASTIAN

"Are you okay?" I ask, helping Ivy up a particularly steep embankment of rocks. "You're not too sore from surfing, are you?"

"Not yet," she says. "But after a few hours of that and now this, I'll be surprised if I can get out of bed tomorrow."

"Then maybe you shouldn't." I wink at her. "I've been told I give very good massages, you know. And we've been pretty busy these past few days. Maybe we could take tomorrow off and hang out at one of our resorts. Sip Mai Tais, get tan, and play our guitars."

"I'm not playing guitar for anyone, let alone the prodigy from Juilliard."

I laugh. "I'm no prodigy. Just a guy who likes to play guitar. It'll be fun."

"I don't know," she says, looking like she swallowed a bug.

"Remember the rules. You have to do everything I say for the next eleven and a half days."

She looks at me from under her lashes. "Everything?" she asks.

"Shit, Ivy," I say, looking around. "You're going to make me hard. And it's not like I'll be able to hide it in my hiking shorts." I adjust myself through the thin material.

There aren't a lot of people hiking this trail, but enough so I can't press her against a rock and kiss her. But that's exactly what I want to do. Because I can't stop thinking about last night. It was unreal. While the first time was quick and dirty, the second was everything but. She let me have my way with her, any way I wanted. It was almost like she'd never been with a man before, even though she assured me she had. Being with her like that satisfied every fantasy I've ever had. But now that I've had a taste of her, I can't help but crave more. And if she's only giving me eleven and a half more days, I plan to taste as much of her as I can.

We come to another difficult climb on the trail and I have to help her once again.

"Are you sure you want to do this with me?" she asks. "I'm just holding you back. You'd probably be there and back by now if you didn't have me to slow you down."

"Hiking is more than just getting there and back. It's about the beauty along the way."

There is unbelievable beauty around us. The rocks, the canyons, the trees and flowers. But I wasn't talking about any of that. And I think she gets it based on the way she's looking up at me right now.

"Besides, there aren't many people who could keep up with me," I tell her. "I'm trained to climb dozens of flights of stairs with almost one hundred pounds of gear."

"A hundred pounds?"

"You know, oxygen tanks, axes, and hoses. That's some heavy shit. Not to mention our turnout gear."

"What's turnout gear?"

"Our coats, pants, and boots along with our hoods and helmets. Those alone are substantial even without all the other stuff we have to carry."

"That must be very difficult," she says, finding a rock to sit on once we get to a level spot.

"It was torture at first. And during training, we had to do it over and over. It was so hard that a lot of guys would have to stop and puke. But you get used to it. We still run drills like that every week, just to make sure we don't get soft or rusty."

"I have a question," she says. "In every picture I've seen of firefighters, like the ones in those calendars, they always wear suspenders. Is that a real thing, or do they wear those just to look sexy in the photos?"

I laugh. "You think the suspenders are sexy?"

She shrugs.

"Actually, they're an important part of the turnout gear," I say. "The bunker pants we wear are pretty heavy and we have to crawl around a lot. If we don't wear the suspenders, our pants could slip down and then our knee pads wouldn't protect our knees and we could get injured or burned."

She doesn't say a word, she just stares at me as I hover over her.

"Are you picturing me in suspenders, Ivy Greene?"

"Wouldn't you like to know?"

"Actually, I would. And that could be arranged, you know. I'm sure I could get my hands on some. Or maybe you could just come by the firehouse after we get home."

"Sebastian," she scolds me with a hard stare.

I hold up my hands in surrender. "Okay, okay. You can't blame a guy for trying."

I finish my bottle of water and then realize I have to pee. I point to a tree. "I'll be right back, nature is calling."

"Sometimes it's really convenient to be a man, isn't it?" she says.

I laugh as I make my way behind the tree to take care of business. While I'm there, I come across a bunch of brightly-colored flowers that look almost like sunflowers or daisies except they're pink. I pick one of them off at the stem and bring it back to Ivy.

I hold it out to her. "A beautiful flower for a beautiful lady."

"I … I …" Her tanned face turns ashen and she stares at the flower like it might burn her.

"You do like flowers, don't you? I mean, you are in the business." I turn the flower over in my hands. "I thought maybe it was a sunflower, but aren't those yellow?"

She shakes her head. Then she closes her eyes. "This isn't a sunflower," she says, obviously struggling to get the words out.

"Oh. Then what is it?"

Her eyes open again, and she looks at the flower once more. Then she looks away, a tear rolling out of her eye. She tries to hide it, but it's too late. I already saw it.

"It's … it's a d-dahlia," she stutters. Then she stands up suddenly. "I'm s-sorry, I have to pee, too. I'll be back in a m-minute."

I'm left staring at the flower, wondering what the hell just happened here.

I put the flower down on the rock Ivy vacated and then I lean against another one, waiting far longer than a minute for her to return. When she does, her eyes are red-rimmed and bloodshot.

"Are you okay? Can you tell me what happened?"

She shakes her head.

"Come on, Ivy. Please. Because whatever I did, I don't want to do it again."

She glances at the flower on the rock before she walks away. "Just don't bring me flowers and we'll be good."

I want to ask her more questions. Why is she bothered by this particular flower and not the one I bought her on the beach? Or the one the concierge gave her? Maybe whoever she's running from used to bring her those flowers.

But I don't ask her. Because her sad eyes are back. I hadn't seen them all day. Maybe for a minute the first time we paddled out on the surfboards, but I thought that was because she was scared.

She walks ahead of me until we get to the top of the large rock face—the one we saw people standing on from the helicopter the other day. It's a bit off the beaten path, so nobody else is here at the moment. I take a minute to stare at the picturesque canyon.

When I turn to Ivy to say something about the view, my heart lodges in my throat and adrenaline shoots through my body. She's dangerously close to the edge of the cliff. There are no fences here. No walls or railings to keep people from falling. *Or jumping*. She's literally inches from going over. One shift in her stance; one falter in her step; one strong wind, and she'd plummet hundreds of feet into the canyon below.

I carefully lunge forward and wrap my arms around her stomach, all too aware that if I make one wrong move, I could be the force that pushes her over. I quickly haul her back as we both fall onto the ground behind us.

She stares into my eyes, but she's not looking at me. It's like she's looking *through* me. Then one of her hands grabs my dick through my hiking shorts. I'm more than a little shocked and confused based on what just happened, but that's not going to stop me from letting this—whatever this is—happen. No matter what her reasons are for doing it, the bottom line is, I want her.

I quickly glance behind us to make sure nobody is around. Ivy, however, doesn't even seem to care. She just looks at me with that blank stare as she frees my erection from my shorts. Then she rolls on top of me, mounting my body, and without any pomp and circumstance, she moves her shorts and panties aside and sinks herself down onto me.

It doesn't take long before we're both breathing heavily. It could be the forbidden excitement of the public venue we're in. It could be the pure desperation in her eyes. It could be that I want her more than I've ever wanted anyone. But whatever the cause, we're both brought to climax in record time.

She slumps over onto me, her body shaking. I'm just not sure it's shaking from her orgasm. I think she might be crying. But I don't ask her, because although I don't know her very well yet, I know in my gut she needed this. She needed this random, intense encounter. Maybe she even needed it to keep herself from going over that cliff.

I can't deny that sex, however we may have it, is amazing with Ivy. But as I feel her body shake on top of me, it has me wondering if she needs it more than she wants it.

She sighs deeply before getting on her knees and righting her shorts. I hand her a small towel from my pack, knowing she'll need to clean herself up. She does, discreetly. Then she looks out into the deep canyon. "I know what I'm doing, Bass. I don't need you to save me, you know."

I'm not sure what she means by that. And at this point, I can't tell if she's just fearless, or suicidal.

When we went surfing this morning, she got way too close to the rocks, even after I told her how to avoid them. And when I caught a wave without her, she paddled out even farther, far past the break point, where she just sat on the surfboard looking out into the vast ocean.

"Look at the helicopter," I say, as another one flies through the canyon. "Two days ago, that was us. We were looking down here and seeing the people who looked as small as ants. And now *we're* the ants, and we're looking at *them*. We've been on both sides of the coin, and it's amazing how different they are. Down here, we feel small, insignificant, almost invisible. But up there, we felt larger than life. Invincible. Isn't it amazing how seeing the same thing from two viewpoints can change your perception?"

She nods. I think she gets what I'm trying to say. But that doesn't mean she'll change the way she feels about whatever happened to her. And after what just happened with the flower and the cliff, I'm sure whatever happened to her was life-altering. She's experienced profound loss—that I'm sure of. I've seen a lot of loss over the past ten months. In my line of work, I'm always seeing people get injured. People dying. People getting pulled away from loved ones. Ivy's got that same look. And it guts me.

"I can see why they call this the Grand Canyon of the Pacific," she says, standing up, but keeping a respectable distance from the edge.

"It's pretty fantastic, isn't it? I was told that if I was coming to Kauai, I had to hike Waimea Canyon."

She looks sad when she stares at the ground. "Yeah, I was told that, too."

I reach out and grab her hand, grateful that she doesn't pull away.

"Come on," I say. "Let's head back before it gets dark."

CHAPTER EIGHT

IVY

Yesterday was exhausting. Physically. Emotionally.

And I think Bass knew it. He walked me home after dinner, kissing me at my door without asking to come in. I wanted him to come in. I needed something to numb the pain. But I wasn't going to beg. He's already getting closer than I want.

I know he thinks he can change my mind about what happens when we get back to New York. But what he doesn't know is that he won't want *that* Ivy. The Ivy who doesn't get out of bed. The one who doesn't go on helicopter rides and canyon hikes.

I cried myself to sleep last night after taking a sleeping pill. I don't dream when I take them. And after the day I had, there was no way I wanted to dream.

Bass didn't know it, but everything we did yesterday were things I was supposed to do. Things I promised to do. Things that gutted me to do.

I roll over in bed and grab the picture frame. I run my fingers across the face inside. "I'm trying," I say. "It may have taken me a while, but I'm doing everything you wanted me to do. And it's just as beautiful as we thought it would be. All of it. The waterfalls, the ocean, the canyon. I know I promised to enjoy it. And sometimes I do. But when I start to enjoy it too much, I feel guilty. Do you think that's crazy? Do you think I'm crazy to feel guilty when things make me happy?"

Bass's face pops into my head and I sigh. "I know he thinks he can make me happy. And maybe he can for a minute or an hour even. But then when I remember …"

I realize what I just said, and a tear escapes my eye. "Oh, baby. It's not that I forget you. I could never forget you. Not in a million years. But sometimes there are moments. Fleeting moments where I think I might feel normal. But those are the moments that make me feel terrible because you're not here. I'm sorry, I know that's not what you wanted for me. But I'm trying. I promise you, Mommy is trying."

I trace my fingers across the curve of her smiling lips. Her chocolate eyes dance with laughter. I don't know how she was ever this happy or carefree, knowing what was happening to her. She was so much stronger than I was. Stronger than I could ever be.

I hug the picture frame and stare out the window, remembering the day we said we'd come here.

"Spin it, Mommy," Dahlia says. "And wherever my finger lands, that's where we'll go."

"Okay," I say, giving the globe a big spin.

"Promise?" she asks, watching it go around and around.

I run my hand down the back of her hair. "I promise, baby."

When the globe stops spinning and her finger touches it, she squeals in delight. "Hawaii," she says gleefully.

"Let me see," I say, squinting my eyes to look at which island her finger landed on. "It's Kauai."

Dahlia grabs my iPad off her table, handing it to me. I smile. I know the drill. I Google Kauai and show her the pictures, then she reads the text, me helping her with the bigger words.

"Waterfalls!" she squeals. "Oh, Mommy, can we go? Please, can we go?"

I look at my sick little girl, machines spread across her hospital room. "Of course we can," I say, knowing the only way we would ever get there would be in our dreams.

We spend the next few hours researching the island. After all, we have nothing better to do while Dahlia is tied to her bed as she gets her dialysis.

The needles don't even bother her anymore. She barely flinches when they put them in. But I do. I always have. Every time they stick a needle into my little girl, I feel like it's going straight into my own heart.

"It rains a lot there," she says, after reading it in an article. "That must be why they have so many flowers. It's the perfect place to go, isn't it, Mommy? I think you would look pretty with one of those flowers in your hair."

I take a piece of her short, thin hair into my hand. "I think you would, too."

A nurse comes in to check on her. "How are we doing?" she asks. Then she sees the globe. "Oh, where are you going today?"

She knows us all too well. All the pediatric staff do.

"Hawaii," Dahlia blurts out. "It's so pretty there. They have waterfalls and flowers and lots and lots of rain. We're going there."

The nurse gives her a sad smile. Dahlia has been on the transplant list for months, ever since her first transplant started showing signs of failure. We both know there is a three-to-five-year average wait for a kidney transplant, and even with her being a high priority, Dahlia having a rare blood type means she could have to wait even longer. And everyone knows she doesn't have that long. Including Dahlia.

"That sounds wonderful," the nurse says. "Will you wear grass skirts and leis made of flowers?"

Dahlia nods excitedly. "Mine will be made out of daisies," she says. "They're my favorite."

She starts to tire when her dialysis is almost done. I crawl into bed with her and cradle her in my arms.

My little girl yawns. Then she snuggles into me. "I want you to go, Mommy. Please say you will. Please say you'll go no matter what."

"Okay, baby." I kiss her soft hair. "Okay."

"No matter what," she says, her soft words trailing off as she fights sleep. "You have to promise."

A single tear rolls out of my eye as I watch her drift to sleep. "I promise, baby girl."

My phone pings with a text.

> **Sebastian: Are you ready? You'd better hurry or you'll miss it.**

I kiss Dahlia and put the frame back in its place. Then I roll out of bed, splash some water on my face and throw on a romper to meet him for our sunrise walk on the beach.

~ ~ ~

Listening to Bass play guitar at sunset is becoming my favorite part of the day. Last night, we just made it back from Waimea in time to see the sun go down, and a guy named Tua brought his ukulele, and together, they drew quite a crowd.

Today, however, there's a large turtle on the sand just down the beach that has drawn people away, so Bass and I sit by the fire pit, just the two of us, as he strums away.

I recognize the tune he's playing. It's the one he wrote for me. Or about me. I'm still not sure which. It sounds even better tonight. Every time he plays it, he adds something. A chord here, a note there. And unlike me, he doesn't have to look at the guitar as he plays it. He looks at me. It's like he's making love to me with the song.

I squirm around on the bench, anticipating what will happen after we go back to my place for dinner. I wanted to cook for him tonight. He's taken me out the past two nights and neither time would he let me pay. I don't imagine he makes a lot of money as a first-year firefighter. And he's right about one thing, my parents sell a shitload of flowers.

They took over a single flower shop from my dad's parents when Grandma and Grandpa decided to retire. Then they turned it into a chain about twenty years ago. Fortunately, the stores have been quite successful. So, money has never really been an issue for us. They have three stores now. Three stores they plan on leaving their three children someday. One for each of us to run.

The thing is, I'm not sure I want to run one.

I still love flowers. Being surrounded by their beauty. Smelling their sweet fragrance. But now, they just remind me of my daughter. Especially certain ones.

"Oh, shit!" Bass says, putting down his guitar and running to the edge of the water. "Hold on, miss!"

I look to see who he's shouting at. There's a surfer who's hung up on the rocks that line the beach to the right of us, her board being pounded into them and she can't seem to stand up or get herself out of it. She looks completely exhausted and I wonder how long she was stranded there before Bass noticed her.

Bass takes off his flip-flops and carefully navigates through what I know are sharp and slippery lava rocks.

"Don't move," he tells her. "I'm coming to you."

The water is only a few feet deep where she is, but I suspect she's too worn out to try and stand and bring her board back in with her. And the bottom of the sea where she's hung up is lined with more jagged rocks. It's the spot Bass told me to stay away from yesterday when he gave me my first surfing lesson.

I watch him expertly work his way over to her and help her off her board onto a large rock. While she's sitting there, practically in a state of shock, he grabs her board and pushes it over the rocks so it won't be taken out to sea. Then he picks her up and carries her back across the dangerous bed of rocks to bring her to safety. And after all that, he goes back out to get her surfboard.

She finally calms down enough to thank Bass for his efforts. In fact, she calms down enough to ask him on a date.

"You have to let me take you out to dinner. I owe you big time for rescuing me. I'm not sure I would have ever had the strength to get myself out of that." She looks at him with doe eyes. "You're so strong."

I study the woman. She's young. I'd be surprised if she were a day over twenty-one. But even dripping wet, I can tell she's beautiful. And she's smiling at him. And I'll bet *she* doesn't hide behind trees and break down in hysterics on hikes. Or have to take sleeping pills to stop dreaming. Or cry every time it rains because she sees her dead daughter dancing in puddles.

He should be with someone like that. Not someone broken like me.

I walk back over and sit on the bench, giving him some privacy to answer her.

A few minutes later, the woman walks away, her surfboard tucked under her arm.

Bass sits down across from me, picking up his guitar and playing another song like what just happened was no big deal.

I can only stare at him.

"You okay?" he asks.

"I'm fine." I nod to his feet. "The question is, are you? Surely you cut your feet when you walked over the rocks."

"Nah. They're tough as nails," he says.

"Bass, you just saved that girl."

"That was nothing, Ivy. I run into burning buildings and hang off sides of bridges."

I gasp. "You hang off sides of bridges?"

"Yeah. Once when we got a call about a jumper. Don't worry, I was anchored. I wouldn't have fallen off."

I sigh. I try not to reveal too much with my eyes. I try not to think about how often I've driven over bridges in the city, contemplating getting out of my car and diving head-first into the water below.

"Are you going to go to dinner with that girl?"

He narrows his eyes at me. "Of course not."

"She's pretty. Why wouldn't you?"

He scoffs at my question. "First of all, rule number one of firefighting is not to get involved with rescues. They look at us as their saviors. It's not any way to start a relationship. And second, I already have a date for dinner—tonight and every other night I'm here."

I can't help the relief that rushes through me, and I scold myself for feeling jealous over another woman.

"So you're not allowed to date the people you rescue?" I ask.

"It's frowned upon," he says. "But it happens." He pats the bench beside him. "Come here."

I get up and walk around the fire pit and sit next to him. He hands me his guitar.

"Oh, no," I say, pushing it back at him.

"You said you don't play very well. I want to teach you. Please?"

"Fine." I pout.

He scoots me to the front edge of the bench and then hops behind me so I'm sitting between his legs. Then his arms come around me as he shows me how to play some chords. We take turns fingering the chords and strumming the strings. We play like this until the sky is black and the only light we see is coming from the fire pit and the tiki torches that illuminate the grounds.

When we stop playing, I lean back and relax into him.

"At the risk of sounding cheesy," he says. "We make beautiful music together."

I giggle as I turn my head to look at him. Then he kisses my cheek.

"I think I like this," he says. "Having you and the guitar in my arms."

I nod. I like it too. But I don't tell him that. It could give him false hope. "Are you hungry?" I say instead.

"Starving," he says, staring into my eyes. "But not for food. Come on, let's go stash my guitar and head to your place. You can cook me dinner and then I can have you for dessert."

My face heats up at the thought.

He leads the way to his room, holding my hand in his, rubbing his thumb across my knuckles the entire time. It's a tiny movement. One I'm not even sure he's aware of. But it's sending pulses through my body, and by the time he lets us in his front door, I'm pulling him across the room.

I push him down so he's sitting on the couch, and then I straddle him.

He laughs as he looks up at me. "Or we could just skip dinner and go straight to dessert."

He pulls my face to his until our lips meet. I kiss him softly. Then I work my mouth down around his jaw to his ear.

"Watching you save that surfer was kind of a turn on," I say, undulating myself on his lap.

"Really?" he says.

"Yeah." I kiss his neck. "Right up until she asked you out."

His body shakes with laughter beneath me. "You're not jealous, are you, Ivy Greene?"

I sit straight up and pull my cover-up over my head. Then I untie my bikini top. "Do I look like I'm jealous?"

He peruses my bare breasts with his eyes and then he explores them with his hands. "I'm sorry," he says. "I forgot the question."

I smile and lean into him, giving his mouth full access to my chest. He takes one of my nipples into his mouth as he works the other one between his fingers. A moan escapes me when I realize how hypersensitive I am to his touch.

"Do you know what it does to me when you make that noise?" he asks.

I grab the hem of his T-shirt and pull it over his head. I can feel his erection pressing into me through his board shorts.

"I missed this last night," he says. "You have no idea how much I fantasized about you when I got home."

I look down at him and boldly ask, "Did you … do anything about it?"

He smiles a crooked smile. "I might have."

I'm not sure why that makes me feel like high-fiving someone, but it does. I'm not supposed to want him to want me too much. It will only make things harder in the end. But the thought of him making himself come while thinking of me is really hot.

"What about you?" he asks, rubbing his erection against me. "Have you touched yourself since meeting me?"

I can only look at him and smile. Because I'm afraid if I say anything, he will find out that it was the first time I'd done that in years. And I'm not sure I want him knowing that.

"Shit, Ivy. I wish I could have seen it."

In a very un-Ivy-like move, I pull on the ties of my bikini bottoms, making the small scrap of blue fabric fall away from my body. Then I run a finger down my stomach until it reaches my clit. I rub it in slow, methodical circles as he watches.

Bass's mouth falls open. He's mesmerized by my erotic performance. I'm confused by it. This isn't like me. I'm the girl who lets the guy take charge. I lie back and let things happen. I don't do this. I've never done things like this. Not until meeting him. And the more I do it, the better it feels. And the better it feels, the more I lose myself to the world.

I like losing myself to the world. I like losing myself in *him*.

After a minute, he moves my hand aside, like his is jealous that mine was having all the fun. He pushes a finger inside me, sliding it in and out, searching for that tender spot that will take me to the edge of ecstasy.

"Oh, God," I say, my head falling back at the pleasure of his fingers inside me.

When he looks like he's ready to explode and I can feel his hard-as-steel length jumping beneath me, he stands, picking me up with him. I wrap my legs around his waist and kiss him as he bumps into a chair on his way to the bed.

"You have a condom, right?" I ask. "I know we went without on our hike, but I'm not making another exception."

He puts me down and reaches into the drawer next to the bed and pulls out a strip of condoms. As he tears one off, I eye him suspiciously and ask, "Just how much sex were you expecting on your solo honeymoon?"

He laughs as he lies down beside me. "I'm a firefighter. I'm always prepared. But just so you know, I got these yesterday. And I'm not planning on using these with anyone but you."

I peek inside the drawer as I try to hide my smile. "Just how many are in there?"

"Enough."

"How many?"

"Two dozen," he says.

I raise my brows. "Optimistic, are we?"

He eagerly removes his shorts as he stares at me. "Yes, I am."

The way he says it makes me think he's not just talking about sex. But I push that thought out of my head, because my body is screaming for release. "Mind if I put it on you?" I ask, reaching over to run my hand up and down his steely length.

He gives me the condom and then laces his fingers behind his head to watch the show. "Go right ahead, but after what you did on the couch, I promise you I won't last long."

"That's okay," I say, nodding to the drawer. "We have a lot of spares."

He chuckles. "That we do."

I open the package and roll the condom on a man for the first time in my life. It's oddly erotic. And by the look on his face, I can tell he feels the same way.

"Damn, woman. You about made me come."

I hover over him, teasing him at my entrance, ready to sink myself onto him.

"You drive me insane, Ivy Greene. Do you know that?"

I cock my head to the side. "Why do you like to call me by my full name?"

"In case you were unaware, you do the same thing to me," he says.

"So, that's why?"

He shakes his head. "Actually, no, that's not why."

"Then why?" I say, lowering myself onto him as we both moan at the sensation.

When he's fully seated inside me, I bend over and put my mouth over his, not willing to kiss him until I get his answer.

"Because it makes you smile," he says, right before raising his lips up to capture mine.

CHAPTER NINE

SEBASTIAN

We never made it back to Ivy's place for dinner last night. We ordered pizza up to my room and ate it in bed. Naked.

I asked her to sleep over, but she refused. I know she's trying not to get too close to me. She's holding back. She's holding back everywhere except sex. That's the one place she's incredibly passionate. It's like she's taking all the emotion she's hiding from me and letting it come bursting out when we make love.

I look at the time, willing it to go faster. It's only been eight hours since I've seen her, yet I can't wait to meet her after breakfast for a walk on the beach.

My phone rings and I pick it up to see Aspen calling.

"Hey, Penny."

"It's not too early there, is it?"

"No. I'm still lying in bed. I can't get myself to sleep past five or six with the time difference."

"By chance is anyone lying next to you?" she asks.

"Nope. I'm here all by myself."

"That's a shame," she says, disappointment seeping through the line.

"You were hoping to catch me in bed with her?" I ask, laughing.

"So you've *been* in bed with her?"

"Is this something we should be talking about?" I ask.

"Of course it is!" she shrieks into the phone. "You're my best friend, Bass. This is what best friends talk about. We can do that, right? Without it being weird? It's not weird anymore … is it?"

"If you're asking me if I'm still hung up on you, the answer is no."

"Then, yes, you should definitely spill. I have a half-hour before I need to be in class."

Unlike me, Penny went on to graduate from Juilliard and is now getting her master's in music. She's super talented and can play the piano better than anyone I've ever known.

"What do you want to know?" I ask.

"Everything. All I know is that she's from New York. You've given nothing away in your texts the last few days."

"She works in a flower shop in Brooklyn. Can you believe that? It's only a few miles from the firehouse. In fact, we put out a fire in a neighboring business just a few months ago. Her parents own the shop and two others like it. She has two older siblings. She's agreed to hang out with me here and do everything Brooke and I were supposed to do. So we're pretty much spending most of our days together. But she doesn't want to see me after we leave Hawaii. There, now you know everything I know about her."

"Wait, why doesn't she want to see you after you leave Hawaii?"

I sigh into the phone. "That's the million-dollar question. I have no idea. She's hurting, that's for sure. I think she came here to get away from something. A failed marriage. Death of a boyfriend, maybe. Something big for sure, but whatever it is, she won't talk about it."

"You've spent the last four days together and you don't know anything more about her than what you just told me?"

"Yup."

"What do you talk about?"

"Me, I guess. And stuff. Hawaii. New York. Seals."

"Seals?"

I laugh. "Long story."

"But you're sleeping together?"

I can feel myself getting hard just thinking about it. "Yeah."

"So, what, you're just not going to see her or call her when you get back home even though you live in the same city?"

"I guess. We don't really talk about it. Every time I try to, she changes the subject. Every time I attempt to get closer to her, she brushes me off. But she's so passionate, Penny. And I know she's going through some deep shit. I just wish I could help her."

"Maybe you *are* helping her."

"How could I be helping her?"

"You said you're spending a lot of time together. Maybe when she's with you, she's not thinking about whatever happened to her. Maybe you're her escape or something."

I think about what she's saying. And I remember Ivy telling me she barely even left her hotel room before she met me. Maybe Aspen is right.

"I'm no stranger to being in a relationship with someone who thinks they are damaged, Bass."

"Yeah, I guess you're not. The difference is, you had months to work on Sawyer. I only have ten more days."

"Sometimes it only takes one day, one moment even, for everything to change. Do you really like this girl?"

"I do."

"Then give it some time. Maybe she feels the same way about you but can't admit it to herself yet."

"Maybe."

"I hope you can change her mind," she says. "I'd love to meet her."

"Are you coming to the city soon?" I ask.

"In about a month. Sawyer will be there for four days during a series with the Nighthawks. I'll be on a break from school, so I'm staying longer, a week or two probably, so I can meet with a wedding planner and get a few other things going."

"Are you finally going to put the townhouse on the market?" I ask.

"I'm not sure. Sawyer really likes having a place to stay when we come back. Remember how long we stayed there over the holidays?"

How can I forget? It was their first Christmas together. The first Christmas in years that Aspen and I weren't roommates. They were always kissing, touching, or laughing. And they kept inviting me to do stuff with them. It was torture seeing them together like that when I still had so many feelings for her. But I'm glad it happened. It was something I had to go through in order to get over her.

And I am. I'm over her. Because all I can see when I think of myself with a woman, is the one with the sad eyes.

"I'm really happy for you, Penny."

"I know you are. And that means a lot to me."

I look at the clock and see it's almost time for me to go. "I have to meet Ivy in twenty minutes. I'd better hit the shower."

"Good luck with her," she says. "Don't push her too hard. But don't go easy on her, either. Sometimes people just need to talk about what happened in order to get through it. Hopefully you can find the right balance."

"I'm a firefighter, Aspen, not a social worker."

"You don't have to be. All you need to be is the person she feels safe enough with to open up to."

"Thanks, Dr. Freud."

"Anytime, *Sebastian*."

~ ~ ~

An hour later, Ivy and I are strolling along the beach.

"What's your favorite food?" I ask.

"Seafood, why?"

"Do you want to go into town tonight for dinner? I'm sure there are a lot of seafood places."

"What happened to me cooking for you?"

I squeeze her hand. "I guess we got a little sidetracked last night, didn't we?"

Her lips twitch with the hint of a smile. "I still have all the food I bought. It'll go bad if we don't eat it. So let's just eat at my place."

"Sounds good to me."

"What's your favorite movie?" I ask.

"Do you want to rent one tonight?"

"Not necessarily. I was just wondering."

She looks out at the ocean. Then she sighs. "You'd probably laugh if I told you," she says.

"My favorite movie is *Shrek*," I say. "It can't be any worse than that."

"Shrek? Really?"

"Yeah, why?"

"My favorite is *Frozen*."

I laugh. "So we're both fans of animated movies. Maybe we could have a movie night and watch them."

She shakes her head fervently. "No, I don't want to watch them."

"Who doesn't want to watch their favorite movie?" I ask.

"*I* don't," she says curtly, pulling her hand away from mine and walking out to put her feet in the water.

I'm beginning to think conversations with Ivy are like walking through a field of land mines. I just never know what's going to set her off. Flowers. Movies. Two seemingly benign subjects, yet she won't talk about them.

"Okay, then," I say, walking up next to her. "No movies. How about games? Do you like games? We could play one. What's your favorite?"

She looks over at me, pursing her lips. "I know what you're doing, Bass."

"What am I doing?"

"You're asking me all of my favorites so you can get to know me better."

"So what? Isn't that what people do who spend time together?"

"People who have a future, maybe."

"Come on, Ivy. You have to admit we're pretty great together."

"Yeah, we are. *In bed,*" she says.

"It's more than that and you know it. We both like the guitar. We work in Brooklyn. We've had fun together, haven't we?"

"Yes, but you must admit, I'm sure you'd have had fun hiking, surfing, and tubing with *anyone* here. It's not me who's making this a good vacation—it's all your adventures."

I want to tell her that it *is* her. That *she* is the adventure. That without her, all those things would have been far less meaningful. But I don't. Because it might push her away.

A dark cloud quickly overtakes the sun above us and I feel droplets of rain on my arms. I grab Ivy's hand. "Come on, let's head up."

"No. You go ahead. I'm going to stay here."

I watch as her head leans back and her mouth opens. Just the way it did when it rained when we were tubing. Her tongue comes out to catch a few raindrops.

I stand back, studying her as she tastes the rain. Then she twirls around in it.

It starts to come down harder, and my instinct is to take cover. But something is happening to her and I feel like I need to let it. Her body starts to shake. I don't think she's cold. I think she's crying. But I can't see the tears through the sheets of rain soaking her body.

My hair is matted to my head. My clothes are drenched. But I have no choice other than to watch this woman experience some kind of catharsis right here on the beach in the rain.

When a loud crash of thunder startles her, she finally looks over at me, gauging my reaction to her silent breakdown.

I reach for her hand and pull her up to the sidewalk so we can find cover.

"Wait!" she says, pulling me to a stop.

She wriggles out of my grasp and walks over to a puddle on the sidewalk. Then she jumps up and splashes down in it, just like a child might do. Then she closes her eyes again, lifting her arms into the air as if to summon something.

When a second crash of thunder assaults our ears, I run over and scoop her into my arms.

"Are you crazy, Ivy? You can't stand in water during a storm."

I carry her up to a covered lanai just outside of a neighboring resort. I set her down on her feet and she looks longingly out at the storm.

"Don't you like the rain?" she asks.

"Only when I know it won't kill me," I say. "What's so special about the rain?"

She looks at me, her hair dripping wet and her clothes stuck to her body. She cocks her head to the side, opening her mouth like she wants to say something. But she doesn't.

"What is it?" I ask.

"It's nothing. Just something someone used to say to me."

I smile softly at her, not prodding or pressing her, but letting her know it's okay to say what she wants to say. Letting her know it's safe.

She looks back out at the rain, then at me. "Rain is like a magic potion that makes the flowers grow."

Then she walks to the edge of the lanai and sticks her hand out to catch some more drops.

And that's when I know. I know that although it's only been four days and it's not really possible, I know I'm falling in love with her.

CHAPTER TEN

IVY

The past few days have been a whirlwind of activity. I've barely had two minutes to have a thought in my head. And that's exactly the way I like it. We've gone surfing a few more times. Hiked a different trail. Saw Kauai's largest blow hole. And went zip lining.

And the sex—it's only gotten better. We're learning about each other's bodies. What we like. What gets us there quickly. What drives us crazy with desire.

Eli and I never took the time to do that. We never got creative. We pretty much had sex on a bed—with him on top. It never would have occurred to us to have sex on the kitchen counter, or on a hike behind a large rock, or on the beach at midnight. I think one time in high school Eli and I did it in a car, but that was our only anomaly. He made me come sometimes, but not every time, and I was okay with that. I was okay with it because I had no idea something like *this* even existed.

For years, Holly has been regaling me with tales of her sex life. But I thought maybe she was different than me. That her carefree spirit made it easier for her to be with men.

I guess I never knew what I was missing. And it does kind of make me sad knowing I'll be missing it again when I go back to reality. Because the truth is, the only reason I'm able to be like this now is because this, here on Kauai, this is not reality. Some days it even feels like I'm not me. Like I'm having an out-of-body experience. Like I'm living someone else's life. Someone who isn't consumed by sorrow. Depression. Guilt.

I'm not a fool. I know as soon as I get back on that plane, everything will change. Once I get home and walk into Dahlia's room with her flower-painted walls decorated by her drawings, I'll be right back where I was a few weeks ago.

But right now, I'm in a fantasy world. And I know it has everything to do with the guy driving up in the white Jeep. As I watch his car come down the long resort driveway, I think of how he looks at me differently now. I'm not sure what changed, but in the past few days, he no longer pushes me. He doesn't ask me as many questions. He doesn't look at me with as much pity.

Maybe Bass has accepted the fact that this will all end in seven more days. Perhaps he's finally realized he doesn't want to get stuck with someone so broken. Whatever it is, I'm grateful.

I put the small cooler in the back seat of his car. I packed some sandwiches so we can have a picnic lunch while out exploring the island.

"Miss me?" he says when I hop in the passenger seat.

"Hardly," I joke, not wanting to admit, even to myself, that I did. "My lady parts needed some recovery time."

He reaches a hand over and runs it down my bare thigh. "I happen to be quite fond of your lady parts."

"Which is exactly why they are exhausted," I say.

"Where do you want to go today?" he asks when we approach the exit of my resort.

"Let's go right and take the tree tunnel over to the fifty."

There is a road, Route 50, that is the main artery on Kauai. The locals call it *the fifty*. Anywhere you want to go on the island, you pretty much have to use the fifty to get there.

"Right it is."

"Good. I love going through the tree tunnel."

In order to get to Poipu Beach, where we're staying, you have to go through an iconic tunnel of greenery. The road gets completely covered by a canopy of eucalyptus trees, leaving just enough room for cars and trucks to pass through. Last week, when we were on the helicopter, our pilot flew over it and we could see cars disappearing into one side and emerging from the other. And now we're one of those cars.

I sit back and wait for Bass to deliver another speech to me about how great it is to look at things from more than one perspective. But he doesn't.

We drive through a brief rain shower and he reaches over to grab my hand. I think he gets my love-hate relationship with rain. But again, there are no questions, not even when I become silent and stare out the window.

A half-hour into our drive up a winding road, Bass slows, pointing to a sign. It's a sign for a waterfall. Oh, God. I really don't want to see another waterfall. Luckily, I've been able to avoid them on our hikes. Seeing hundreds of them from the helicopter was almost too much to take. Waterfalls were one of the reasons Dahlia picked this island. And they are far worse than rain.

Before I can protest, Bass turns down the road, looking excited. "I've never seen one up close and personal before. Have you?"

All I can do is shake my head.

He finds a place to park along the side of the road that is lined with lots of other cars. He turns off the Jeep and gets out. When I don't open my door, he comes around the side of the car to open it for me. But I sit, frozen to my seat.

"Are you okay?" he asks.

"You go ahead. I'll wait here for you."

"You don't want to see it?"

I shake my head.

He sighs, probably wondering why I don't want to go, but not questioning me about it. He watches the other people making their way to the falls that we can't see yet from where we're parked. He clearly wants to check it out. He starts to make his way back to the driver's side. He's going to leave. For me.

"No," I say, feeling guilty. "You should go. We're here and you should see it."

"I really don't need to. It's fine."

"Bass, go. I promised my brother I'd call him today," I lie. "I really just want to stay in the car and make that call. I'm okay."

"Are you sure?"

I nod. "Yeah."

"Okay, I'll only be a few minutes."

"Take all the time you want."

I watch him walk away. Then I see a family pass by on the way back to their car. A little girl is holding her mother's hand, squealing about how wonderful the falls are. The girl has a flower in her hair. She must be about six years old.

Through my tears, I follow the family with my eyes until they are out of sight. Then something happens. I feel the strongest urge to get out of the car and go see the waterfall. I don't want to, but it's almost like I have to.

I slowly walk around the bend in the road, hearing the rushing water get louder and louder as I make my approach. I see dozens of people lining the railing that separates them from the valley below. I look over to see Bass talking with a man. I hang back, walking to an unoccupied viewing spot far from the crowd.

When the falls come into full view, I gasp. The power of the rushing water is incredible. And the mist it creates as it hits the rocks below fills the valley.

My emotions overwhelm me, and I have to turn my back to the waterfall and sit on the ground. I sit here and listen to the sound of the falls with my eyes closed, wishing for the millionth time that Dahlia were here to see it.

To my left there's a break in the fence, like someone had cut through the wire to make their way down to the waterfall. There is a flimsy rope that is attached to try and prevent anyone from going through.

I stand up and walk over to investigate. When I look beyond the fence, I see a trail that cuts through the brush. It disappears beneath the heavy foliage. I'm not sure anyone standing at the railing would even see someone walking on the trail.

I look at Bass to see him still talking to the man as they both admire the falls. Then I look back at the water, being drawn to it like I am to the rain. I feel the need to touch it. As if somehow touching it will bring me closer to her.

Without thinking too much about it, I untie the rope and slip through the break in the fence. The first part of the short trail is easy to manage, but I stop walking when something catches my eye. It's a flower. But it's not just any flower, it's a daisy. A single daisy. I look around for more, knowing daisies grow in bunches. In fact, they grow in such hearty masses that they invade gardens because they're resistant to bugs and pesticides.

I stand here, staring at the flower, wondering how a single daisy came to grow here all on its own. And even over the loud drone of the waterfall, I can hear her words. *'Daisies gonna make everything better.'*

As I get closer to the falls, I have to be careful not to lose my footing. I navigate my way down by holding on to tree branches. And a few minutes later, I find myself standing on a slippery rock behind the falls, about halfway between the top and the bottom.

I can just barely touch the water if I extend my arm out. I can't hear anything but the water rushing by me. It's loud and I find that I like it, because the loudness of the water quiets the voice in my head. It quiets *her* voice.

I stand here, letting the water rush over my hand, wanting so desperately to stand underneath the falls and let them engulf me. But I know if I make one wrong move, I'll end up falling thirty feet to the rocks below.

Suddenly, arms come around me and I'm hauled back against the wall of rocks behind me.

"Ivy, what are you doing?" Bass screams at me.

I can't answer him. Because I'm not even sure myself.

"You're not fearless, are you?" he yells over the loud sound of rushing water. "You want to die, don't you?"

I slip down the face of the rock until my butt hits the ground. I pull my knees up to my chest. My eyes are so blurry with tears, I can't even see his face anymore. And maybe not being able to see his face makes it easier for me to be honest. Honest with him. Honest with myself.

"Yes," I say, probably not loud enough for him to hear. "But I can't. Because I made a promise to live."

"Promise to who?" he says into my ear, sitting down next to me.

I just shake my head.

"Ivy!" he shouts. "Tell me. You can't hide from your pain forever. You need to let me in. Can't you see how much I care about you? Can't you see that I love you?"

My eyes snap to his. *He loves me?* He's only known me for *one* week. That's ridiculous. Not to mention how someone falling in love with a shell of a woman is unlikely.

I stand up and face him. "I don't want you to love me!" I shout.

"Why?" he yells back. "Why won't you let me love you? Who did you lose, Ivy?"

I ignore his question and walk over and reach out to run my hand through the water one last time. He holds on to me so I don't fall.

Then I turn and make my way back up to dry land. On my way, I pluck the daisy from its root and throw it to the ground. Dahlia was wrong – daisies don't make *anything* better. Nothing can make anything better.

As we emerge from the broken fence, people watch us. We're dirty and wet and I wonder if I'm going to get in trouble for trespassing. But nobody approaches us as we walk back to the car.

"Take me home," are the only words I say to him.

We drive in silence back to my resort. And when I get out of his car, I don't even bother getting the cooler I put in the back seat. I want away from this. From him. From everything.

"Ivy!" he calls after me as I shut the door and walk away.

But I don't stop. I don't even turn around. I just keep walking. I walk up to my room and collapse onto my bed, not even bothering to clean myself off. And I cry. I cry harder than I've ever cried before. I cry a waterfall of tears.

~ ~ ~

"That's it, Ivy," the doctor says. "Just one more push and your daughter will be here."

Eli grabs my hand and tells me I'm doing great. I'm excited, but terrified at the same time. The last time I did this, it was anything but a happy occasion. Waiting for my dead child to be born was every woman's nightmare. One I lived through. But this is different. She has a heartbeat. I could hear it on the monitor just a little while ago. She's alive. I'm going to have a baby.

"Just a little more, sweetie," the nice nurse says.

I shake my head, not having any strength left in me.

"Come on, you can do better than that," the bitchy, condescending nurse says, trying to do her job even though she clearly has a problem with me becoming a teen parent.

I muster up all my strength and give one final push, feeling the overwhelming relief of my baby's body slipping out of mine. Eli is asked to cut the cord. But I still can't breathe. I can't breathe until I hear her breathe.

When her little cries bounce off the walls of my room, I cry out myself. She's here. And she's alive.

Eli leans down to kiss me, his tears mixing with my own. "You did it," he says.

"We did it," I reply.

The nurse places our tiny baby girl on my chest and I wrap her in my arms as the doctor finishes his job. I look up at Eli. "Dahlia," I say. "I want to name her Dahlia."

For months, Eli's been asking me to pick a name. But I couldn't do it. I couldn't name my baby unless I knew she was going to be okay. Because last time when we picked a name early in my pregnancy, everything went wrong.

"Dahlia sounds perfect," he says, leaning down to kiss her.

One of the nurses comes over after we have a minute to bond with our new daughter. "We need to clean her up now," she says. "Don't worry, you can have her back shortly."

Someone else places wristbands on Eli's and my wrist just as the doctor tells me everything looks good 'down there.'

My huge smile feels like it could split my face in two. Not even the looks from that second bitch of a nurse bother me. The one who thinks Eli and I are too young to start a family. But she doesn't know. She doesn't know what we went through. She doesn't know Dahlia is a gift. She's not a replacement—she's a miracle.

Suddenly, there's some commotion around the doctor who came into the room to examine Dahlia.

The nice nurse comes over to us, not looking as happy as she did a moment ago. "They need to take your daughter for some tests," she says.

"Tests? Is she okay? Wait!" I cry as the other nurse wheels my baby out of the room. "You said I could have her right back."

The doctor comes over. "I'm Dr. Halburn, a pediatric resident. Dr. James just informed me that you experienced a stillbirth last year. Did they perform an autopsy?"

"Oh my God! What's wrong with her? She was crying. She's alive, right?"

He puts a hand on my arm. "Yes. She's alive. I just noticed some irregularities when I was palpating her abdomen."

"Irregularities?" I ask through my tears.

"It may be nothing," he says. "But if we knew what caused the death of your other child, it might be helpful."

"Death? She's going to die?" I scream.

"No. No," he says. "She looks good. We're just trying to cover all the bases."

Eli shakes his head. "They didn't do an autopsy. We were told that sometimes those things just happen."

"Sometimes they do," the doctor says. "I don't want you to worry. Your baby is in good hands. We're just being cautious."

"Dahlia," I say. "Her name is Dahlia. Please. I can't go through that again."

He gives me a sympathetic nod. "I'll be back as soon as I can. Try to get some rest."

"Oh, Eli," I cry. "What if—"

"It's not like before, Ivy. I promise you. She's big and healthy. You saw her. She was crying. Her eyes were open. She's going to be fine. They are just being cautious like he said."

He sits on the bed next to me and I cry in his arms until I fall asleep from exhaustion.

CHAPTER ELEVEN

SEBASTIAN

I haven't seen her since yesterday afternoon. She won't answer my calls. She won't respond to my texts. She didn't even go for a walk on the beach last night or this morning like she has for the past week. I should know. I've done nothing but stalk her resort, watching for her to emerge.

By dinnertime yesterday, I was going crazy and finally convinced Leilani, the concierge, to go check on her. She reported back that Ivy was okay.

But it's not true. She's anything but okay. I pushed too hard. Asked too many questions. And when I said I loved her—I'm sure that was the nail in my coffin.

Why did I say it? I'm not even sure I *do*. Maybe it's just the fireman in me trying to protect her. But, holy shit, was I scared that she was going to do something reckless.

And now she's shut me out completely.

I'm an idiot. First, I go for years without telling the woman I loved how I felt about her, and now I go and do just the opposite, spouting it out after only seven days of knowing Ivy.

I pick up my surfboard and head back out for another set. Every time I catch a wave and come close to shore, my eyes scan the beach for a certain blue bikini.

Late in the afternoon, I head back to my resort, trading my surfboard for my guitar, taking my usual spot by the fire pit.

"Aloha, Mr. Briggs. Where is your beautiful lady?" Tua asks, catching me sitting alone.

"She's not feeling well," I lie.

He nods to my guitar. "Maybe I'll come play with you later."

I shrug. "I'm not sure I'll be here. I'm not feeling so great myself. I might turn in early."

He raises his eyebrows at me. "A lovers' quarrel?"

"Something like that."

He puts a fatherly hand on my shoulder. "Not to worry. Nobody can stay mad for too long on Kauai. It's paradise."

I glance out over the water, but it's not as blue as it was a few days ago. I look inland at the mountains, and they don't seem as green.

"I hope you're right, Tua."

"Tua always right," he says, going back to his job of stacking some beach chairs as people are leaving for the day.

I take one last look down the beach before I stand up and start to walk away.

"Help!" I hear a lady scream.

I throw my guitar on the grass and run over to the woman who is clearly in a panic.

"My daughter. She was playing in the surf right over there, but now she's gone. I don't swim very well, so I didn't go in with her. I looked away for just a minute."

"How old is she?"

"Six." She covers her mouth in a painful cry. "Oh my God. Where is she?"

"Ma'am, she probably just went to the bathroom or for a drink. What's her name and what color is her bathing suit?"

"Bright pink with yellow flowers. Her name is Misty."

I call out to Tua. "Get some people and search the grounds for a six-year-old girl wearing a bright pink bathing suit with yellow flowers. Name's Misty."

He throws down the chair he's holding and runs to the nearby bar to do what I asked.

The mother screams again and runs toward the water. "There she is! Oh my God, she's drowning! Someone help!"

I see a momentary flash of pink, and then nothing.

I throw off my shoes and yell to Tua. "Call nine-one-one!" I look at the gathering crowd. "Someone run and get the lifeguard."

I grab the mother who is trying to go in the water. "Hold her," I say to a few other women. "If she comes in, I'll be rescuing *two* people."

A man runs up alongside me as I'm running into the water. "I can help. I'm a good swimmer," he says.

I point to where I saw the girl. "I'll come in from the left, you take the right, and we'll work our way around the area. She could be on the bottom, possibly being dragged out, so use your feet to feel around, too."

"Got it," he says before we both dive into the deeper water.

I try to stay calm and remember my training on drowning victims, something we don't see a lot of in the city. I dive down and attempt to search in a methodical manner, but it's hard with the surf coming in. It's only about four feet deep, but in the twenty seconds it took us to get out here, the girl could be anywhere.

It guts me to hear the mother screaming back on the beach every time I come up for air. I see a few more people swimming out to help with the search.

My foot touches something soft and my heart thunders. I reach down and feel a small foot. I pull the girl up and into my arms as I wade as fast as I can through the water to make it back to the beach.

A lifeguard is running toward me with a backboard. "Put it on the beach," I say. "I need her on a flat surface."

"I can handle this, mister," the lifeguard says, looking like he might pass out from fear.

"I'm a trained paramedic and a firefighter. Unless you've been to medical school, I'm taking point on this. Do you have an ambu bag?"

"Yes," he says, reaching into his pack.

"Good. She's not breathing. I'm going to start CPR and you breathe for her whenever I nod."

I hear so many things in the background as I try to bring her tiny, blueish body back to life. I hear sirens in the distance. I hear people crying. An officer arrives and is yelling at people to stand clear. But what I know I'll always remember about this moment are the blood-curdling screams of a mother who thinks her daughter is dying right here in front of her.

"Please, please," I hear myself chant as I press on her chest.

Then, just as the paramedics come on the scene, the girl coughs and water spews out of her mouth. I turn her on her side to help the water drain out of her. She coughs and coughs, water spurting out with each forceful ejection of air. Her mother drops to her knees, cradling the child in her arms as the paramedics try to peel her away to do their assessment.

The girl is moving her arms and legs, crying and scared.

The mother wraps me into a hug. "Thank you. Thank you. Thank you," she cries. Only now, she cries tears of joy.

One of the paramedics asks me for my name and number for their report and I give it to him and the police officer. I tell them every detail of the rescue. I know the drill. They need to document all of it.

They load the girl onto a gurney on the sidewalk, but before they leave, the mother pulls me in for another hug. "You've given me my life," she says. "I hope you know that."

I nod, swallowing the burning sensation that's rising in my throat.

I look over the woman's shoulder and see Ivy, frozen in place on the beach. Then I watch her lean over, hold her stomach, and wretch into the sand.

When she sees me, she tries to run, but her feet give out from under her and she collapses.

"Ivy!" I make my way over to her and put my hand on her shoulder. "Are you okay?"

Her body is silently shaking. She's almost in hysterics.

"Do you need help?" the lifeguard asks, no doubt seeing her pale face.

"No. I'm good. She's just upset by what she saw. Thank you."

She watches, her body heaving, as the paramedics wheel the girl away through the property.

"It's okay," I say. "The girl is going to be fine."

"The mother," she says with a shaky voice. "I wonder if she has any idea what you saved *her* from."

"I think she does. When she came up to me, she said I'd just given her her life."

Ivy nods over and over, tears falling onto the sand beneath her. Then she looks up at me. "I wish someone could have given me mine."

All of a sudden, my heart sinks into the pit of my stomach and my throat burns. "Oh, Ivy. Did you …" I can barely get the words to come out. "Did you lose a child?"

She swallows hard as her eyes close. "Not just one," she says, choking on her words. "I've lost two."

Her body wretches with sobs, as if saying those words was the hardest thing she's had to do.

She goes limp in my arms and I pick her up, carrying her through the grounds of my resort as I try to navigate the sidewalk through my blurry vision.

When I get her to my room and put her down on my bed, she cries. She cries long and hard. I'm not sure what to do. I've seen profound loss in my job, but I've never experienced it. I've never witnessed the extent of pain that I'm seeing right now.

I get in bed next to her, pulling her back against my front. I rub a hand along her arm then through her hair. I try to comfort her with a soothing touch, knowing she's probably dying inside. And she lets me hold her. She lets me hold her until she falls asleep from exhaustion. Then I hold her some more. I hold her until the sun comes up twelve hours later.

CHAPTER TWELVE

IVY

I squeeze my eyelids tightly shut, trying to stave off the light that's coming through the window. Something feels different. Something smells different.

I open my eyes and see Bass sleeping soundly on the pillow next to me and everything comes rushing back. He saved her. He saved that woman from a lifetime of pain.

He carried me up to his room and took care of me. I vaguely remember having a nightmare last night. He pulled me close and comforted me until I fell back to sleep.

He said he loves me. But I know all about trying to love someone who is broken. It doesn't work. It's why Eli and I split up years ago.

I lie here, staring at Bass, wondering what he could possibly see in me that would make him love me.

Maybe it's Hawaii. It's a magical place. I wonder if he would have fallen in love with *anyone* he met here. Maybe that's what he does—fall in love. He did, after all, fall in love with his friend. He could be one of those guys who is attracted to unattainable women.

Or it could be that he's a protector. He saves people by profession. He probably thinks he can save me. And part of me wants him to, even though I know I can't be saved.

He thinks I want to die. They all do. And maybe I *am* reckless, but I'm not about to fail Dahlia like that. So even though I've thought about it—I've thought about it a thousand times in the past seven months—I'm not going to break the promise I made to her.

She wanted me to live. She wanted me to live for her. She even wanted me to love. I think she knew, even at her tender age, that her father and I were better as friends. She would talk about me finding my prince. She would talk about him saving me. Tears well up in my eyes. I always assumed that when she talked about it, she meant save me from an evil witch, or a dragon, or from a tower in a castle. We did watch a lot of Disney movies, after all. But as I lie here looking at Bass, I think of how she was wise beyond her years. Could it be that she was talking about a *different* kind of saving?

I watch his eyes flutter open. "Good morning, beautiful."

I wipe a tear from my eye, knowing I look anything but. "Good morning."

He reaches out to grab my hand. "Are you okay?"

I nod, my head still on the pillow.

I lie here and wait for him to ask me about my breakdown. About my many breakdowns. But he doesn't. He just rubs his fingers across my knuckles, staring at me with a sympathetic smile.

When he opens his mouth, I brace for his inevitable questions.

"What's your favorite breakfast food?" he asks.

I laugh. "Pancakes."

He reaches over for his phone, calling in an order for room service. Then he scoots closer, pulling me into his arms, spooning me. I relax into him, liking the way it feels to be held this way. His arms are strong. I should know, I've been in them more than a few times.

I realize we're both still wearing our bathing suits, and when I move my foot back to hook it around his, I feel sand in the bed. He must have put me down and lay here all night. He slept in a sandy bed with a wet bathing suit—for me.

I wiggle my toes against his. "I think we need to change your sheets."

"Don't worry about that," he says in my ear. "Housekeeping will take care of it."

"I'm sorry you got such a bum deal when you came to Hawaii. I know you expected a lot more from your vacation."

He pulls me closer to him if that's even possible. "You got one thing right. I didn't get what I expected when I came here. I never expected to meet a beautiful woman. One with sad eyes who compels me to write songs about her. I never expected to experience all the great things on this island with someone who looks at everything with so much emotion, it's breathtaking. I never expected any of it. I never expected to feel this way. I never expected *you.* And I wouldn't change a thing, Ivy Greene."

I turn my head so he can see me smile. "Thank you."

"For what?" he asks.

"Just … thank you."

Bass hops out of bed when we hear a knock on the door. He directs room service to put our breakfast trays on the balcony. Once the server is gone and Bass ducks into the bathroom to wash up, I get out of bed and search for something to change into before heading outside.

Bass stops dead in his tracks when he opens the balcony door. "Wow," he says.

I put down my orange juice. "I hope you don't mind my borrowing some clothes."

"Some?" he asks, his eyes raking over my legs that are bare from toe to thigh. "It looks to me like you've only got on a shirt."

I flash him a peek at the boxer briefs I took from his drawer. They are under the Hawaiian shirt I stole from his closet.

"Shit, Ivy," he says, adjusting himself through his shorts.

"So you *don't* mind my rummaging through your clothes? Good," I say, smiling.

"Woman, you can rummage through my clothes anytime you want if it means you'll come out looking like this."

He leans down to plant a kiss on my head, then he grabs the bottle of champagne he had delivered with breakfast. He pours some into our glasses of orange juice to make mimosas.

He lifts his glass. "To a new day filled with new possibilities."

"I'll drink to that," I say, clinking my glass to his.

He pulls my legs up onto his lap and we sit and eat pancakes and drink mimosas. He looks happy.

He catches me staring at him and runs a hand up my thigh. "Let me spend the rest of the week with you," he says. "I have five days left and after all we've done together, I can't imagine being here alone."

"I—"

"Before you say anything, I want you to know I won't pressure you. There won't be any mention of the future. Or of that L-word. I just want to be with you for as much time as I have left here."

I study him, wondering if I've ever met anyone else as kind as he is. Or as handsome. Or strong. I think Aspen must have been crazy not to love him back. Heck, *anyone* would be crazy not to love this man.

Suddenly, I feel my stomach tighten and my breath hitch.

"What is it?" he asks, feeling me tense up.

"It's nothing," I say, not wanting to reveal that somehow, some way, in the last ten seconds, I think I fell in love with Sebastian Briggs.

CHAPTER THIRTEEN

SEBASTIAN

"So, five more days?" I ask, running my hand up under her shirt to feel her wearing my boxer briefs.

Damn, that's sexy—her wearing my underwear. But what would be even sexier is seeing them on my floor.

She smiles and nods.

I'm not sure what just happened, but it's almost like I saw something shift behind her eyes. I might have even seen them soften. I suppose it's because I promised not to push. Not to tell her I love her. Maybe without that pressure, she's willing to give me these last few days.

I can't imagine going back to New York and knowing she's there without being with her. But that's a problem for another day. Today, and for the next five days, she's all mine.

I can tell she likes where I have my hand. But she pretends like she doesn't notice it, taking the last bites of her pancake despite my fingers working their way under the thin material.

I laugh, watching her eat. "You really do like pancakes, don't you?"

"Yeah, I really do."

I remove my hand from under her shirt and make us two more mimosas. I pass one to her and then she climbs on top of me, straddling me right here on the balcony.

I pull the back of her shirt, *my* shirt, down so it covers her ass. Although we're on the top floor, I still don't want anyone from across the complex getting a peek at her—even in her underwear.

I take a long sip of my drink before putting it down and unbuttoning her shirt. I push the halves of the shirt aside, revealing her chest. With a finger, I trace the tan line underneath, around and over her amazing breasts.

Her breathing accelerates, and she starts to squirm in my lap. When I pinch her nipples between my thumbs and forefingers, she tosses her head back and moans.

I stand up with her in my arms. "We'd better go inside before we get charged with public indecency."

"Do we have to?" she asks.

"Why, Ivy Greene, are you an exhibitionist?"

She laughs, and it takes my breath away. "I've never had sex on a balcony before," she says.

I raise my eyebrows. "Well, shit. Now we have to." I look around the resort and see people bustling about. "But I'm thinking we'll wait until dark. And maybe we should use *your* place since it's right on the beach."

She bites her lip. "That's a date, Sebastian Briggs."

My cock jumps just thinking about it.

I carry her inside, whispering into her ear all the things I want to do to her.

When I put her down on the couch and look at her like I want to devour her, she says, "I'm feeling kind of dirty."

I raise an eyebrow. "I think I've created a monster."

She slaps my leg. "Not *that* kind of dirty. After sleeping in my bathing suit, I feel like I have sand in … unmentionable places."

I get even harder thinking of her unmentionable places. "Then why don't we go take a shower?"

"We?" she asks, biting that lip again.

"Definitely."

I hold out my hand, helping her off the couch, then I grab a condom out of the nightstand on our way to the bathroom.

"As much as I like seeing you in my clothes, seeing you out of them will be even better."

I push my shirt off her shoulders and then slip the boxer briefs down her legs. It's the first time I've seen her completely naked in full daylight and I have a hard time not staring at her incredible body like a driveling fool.

"You're gorgeous, Ivy."

She blushes. "Now you," she says, nodding to my shorts.

I remove my clothes and stand naked in front of her.

"You're the gorgeous one, Sebastian."

I've never liked being called by my given name. It's always sounded too old and stuffy to me. But I love the way she says it. I love the way she *looks* at me when she says it. Nobody has ever looked at me this way before.

"Come on," I say, leading her over to the shower.

I reach in and turn it on, placing the condom on the shelf. As the water warms up, Ivy wraps her hands around me, pressing herself into my back. I move a hand behind her and caress the soft skin of one of her butt cheeks.

"Is it warm yet?" she asks, impatiently.

I laugh at her eagerness before pulling her into the shower with me.

I watch as she stands under the stream of water, letting it wet her long hair as she arches her back into it. When her eyes open and she sees my heated gaze, she reaches over for the bottle of body wash. She squirts some into her hands. "I want to wash you," she says, looking down at my hard cock.

I smile, knowing I'm about to live out every adolescent fantasy I ever had. I hold my hands away from my sides in an invitation. "Be my guest."

She starts at my shoulders, forgoing the washcloth and using only her hands to lather me up. She soaps up every inch of my arms before moving on to my chest. She takes special care to wash my nipples, pinching them as I was pinching hers just minutes before.

She turns me around, running her hands along every ridge of my back, massaging me as she goes. Her hands run over my butt cheeks, kneading them in slow circles. When she uses a few fingers to wash the crack of my ass, I have to resist taking my cock into my own hands. I need a release like I've never needed one before.

But she doesn't touch me where I need to be touched. She finishes washing my thighs, my knees, my feet. She washes every inch of me before she washes the inches I crave her to wash. And by the time she makes it to my dick, I know I'm about to blow.

She squirts more body wash into her hands, watching the anticipation on my face as she lathers them up.

"Shit, Ivy. I'm not going to last long."

"Good," she says. "Because *I* need a good washing myself."

I groan at her touch when she takes me into her hands. She uses both hands to lather me up, taking time to make sure my balls get good and clean, too. She grips me harder and her movements become faster. I brace myself against the wall behind her as I watch what she's doing to me.

It doesn't take her long to bring me to a powerful orgasm and I shout out, her name echoing off the tile walls.

Her gaze follows the trail of my come as it drips down the wall and onto the floor before it swirls down the drain.

"Best. Shower. Ever," I say, when I regain my ability to speak.

She does a small curtsey and then leans provocatively against the wall, awaiting her turn.

"Payback is hell," I say, reaching for the shampoo.

"I'm counting on it."

I turn her around and lather up her hair, massaging her scalp as I go. I've never washed a woman's hair before, so I have no idea if I'm doing it right, but based on the moans coming from her, she doesn't seem to mind. I gently push her under the stream of water and rinse her hair until it's clean. My hands glide easily over her arms. Her stomach. Her creamy breasts.

I grab the body wash and squirt a good amount into my hands, torturing every inch of her body like she did mine. I take special care not to touch the area between her legs until the rest of her is clean.

She squirms around, her movements begging my hands to touch her there. When I finally allow myself to touch her center, she almost buckles at the knees. I use my body to hold her up as my hand explores her silky folds. I'm already growing hard again when I circle a finger around her clit. I push another one deep inside her. She calls out my name when I hit her G-spot. My *real* name.

I crook my fingers and rub that spot over and over until she not only calls out my name, she screams it.

Then, before she can come down from her release, I turn her around, pinning her to the wall before I tear open the condom, put it on, and push inside her from behind.

She bends over slightly and puts a knee up on the bench, giving me easier access to push in and out of her. The wet slapping sounds coming from our drenched bodies is erotic and quickly brings me to a second orgasm.

Ivy's pleasured cries mingle with my own and I wonder if she's still riding the wave of her first orgasm, or if she's having another.

I brace myself on the wall as I pull out of her, my body languid and wanting to collapse on the shower floor. Ivy sits down on the bench, apparently feeling the same way.

I toss the condom over the shower door and hastily wash my hair, rivulets of water cascading down my chest and over my sensitive cock.

I shut off the tepid water and then open the door to grab two towels, wrapping one around Ivy before I secure the other around my waist. I lead her over to the vanity, pulling out a stool that resides underneath. "Sit," I say. "I'm going to comb your hair."

"It's just like a day at the spa," she says.

I look over at the shower. "Just what kind of spa do you go to?"

She giggles. Our eyes lock in the mirror. I smile.

I get another towel and scrunch it around her hair to absorb the excess water. Then I get my comb and carefully work it through from her roots to the ends. It takes me a while. Her hair is long, and I don't want to hurt her by yanking the comb through it.

Every time I glance in the mirror, I see her staring at me, studying me as I work meticulously on her hair. But she's so lost in thought she doesn't even realize I'm watching her.

"All done," I say, giving her a rub of the shoulders.

She finds my eyes in the mirror and holds my gaze, taking a deep sigh.

"She wanted me to come here," she says.

"She?"

"My daughter. Dahlia. I'm in Hawaii because of her."

My stomach turns when she says her name. No wonder she had such a bad reaction when I gave her the flower of the same name on our first hike.

I can see she's trying to hold it together. I lean down and place a kiss on the top of her head. "How old was she?"

"She would have turned six last month."

"I'm so sorry."

She nods over and over as I calculate in my head how old Ivy must have been when she had her daughter. Eighteen. She was eighteen when she had her. And she's had *two* children.

"And the other one?"

She looks down at her hands. "I … I can't talk about it. I guess I just wanted to tell you why I'm here."

I turn her around and kneel down so I'm on her level. "Thank you for telling me."

She gives me a sad smile. But I swear, in that smile, I can see the first hint of something. And I'm pretty sure it's called *healing*.

"I'm here if and when you want to talk. And I've got a pretty big shoulder you're welcome to use anytime you want, Ivy Greene."

She leans forward and falls into my arms. And as I hold her, I know for sure I never want to let her go.

CHAPTER FOURTEEN

IVY

I'm not sure why I felt compelled to tell Bass about Dahlia. I hadn't planned on it. I don't tell anyone about her. Or about *him*. But the way he took care of me last night. And then this morning in the shower. He's so gentle, in a commanding kind of way. He's compassionate, in a charming kind of way. And he's protective, in a seductive kind of way.

He's everything I never knew I needed.

I look over at him as he's singing along with the radio while we drive to our evening destination.

Do I need him? *Should* I need him?

He catches me watching him and reaches over to take my hand. And suddenly, I'm sad. Not just about Dahlia and everything else that's happened to me, but about the fact that we only have four more days together.

I've thought about things. All day today when we laid out on the beach, I thought about things. About trying to be with him when we go back to New York. I know he wants it. And deep down, I want it, too. But I'm just not sure it can happen. I'm afraid that when we leave here, we'll leave behind everything we've found in each other.

"Don't think too hard, you'll hurt yourself," he says, squeezing my hand.

He turns onto a private drive, following signs to what's reported to be the best luau in Kauai—something he already had tickets for, courtesy of his ex's parents.

"Are you sure you want to do this?" he asks.

We talked about it earlier. He was afraid I'd be upset by all the flowers that will be here. But the truth is, I miss flowers. And other than being bothered by the one flower that bears the same name as my daughter, I love them. Everyone thinks the reason I stopped working was because of the flowers. The flowers Dahlia loved so much. The ones she helped me arrange whenever she came into work with me. It wasn't because of the flowers. It wasn't even because every time I set foot in the shop, she was everywhere. It was because I could barely get myself out of bed. It was because I knew nobody wanted to buy flowers from someone who couldn't even bring herself to smile.

Then thoughts of the past ten days shuffle through my head. I think I've done more smiling in these ten days than I've done in the past ten months.

"Because we can blow this popsicle stand and go take another shower," he says.

I look over at him, feeling the edges of my mouth turn upward. "I'm sure."

We lock elbows as we walk up to the reception area. Bass hands over our tickets and the man scans them in, giving us a welcoming smile.

"Aloha, Mr. and Mrs. Briggs," the large Hawaiian man says. "And congratulations."

"Oh, we're not—"

Bass squeezes my hand. "Thank you," he says, not letting me finish my declaration.

"Are you enjoying your honeymoon on Kauai?" the man asks.

Bass winks at me before he kisses the side of my head. "We're enjoying our honeymoon very much."

The man motions to our left. "Please follow the path for your greeting."

"Thank you," I say. Then I turn to Bass. "Did the tickets really say you were on your honeymoon?"

He nods. "Yes. They're premium tickets that allow us to sit up front at a special table for two."

"The VIP treatment?" I say. "Nice."

We approach two ladies in traditional grass skirts. One of them holds out a lei made of shells for Bass, and the other, a lei of flowers for me. Bass waves away the lei of flowers. "The lady will take the shells too, if that's okay," he says.

"It's fine, Bass. It's made of orchids."

"So orchids are okay?" he asks with a raised brow.

I nod, leaning down so the small woman can put them over my head.

"Good to know," he says.

We make our way into the large covered pavilion with a raised center stage surrounded by what looks to be a hundred tables.

"It's really just the one flower I have issues with," I tell him.

He smiles at me, glad to be getting another piece of information. "Okay."

"What's our table number?" I ask.

He looks at his ticket stub. "Table number one."

"Really?" I look around at the huge venue. "Out of all these?"

He shrugs. "Only the best for our honeymoon, Mrs. Briggs."

I roll my eyes at him.

We stop at the open bar to get a few colorful drinks before finding our table.

"Not bad," I tell him when we find it front and center, along with six other identical tables for two.

Our table is decorated with flowers that have been cut high up off the stem. I look around at the other tables, confused as to why our table seems to have quite a few daisies when the others don't. Daisies are not what I'd call a traditional Hawaiian flower. I look at Bass suspiciously. Did *he* have them put here? No—I haven't told him about the daisies. He would have no reason to.

I walk over to another table and sift through the flower petals.

"What are you doing?" Bass asks. "You don't like our table?"

"It's fine. I was just, uh … looking at the flowers." I finally find a daisy hiding under some other flowers on the neighboring table and shake my head at myself for acting so strangely.

Bass nods to the vendors just outside the pavilion. "Want to get a souvenir? They said we had some time before dinner."

We take our drinks and peruse the booths that are filled with various products. One has amazing photos of many of Kauai's landscapes. Another holds perfumes made from island flowers. Another, souvenirs created from shells and lava rocks.

"Take your pick," Bass says.

Something catches my eye and I walk over and pick up a large framed photo. "Is this …?"

Bass looks at it. "That's the big waterfall we saw from the helicopter. The one from those movies."

I run my fingers over it. It's the reason I went on the helicopter. Dahlia wanted me to see this specific waterfall and the only way to get there is by flying.

Tears well up behind my eyes as I remember seeing it from up in the sky. "She wanted me to see it," I say. "And because of it, I met you. It's almost as if …"

"As if what?" he asks.

"Nothing." I turn to the proprietor. "I'll take this one."

Bass pulls out his wallet, but I push it back at him. "You've done so much. I'm taking care of this one. And I want to buy one for you, too."

"It'll be a tough choice," he says, perusing the beautiful photos. But then he stops when he comes across one. "This is it. This is the one."

He pulls it from the stack and I look at it. It's a brilliant sunset over the beach. There are palm trees and lava rocks, and everything we've seen on our nightly walks. But I'm not sure that's why he wants it. I think the reason he picked this one is because there is a silhouette of a couple walking hand in hand along the shore. Maybe he thinks if he can't have me, he can at least have the memory.

I rein in my emotions and hand some cash over to the vendor.

"They're both perfect," I say, as we take our purchases and walk away.

Everyone is directed to the fire pit where the roasted pig is being uncovered. Then we're herded through the buffet line to get our dinner before the show starts.

The show is wonderful. They have fire dancers, women doing the hula, an old man telling a story with his body while someone narrates over the loudspeaker. Then, just before the show is over, all the girls under the age of ten are invited up onto the stage to dance with the hula dancers.

My hand covers my mouth, holding in the sob that begs to come out knowing my daughter will never be one of those girls.

Bass stands up and offers me his hand. "I think it's time to go," he says.

He wraps his arm around me and doesn't say a word as we make our way to the car. He opens the door for me, letting me in. And when he gets in and starts the car, he puts a supportive hand on my knee. We drive home in silence. I think he knows I need a minute.

"She would have loved that," I tell him, when the knot in my throat clears enough for me to speak.

"Did she want you to go to a luau?" he asks.

I nod. "She wanted me to do it all," I tell him. "She wanted me to go everywhere you've taken me."

He squeezes my hand. "Of course she did," he says. "She wanted you to be happy."

Happy. It's not a word that's been in my vocabulary. Not in a long, long time. But over the past ten days, I've seen *hints* of happy. Maybe even *promises* of it. I look at the man sitting to my left, wondering if some way, somehow, he was sent here to me. Sent here to me from her.

~ ~ ~

"Something's wrong," I tell Eli. "The nurses keep saying Dahlia will be brought back to us any minute. But you see the way they're looking at us. It's almost like the way they looked at us when we lost—"

"It's not like that," he says. "You saw her. You heard her cry. She's fine. That pediatric guy said they were just being cautious."

"Maybe the tests they wanted to run take a long time," Holly says.

Mom comes over and sits on the edge of my bed. "When you were born, a similar thing happened. They whisked you away quickly. They didn't even let us hold you. They said you were having trouble breathing. We were devastated.

But a few hours later, when the nurse came walking in, rolling your bassinette, I think that was one of the best moments of my life." She pats my hand. "Be patient. I know it's hard to wait. Everything will be okay, honey."

"But why aren't they telling us anything? If she were okay, they'd be telling us not to worry."

"It's all about covering their asses," Eli's dad says. "They're all afraid of lawsuits. They will spend your money running unneeded tests just so they don't get sued. I'm sure that's what's going on here."

There's a knock on the door and then two doctors come through. The one I recognize from before looks at the crowd of people in my room. "Mr. and Mrs. Greene, I'd like to discuss Dahlia's condition with you. Perhaps we should clear the room."

"It's not Mr. and Mrs. Greene," Eli's mom says. "They aren't married."

"Mom, who cares about that right now?" Eli tells her.

"Her condition?" I ask, a sick all-too-familiar feeling washing over me. "What condition?"

The doctor looks around at the other five people in the room.

"It's okay," Eli says to him. "They are all family."

The doctor nods. "I'm Dr. Halburn, a pediatric resident," he says, introducing himself to the others. "And this is my attending, Dr. Hasaan. Earlier, during my initial assessment of Dahlia, I discovered that her kidneys were enlarged. So we took her for some tests."

"Enlarged kidneys?" Eli says. "What does that mean exactly?"

"Are you familiar with recessive genetic disorders?" he asks.

Eli and I look at each other and then shake our heads.

"A recessive genetic disorder is a condition that a child can inherit from their parents even though their parents do not have the condition themselves."

"I don't understand," I say. "Is she sick? Does she have cancer or something?"

"It's not cancer," he says. "It's called ARPKD. That's short for autosomal recessive polycystic kidney disease and we believe it was most likely the reason for the stillbirth you experienced last year."

"Oh my God." My hand covers my mouth, sobs pouring out of me. "Is she going to die?"

"ARPKD is a serious disease and can be life-threatening," he says. "In about thirty percent of newborns, it's fatal. I'm so sorry to have to deliver this news."

Gasps are heard around the room. I hear my mother cry out in agony. Holly runs over to me and takes my hand. "That means there's a seventy percent chance Dahlia could survive, right?" she asks Dr. Halburn.

"That's correct. But typically, children who survive infancy can develop many issues. Worsening kidney function will often lead to renal failure. Many ARPKD patients require kidney transplants in early childhood. There are also other life-threatening issues such as feeding and breathing difficulties due to enlarged kidneys. She'll have to stay here for a while until we can figure out the extent of the disease. High blood pressure is particularly difficult to manage in cases like this. And we could run into other complications with her liver and spleen."

As the doctor runs down the list of horrible things that could happen to my beautiful baby girl, my body shuts down. All I can remember is the time when, a little more than a year ago, I was in this same hospital, on this same floor, holding the tiny lifeless body of another baby. My son.

This can't be happening.

Not again.

I jolt awake, drenched with both sweat and tears. I grab my pillow, searching for comfort. I try not to remember the day she died only a short five and a half years later. I can barely remember the days and months afterward. I went through the motions of living, but I wasn't alive. My family tried to help. Eli tried to help, even though he was hurting, too.

And sometimes he did help. Sometimes we were able to comfort each other. Like on what would have been Dahlia's sixth birthday. We spent the day together—talking, crying, comforting. Numbing our pain.

But as I lie here now, I think about the past few weeks. I think about Bass and how good it's felt to be in his arms. In some strange way, without even knowing what happened to me, he provided me more comfort than my parents. Than my sister. Than Eli.

I look at the clock and see it's almost 2:30 a.m. It's the middle of the night. But this can't wait. I throw on some clothes and grab my room key before I head out the door.

CHAPTER FIFTEEN

SEBASTIAN

I rub my eyes and look at the clock, wondering who would be knocking on my door at this hour. Drunk teenagers probably. I roll out of bed and curse as I run into the end of the couch in the dark room on my way to the door.

I look through the peephole and see Ivy. I open the door.

"She loved pancakes," she blurts out, her eyes swollen and red-rimmed. "I used to make them in the shape of flowers. Dahlia would help stir the batter and then after they cooked, she would put a blueberry or raspberry in the middle as its colorful stigma."

I pull her into my room and she falls into my arms. I flip on the light and walk her over to my bed and sit her down. Then I fetch a bottle of water from the mini-fridge and hand it to her.

She takes a drink. "I'm sorry. I know it's late."

"I don't care what time it is, Ivy. I'm glad you came over."

"I had a bad dream," she says. Then she laughs half-heartedly. "I have a lot of them actually. Sometimes I take sleeping pills because I don't dream as much when I do."

I run a hand down her arm and sit next to her. "That's understandable."

"She died just before Christmas last year."

I blow out a long sigh. "I'm so sorry."

"It was her favorite time of year. She loved to decorate the tree. I put it up early, in September, because I knew I didn't have much time with her. Her transplant was failing and we couldn't find a match. Parents don't make a good match for donating organs, did you know that?" She laughs a painful laugh. "But in a sick twist of fate, siblings do. But Eli and I couldn't risk having another child to help her knowing what happened with the first two."

Ivy takes her shoes off and scoots up the bed to sit against the headboard. I get myself some water and turn off the main light, flipping on the light in the bathroom to give the room a dim glow. Then I crawl up the bed and sit next to her, holding her hand in silence.

"How come you're not asking me a bunch of questions?"

"Because you're going to tell me what you want me to know. I'm not going to pry, Ivy. Something horrible happened to you and you need to tell me at your own pace."

She nods. "I think I'm ready to talk about it. I feel safe with you, Bass. It's okay if you want to ask me things."

She has no idea how relieved I am to hear her say that. I've been wanting her to open up to me since we met. I was beginning to think it wouldn't happen.

"Okay. Is Eli your ex-husband?" I ask.

"Ex-boyfriend. We were never married. Boy did his mom hate that."

"How come you never married?"

She shrugs. "I guess we always planned to, but we were so young. He wanted to wait until he graduated college. Then when Dahlia was born and we had to deal with all her medical issues, we drifted apart. It's hard to put all your energy into your sick child and have anything left to give a partner. But I'm glad we never married. We didn't have to go through a divorce. And we're still friends. He's one of my best friends, in fact."

I realize she's not crying. But maybe it's because she's talking about her ex and not so much her child. Or one of her children.

"You said you lost two children. Will you tell me about both of them?"

She nods, swallowing what must be a lump in her throat. "How much time do you have?" she says with a sad smile.

"All the time in the world."

She takes another drink and sinks down into the pillow. I lie next to her and pull her head onto my chest as she wraps an arm over me.

"Eli and I were high school sweethearts. We started dating when I was sixteen. Senior year, I got pregnant by accident. But we were excited about having a baby all the same. We had so many plans. I was going to work for my parents, of course, and Eli was going to get his teaching degree at a local college. We lost the baby shortly after graduation. I was only thirty-one weeks along."

She tenses up and I feel hot tears drop onto my chest. I squeeze her tightly. "It's okay, sweetheart. You don't have to talk about it."

"No, I do. I … I want you to know."

I kiss her on the top of her head. "Okay."

"When I got to the hospital, they told me the baby had died. They couldn't find a heartbeat. The worst part was that I had to go through labor knowing I was going to deliver my dead child. But he was perfect. Tiny, but perfect. He had ten fingers and ten toes. They let me hold him. They even let us bury him. They said it would help with the grieving process."

She shakes her head and I feel more tears drop on my chest. "It didn't help. I know some people thought it was a blessing. That we were too young to have a baby and this was nature's way of righting a wrong. But it wasn't wrong, Bass. I loved him. I loved him so much."

"Of course you did," I say, running a soothing hand down her back as she sobs into me.

"Nobody could understand why I was so sad. Nobody but Eli. Because he's the only other person who loved Jonah as much as I did."

"Jonah," I say. "That's a good name. A strong name."

She nods. "I thought so, too. Eli wouldn't let me name him anything like what my parents named my siblings and me. When I first got pregnant, he used to joke about me naming our son Oak or Maple."

I laugh. "I'm going to have to agree with Eli on that one."

"I think you'd like him, Bass. He's not big like you. And he's not anything fancy like a firefighter. He teaches middle-school English. But he's a good person."

"Of course he is. He chose you."

"I … I don't love him anymore if that's what you're wondering."

"I wasn't wondering."

"I did, though, back then. As much as teenagers can love one another. And I really did think we made the right choice to have another baby. Everyone else was mad at us, barely eighteen years old and choosing to get pregnant. But we were happy again. We knew another baby wouldn't replace Jonah, but it would bring us joy, and that's what we needed."

Her body trembles almost uncontrollably. She has a hard time getting her words out. "We … we had n-no idea we were making the w-worst decision of our lives. Eli and I did it to her. *We* made Dahlia the way she was."

"I'm sure that's not true," I say, holding her tightly against me. "I'm sure that whatever happened wasn't your fault."

She shakes her head. "No, it was. It was entirely our fault. And it's just one more reason why Eli and I can't be together."

Sobs bellow out of her and for minutes she cries, clawing at me like she can't get close enough. I kiss her hair. I run a hand down her back. I massage her shoulder. And eventually, her breathing evens out and she falls asleep.

I lie awake, stunned. I don't even know the entire story yet, but what I do know is she has been through two horrible tragedies. No wonder she is the way she is. I have no idea how to comfort her. I see a lot of tragedy in my profession. But we never get to hang around to offer more than a few minutes of comfort to our victims or their families. I want to help Ivy. But I'm not sure how to do that without making things worse for her.

When Ivy rolls off me and onto the pillow, I grab my phone and head to the balcony. I know exactly who to call for advice. It's still the middle of the night here, but it's 9:30 a.m. back in New York.

Brady answers on the first ring. "You miss me so much you had to call all the way from Hawaii?"

I laugh quietly, not wanting Ivy to hear me. "You wish. No, I've got a big problem, man."

Brady Taylor is best friends with Penny's fiancé. He plays ball for the New York Nighthawks. We've become friends ourselves over the past year. And he's been through more tragedy than anyone I've ever known. Until meeting Ivy, that is.

"What's up?" he asks.

"I don't mean to dig up old demons, but I need help. Someone important to me has suffered a huge loss. She's lost two children. She just started to open up to me about it tonight. And I don't want to push her away. But I also don't want her to keep it all inside because I can see it's killing her."

"Damn." I can hear the pain in his voice. "I'm sure it *is* killing her. I know we all grieve differently, and I only have my own experience to go by, but what I can tell you is I didn't start to heal until I talked about it. And I almost lost Rylee because I didn't want to let her in. I guess what I'm saying is that sometimes people might need a little push to get them where they need to be."

I nod. "Thanks, man."

"Just how important is this woman to you?"

"Very," I say. "I'm pretty sure I'm in love with her."

"Just how long have you *been* in Hawaii?" he asks.

"Eleven days. I know it's fast, but—"

"Hey, when you know, you know. There's no set time limit on how long it takes to fall in love, Bass."

"I guess. The problem is, she doesn't feel the same way."

"Are you sure about that? You said she started to open up to you. People who have lived through what she did, what I did—we don't talk to just anyone about it."

"I can only hope you're right. Hey, thanks for the talk. I have to go. I have some flower pancakes to order."

"Some what?" he asks.

I laugh. "Nothing. Thanks, Brady."

"Anytime."

I sit on the balcony for hours, waiting for the sun to come up, thinking about the woman sleeping in my bed, wondering if I'll be able to push her just enough, but not too far. Then I pick up my phone and call room service, hoping they will be able to honor my crazy request.

CHAPTER SIXTEEN

IVY

I awaken to the smell of my favorite breakfast. I look around the room as the events of last night come rushing back to me. Bass is sitting on the couch, tapping around on his phone. He looks up at me and gives me a sympathetic smile.

He knows I'm broken. And he hasn't even heard all of it. I wonder if he will think I'm too much of a basket case to take on. Maybe this whole time, when I've been falling in love with him, he's been realizing he's not so disappointed anymore about not being with me when we go back to New York.

He puts down his phone, looking somewhat nervous.

"I ordered breakfast," he says.

I smile. "I can smell it. Thank you."

"Don't thank me yet," he says.

I cock my head to the side and then get out of bed and walk over to the table with the domed silver tray. I laugh before I remove the lid. "Why, did you eat them all?"

The lid comes off to reveal a plateful of pancakes in the shapes of flowers. There are even small pieces of berries in the middle of each one.

I swallow my tears and take in a deep breath. "Well, are you going to join me?" I ask.

"Absolutely," he says.

Bass gets off the couch and picks up the tray, carrying it out to the balcony.

"I'll be right out," I tell him. "Just let me wash up."

I use the toilet and then when I'm washing my hands, I notice how puffy my eyes are. I splash cold water on my face, wishing I had some makeup here to cover the bags under my eyes. I take a few calming breaths and study myself in the mirror. "You can do this," I say to my reflection.

I wanted to tell him everything last night, but I was just too exhausted. He needs to hear it. I need to say it. And then maybe we can both figure out what to do next.

"There you are," he says when I open the balcony door to join him.

I see a vase on the balcony table. And it's got a bunch of daisies in it. "Did you get these?" I ask.

"Well, I requested roses. But they said this was all they had at seven in the morning. I hope it's okay."

I pluck one of the flowers from the vase and study it, thinking about how these particular flowers keep finding me. It's like they're *following* me.

"Daisies were her favorite flower," I tell him. "You'd think dahlias would have been. I mean they smell better and they're prettier, not to mention she was named after one. But no, my daughter picked the flower a lot of farmers despise because it can overrun their pastures."

Bass reaches out to grab my hand, then he tugs me down onto his lap. "You're so sexy when you talk shop. Tell me more."

I giggle and shimmy around on his lap. "Okay—did you know that daisies grow everywhere except Antarctica? Also, a daisy is actually two flowers in one. The white petals are one flower and this yellow cluster of tiny disc petals is another. Oh, and did you know you can eat the petals? They're high in vitamin C." I trace the petals with my finger. "The daisy represents purity and innocence."

"I think your daughter had good taste," he says.

I nod. "I think you're right."

I stare at the daisy, remembering her words. Then I look at Bass. Maybe Dahlia was right. Maybe daisies do make things better. Things are better. *Aren't they?*

Bass pours some syrup on the pancakes and then cuts a piece off, feeding it to me.

I try not to cry as I eat. This is the first time I've eaten flower pancakes since she died. I think he gets that I can't talk right now. He alternates feeding himself and me, and we eat our entire breakfast in silence. I know why he did this. He wants me to see I can still do the things I enjoyed with Dahlia. He wants me to see I didn't die along with her. With Jonah.

When we're done eating, I settle back into his arms and look out at the view. "She planned this entire trip," I tell him. "We spent a lot of time in the hospital, and one of the things we would do to pass the time was fantasize about places we wanted to visit and research them. She didn't go to pre-school or kindergarten like other kids. She was in and out of hospitals too much. So Eli and I taught her how to read and write. She was way ahead of other kids her age. God, she was smart."

A lump forms in my throat.

Bass runs his hand up and down my back. "So she picked Hawaii. Did she specifically choose this island?"

"She did. And when we researched it and saw all the waterfalls, she fell in love with Kauai. And of course, she loved flowers, so that was just an added bonus. She made a list of everything we were supposed to do."

I close my eyes, trying to stave off the tears. "But she was smart. I think she knew what was happening to her before we did. She knew she would never go on this trip. She knew she was planning it just for me."

Bass kisses the side of my head. "It sounds like she was one hell of a little girl."

I nod over and over. "She was incredible."

"Ivy, why did you say it was yours and Eli's fault that your children died?"

"Eli and I both carry a recessive gene for polycystic kidney disease. When that happens, and you have a baby, they can end up with the disease. Not all the time. Half of the time the babies will only be a carrier. Twenty-five percent of the time they won't be a carrier and will be perfectly fine. But the other twenty-five percent will get the disease."

"And you both knew you were carriers?" he asks.

"No, we didn't."

"Then how could you be to blame? Hell, you wouldn't be to blame even if you *did* know."

I get what he's saying. It's the same thing my parents and the doctors said. But the truth is, *I* did this to her. To *them*. If they'd had other parents, they would have lived.

"When Jonah was stillborn, they told us that sometimes those things happen. They asked if we wanted an autopsy, but they said it wasn't necessary. They said most people don't get one because it just delays the grieving process. So we didn't get one. If we had, they would have found out why he died. But part of me is glad we didn't. Because if we'd known, we might not have had Dahlia. And as guilty as I feel for putting her through what she went through, I can't imagine never having those years with her." I belt out a sob. "She was the best thing that ever happened to me. And also, the worst."

"You said something about a transplant?" he asks.

"She had a kidney transplant when she was two. But when she was five, it started to fail, and … and …"

Bass grips me tightly. "It's okay. You don't have to say anymore. Thank you for trusting me with your story."

"I had to tell you," I say. "I had a dream about her last night and when I woke up, I knew I wanted you to know. I wanted you to know all the worst things about me. Because I lied when I said I didn't want to be with you longer than in Hawaii. But it wasn't fair of me to ask you for more unless you knew how … broken I am."

"Ivy, you're not broken. Terrible things have happened to you and the ones you loved. And it's still very fresh. You can't be expected to bounce back from losses like that and be a normal twenty-four-year-old."

"If my brother were here, he would tell you I wasn't normal even before that," I say.

"A joke?" he says, laughing. "You made a joke?" He looks at me with sympathy. With passion. With love.

Then he takes my face into his hands and stares into my eyes. "I know I promised not to use the L-word, but I'm not sure it's a promise I'll be able to keep."

"Good," I say, a happy tear escaping my eye. "Because I just might want to use the L-word myself."

He pulls my face to his. He kisses me softly, gently, passionately. And his kisses tell me far more than any words ever could.

When we finally break apart to catch our breath, I ask him, "Stay with me."

"You want me to stay at your place for the next four nights? Because I'm totally down with that. Nothing would make me happier."

"Stay with me even after that," I beg. "Can you? Can you extend your vacation? Can you stay with me for another week? Longer even. You don't need any money. I'll pay for everything."

He looks at me sadly. "Sweetheart, I have a job to get back to. One that I love. And they need me. If we're short on shift, lives could be at stake. I wish I could say yes, but I can't. I have to go back on Friday."

I turn around in his lap and lean back into him as he wraps me in his arms again.

"I'm scared," I say. "Everything is different here. *I'm* different here. As bad as I am now, I was worse back home. Most days, I couldn't get out of bed. What if … what if I can't do this back in New York?"

"If you don't feel you can do it, I'll wait."

I crane my neck around and look into his eyes. "But for how long?" I ask. "How long are you willing to wait?"

"Long," he says, running his thumb under my eye to catch another tear. "Because I'm pretty sure you're worth waiting for, Ivy Greene."

CHAPTER SEVENTEEN

SEBASTIAN

I stare at the screen on my phone, wondering how anyone could watch a child go through five and a half years of what Dahlia went through. ARPKD is a horrible disease that can affect almost every major organ in the body. It's not just kidney disease, it can cause liver failure, abnormalities of the heart, breathing problems, hypertension, anemia, and a long list of other complications.

My heart goes out to Ivy. She was looking for joy. For a way to overcome the sadness she felt after losing her first baby. And all she got was heartache. She went through hell. How does someone come back from that?

Then I think about Brady Taylor and everything he lost. It's not that he's forgotten what happened, he's just learned to deal with it in a way that allows him to live a happy life.

I've seen Ivy smile. I've heard her laugh even. And there are fleeting moments when I swear she's happy. But then it's like a light switches off. I think whenever she catches herself being happy, she must feel guilty. I promise myself to do everything I can to help her get past that guilt. It's the guilt that is holding her prisoner, I'm sure of it.

I pack up the rest of my things and head down to the parking garage with my one large suitcase, my backpack, and my guitar. I plan to get the most out of these last four days with her. I have no idea what to expect after we go home. She doesn't want to leave the island, that's for sure. I think if she had her way, she'd stay here forever. Maybe she will. Maybe she'll decide going back to where her daughter died is too painful.

My phone rings before I start the engine. It's Aspen.

"Hey. What's up?"

She squeals several unintelligible sentences into my ear.

"Slow down, Penny. Is everything okay?"

"Everything is great!" she shrieks. "They caught them, Bass. They caught the two guys who set up Denver. He's free. Can you believe it? He can go back to being a normal person now."

"What? How?"

"I just found out myself. Denver didn't want to tell me and get my hopes up, so he didn't say anything until they had their trial. It just ended today. And one of the guys provided detailed emails that proved Denver didn't know a thing about it—that he thought everything was legitimate. One of the email exchanges between the two scumbags even talked about how easy it was to fool Denver into believing it was real. A phone conversation the guy recorded had them joking about Denver having to pay restitution to the victims when *they* had all the money. Their sentencing is next week. I hope they go to prison. Oh my God, he's free, Bass! And in three weeks, it will be like it never even happened. That's about how long it'll take to get his record expunged. He can come to the wedding. He can go *anywhere!*"

It's hard not to get caught up in her excitement. Being twins, Aspen and Denver are as close as I've ever seen two siblings. I know how hard his conviction was on her, especially since she's always maintained he was innocent. I wanted to think so, too. But in my line of work, the simplest explanation is usually the right one. And all fingers pointed to Denver Andrews.

I couldn't be happier for them.

"That's the best news, Penny. Please give him my congratulations. He must be so relieved."

She spends the next few minutes giving me more details about it and then tells me she's got to go to class. I sit in the car and think of how quickly someone's life can turn around. Yesterday, Denver was a criminal with a felony record, and today, everything has changed. A complete one-eighty.

I find myself hoping Ivy can find that same kind of change in her life. And that I'm going to be a part of it.

I trade the hangtag on my rearview mirror for the new one Ivy got me for her parking garage, then I drive over to her resort, making a stop along the way.

She opens the door, seeing what I have in my hands. She raises her eyebrows at me.

"It's made out of orchids," I say, draping the lei around her neck. "I just really wanted you to know how much I was looking forward to you getting *leid* today."

She laughs and the sound is music to my ears. She pulls me through the doorway, kissing me before I even have a chance to grab my things. "I think that can be arranged, Sebastian Briggs."

"Good, but it will have to wait until later. We have plans."

"Plans?"

I pull our tickets out of my backpack. "We're going on an ATV adventure in one hour. And we'll get dirty, so don't wear anything nice. But wear a bathing suit underneath your clothes because there may be swimming involved."

"Is that the one that goes to the rope swing they used in that Harrison Ford movie?" she asks.

"You really did do your research, didn't you? Yes, that's the one."

She sighs. "I think it also goes to a waterfall."

I nod. "It does. But we don't have to see it if you don't want to. We can hang back with the ATVs and wipe the dirt off each other's body."

"Gross," she says.

"Okay, we can hang back with the ATVs and make out."

"I'll take option number two. Just let me go and get ready. You can unpack your things if you want. There is plenty of room in the dresser and closet in the bedroom."

I put my guitar down next to hers and then wheel my suitcase into the bedroom. I open a drawer to find Ivy's undergarments inside. I hold up a pair of her panties and run my fingers along the lacy edges.

I open another drawer and see a bunch of folded T-shirts. Another has a stack of shorts.

I smile when I get to an empty drawer and fill it with my things. I like this. I like my things being next to hers.

I throw on an old shirt, one I don't mind getting dirty, just as Ivy emerges from the bathroom.

Her eyes rake over me.

"What is it?" I ask.

She walks over and puts her hand on my chest, tracing the FDNY letters on my left pec. "I really like this shirt," she says. "It would be a shame to get it all dirty."

I immediately take it off and hand it to her. "Do you want it? It was one of the first shirts I was given when I joined the department."

She turns it over, studying my last name printed across the back. Then she puts the shirt in the same drawer as her panties. Lucky shirt.

"I think I like you wearing my clothes," I say. "Feel free to wear whatever you want whenever you want."

"I hope you don't mind if I don't extend the same invitation to you," she says with a smirk.

"Another joke?" I say. "I think there must be a comedian hiding somewhere in there."

I put on another shirt and then kiss her. "I look forward to seeing you in that shirt later tonight. And then I look forward to seeing you *out* of it."

~ ~ ~

I'm not sure how Ivy makes a helmet, goggles, and bandana look sexy, but she does.

They were right. You do get dirty on this excursion. In fact, we both have clean spots running diagonally down our shirts where our seatbelts cross our bodies, but the rest of us is covered with a layer of dirt.

I love driving the ATV. Each couple or family got their own. We play follow the leader through the center of the island on narrow back roads and steep hills. We stop along the side of the road a few times so the tour guides can give us some history of the island or point out interesting spots that were used for filming movies.

We get to our first destination and Ivy pulls her bandana off her face. I laugh, reaching over to try and wipe some dirt that collected on the strip of skin between her bandana and her goggles. But it doesn't matter. Dirty or not, she's still beautiful.

We hike down a short trail to a river. The tour guide grabs a rope swing. "This is the exact spot where Indiana Jones swung on a rope out into the river where his biplane was waiting for him in *Raiders of the Lost Ark*." He points up to the embankment. "Harrison Ford came right down there and did the stunt himself. You all can experience the same thing right now if you want to."

Our guide gives us a demonstration and then asks who wants to try it.

"Hell yeah," I say, getting in line.

I raise my eyebrows at Ivy.

She shakes her head and takes a step back. "I think I'll just watch."

The other guide plays the theme song from the movie loudly over his Bluetooth speaker as some of us swing out and drop into the water.

I climb out of the water and go over to Ivy. "Come on. You're the fearless one."

She gives me a look. "Fearless or stupid?" she asks.

I reach up and cup her chin. "You're not stupid, Ivy. Those things you did—getting close to the edge of the canyon, going behind that waterfall—I don't think you did those things because you're stupid. I think you did them to help you feel alive."

She studies me. "You're pretty terrific. I hope you know that."

"Come on." I grab her hand and lead her over to the rope swing. "Let's go feel alive."

~ ~ ~

Two hours later, after a picnic lunch and more exploring, we reach our final destination. Everyone else exits their vehicles and follows the guide down the long path to the base of the waterfall where there is a swimming hole.

I reach over and grab Ivy's hand. "Want to make out?" I ask.

She looks at my filthy face and clothes and scrunches up her nose.

I use my bandana to wipe my face. "Oh, come on. I'm not that dirty."

She looks over to where everyone disappeared down the path. "Maybe we should go see it," she says. "You know, just so you can wash off all the dirt and grime."

"I'm fine up here or down there," I tell her. "I'll do whatever you want to do."

She nods. "I think I want to go see it."

We get out of the ATV and walk over to the descending stairway that's been built from tree branches and rocks. It's steep, and we hold on to each other to keep from falling. The path winds around in S-curves as it takes us lower and lower. We are becoming engulfed by the large bamboo trees lining the trail.

Ivy stops her progress, looking up at our surroundings. "I feel like we're in that movie where the people get shrunk down and are walking through blades of grass."

I look up at the tall, green bamboo surrounding us, and damned if that's not exactly how it feels. I grab my phone and snap a picture of her.

After I put my phone away, I see Ivy staring at a small grouping of flowers at the base of the bamboo. I swear I can see the hint of a smile cross her face as she regards them. I reach out to pluck one of the flowers at the stem to put in her hair, but she stops me.

"No, don't," she says, pulling my hand back. "Let it live."

She runs her finger down the petals of some of the flowers. "Come on," she says, standing up and leading the way.

We turn a corner and finally the falls come into view. They aren't huge falls like the ones we saw from the helicopter or the one we climbed behind the other day. It only goes up twenty or so feet, the water coming down into a lagoon below where people are swimming. Kids are going under the falls, letting the water drench them from above.

"It's so pretty," Ivy says.

But she doesn't go any closer. She just sits down on a large rock, watching people take their turns going into the falls. She sits in silence for twenty minutes, staring. I stand behind her, rubbing her shoulders the entire time.

When the guides tell everyone to wrap it up because it's time to go, Ivy finally stands up. She looks over at the falls and then back at me. "I … I want to …" She takes a few steps toward the waterfall, looking at it longingly. "But it's too late."

"Come on, folks," the guide says, walking past us. "Let's head back up."

I reach into my pocket and pull out some money, handing it to him. "Can this buy us ten minutes?" I beg him. "Please? It's important."

He nods. "Ten," he says. Then he herds the others back up the windy path and out of sight.

I take my shirt off and drop my phone and wallet onto it. Then Ivy lets me take her top off. She looks at me warily as she removes her shorts, leaving her standing in her bikini.

I grab her hand and lead her to the entrance of the lagoon. We wade in and make our way over to right in front of the waterfall. She reaches her hand out, palm up, to feel the water as it cascades over it. Then she closes her eyes and steps forward until her body is completely under the falls. Her head falls back and the water rushes over her face and chest before rolling off to join the water in the lagoon.

I watch her stand beneath the falls. I wonder what she's feeling. I wonder what she's thinking. Whatever it is, she needs it.

Her shoulders start to shake. She's crying. And I stand back and let her. It's like she's becoming one with the waterfall. But then something miraculous happens. Her crying turns to laughter. She's spinning around beneath the falls, laughing like a child.

When I can't stand not touching her any longer, I come up behind her and wrap her into a hug, both of us standing in waist-deep water. I turn her around and we stare at each other as the gentle falls roll over us.

"Thank you," she says, running her fingers down the side of my arm. "I will never forget this moment for as long as I live."

"Me neither." I raise my hands to her face, putting one on either side of it. "I love you, Ivy Greene. And if you'll let me, I'm going to tell you that every day for the rest of your life."

"I think I might like that," she says, smiling. "Because I'm pretty sure I love you, too, Sebastian Briggs."

CHAPTER EIGHTEEN

IVY

The past few days have been unlike any I've ever known. I've been happy—something I never thought I'd be again. I stare at the pictures we bought at the luau that are perched side by side on the dresser. These two pictures are the epitome of our time here. I'm so glad I bought the waterfall one. I wanted it because waterfalls were Dahlia's favorite thing about this island. But now it has two meanings to me.

I look at Bass, still asleep on the pillow next to mine, and I think of how my life has changed these past weeks. I look at the picture of Dahlia on my bedside table. The picture I don't have to hide from him anymore. Because with Bass, I don't have to hide my pain. He lets me show it. He lets me experience it. And in some strange way, that has seemed to lessen it.

I study every curve of his chest. Every angle of his face. I don't want this to end. I want to wake up to him every day. But today is our last full day together. I only have one more morning to wake up next to him. Then everything changes.

"Stop it," Bass says, waking up to catch me staring at him.

"Stop what?"

"Thinking about how today is our last day together." He pulls me into his arms. "Because it's not. It's just the beginning."

"Do you really think we can make this work?" I ask.

"Yes. I do."

"Last week you told me firefighters shouldn't get involved with people they rescue. I feel like you rescued me, Sebastian."

His finger traces the edges of my cheek. Then he leans in and gives me a gentle kiss. "It's quite the opposite, sweetheart. I've been running on autopilot for a long time, just going through the motions. I love my job, but I knew there should be more to life than that. You're my more."

I smile at him before resting my head on his chest. "Tell me about your job. I think I'll always worry about you getting hurt in a fire."

"Fires are actually a very small part of the job," he says. "Seventy-five percent of our calls are medical."

"Don't you have ambulances for that?"

"We do have an ambulance in our firehouse. We call it a bus."

"A bus? Why would you call an ambulance a bus?"

I laugh. "Depends on who you ask. Some people think it goes back to the days when ambulances would transport multiple people at a time. Then there are the stories of an old company that built buses for the city, but they also built ambulances. Others just think it's a shortened version of the word ambulance. It's really just a story of legend at this point."

"So, the *buses* must stay pretty busy if so many calls are medical," she says.

"They do. But even if a call is medical, they still dispatch my engine company a lot of the time. We never have a full idea of what we're getting into because most callers are frantic and the information is minimal. And even if it's not a major medical emergency, the patient's weight or placement may be an issue and extra manpower may be needed."

"But what about the other twenty-five percent of your calls? Those are the ones I'll worry about. That's a lot of fires."

"Most of those calls aren't even fire related. They consist of traffic accidents and fire alarms mostly. And we get a lot of calls about people stuck in elevators. When we do get calls about fires, most of them are kitchen fires, or fires in a garage or workshop due to mishandling of gasoline or chemicals. True fires, like what most people think of when flames are coming out of windows and smoke billowing into the sky—those only happen about once a week or so."

My heart races just hearing him say it. "That's enough for me to worry about you, Bass."

He kisses my head. "Don't worry about me. I'm good at what I do."

"Do you think one day when we get back, I could come by the station and see where you work?"

"I'd like that," he says. "And what about you? Do you think I can come see where *you* work?"

I know what he's really asking. He's asking if I'm going to go back to work. I've thought about that a lot during my stay here. I know I should. I know I probably need to. I can't go back to the way I was before I came to Hawaii. I can't go back to lying in bed all day watching mindless television while my parents support me.

I think about trying to go back to the flower shop—the place that reminds me of Dahlia almost as much as her bedroom does—the bedroom I would sit and cry in every day while staring at her flower-lined walls. She would often come to work with me and help me arrange flowers. And when I was on the computer, or doing paperwork, she would draw. She drew so many pictures of flowers that we ran out of wall space in her room to pin them up.

Then I think about the waterfall and how sad I was to see it. But when I gave myself a chance, when I let myself think about how happy it would have made her, it became something different. Something unexpected. It became a happy memory, not a sad one. And although I know going back to work will be hard, because all I will see is Dahlia sitting at her little table in the corner, drawing pictures, I wonder if eventually it will feel like seeing a waterfall.

"I … I think I might like that, too," I say hesitantly.

He turns me over and pulls me up so I'm lying on top of him. I can feel his erection come to life beneath me. He smiles up at me. "I think we're going to be just fine, Ivy Greene."

~ ~ ~

After spending the day at the beach, we're enjoying Bass's last Hawaiian sunset in our usual spot by the fire pit. I'm sitting between his legs as we play his guitar together. It's become my favorite thing to do.

"Will you play me a song?" he asks. "When we first met, you said you knew a song or two. Will you play one for me?"

I look down at the guitar, knowing the only other person I've ever played for was her.

"Okay," I say quietly. "But I'm not singing."

I start playing the song I used to play every time Dahlia was in the hospital. She always had trouble falling asleep in a bed that wasn't hers, so I would play and we would sing. *'Play the sunshine song, Mommy,'* I can almost hear her say.

I start to strum out the tune, my fingers shaky as they try to hold the chords I haven't played in so long. I'm not sure what I was thinking when I bought the guitar at the second-hand shop. I knew I wasn't going to play *You Are My Sunshine* again. And it was the only song I knew. I guess I just thought having the guitar would make me feel closer to her.

I fumble a few times, because it's hard to see where to put my fingers when my vision is so blurred with tears. But I push through. I play the song. And when I hear Bass sing the words that I can't, my heart expands with more love than I'd ever thought possible.

And through my tears, I feel myself smile. I feel myself smile, because even though he won't admit it, the man sitting behind me *has* rescued me. He's saved me from a life full of guilt and self-abhorrence. Instead, he's shown me a life of precious memories and hope.

When the song is finished, I put down the guitar and relax into his arms. He kisses me just below my ear. "You are the strongest person I've ever met," he says, just as we watch the last rays of the sun be eaten up by the sea.

CHAPTER NINETEEN

SEBASTIAN

I try not to wake her, but it's hard because I have to touch her. I'm not sure when I'll get to touch her again. It'll be at least two weeks, that's how much longer she's staying in Hawaii. But even after that, who knows what will happen.

We stayed up all night talking. Well, in between our marathon love-making sessions that is. We couldn't get enough of each other. It's more than evident that she's afraid of my leaving. I'm worried about her staying. I've asked her to come home with me, but she won't. She says she needs more time.

She's done so much healing this past week, particularly after she went under the waterfall. It's a transformation I've been fortunate to witness. I just hope after I leave she doesn't sink back into a depression.

"Don't go," she says, waking up to see me watching her.

"Don't stay," I say back to her.

It's the same thing we've said to each other for days.

I wrap her in my arms. "Thank you for giving me the best vacation of my life."

She snuggles into my shoulder. "There aren't enough words to thank you for what you've given me."

"We're good for each other, aren't we?"

She nods but doesn't respond.

"We're good for each other here and we'll be good for each other back home," I say.

"I hope you're right, Bass. I really do."

Ivy's phone rings and she reaches over to check it. "Do you mind?" she asks.

"Go ahead," I say, reaching for my own phone to check for messages.

"Hi, Eli," she says.

My ears perk up when I hear her ex's name. I know they talk. She said they're friends. But something about him calling her when we're in bed together just rubs me the wrong way.

I fiddle with my phone as I listen to her side of the conversation.

"No, he hasn't left yet," she says into the phone. Then she's quiet as she listens.

"I'm fine, Eli." Another pause. "Two weeks from Thursday." A longer pause and I can almost make out the male voice on the other end. "That's okay, Holly said she'd pick me up."

She moves the phone to her other ear. "I can't really talk about that. He's lying right next to me." She looks over at me and I try to pretend like I'm not listening, but she must know I am.

"We're adults, Eli. It's fine. Listen, I'll call you later."

She says goodbye and hangs up the phone.

I turn to her, raising myself up onto an elbow. "Well, that wasn't awkward in the least."

She rolls her eyes. "Sorry. He can be a bit protective of me."

I straighten my spine. *I* want to be the one protecting her.

"You talk to him about me?" I ask.

"Sure, he's one of my closest friends."

"What did he say when you told him I was in your bed?"

"He said he thinks I'm rushing things."

"Maybe he's jealous," I say.

"I don't think so. He's dated other people since we broke up."

"That doesn't mean he's not still in love with you, Ivy. I should know, I hid my feelings for my best friend for years while dating other women."

"It's not like that. He's moved on. We really are just friends."

I study her, hoping she's being straight with me. Then I look at Dahlia's picture next to the bed. "Do you think you'd still be together if you didn't both carry that recessive gene?"

She shrugs, staring at the picture. "To be honest, I don't know. We didn't break up because of that. We broke up because it was too hard to be together when Dahlia was so sick. And then after … well, I'm not sure either of us had the energy to be with *anyone*."

"Do you want more children, Ivy?"

She reaches out to touch the picture of her daughter. Then she nods. "I do. But not for a long time. And not unless he gets tested for the gene."

I grab her hand. "Not unless *I* get tested," I say. "*I'm* the one you're going to have babies with. I hope you know that."

She doesn't respond. She doesn't smile or swoon like most women would when hearing that declaration. She just looks scared. Terrified even.

I pull her down on the bed so she's lying under me. I hover over her. "We have all the time in the world, sweetheart. We won't do anything until you're ready. But it sure will be fun getting in the practice."

Finally, I see the hint of a smile. It's my green light to devour her once again. And for the next two hours, we do nothing but practice and practice.

~ ~ ~

Tears roll down her face as she walks me up to the security line outside Lihue airport. When it's almost my turn to go through, her grip on me tightens.

"You go ahead," I say to the people behind me, stepping out of line and pulling Ivy over to a nearby bench.

"I'm sorry," she says. "I'm a blubbering idiot."

"It's okay. It just means you love me."

She nods. "I do, you know. I'm not sure how it happened like this, Bass. It's only been two weeks. But I love you so much. More than I thought I could ever love someone after …"

"Me, too," I say. "But it didn't take me two weeks, Ivy. I fell in love with you long before that."

"When?" she asks.

"I think it was when you were dancing in that puddle during the storm."

She looks walleyed at me. "Really?"

I laugh. "Yeah. Really. I had never seen so much emotion pour out of one person. You were so beautiful. And when you told me about the rain being a magic potion that makes the flowers grow, I knew you were the one for me." I squeeze her hand. "It was Dahlia who said that, wasn't it?"

She nods. "She loved the rain. She loved going outside to splash in the puddles and catch drops on her tongue. She loved watering the plants and flowers at the shop. She … she said she wished there was a magic potion that could help her grow up and be a mommy like me." She chokes out her next words. "Because she knew she never would."

"I wish I could have met her," I say. "She sounds like an amazing girl."

"She was." Ivy puts her head on my shoulder. "I can show you her bedroom if you like, you know, sometime later after I get home. You'd think a paint truck vomited on the walls with all of her colorful paintings."

I'm reeling on the inside knowing she's thinking of the future. A future with me in it.

"I'd love to see it," I say. "I'd love that more than anything."

She catches me checking the time. "I know you have to go. I guess I'm just trying to hold on to the fantasy a little longer."

We stand up and I kiss her. I don't care who is watching and how indecent it is. I need her to know how much she means to me. That when I walk away, I'm not walking away from her. From this.

"The fantasy is not over," I say. "It's just the beginning. Everything is going to be okay. I promise."

She nods, a tear running down her cheek as I walk away.

"I'll see you soon, Ivy Greene."

She tries to smile and then she blows me a kiss. And all the while I'm saying a silent prayer that the woman I love will find the strength to heal and come home.

CHAPTER TWENTY

IVY

I lie here in bed, staring at Dahlia's picture like I do every morning. But now I have another face to stare at as well. I pick up my phone and page through the pictures of Bass—the pictures of *us*—just to make sure I didn't dream the entire thing.

I know I didn't, because when I look at the photos we bought at the luau that are still perched on my dresser, everything comes rushing back. He left his photo here. I think he did it on purpose. He wanted me to look at them and remember. How is it that after only two weeks, he gets me so well?

I was worried about all the alone time I was going to have here after he left. But I also knew I needed it. I needed it to figure out if it was just being with Bass that changed me, or if I had really changed. And the past few days have given me hope. Hope I never knew existed.

Even Holly said I sounded different when we talked on the phone yesterday. She said different was good. She said different is what I need and that everything will be different when I come back next Thursday. I'm not sure what she means by that. Does she think when I get back I will have miraculously forgotten about the last seven years of my life?

My phone rings and I smile when I look at the screen and see Bass's picture. We've been texting a lot, but this will be our first call since he left a few days ago.

"Good morning," I say.

"Hey, beautiful. I didn't wake you up, did I?"

"You'd think after almost a month here I could sleep past six, but no, you didn't."

"You'll be happy about that when you get back to New York. It'll be easier to adjust to the six-hour time difference."

"So, it's one o'clock there. Are you on your lunch break?"

"We don't have official lunch breaks around here, but, yeah, I just ate lunch."

"What did you make today?" I ask, knowing as the newest member of the firehouse, he's often tasked with kitchen duty among other things.

"Spaghetti and meatballs."

"I bet you'll be happy when you don't have to cook so much, huh?"

"Good news on that front, we have someone retiring this week, which means we'll get a new guy. I won't be the *probie* anymore. God, it seems like I've been one forever."

"Yeah, but in a way, you'll be a better person for having gone through it. I mean, sometimes we need to experience hard times so we can appreciate everything that happens after."

"Words of wisdom, Ivy Greene? I thought that was *my* job."

"Sorry," I say.

"Don't be. Your saying that is everything I wanted to hear."

I can practically *hear* his smile over the phone.

"So, what have you been doing for the past few days?" he asks.

"I've been playing a lot of guitar. Tua and I have become friends. He meets me by the fire pit every night at sunset and we play together."

"Do I need to worry that I've been replaced?" he jokes.

"Yes, Bass, you've been replaced by a short, stocky, forty-something native Hawaiian who plays the ukulele. Oh, and he has a wife and four kids, by the way."

"I'm glad to hear it," he says. "And speaking of the guitar, I've been thinking lately about the song you sang to Dahlia. You see the irony, right?"

"What, that she loved the rain and I sang her a song about sunshine?"

"Yeah, that."

I think back to when Dahlia was barely two years old and decide to tell Bass the story. "She was in the hospital after her transplant. Volunteers would come around the pediatric wing and entertain the kids. There was a guy who played guitar. Dahlia would perk up every time he would play for her. She asked me to play, too. So every time he came in, he would teach me a little more of the song. Then when Dahlia came home, my dad bought me a guitar so I could keep playing. I'm still not sure if she really loved that particular song, or if she just knew I couldn't play any others, but it became our thing."

"Thank you for sharing that memory with me," he says. "Ivy, are you crying?"

I close my eyes to squeeze out the tears that never came, and I realize that was the first time I've talked about her without choking up.

"No. No, I'm not," I tell him. "I think I might be smiling a little."

"I wish I were there to see it. I miss your smile. I miss everything about you."

"I miss you, too. But I'm trying to stay busy. Oh, you'll never guess who I had lunch with yesterday."

"Who?" he asks.

"Erma."

"The seal lady?"

I laugh. "Yeah. Did you know she's only seventy-six?"

"Really? I would have guessed ninety or more."

"I think it's being out in the sun so much that has aged her. But she's fantastic. I know we learned a lot about the island from all of our excursions, but hearing about it from someone who has never left Kauai gave me a whole new perspective."

"She's never left the island?" he asks.

"Not once."

"I can't imagine being stuck in one place for so long. But maybe if you don't know what else is out there, you would never miss it."

"I'm glad I found out what else is out there, Sebastian."

"Me, too, Ivy. You sound good. I'm really happy—"

I hear a loud siren go off in the background and then someone's voice comes over a loudspeaker shouting out numbers and stuff. "I have to go, sweetheart. I love you."

"I love you, too. Please be safe."

"Always," he says right before the line goes dead.

My heart races. I'm not sure I'll ever breathe easily knowing he's out there risking his life to save others. I worry about him. And I'm not sure I could take any more loss.

But then I think about what Alder's wife, Christina, keeps telling me. She says that God never gives you more than you can handle. And if that's true, the rest of my life should be a cakewalk because no way could I handle anything else.

Christina grew up going to church. She still goes every Sunday, making sure to bring Alder and their two-year-old son, Ricky. I appreciate all her words of wisdom even though I don't always agree with them.

After Dahlia died, she tried to get me to go to church with them. But I couldn't. I found it difficult to pray to a God who took away my children. My life. I also found it difficult to be around Ricky. But lately, I've found myself wishing I could start praying again. Praying that Bass doesn't get injured. Praying that I'll be able to start living.

I've promised myself that I'm going to be a better friend to Christina. She married my brother five years ago and we became instant friends. She fit right in with Holly and me. We did everything together. Right up until she had a healthy baby boy and I became a terrible friend.

I just couldn't be around her when she was with Ricky. I couldn't watch him reach milestones that Dahlia hadn't reached. I couldn't watch him have playdates when she was cooped up in the hospital. I couldn't witness how happy they were as a family.

I don't think Christina has ever held it against me. I'm sure she could imagine how things would be if her child were as sick as mine was. And she made a lot of effort to make sure we could have plenty of girls' nights. But family gatherings were hard, and the sicker Dahlia became, the fewer I went to. In fact, last Christmas, my family had two holiday celebrations, one for all of them and one for me because they knew I couldn't be around Ricky. I told them not to bother, that I wasn't in the mood for celebrating when my child had just died weeks before. But they insisted.

I wonder what this year will be like.

I get out of bed, not wanting to think about the anniversary of Dahlia's death. Getting through her birthday last month was hard enough. But one thing I do know—I don't want Eli to be the one to comfort me anymore. Bass is the one I want. He's the one I need. He's the man I want to spend my life with.

I head for the shower, taking off the FDNY T-shirt with his last name on the back. I stare at it, wondering, hoping that someday maybe it will be mine.

CHAPTER TWENTY-ONE

SEBASTIAN

Brett raises his glass. "Out with the old, in with the new."

The rest of the guys raise their glasses, too, waiting for me to complete the ceremony. I reach behind me, grabbing the large box I put together for Noah August, Engine 319's newest addition.

Inside the box is a bunch of stuff I threw together: a soup ladle, a bottle of laundry detergent, a toilet brush, some turtle wax. I pick it up and hand it to Noah.

"I like my shirts lightly starched, Probie," I say, thinking how good it feels to be able to call someone else by that name.

Noah's eyes go wide. "I have to do your laundry, too?" he asks.

The entire company laughs. Noah has no idea what he's in for. Well, maybe he does. Being a probationary firefighter is a bit like rushing a fraternity. While technically, we can't haze him, we can make him do all the scut work around the firehouse. Like cooking, cleaning the toilets, and washing the rigs.

I raise my own glass. "Welcome to the brotherhood, Noah August." But before I drink, I stare at him. "Anyone ever call you Auggie?"

"Not in all of my twenty-three years," he says, looking slightly annoyed.

"To Auggie!" I shout, before taking a drink of my soda.

"To Auggie!" everyone else replies.

Noah shakes his head. But he doesn't say anything. There's not much he can say. Once you've been given a nickname, it tends to stick. Some of us never got a nickname. I was always just called *Probie* or *Briggs*. But some of the guys weren't so fortunate. Like Duck, whose real name is Steve Hanson. Steve can't seem to walk without his toes pointing out. Or Miles Nelson who everyone calls *Stache* because his facial hair makes him look like a seventies porn star.

The alarm sounds, but it's only for EMS, so Debbe and Ryan leave their lunch on the table and take off.

"I'm really happy to be here, guys," Noah says.

Brett stands up with his dirty dish and pats him on the back. "Let's hope you still feel that way in a week or two," he says with a sarcastic grin that has Noah looking a little green around the gills.

Lieutenant Brett Cash is second-in-command here. He's on Squad with Justin, Cameron, and Miles. They go on a lot of the same calls as my engine company, but in addition to everything we do, they also deal with heavy extrications and entrapments.

"Come on, Squad, let's go gas up the rig," Cash says.

The four of them finish their lunch and head out. Any time one of our trucks goes anywhere, the entire team has to gear up and be ready for a call. It's the nature of the business. If one of us needs to go to headquarters to be questioned about a report, or if we want to check up on an injured colleague, we all go. We are together with our team the entire time we're on shift. We know each other's business better than our mothers, girlfriends, or wives do.

We are family.

And Noah August is now part of that family. I finish my lunch and hand him my plate, just because I can. "Welcome to the jungle, Auggie."

I head up to the bunk room, hoping to get an hour or so of shuteye, but all I can think about is Ivy. She's coming back in a few days. I wish I could be there to welcome her home, but I can't. I'll be on shift. And I've used up all my favors for a while.

I can't wait to see her again. She sounds good when we talk. Happy even. And it makes me relieved to think that whatever she went looking for when she went to Hawaii, she found. I just hope that *whatever* is me.

"Briggs," Noah says from over the partition that separates our bunks.

"What is it, Auggie?"

"So, yeah, about the name. I didn't want to say anything in front of everyone, but when I was a kid I wasn't as big as most of my friends. I got picked on by the bullies at school. Kids who called me that name. So it kind of brings back bad memories if you know what I mean."

I stand up and stretch my arms, giving up on sleeping. I give him a sympathetic look and pat him on the shoulder. "Yeah. Yeah, I do. I'm sorry about that, man."

"Thanks," he says, as I walk away.

I pull my phone out of my pocket and text Katrina at headquarters. She's the one in charge of outfitting all of us in FDNY gear. I ask her if she can get me a dozen shirts. Then I make sure she gets the spelling right. "It's Auggie with *two* Gs," I tell her.

J.D. waves me into his office as I walk by.

"What's up, Cap?"

Jim Dickenson is the officer in charge of the firehouse. He's also the OIC for Engine 319. He's part of my team, along with Steve and now Noah.

Technically, Battalion Chief Mitzel is in charge, but he's in charge of five firehouses and his office is over at Engine 71/Ladder 12. We only see him if there's a major fire or other life-and-death call.

"You happy to be out of the hot seat?" J.D. asks.

"Hell yes, Captain."

"Good. You've done a great job here, Briggs. I just wanted you to know it hasn't gone unnoticed."

I reach out to shake his hand. "I really appreciate that."

He has no idea just how much. My whole life, I've dreamed about being a firefighter. I may have gotten sidetracked for a few years, following what was my parents' dream for me, but as I look around J.D.'s office, seeing all the pictures of the firefighters who have served in this house, I know I made the right choice.

The alarm sounds, calling us into action to respond to a residential structural fire.

J.D. runs out from behind his desk and shouts up into the bunk room. "Engine Company 319, you have exactly fifty-two seconds to get your asses in gear!"

I laugh, knowing that was meant for Noah. The rest of us know all about the captain's fifty-two-second rule. It doesn't matter if we're in the middle of taking a shower or taking a dump, there are no exceptions if you want to stay off his shit list. He's one of the toughest captains at FDNY. But he's also one of the best. And I'm a better firefighter for it.

I run out with him and we suit up in our turnout gear that sits next to our rig. I take my place in the back seat, along with Noah, helping him adjust the straps on his coat. Then as we pull out onto the street, I stare out the window, listening to the siren and waving to the kids who stop and stare. And I smile because I know I'm exactly where I need to be.

~ ~ ~

I look up at the awning over the front door. *The Greene Thumb.*

How many times have I jogged past here over the last year? My apartment is about a mile away and this street is part of the route I take on my runs. I look through the window, wondering if one of those times when I was jogging by, Dahlia was in there with Ivy, painting pictures of the flowers she loved so much. Painting pictures of the rain.

I open the front door and walk through, my nose being assaulted by a dozen different fragrances all at once. There is a man being waited on, so I hang back and look around. I stand shielded by a tall floor display and watch the woman behind the counter. No doubt the woman is Ivy's sister, Holly. The resemblance is remarkable. She has brown hair like her younger sister, although it's not quite as long. She has the same heart-shaped face, though it's not as thin. She has the same eyes, but they aren't nearly as sad.

Holly acknowledges me, saying she'll be with me in a minute. I lift my chin at her.

She keeps glancing over at me while she helps her customer. When the man leaves, she walks over to me, holding out her hand. "Sebastian Briggs, I presume?"

"Bass," I say, shaking her hand as I look down at my FDNY T-shirt. "What gave it away?"

She laughs. "I was wondering if you were going to come in."

"Why were you wondering that?" I ask.

"You're in love with my sister, aren't you?"

"Well, yes. But she's not back from Hawaii yet."

"Not until tomorrow," she says. "But I knew if you were the one for her, you'd come here even before she got home."

"Why?"

"Because if you love her, you know how broken she feels, and you'd probably want to meet someone close to her to find out how you can help."

I cock my head to the side and stare at her.

"Sorry," she says. "I guess I haven't introduced myself properly. Holly Greene, co-manager of this fine establishment and certified single lady if you have any bachelor friends at the firehouse you want to introduce me to."

I laugh, thinking of several who would be interested. She's beautiful like her sister. And spunky. It makes me wonder if Ivy used to be spunky, too. Before her world was destroyed.

"I might be able to arrange that," I say.

"A double date maybe," she says, nodding to a calendar on the wall—the FDNY charity calendar. "One of them can put out my fire anytime."

"We did, you know. Earlier this year," I say. "Put out a fire here, I mean."

She rolls her eyes as if she just ate a decadent piece of chocolate. "I know. I thanked the owners next door for having a faulty stove. I got to sit here for hours watching your unit tear through walls to make sure the fire was out."

I laugh.

She walks over and pounds the wall with her palm. "Good as new."

"I'm glad there wasn't much damage to your place."

"That's because you arrived so quickly."

"We do what we can to help."

She nods and smiles at me, studying me for a second. "You don't need to be asking *us* how you can help her, you know. You helped her more in those two weeks than any of us could in seven months."

"I'm not so sure it was me," I say. "She did all the things Dahlia wanted her to do. I think it made Ivy feel closer to her, but in some strange way—"

"It also helped her let Dahlia go."

"That's what I was thinking, too."

"You're too modest," Holly says. "It *was* you."

"She took the first step by getting on that helicopter. That's where we met."

"I know." She smiles brightly. "I know everything about it."

I raise my eyebrows.

"Everything," she says. "Ivy's not just my sister. She's my best friend."

I try to look embarrassed. "Excuse me while I blush then."

She laughs at my dramatics. "No need to be embarrassed. I never thought *anyone* would ever get through those cob webs she had growing between her legs. Well, except maybe Eli, but he doesn't count anymore. Anyway, we all think you're a saint."

I want to ask her about Eli, but I don't. "All?"

"Mom, Dad, Alder, Christina. We're all very grateful to you. They can't wait to meet you. Uh, unless you've already been to the other shops today. Are you making the rounds?"

I shake my head. "You're the only one I've met so far. I was wondering if you could do me a favor."

"Sure, name it. I mean, I'm going to owe you big time after you set me up with a hottie from the firehouse. Wait, do you have any pictures?"

"Sorry, no."

"Shame," she says. "So, the favor?"

"I'm not able to meet Ivy at the airport. I'll be on shift. I know she said you were picking her up and I was wondering if you could give her something for me."

"Of course."

"Do you know how to make leis?" I ask.

She smiles. "As a matter of fact, I do. We've done some Hawaiian-themed weddings before."

"Great. Can you make it out of purple orchids?"

"Whatever you want." She nods to some notecards on the counter. "Want to send a note with it?"

I look at the small cards. "Uh …"

She picks one up and hands it to me. "Come on, Casanova, it would be romantic."

She hands me a pen. I pull up a nearby stool and sit down, staring at the blank card.

"You love her, Briggs. It shouldn't be that hard."

"I'm a firefighter, Holly, not a poet."

I think about our time in Hawaii and then I scribble out the note and put it in the small envelope before handing it back to her.

She immediately opens it and reads the card as she pops her gum. I get the feeling this woman knows no boundaries.

Her eyes tear up then she walks around the counter and hugs me. Hard.

"What was that for?" I ask.

"For being the one for her. I wasn't sure before, but I am now."

"Why are you sure?"

She nods to the note I wrote. "Because only the man she loves would be able to write these things. Believe me. I know her better than anyone."

"Sorry, Holly. I'm hoping to strip you of that honor," I say, handing her my credit card.

She runs my card and hands me the receipt. "You know, I think I might be okay with that. Especially seeing as I'm going to be very busy once you introduce me to your friends."

I shake my head at her and laugh as I make my way to the door. "Nice to meet you, Holly."

"We're going to be related one day, you know," she shouts after me. "I'm calling it first."

"No," I say, pushing the door open. "Actually, you're not."

CHAPTER TWENTY-TWO

IVY

Even though I'm in first class, I hang back, staying on the plane while everyone else gets off. I stay seated by the window as I pretend I'm searching for something in my purse. But I know I'm just prolonging the inevitable. I'm going to have to step off this plane in a minute. I'm going to step out of my fantasy and back into reality.

"Miss?"

I look up to see the flight attendant staring at me.

"Sorry," I say, grabbing my carry-on. I walk out of the plane as the crew thanks me for flying with them.

I walk through the gate and enter the busy airport. I follow the other passengers to baggage claim. When I get there, I'm looking around for my sister when I get hugged from behind.

"Ivy!" Holly squeals. "I've missed you."

I turn around to give her a proper hug. "I've missed you too, Hol."

She takes a step back, still holding on to my arms. "You look radiant."

"I do?"

"Absolutely. Hawaii was good for you," she says. Then she elbows me. "Or *something* was." She reaches into her purse. "Hey, speaking of *something*." She puts a lei made of purple orchids around my neck.

I laugh. "Hol, leis are for *arriving* in Hawaii, not coming home."

"It's not from me, it's from Bass. Maybe he wants you to feel like every day is Hawaii." She hands me a small envelope. "And he wrote you a note. He was bummed that he couldn't be here."

"He's on shift. He told me."

I see my suitcase coming around the carousel. "That's mine."

"I'll get it," Holly says.

As she works her way through the crowd to get my bag, I open the envelope. My eyes mist up as I read his words.

> You are my sunshine.
> My waterfall.
> My puddle in the rain.

I hold the note to my chest, wanting so desperately to see him again. I know it's only been a couple of weeks, but it feels like forever.

"I like him," Holly says, dragging my suitcase behind her.

"He's taken," I say with a smile.

She cocks her head to the side, studying me. "You're different."

"I hope so." I nod to the outside doors. "But I'm not sure what will happen when I go out there. When I go home. I don't want this feeling to go away."

"You're not going home," she says. "Well, you are, but you're not."

"What does that mean?" I ask.

"Don't be mad, Ivy."

I narrow my eyes at her. "What have you done?"

"Something that needed to be done. You'll see."

She hails us a cab and gives the driver her address. Then I get it. I'll bet she's planned some kind of welcome home party for me at her place. She's probably got the whole family there. Maybe she's even going to surprise me with Bass. My sister is sneaky that way.

When we get to her building and onto the elevator, she pushes the button for the fourth floor instead of the seventh. I reach out and press the correct button. "You pressed the wrong one," I say.

"No, I didn't. I moved."

"You moved?"

She shrugs. "A bigger place became available, so they let me switch the lease."

"Why do you need a bigger place?"

The elevator dings, arriving at the fourth floor. "Come on," she says, pulling my suitcase behind her.

We pass by two other doors on the way to hers. Then she gives me a look before opening her door. It's a guilty look if I ever saw one.

She holds the door open for me and we put my bags inside. Then I see my favorite chair in the corner of her living room.

"What's my chair doing here?"

She digs around in her pocket and pulls out a key. She hands it to me. "It's here because *you're* here. You live here now. With me."

"I *what?*"

"We—Mom, Dad, Alder, and Christina—we all thought that you being in your apartment was not good for you anymore. All you did was lie around and be depressed. You hardly ever left her room, Ivy."

"Her room was the only thing I had left of her," I say, turning around and heading for the door. "I'm going back there. Right now."

"It's gone," she says.

"What do you mean, *it's gone?"*

"Your old apartment. The lease was in Dad's name, remember? He broke it and paid the early termination fee. Someone else is already living there."

Tears well up in my eyes. "It's *gone?* What did you do with all her stuff?" My hand comes up to my mouth to cover a sob. "Oh, God. Did you throw it away?"

I drop my purse on the floor and run through the apartment, looking for Dahlia's room, but knowing there won't be one. I rip open the bedroom doors until I find the one with my furniture. And that's when I see it. I see Dahlia's favorite blanket lying on the foot of my bed. I grab it and sink down onto the bed, holding the blanket tightly against me.

Through my tears, I look around the room, the only evidence of my daughter being the framed pictures of her on the wall.

I look back at Holly standing in the doorway. "How could you do this?" I shout. "You had no right."

"Ivy—"

"Get out, Holly. I can't even look at you."

She walks into the room and picks something up off the dresser. Something I've never seen before.

"Here, you should look through this," she says. "And we didn't get rid of anything. It's all in storage."

Then she turns around and walks out the door, closing it after her.

I look down at what she placed in my lap. It looks like a scrapbook. It's got a picture of a flower on the cover. A dahlia. I open it and instantly big balls of tears roll down my cheeks. Inside the book looks to be just about every picture my daughter ever sketched, drew, or painted. The ones from her bedroom walls. The ones she created at the shop. The ones she slaved over in the hospital. Holly had them all laminated and bound together in one large book.

The tears, the memories, the jet-lag—it all has me feeling exhausted and I curl up with Dahlia's blanket and go to sleep.

~ ~ ~

Holly is sitting at the kitchen table, sipping a beer, when I emerge from my bedroom. She runs her hand down the side of the bottle, her finger catching the condensation as she looks up at me guiltily.

"I'm sorry," she says, at the same time as I say, "Thank you."

"Wait, what?" she asks. "Thank you?"

I fetch myself a bottle of water from the refrigerator and sit next to her. "If you'd done this before, I would have hated you. Before, I was frozen in time. I was unable to move forward. I had nothing but her memory. But now …" I look down at the lei that's still around my neck. Then I nod back to my room. "The book. It's … it's perfect. Thank you so much."

Holly lets out a long, relieved breath. Then I pull my chair next to hers and make her sit here as I page through the pictures I took in Hawaii. I tell her all the things I hadn't already told her on our phone calls. The sun has gone down by the time I finish talking.

My sister wraps me in a hug. "I've missed you."

I laugh. "You already said that at the airport."

"Yeah, but that was me missing your *physical* presence. I've also missed my sister. My best friend. The talks we used to have. The things we used to do. That person is back now. And I'm pretty sure I know who to thank for it."

I smile thinking of Bass. Then I check the time. He wanted me to stop by the firehouse to see him tonight. And even though the long flight and the time change has me feeling off, I still can't wait to see him.

"Just let me change and freshen up. Then you can come to the firehouse with me and thank him in person."

"Seriously?" she says, smiling and looking down at her clothes. "Well, shit, I guess I'd better put on something that shows a little more cleavage then."

I laugh. "Men don't like you for your boobs, Hol."

She pats my hand in a motherly fashion. "Oh, my sweet, innocent, baby sister." Then she darts to her bedroom to, no doubt, put on something that will have Bass's coworkers drooling over her.

CHAPTER TWENTY-THREE

SEBASTIAN

"Briggs!" Cameron yells from the garage. "Someone's here to see you."

I smile, walking down the hall with an extra spring in my step.

"*Two* someones, actually," Cameron says as I round the corner. "Two *hot* someones."

We just finished eating dinner, so everyone is in the main room. And they are all looking at me.

"What?" I say. "I couldn't wait until tomorrow to see my girl. So sue me."

I push through the doors out into the garage where Justin is already greeting our guests.

Ivy and I lock eyes. *Damn.* I wish everyone wasn't watching. Because all I want to do is pick her up in my arms and kiss her.

Oh, what the hell.

I stride over to her and lift her off the ground and into a hug before my lips come crashing down on hers. Her legs clamp around my waist as we taste each other for the first time in two weeks.

The laughter and whistles I hear in the background don't even bother me. I don't care about anything other than the fact that I'm kissing this woman and she's kissing me back. I know she just got back from Hawaii this afternoon, but with this one kiss, I could swear she's telling me she's okay.

When we finally break apart, I put her down. "Hi," I say, brushing a stray hair behind her ear.

"Hi, yourself."

I nod to her sister. "Hey, Holly."

She smiles at me. "Bass."

"Justin Neal," Justin says, coming to stand between Ivy and Holly. He holds out his hand to Holly, checking out her cleavage.

"Holly Greene," she says, shaking his hand while she blatantly peruses the muscles on his arms. She looks over at Ivy and raises her eyebrows in appreciation.

"Looks like a match made in heaven," Ivy whispers to me.

She has no idea how right she is. Justin is the playboy of Squad 13—hell, he's the playboy of the firehouse, maybe the entire battalion.

"Come on. Let me introduce you to the guys and then I'll give you a tour."

"So, Justin," Holly says, looking over at the rigs. "Which one of these do you work on?"

He points to it. "That one. I'm the engineer, uh, the driver."

"Oooooh, really? I'd love to see your … *truck*," she says with a sultry grin.

He laughs. "I'd love to show it to you. Right this way." Justin looks over at us. "Catch you later. Nice to meet you, Ivy."

"You, too," Ivy says to him as they walk the other way. Then she turns to me. "Did we even meet? I think once he saw Holly, he didn't even know anyone else was in the room. That tends to happen a lot."

"Sweetheart, your sister has *nothing* on you. You're both gorgeous."

"She got more in the boob department."

I look at Ivy's chest. "Your boobs are fantastic." I shift myself around. "Shit, now I'm getting hard."

She giggles.

God, I can't wait to get her alone.

I take her inside and introduce her to the guys from Engine and Squad. When she meets Lieutenant Brett Cash, the OIC of Squad, she whispers in my ear, "Wow. Holly will be disappointed she didn't see *him* first."

I elbow her. "Oh, you think he's good-looking, do you?"

She shrugs. "He's all right, I guess. But I'll bet he doesn't play guitar the way you do."

I shake my head and smile. "I'm the only one here who plays. Besides, Cash is married. Has a baby, too."

Debbe and Ryan come through the doors. "Guys, I'd like you to meet Ivy Greene. Ivy, this is Debbe Kane and Ryan Reed. They're our paramedics."

"Nice to meet you."

The alarm sounds, but just for EMS.

Ivy watches Debbe and Ryan head out the door and then she looks back at me and the rest of the guys who aren't bothering to move. "Don't you have to go?"

"No. They didn't call for Engine or Squad. We're good for now. The paramedics go on more calls than the rest of us."

"Oh, good," she says. "You used to do that, right?"

"Yeah, before I went to the fire academy."

"What's the difference between a paramedic and an EMT?" she asks.

"Well, paramedics have a lot more training. Whereas EMTs can do basic things like administer oxygen and splint broken limbs, paramedics are trained to put in IVs, push meds and intubate."

"You know how to do all that?" she asks. "Put tubes down people's throats and help them breathe?"

"I do."

"Wow. Is everyone here a paramedic?"

"No. Most of them are EMTs with the exception of J.D., Cash, and me." I wave my hand around the room. "Do you want a tour?"

"Yeah, sure."

"Well, this is the day room. It's pretty much where we hang out when we have nothing else to do." I walk her past the recliners, the large TV, and the huge table that seats all of us. "And over here are some games." I show her the foosball table and the dart board.

Then we head down the hall. "In there is our weight room. We work out a lot. Over there are some offices." We climb the stairs. "And here is the bunk room."

She looks around at the large room with beds separated by chest-high partitions. "I've wondered what this would look like," she says. "It's pretty much how they show it in the movies."

"Some of the newer houses have separate cubbies for each person, but this is how most of the houses in the city are set up."

"Where is yours?" she asks.

I walk her to the back wall and motion to my space. She steps in and sits down on my bed. Then she smiles when she sees what's on my side table. She picks up the framed picture of her, one I took when we were on the beach.

"So I can wake up to your beautiful face every day," I say, reaching out to her.

She puts her hand in mine. I want nothing more than to tackle her onto my bed and make love to her. I've thought about nothing else this past week.

"Are you … okay?" I ask.

I know she knows what I mean. We've talked a lot over the past week about her coming back to New York. About her coming back to reality. She was so worried about sinking back into depression. It would kill me to find out that all the progress she made in Hawaii was for naught.

She squeezes my hand. "I think I just might be getting there."

I lean down and kiss her forehead. "Come on, we'd better finish the tour before I have to go on a call."

Walking out of the bunk room, she notices something. She points to the pole in the corner. "You actually have a pole? I thought maybe that was just in the movies."

"All of the older firehouses have them," I say, walking her over to it. "But most don't use it anymore. See how this one is fenced off?"

"Why don't you use it?"

"You'd be amazed how many ankle and leg injuries firefighters got from landing the wrong way. And in some cases, people would fall through the opening when they were in a hurry at two or three in the morning."

"Really?"

"Yeah. As a whole, the fire service has tried to go away from poles, and outside the city, most new stations are now only one story."

"Darn," she says with a smirk. "I was kind of looking forward to seeing you slide down the pole."

I laugh. "I wouldn't mind seeing you on a pole, either."

Our heated stares burn into each other. I grab her hand. "Let's go before we get indecent."

Down in the garage, I show her the truck I work on. "This is Engine 319."

She looks at it. "Where's the ladder?"

"Engines don't have them. Those trucks are called *Ladders* and we don't have one at this station. Engine trucks are the first line of fire suppression and we also go on a lot of medical calls. Ladder trucks are for aerial suppression. And then there's Squad." I point to the squad truck only to see Holly and Justin making out in the front seat. I shake my head and laugh.

"Looks like we might have to make it a double date tomorrow night," Ivy says.

I pull her close to my side. "As long as I get to take you home after."

She smiles up at me. "I think that could be arranged."

Her smile and her declaration have my cock stirring. I tug on her hand. "There is one more room I want to show you," I say, pulling her back to the equipment room.

Her eyes go wide. "There's so much stuff in here." She reaches out to touch some gear. "What is this used for?"

I don't answer her question and she doesn't ask another because my lips collide with hers. I devour her mouth like I'll never get to kiss her again. I pull her tightly against me and then lift her up and pin her against the wall. Her legs wrap around me and the friction on my pants makes me hard.

"Shit, Ivy. I've missed this."

She moans into my mouth when I kiss her again. Her hips undulate into me, making me crazy for her. I put a hand over her

T-shirt and caress her left breast while I suck on a spot on her neck.

"Oh, God," she whispers to the ceiling.

Then we hear the alarm. I go still and listen. It's for both Engine and Squad. "I have to go," I say, putting her down and pulling her to the door. "I'm sorry."

"Don't be sorry. Go," she says. "I'll see you tomorrow night."

I run to the truck and pull on my turnout gear, all too aware of the full-on erection that I'm hoping goes down quickly. "Tomorrow," I say, as I hop in the back of the rig. Then I watch her watch me until the truck is out of sight.

J.D. and Auggie stare at me. Even Duck takes his eyes off the road and gives me a look.

"What?" I bite at them.

J.D. shakes his head at me. "You might want to wipe the lipstick off your face before we get to the call. Someone might mistake it for blood and leave you for dead."

"Shit," I say, wiping my mouth on the sleeve of my coat as they all share a laugh.

~ ~ ~

"So what do you guys do all day when you aren't fighting fires?" Holly asks, as the waitress brings our first round of drinks.

"Well, first of all, fighting fires is actually a very small part of the job," Justin tells her. "We deal with a lot of other shit, too."

"Yeah, but you can't be out on calls *all* the time, can you?" she asks.

"We're not," he says. "But there's still plenty to do. We check the equipment on the trucks, we clean, we test fire hoses, do building walk-throughs. And we work out a lot."

Holly puts her hand on Justin's bicep. "Yeah, I can tell."

Ivy rolls her eyes at her older sister. "So, what's the difference between the two trucks you work on?" she asks.

"Squad and Engine both go on a lot of the calls, and we both fight fires, but Squad is equipped to perform heavy extrications, entrapments, and forcible entries. They have to go through more specialized training than engine companies do. And our lieutenant, Brett Cash, even has hazmat training."

"Impressive," Holly says.

"Brett has pretty much gone through all the training available to firefighters. He lost his mom in 9/11 and vowed to help as many people as possible."

"Oh, gosh. That's horrible," Ivy says.

"It's not unusual to have at least one person in every house who lost someone that day," I tell her.

The waitress brings our dinner and we eat as Holly continues to ask questions about what we do, batting her lashes at Justin the entire time. I wonder if I should tell her she doesn't need to try and impress him. She's got boobs and a nice ass—the only two requirements in his book.

All through dinner, Ivy and I tease each other under the table. She's wearing a dress she bought in Hawaii. I should know, I've already peeled it off her once before. I plan to do it again in about an hour. Less if we eat faster.

I run my hand along her thigh, feeling her shiver through the thin fabric. When I just about reach her panty area, she clears her throat and shifts in her chair. Then she grabs the table, nearly toppling over our drinks.

"You okay, Ivy?" Holly asks.

"Hmmm? Oh … uh, I'm good." She bites her lip as I give her leg a squeeze.

Then she picks up my hand and puts it back on my leg, but she doesn't remove her hand. And I find she can give as good as she gets. Her fingers lightly graze the fly of my pants as I try to hold a conversation with Justin. But talking with a co-worker is not exactly what I want to do with the rising problem in my lap.

I turn my attention to Ivy, pushing her hair behind her ear as I lean in close. "I can't wait to get you alone."

"I was thinking the same thing," she says.

"Stay with me tonight, Ivy Greene," I whisper. "I've missed waking up next to you."

She gives me a half-smile and then looks to see if Holly and Justin are listening. They aren't. They seem perfectly happy ogling each other over their glasses of wine.

"I go back to work tomorrow for the first time in a long time. Everything's finally falling into place. I'm starting to feel, I don't know … normal again. I have you to thank for that. So I'll come back to your place. Of course I will. But I'll be going home by midnight. I hope you're not mad about that."

I rub my finger across the bare skin of her back. "I'm not mad about that. I couldn't be happier that you are getting back to normal." I look at the time on my phone. "It's not quite nine o'clock. That means we have three hours before you turn into a pumpkin. We can do a lot in three hours."

Her face lights up and she squirms in her seat.

"Justin and I were thinking of heading to a club," Holly says. "I was going to invite you, but with all the eye-fucking going on over there, I'm guessing you'll pass?"

"Do you have to be so crude, Hol?" Ivy says.

"Well, what would *you* call it when the two of you can't keep your hands off each other? I mean, based on the look on your face a minute ago, I wouldn't be surprised if you went all Fifty Shades and took off your panties right here at the table."

"Holly!"

The three of us laugh while Ivy blushes.

"I think we'll skip the club," I say. "Ivy and I have other plans."

We pay the check and say goodbye to Holly and Justin. I hail a cab and open the door to let Ivy inside. I scoot in next to her. Then I lean close. "You're mine for the next three hours."

"Just for the next three hours?" she asks.

I take her hand in mine. "No. For the next three hours and seventy years if I have anything to say about it."

The smile that lights up her face lets me know so much more than any of her words. It lets me know just how much she's healed. And for the first time since I met Ivy Greene four weeks and two days ago, I breathe easily.

CHAPTER TWENTY-FOUR

IVY

I look at myself in the mirror, thinking I look kind of green. I'm not sure why I woke up feeling so crappy. Last night was incredible. It was even better than Hawaii. It was better because I think we both knew last night was only the beginning. Maybe the reason I look like death warmed over is because today will be my first day back at work.

I know Dahlia will be everywhere. At the table in the corner that I had set up with arts and crafts. At the counter, charming customers. In the back, putting together flower arrangements with Aunt Holly and me.

I walk back into my bedroom and sit on my bed, pulling Dahlia's blanket into my lap. I page through the scrapbook of her drawings. *Did she always make this many pictures of daisies?* I don't even remember some of them. Then again, they were her favorites, so maybe I was just blocking it out—my subconscious' way of protecting me.

I think about how in Hawaii, daisies seemed to be everywhere. I trace the outline of one of her creations, remembering her.

I look up and study my favorite picture of her hanging over my bed. The one where she's all dressed up and smiling for the camera. I remember that day like it was yesterday. It was Valentine's Day and Eli took Dahlia on a *date*. We went out and found a pretty red dress for her. I did her hair in the fancy braids she always liked. Eli brought her flowers and took her out to dinner. It was one of her good days. She wasn't quite five years old and we hadn't yet found out that her transplant was failing.

I think of what a good father Eli was. He really knew how to make Dahlia laugh. While I was the one she lived with, the one who managed all of her appointments and hospital stays, he was the perfect part-time dad—the person who always made her smile even when there was nothing to smile about.

I make it a point to remember to call him later. We haven't spoken in a week.

"Ready?" Holly asks, peeking her head in my doorway.

"Just about."

I fold up the blanket and put it on my pillow. I'm not sure why I keep it there instead of on the foot of my bed. I guess I like the idea of her lying close to me. I run my hand over the soft material. "I love you, baby girl, but please, please don't come to work with me today. I'm not sure I could handle it."

"Who are you talking to?" Holly asks from down the hall.

"Nobody," I say, grabbing my purse.

She narrows her eyes at me. "You still talk to her, don't you?"

I shrug.

"Does she talk back?" she asks warily.

"I'm not crazy, you know."

"I never said you were. I was just wondering."

"She talks to me in my dreams sometimes," I admit.

"She does me too."

"Really?"

She nods. "She's the one who told me to get rid of your apartment and move you in with me."

"It's not really her, Hol. You know that, don't you? Our dreams are just our subconscious talking."

"Believe what you want to, little sister. But I'm telling you, my niece and I have had some pretty interesting conversations."

I roll my eyes at her.

"What? It's true. And Grandpa Joe—he stops by, too. We party sometimes."

I laugh at her as I grab a muffin off the table. "Come on. I don't want to be late for my first day back."

Twenty minutes later, I stand on the sidewalk as Holly unlocks the gate that covers the storefront windows. I watch her push it to the sides and then open the front door. I haven't been here in months. I tried to come back to work in February, and then again in April, but both times I had anxiety attacks and had to leave.

The first thing I notice when I enter the shop is that Dahlia's corner table is gone. I wouldn't let anyone move it before, but now, just like she did with my apartment, Holly has taken it upon herself to change things. I walk over to where it was. Tears well up in my eyes when I look at the wall. It has photos of Dahlia when she was painting. And there are framed pictures of her artwork, similar to the artwork Holly bound in the scrapbook at home.

I turn around to see Holly staring at me.

"Thank you," I say.

I reach out and touch Dahlia's face. "Mommy is going to be okay."

The back doorbell chimes with our morning delivery and Holly runs back to get it. I set about checking on which flowers on the floor are still good enough to sell and which aren't. I go around the store with my plastic bin, throwing the old ones into it, knowing they will be put to good use. We have a lady down the street who buys our older flowers, using the petals to make soap, bath bombs and perfume.

I walk into the back and see Holly finishing up with the delivery guy. I start to unwrap everything when I notice something. "Holly, since when have we ordered this many daisies?"

She shrugs. "I'm not sure. A month or so maybe. We've started to have a run on them for some reason."

My lips curve up into a smile. I can't help but remember my daughter and her love of daisies. *'Daisies gonna make everything better,'* I can almost hear her sweet voice say.

Then my hand comes to my mouth and I feel sick. I quickly grab a bottle of water from our refrigerator and drink it to tamp down the acid in my throat. Then I hold the bottle to my forehead.

"You okay?" Holly asks, putting a supportive hand on my arm.

"Yeah. Just dealing with memories, I guess."

I busy myself cutting stems and arranging flowers. "What did Janie say when you told her I was coming back?"

"She was happy for you. She's working over at the Manhattan shop now."

I give her an accusing stare. "You mean she's waiting for your call after I freak out and leave."

"That's not how it is, Ivy. She's helping out Mom and Dad. They are trying to cut back on their hours. They aren't getting any younger, you know."

"Whatever."

It's a lie. My parents haven't even hit sixty yet. They love to work. Everyone is waiting for me to fail.

At nine o'clock when the shop opens, I help the first few customers, happy to be back in the swing of things. I glance over to catch Holly smiling. She nods at me. Then I see her pull out her phone and tap on it. My bet is she's sending a progress report to Mom, Dad, Alder, and Christina.

"Tell them everything is A-Okay," I shout from across the room.

She laughs and gives me a thumbs-up.

By lunchtime, it feels like I never left. I even managed not to break down when a long-time customer expressed her sympathies over Dahlia's death.

I can't wait to tell Bass about my day. He's going to be so proud of me.

"Are you okay here while I run out and grab lunch for us?" Holly asks.

"Of course."

"Any requests?"

"Whatever you get will be fine."

"Okay. Be back in fifteen."

While she's gone, I help a few customers and then I start on a new flower arrangement. It's a mixture of dahlias, daisies, and baby's breath. By the time I'm done, I know I won't be selling this one. I set it aside to take home with me later. I have just the spot for it in our apartment.

Holly comes through the door, carrying our lunch. As she takes it into the back room, the pungent smell of barbeque assaults my nose, making my stomach turn. I race past her and into the bathroom, just in time to heave over the toilet.

Holly comes up behind me, holding my hair until I'm done. Then she hands me a wet paper towel and rubs my back as I clean myself up.

"I'm sorry," she says. "I know how hard this must be on you."

I shake my head. "It's not that. I'm fine, Hol. Today has gone much better than I imagined. I mean, I felt a bit nauseous this morning, but it was to be expected." I look over at the bag of takeout and nod to it. "It was the smell of the food. It was the strangest feeling. When I got a whiff, I just knew I was going to throw up."

Holly closes the lid of the toilet and sits down on it. "Shit, Ivy, really? You don't think you're pregnant, do you?"

"Pregnant?" A maniacal laugh escapes me. "Are you crazy? I'm on the pill, Hol."

She raises an accusing brow. "We both know you suck at taking it, Ivy."

"But Bass and I used condoms, too," I say.

Except for that one time on the cliff, my subconscious tells me.

"Think about it," she says. "The same thing happened to you the last two times. The first time, you couldn't stomach the smell of bacon. Mom couldn't make it for months. And what was it with Dahlia?"

I close my eyes as my heart sinks. "Fish," I say. "I couldn't stand the smell of fish." I look up at her. "Oh my God, Holly."

My throat becomes thick. *It couldn't be.*

"Wait here," she says. "I'll be back in two minutes."

I hear her go through the front door and lock it. Then a minute later, I hear her unlock it and then lock it again from the inside. She runs back into the bathroom, handing me a bag from the small market next door. "I bought three tests," she says, walking out the door and closing it behind her.

I stare at the pregnancy tests, not wanting to take them, but knowing I should. I think about the past few days, how I've been feeling off, but I did just come back from Hawaii, and my body is still getting used to the time difference. I try to remember the last time I had my period, but even on the pill, I'm not sure I've had a normal one since Dahlia died, so it's hard to tell.

Then I reach up and grab my breasts, thinking of how they've gotten heavier lately. But I guess I just thought it was all the food I consumed in Hawaii.

No. I'm not pregnant. No way.

By the time I've peed on all three sticks, I've convinced myself that Holly and I are crazy to even think it. I open the door and hand her the sticks. "No way am I pregnant," I say, giving dirty looks to the takeout food on the counter as I make my way across the room for a bottle of water.

Then I watch her as she looks at the clock on the wall for two more minutes.

She looks down at the tests and then at me. "Then we better go get some more tests, because all of these are faulty."

I calmly walk back over to her, thinking she's pranking me. But when I look down at the tests and see what she sees, I drop my water and run back to the bathroom to vomit once again.

I sit down on the floor of the bathroom, wanting to shrivel up and make it all disappear.

"I'm not surprised," Holly says. "With all the sex you guys had in Hawaii. According to you, you fucked like rabbits."

Tears blur my vision and I close my eyes, causing warm droplets to fall onto my cheeks. "I-I can't, Hol."

She takes a seat on the floor next to me and grabs my hand. "This won't be like the others, Ivy. Maybe this is a blessing."

I look up at her, wanting so desperately to believe that's true. "I'm terrified."

"It's going to be fine," she says. "You'll see."

"What am I going to tell Bass? We've only been together for a few weeks."

"He loves you, Ivy. Everyone can see that. He'll be okay with it. I promise you."

I squeeze my eyes shut and shake my head in denial. "I can't tell him. Not until I know for sure. I have to know for sure, Hol."

She stands up and holds her hand out to me. "Okay, then. Come on, let's go find out for sure."

"What do you mean? You know it takes weeks to get in to our gynecologist."

"We're not going there, we're going to the emergency room."

"This isn't exactly an emergency," I say.

"Look at you," she says, eyeing my face that's smeared with mascara. "You're a mess. You're shaking uncontrollably. I'd say that's an emergency. We're going."

She wipes my face with a wet paper towel and then grabs our purses on the way to the door. She puts up the closed sign in the window and locks up. Then we walk four blocks over to the nearest hospital.

It's the longest walk of my life.

~ ~ ~

I stare at the tiny blob on the ultrasound screen, unsure if I want to laugh, cry, or scream.

Holly squeezes my hand. "It's okay, Ivy. Everything will be okay."

Then I realize I'm feeling something I didn't expect. I think I'm feeling … happy.

"I can do this," I say, already in love with the little life growing inside of me. "Even if he doesn't want to do it with me, I can do this. Maybe this was meant to happen."

She smiles at me. "I think it absolutely was."

I can't stop staring at the screen and the tiny pulsating heartbeat. But then I see something that makes me feel sick all over again. I see Dahlia's birthdate in the corner of the screen. "What's that?" I ask the technician, pointing to it.

"That's the EDC," she says. "The day you got pregnant."

"What?" I try to sit up, but she's still got the ultrasound wand stuck up my vagina. "No. Get it out," I say, feeling bile rise up in my throat. "Now!"

She pulls the wand out of me just in time for me to hurl over the side of the hospital bed.

The tech rushes out of the room, presumably to fetch someone to clean up the mess I've made.

"What is it?" Holly asks, seeing the terror on my face.

"The d-date," I say, wiping my mouth on my sleeve. "Dahlia's b-birthday. It was weeks before I even met Bass. And Eli and I … We were sad. It just happened. And we didn't use … Oh my God."

"Oh, Ivy," she says, her face falling in understanding. "You slept with him?"

My sister stares at me, knowing my world just fell apart for the third time.

"How could God be so cruel?" I say, bringing a shaky hand to my mouth to cover my sobs.

"There are no guarantees it will happen again," she says. "Odds are the baby will just be a carrier."

Someone comes in to clean up my mess. "Are you okay?" the ultrasound tech asks, peeking around the curtain at us.

"She'll be fine," Holly tells her. "This may not have turned out the way she wanted, but she'll be fine. They *both* will be."

~ ~ ~

Hours later, I'm at home in my room, paging through Dahlia's scrapbook, knowing I'm not strong enough to go through it all again. My first thought after seeing the date on the screen was to admit myself to the hospital so I could have an abortion. But my second thought, the one that kept me from doing it right then and there, was of my precious daughter. Would I have given up my five and a half years with her had I known what would happen? And maybe having an abortion would be selfish. I have to ask myself if I'd be doing it for myself or for the baby.

I stare at my phone with the picture of Bass and me on the beach as my wallpaper. Why couldn't it have been him?

I know I need to make the call. I need to say the words. Get it over with. But I know it will wreck him as much as it has me. Can we even get through this?

I dial the number.

"Hello?"

I break down in sobs. I can barely even breathe.

"Ivy, is that you? What is it? Are you okay? Tell me."

"I … I'm p-pregnant, Eli."

CHAPTER TWENTY-FIVE

SEBASTIAN

It's not like Ivy to ignore my texts and calls. For two days now, I've been waiting on her to reach out to me. I was giving her some space because I know how hard it must be for her to be back in these surroundings and have all the memories she must be having.

But two days?

I push open the front door to *The Greene Thumb* and look around. Nobody is behind the counter, but I hear someone in the back.

"Be right there!" someone shouts after hearing the bells over the door ring.

It's not Ivy's voice. A second later, Holly comes around the corner. When she sees me, her look says a thousand words. It's the same look Aspen gave me when I said I loved her. It's the same look Brooke's dad gave me right before he said there wasn't going to be a wedding.

"What's going on, Holly?" I ask.

"I think you need to ask Ivy."

"Don't you think I've been trying to?" I say. "I've been texting and calling her for days. What happened? Why isn't she at work today? We had a great night the other night and then complete radio silence."

"Bass, you really need to talk to her. It's not my place to say."

"How can I talk to her if she won't take my calls?" I shake my head. "I don't even know where she lives because the address she gave me when we were in Hawaii isn't valid anymore since she moved in with you."

Holly grabs a note card off the counter and scribbles something on it. She hands it to me. "Here's our address. She should be there now. The code at the bottom is for the front door of the building."

"Is she depressed?"

"Bass," she says, looking irritated.

"Holly, I love her."

"I know you do. But you need to understand there is only so much loss a person can take. When you see her, please remember that."

"Loss? What loss?"

"Just go see her." She turns me around and pushes me toward the door.

My mind is spinning, wondering what could be going on. Did she lose someone? Obviously not a family member or Holly would have been devastated as well. My walk turns into a jog and then I find myself practically sprinting to the address Holly wrote down for me.

I have to punch the code in three times before the door unlocks, because each time I mess it up. I don't bother with the elevator. I run up the three flights of stairs to the fourth floor. Then I stand at her door, catching my breath before I knock.

When she answers, my heart sinks. Her eyes are red-rimmed and she's wearing nothing but a T-shirt under a robe that she pulls around herself when she sees me.

"Sweetheart, are you okay?"

I take a step forward, wanting to take her in my arms, but she takes a step back.

"What's wrong, Ivy?"

She looks over her shoulder and then back at me, doing her best to avoid direct eye contact. "I don't want to hurt you, Bass."

"So don't."

"Sometimes it's not a choice," she says, shifting her weight nervously from foot to foot.

Then a guy walks down the hallway and goes into the kitchen. He eyes me, but he doesn't come to the door.

"Who the hell is that?" I ask, my blood pressure rising as I look at her skimpy attire once again.

"It's Eli," she says, with a low, long sigh.

I look between the two of them, feeling nauseous. "Why do you look so guilty, Ivy? And why aren't you dressed? Are you fucking him?"

Ivy cringes before I notice a quiver of her chin.

Eli hears me raise my voice and makes his way over to the door.

"No." She looks down at her nervous hands and then back at me. "I mean, not lately. Um … this is really hard, Bass."

"What's hard? You dumping me? Is that why Holly sent me over here, so I could see for myself how you can just push aside everything we shared in Hawaii?"

"It's not like that, man," Eli says.

"Eli, stop," Ivy says with an emotion-choked voice. "I can handle this. Can you just wait in the other room, please?"

"Not if he's going to stand here and yell at you." He turns to me. "She's been through enough without you adding to the mix."

"What the hell are you talking about?"

"Eli, please," she begs.

He holds up his hands. "Fine. But no yelling or I'm coming back out."

We watch him walk down the hallway.

"Is he going to your bedroom?" I ask through clenched teeth.

She's having a hard time looking at me. Her eyes are glued to the door in a vacant stare. "Bass, I never wanted to hurt you."

"I love you, Ivy. I wanted to spend my life with you."

More tears come streaming out of her eyes. "I know. I thought I wanted that too. But things change. I'm so sorry."

"Things don't have to change. Not if you throw *him* out instead of me."

She looks to the ceiling and rubs the back of her neck. "Eli and I, we've been through so much together. Nobody else can understand. Not even you."

"Look at you, Ivy. You're clearly upset. You aren't thinking straight. Is he making you do this? Does he have some kind of hold on you?"

She shakes her head. "This is my choice. I've made it, Bass. But that doesn't mean I can't feel bad. Everything you and I shared. It was real. You helped me in so many ways. But Eli is the only one who can help me now. I'm sorry. Please, I have to ask you to leave."

"You want me to walk out this fucking door and not look back as if the last four weeks of my life never even happened?"

"Yes," she says, with closed eyes.

I hit the wall. "I'm not leaving."

Eli comes out from the back. "Tell him, Ivy. He deserves to know."

"Eli, no."

"What do I deserve to know, Ivy?"

She shakes her head as her body heaves with sobs.

"Tell him," he says.

"I-I'm still in love with Eli," she says. "I tried to get over him. I tried really hard. And Hawaii was great. But Eli is the one I need to be with."

"Ivy," Eli says, staring her down as if to scold her.

"Eli, this is between Bass and me."

"You still loved him?" I ask, angrily taking a step forward. "When we were sleeping together?"

Eli puts a hand on my chest, pushing me away from her. I'm a lot bigger than he is, but it's obvious he loves her and would do anything to protect her. Just like I would.

"It's no different than you using Brooke to try and get over Aspen," she says. "It didn't work for you either, did it?"

"But you said you loved me, Ivy. We made plans."

Her hands come up to cover her mouth. Her eyes close momentarily. She's hurting. This is tearing her apart. She truly looks to be torn between two men she loves. And I'm clearly the loser.

"Plans change," she says. "I tried to love you. I w-wanted to. But I c-can't. Please, don't make this harder than it already is."

Eli looks pissed. But in some strange way, he looks pissed at Ivy and not at me. He doesn't look at me like the competition—like the way I'm looking at him. He looks at me like he feels sorry for me.

"So that's it?" I ask.

"I'm s-sorry," she says.

She reaches out like she wants to touch me, but she pulls her hand back. I want to pull her into my arms and make her change her mind. But how can a few weeks compete with what they've shared together? High school sweethearts. Kids. Extreme loss.

I back up and cross over the threshold into the hallway. "I'm sorry, too, Ivy. You'll never know just how much."

"Goodbye, Sebastian." She shuts the door and I hear her body thump against it as she cries out in agony. I want to go back in and comfort her. But I don't. Because that's not my job anymore. It's *his*.

I take the elevator to the ground floor, studying myself in the reflective chrome doors, wondering why I always choose women who are incapable of relationships. "Fuck!" I yell to no one. I hit the door, denting it and distorting my face.

When the doors open, I walk outside. And then I run. I run faster and farther than I've ever run before. And when I finally get home, I collapse from exhaustion. But that doesn't keep me from dreaming of her and the life we'll never get to have.

CHAPTER TWENTY-SIX

IVY

It's been weeks since I've seen Bass. Weeks of throwing myself into work to try and forget that the child growing inside of me will make me love him before I have to go through another miscarriage, stillbirth, or worse—bonding for years and then losing another love of my life.

Him. Thinking of the baby as a boy is the only way I can get through this. Because as much as it hurt to lose Jonah, losing Dahlia was a million times worse.

We talked about it, Eli and I. We talked about terminating the pregnancy. But in the end, neither of us could bring ourselves to say we genuinely wanted to do it. It would be like saying we wished we never had Dahlia.

The doctors told us the chances of us having another ARPKD baby are small. But I know better. I know this baby has the same chance of having it as the other two. When Dahlia was born, they said it was unusual for a couple to have two children with the disease since the chances are only twenty-five percent with each one. That's twenty-five percent too high when we're batting a thousand.

They also said there is no way to determine if the baby has it in utero, not unless there is clear visible evidence of enlarged kidneys or cysts. And even if neither of those shows up on an ultrasound, it still doesn't mean the baby is out of the woods.

I had several ultrasounds with Dahlia, mostly because I was scared of losing another baby, and none of them showed any indication of the disease. But perhaps that's because they didn't know they were looking for it.

I sit down in a chair in the shop office and open up a package that was delivered this morning. I put the batteries inside the device and then try using it. Then I start to panic.

"What are you doing?" Holly says, coming around the corner.

"I'm trying to hear the heartbeat," I say, moving the wand thing around my lower, still-flat belly.

"Seriously?"

I shrug. "It will give me peace of mind."

"Except that you look terrified right now," she says.

"That's because I can't find it. Maybe you can help."

Holy lets me give her a demonstration of how it works. Then I lean back in the chair as she moves the wand all over my stomach.

"I must be doing it wrong," she says.

Tears prickle my eyes. "Or maybe there isn't a heartbeat."

"Ivy, you can't beat yourself up like this."

"Try again," I say.

She spends a few more minutes on it, but then the bells on the front door chime. "I'll be right back," she says.

I pull my shirt down, put the fetal Doppler away and grab my purse.

"I'll be back later," I say, when I pass Holly on my way to the front door.

"Where are you going?"

"I need to be sure."

I hear her sigh as I walk out of the shop. I make the four-block trek to the emergency room. I know this will probably cost me at least a few hundred dollars. But at this point, I don't care.

"I think my baby is dead," I tell the intake nurse.

"Is the baby here?" she asks, looking behind me.

"I'm pregnant. I think the baby died."

She gives me a sympathetic look and then takes my information and puts a hospital band on my wrist.

"Right this way," someone says from the other side of the double doors that lead into the back.

The nurse gets me set up behind a curtain and takes my blood pressure and temperature. Then she asks me about the pregnancy.

"A doctor will be in shortly," she says.

It seems to take forever for the doctor to show up, but the clock on the wall tells me it's only been fifteen minutes when an attractive guy wearing a white lab coats walks around the curtain.

"I'm Dr. Stone," he says. "I'm filling in for Dr. Rigdon today, but not to worry, I know my way around this ER almost as well as my own ER across the bridge. I hear you're worried about a miscarriage. But it says in your chart that you haven't had any bleeding. What makes you think you're losing the pregnancy?"

"I can't find the heartbeat," I say.

"Did your obstetrician send you here?" he asks, confused.

"No. I have one of those Doppler things at home and I can't hear the heartbeat."

He nods. "Oh, I see. I assume you bought it over the Internet?"

"Yes."

"Those can be fairly reliable, but only after about fourteen to sixteen weeks. At ten weeks, you're not far enough along to hear it without being a skilled physician."

"Really? They should tell you that when you buy it."

He pulls out a device from his pocket that looks similar to the one I ordered only a lot more expensive. "Let's take a listen, shall we?"

"Please."

He moves the wand around down by my pubic mound and he presses a lot harder than I was pressing at the shop. Ten seconds later, my own heart starts beating again when we hear the fast-paced *whoosh whoosh whoosh* come through the small speaker.

My head falls back against the pillow, relieved to hear the sound.

"Sounds perfect," he says, removing the device.

"Wait. Can I hear it for just a little longer?"

He smiles and puts it back where it was, moving it around again until he finds the heartbeat. I lie here and listen, hoping things will be different this time. But the nagging feeling inside me tells me otherwise.

"Thank you," I say, after Dr. Stone lets me hear for another minute or two.

"Of course. But I think you should wait at least four more weeks before trying this yourself. You'll just cause undue stress if you don't. You need to relax and enjoy your pregnancy. Your little one will be here before you know it."

I don't tell him there is nothing to relax about or enjoy. I don't tell him that I wish I never got pregnant. I don't tell him how much I regret turning to Eli for comfort on Dahlia's birthday. I don't tell him about the two lives I've already lost and the man I've had to push away because of how screwed up this whole thing is.

I don't tell him any of it. Because he obviously thinks I'm just another paranoid first-time mom.

"Thank you, Dr. Stone. You've been very kind."

"The nurse will be in to discharge you in a minute."

A half-hour later, I'm walking back in the shop. Holly eyes me over the top of the package she's looking at. "I'm assuming all is well?" she says.

"Yeah."

She holds out the packaging of the fetal Doppler. "That's because you didn't bother to read the damn directions, did you? It says you might not be able to hear the heartbeat until about sixteen weeks."

"That's what the doctor told me."

She throws the box at me. "Stop doing things to make yourself crazy," she says. "This is hard enough on you as it is without you creating drama."

"I know. I just thought it would help—"

"If you obsess over things that may or may not happen?" She pulls me over to the stool at the counter and sits me on it. "Ivy, you must know that nothing you do at this point will change the outcome. Your job now is to eat properly and sleep and try not to stress over every little thing. That is what you can do to give this baby the best chance."

I lean in to hug her and when I do, I think I see something out the storefront windows. I pull back.

"What is it?" Holly asks.

"I could swear I just saw Bass."

She nods. "I wouldn't doubt it. He walks past here almost every day. Sometimes I see him jogging, too. I've caught him looking through the window more than once. I wish you'd just tell him. You know he must be suffering."

I shake my head. "No. I'm not telling him, and neither will you. I know you're still hooking up with Justin and if you happen to be where Bass is, you can't tell him. Not under any circumstances. Do you hear me?"

"I hear you, little sister, and I'm not going to rat you out, but don't you think telling him you're pregnant with Eli's baby would at least provide him with more of an explanation?"

"I know him, Holly. If he knew I still loved him and just got pregnant by accident before I'd ever met him, he'd still want to be with me. I know he would."

"Would you please tell me what the hell is so wrong with that? I mean, you love him, Ivy. And he loves you. You two should be together."

"There is no way I would put him through this, Hol. Nobody knows better than I do how devastating this can be. I can't risk him falling in love with the baby—the baby that isn't even his—and then going through anything like what we went through with Dahlia. Or even Jonah. And Eli and I have done this before. We supported each other through both of them. We can do it again."

"But you don't love Eli. In fact, he has a girlfriend. One he's very happy with as I hear him tell it."

"Of course I don't love him."

"And why do you think Eli isn't dumping his girlfriend over this?"

I shrug.

"It's because he's thinking rationally, Ivy. Listen to the doctors. The chances of this baby being sick are low."

"Twenty-five percent is not low, Hol. Think about it. If there was a twenty-five percent chance you would die every time you walked out the door, would you ever leave your house? If there was a twenty-five percent chance your plane would crash every time you flew, would you ever book a flight?"

"Geez, well when you put it that way."

"Yeah, it's a huge possibility. And it's happened twice."

"But what if after, if the baby is okay, what happens then? Will you go crawling back to Bass and say, 'My bad, I still love you and secretly hope you've pined away for me these last seven months'?"

"Of course not. I know he's going to move on."

She shakes her head. "You're giving up the opportunity to be happy. And if anyone deserves to be happy, it's you."

"I can't do it to him, Hol."

She runs a supportive hand up and down my arm while staring at my face. "You should go home and rest. You look tired."

"You mean I look like crap," I say with a pathetic smile.

"You look beautiful, Ivy. But tired."

"I haven't been sleeping very well," I admit. "I don't take sleeping pills anymore because I don't want them to hurt the baby."

I don't tell her that because I'm not taking sleeping pills, I dream. Every night I dream about Dahlia. How she was. How she would have been. How she died. I relive that day over and over in my dreams. Her life and death are on a constant loop that plagues me during my sleep. The only thing that's changed since going off the sleeping pills is now I dream of daisies. Every time Dahlia comes to me in my sleep, she has a daisy in her hair, just like the one I wore in Hawaii.

Oh, how I miss Hawaii. I guess Dahlia's just trying to keep that memory alive, too.

Holly grabs my purse and puts it on my shoulder before pushing me toward the door. "I'll close up. You go home and rest, birthday girl, we're having company later."

~ ~ ~

The sound of laughter wakes me. It takes me a minute to remember where I am. The nap I took was longer than I expected. I look at the clock. It's after six. I hear the squeals of a child coming from the living room. Oh, right, everyone is coming over for dinner.

I check my hair and makeup and then head out to join them.

"Happy birthday!" Christina hugs me as soon as I come in the room. "I'm sorry," she whispers. "I couldn't find a sitter for him."

I close my eyes for a minute and think of how the past two years have been for her—walking on eggshells around me because her son is healthy.

"Christina, I've been so selfish," I say. "Of course Ricky should be here. I've been a horrible sister-in-law and friend and an even worse aunt. I'm so sorry."

"You haven't been horrible, Ivy. You've been human. It's understandable—all of it."

"I'm going to be better, I promise. No matter what happens with …" I put a hand on my stomach. "I'm going to be better."

Ricky toddles over and holds his hands up to Christina. I lean down and try to pick him up, but he fusses and wiggles out of my hands.

"It's okay," Christina says, holding him on her hip. "You remember Aunt Ivy, don't you?"

Ricky buries his face in her neck.

She reaches out to touch my arm. "It'll take time. Thank you for trying."

I nod. Then I greet the rest of my family.

It's odd being pregnant and having nobody acknowledge it. It's the proverbial elephant in the room. It's so different than the other times. When I was pregnant with Jonah, everyone was worried about how two teens still in high school would be able to care for a child. When I was pregnant with Dahlia, after people got over the shock that we'd planned it, everyone said what a blessing she would be in the wake of Jonah's death. But now, everyone knows this child isn't a blessing. Everyone is well aware of the months or years of torture we'll have to go through if the baby is like Jonah and Dahlia.

They all know there is a chance of the baby being normal, or just a carrier. But we don't talk about it. Because what if it's not true? What if everyone convinces me that *this* baby will be okay? What if I start to get excited about the idea of raising a child who isn't tied to doctors, hospitals, and dialysis machines? What if I get my hopes up and then—then my world comes crashing down again.

They all know it's better this way.

My mother puts her arm around me. "I saw what you did and I'm proud of you. I know how hard it's been for you to watch them with Ricky."

"It has, but that doesn't mean I should be a bad person. I was pathetic back then. I don't want to be like that anymore, Mom. I'm tired of playing the victim. I was getting so much better. I was almost normal again, and then—"

"Shhhh," she whispers in my ear as she pulls me in for a hug. "Nobody thinks you're pathetic, dear. God works in mysterious ways."

"You always say that. But do you really believe it? Do you think God has a plan for me, and that plan included two of my children dying—and now, this?"

"I do, sweet Ivy. I do."

My dad comes over and kisses me on the head. "Happy birthday, baby."

"Thanks, Daddy."

Over his shoulder, I see a huge flower arrangement on the table. It's not one of ours, I can tell. I go over and smell the daisies. "Who's this from?"

Holly shrugs. "Don't know. But whoever sent them went through our competition." She wrinkles her nose in disapproval.

"Maybe it was Eli," Alder says.

But we all know better. Eli would have used one of our shops.

I know who sent them. I'm pretty sure all of them know, too. And this room is starting to get awfully claustrophobic with *two* elephants in it.

CHAPTER TWENTY-SEVEN

SEBASTIAN

The stadium erupts in cheers when Sawyer Mills steals a base. It's funny that even though Sawyer plays for Kansas City now, New York still loves him.

Brett bumps his fist to mine. "Sweet!"

The next batter for the Royals strikes out, ending the inning. The Nighthawks come up and score a run, making them up by three after the bottom of the eighth, so as long as they can hold the lead, they'll solidify the win without even having to bat again.

"We're all meeting up at Sawyer's place after the game if you want to come hang for a while."

Brett shakes his head. "Thanks, but these days, a few hours away when I'm not on shift is all I can do."

"Tough being a new dad, Lieutenant?" I ask.

"I told you not to call me that when we're not on duty," he says with a hint of irritation. "Call me Brett, or if you prefer, Cash."

I pat him on the back. "I'm just messing with you."

"To answer your question, it's not tough. I love being a dad. And Leo is four months old now, so it's not exactly new anymore. But I think Amanda has post-partum depression or something. She never wants to be alone with him, which pretty much means she's never alone with *me*. She works all the time. Like *all* the time. I can't tell you the last time we had a meal together. She's even got the nanny living with us now. So I try to be home as much as I can. Hell, I feel like a single parent."

"Hey, sorry. I didn't mean to pressure you into coming to the game."

"You didn't," he says. "I needed this. Yelling at the top of my lungs was just the ticket for getting out all this pent-up frustration."

"So Amanda is for sure keeping her job? I know she was talking about staying home with Leo before he was born."

He rolls his eyes. "Yeah, she's keeping her job. In fact, sometimes I think she likes the job better than Leo and me. And she's been working extra hours now that she's trying to move from assistant buyer to buyer."

"You know, Leo is almost the same age as Caden's twins. Maybe you could get them together for … what do they call it, play dates?"

"Do babies do play dates?" he asks.

"Hell if I know."

Brady Taylor ends the game by striking out the last three batters and the stadium comes alive.

Brett and I walk a few blocks over to where he can catch a cab and then I head to Sawyer and Aspen's townhouse.

When I arrive, it's dark. They won't be home for a while. But I have a key, so I go in and crack a beer from the twelve-pack I brought with me. I come over and check on things from time to time when they're away. I know they've talked about selling it this past year, but Sawyer seems to think they come back enough to justify keeping the place. And it's not like they can't afford it.

I look around the living room, seeing dozens of moving boxes, wondering if they've finally made the decision to sell.

The front door opens and Aspen walks through, followed by her brother. Aspen sees me and runs over, flinging herself into my arms. "Bass, I'm so happy to see you."

I squeeze her tightly. It's been months since I've seen her. We talk on the phone a lot, but it's not the same as having her here. "I'm happy to see you too, Penny." I look over her shoulder. "Nice to see you, Denver."

Once Aspen lets me go, I shake his hand. "Congratulations, man. I was so happy to hear the good news."

"You and me both," he says. "I've never been so happy to leave the place I've always called home."

"I'll bet. So, it didn't take long for them to reverse your charges or whatever?"

"No, it moved pretty quickly. They had their trial last month and one of the guys gave up evidence so they'd go easy on him. He pretty much cleared my name with all the emails he produced. After that, I was exonerated and then it took a few weeks, but my record was expunged."

"That's fantastic," I say, patting him on the back. "Hey, where is everyone else?"

"The Hawks had to stay after for a short meeting," Aspen says. "Sawyer was going to wait for them at the stadium. They'll be here soon. Murphy and Rylee are coming, too. I can't wait to see them."

"How about a drink?" I ask. "I stopped to get some on the way. Didn't know what you'd have here."

"I'll get them," Denver says. "I need to learn my way around the kitchen. Might as well start now."

"What do you mean?" I ask.

"Didn't Aspen tell you? I'm moving into their townhouse."

"You are?"

"It makes sense," Aspen says. "We aren't here much, a month in the off-season and then a week here and there. Denver needs a place to stay and we need a caretaker since Sawyer refuses to sell."

"Are you moving here permanently?" I ask him.

"We'll see. I'm good for a while, now that the court has ordered those scumbags to pay me back for all the restitution I had to pay the others. But I would like to try and get a job here."

"But why leave Kansas City?" I ask. "I mean, now that Aspen is there."

He laughs. "Yeah, kind of ironic, isn't it? But I can't stay there. Even though I was exonerated, the people there have hated me for so long it's not like they're suddenly welcoming me with open arms, you know?"

"So now Sawyer can get traded back and play for the Nighthawks, right?" I ask Aspen.

"It's not that easy," she says. "Plus, even though all of you aren't there, we really like it in Kansas City. I've got school, my volunteer work, and some old friends. And Sawyer likes the change of pace. I guess we don't know what the future will bring, but for now, we're happy with things the way they are."

"That won't stop me from trying to talk you into moving back," I say.

Aspen hugs me again. "I would expect nothing less."

I raise my beer. "Welcome to the city," I say to Denver. "You've got a friend here whenever you need one."

He taps his glass to mine. "Thanks, I appreciate that. Maybe we could see some games together."

"Absolutely. So, what kind of work do you want to do here? Are you thinking NYPD?"

Denver looks disgusted. "Hell, no. I'm not going down that road again. I'm done being a cop."

I nod. "Yeah, I guess being screwed over by your superior leaves a bad taste in your mouth. Aren't you pissed as hell?"

He rubs a hand over his jaw. "You'd think, wouldn't you? And I was. I was pissed for the better part of two years. But now, I'm just so goddamn happy to be free to live my life. And the restitution they have to pay me goes a long way to ease the pain."

"I know you liked the grounds crew job Sawyer got you with the Royals," I say. "Are you considering something like that here? Maybe Caden or Brady could hook you up."

He shakes his head. "I don't think so. Maybe I'll go back to school until I figure it out."

I study him for a minute. "Do you have any other criminal record?" I ask. "I mean, now that they've expunged the felony, is there anything else? What about your DUI charge last year?"

"Those charges were dropped, remember?" Aspen says.

"Getting that DUI dropped was purely a matter of who I knew," Denver says. "Sawyer's attorney found me the best lawyer in KC. He hired a private investigator who found out that the guys at the bar were friends with Kenny Marron. Kenny was the cop who arrested me. He was also the son of one of the guys who screwed me over. Joe, the bar owner, overheard the entire conversation a few days later when the guys were laughing about it in the bar. Apparently, the assholes called Kenny after I mouthed off to them. They saw me take a few drinks and told Kenny to follow me in his police car, because before I left, one of them went outside and punctured my tire. The whole thing was a set-up, so they threw out the case despite the fact that I tested right at the legal limit."

"So there's nothing on your record?" I ask. "Nothing at all?"

"That's right. Why do you ask?"

I glance at Aspen. "Your sister might kill me for suggesting this, but how about trying for FDNY?"

"You want Denver to become a firefighter?" she says.

"Sure. Why not? He was a police officer, so he's not opposed to civil service. And look at him, he's in better shape than *I* am."

Denver laughs. "Yeah, well, with no friends, there was never anything to do after work other than hit the gym." He gives me a serious look. "Do you think they'd take me?"

I shrug. "I don't know, but you have your time as a cop under your belt—they'd like that. And you're in luck, they only offer the test once every four years, and it's coming up soon."

"Really?" he asks, looking more than a little interested.

"Yeah. But don't get your hopes up too high. The waiting list is long. Most guys wait years to get the call. They put you on a list based on your test score, interview, background check, and physical assessment. Then you wait. It took me a few years to get called. I took that time to become a paramedic. They say FDNY is the hardest civil service job to get. But once you're in, it's a brotherhood for life."

"Well, I've got nothing but time," Denver says. "I guess it's worth a shot."

Aspen is looking at us as we talk like she's watching a tennis match. "No way," she says.

"No way, what? To Denver joining FDNY?"

"Den, have you forgotten that the first time you responded to a car crash as a cop, you called me in a panic?" She puts her hand on his. "You told me they put you behind a desk for a week because you froze. And then you said after that, you'd make sure you were put on traffic duty when being called to an accident."

Denver shrugs. "That was almost two years ago. I'm sure I'm fine now. Anyway, how many car accidents could there be in a city where you can barely drive over twenty-five miles an hour?"

"More than you'd think," I say. "Traffic accidents make up a high percentage of our calls. Some of them can get pretty gruesome. Maybe it's not a good idea. I'm sorry I brought it up."

"Definitely not a good idea," Aspen says.

Denver shakes his head at his sister. "You don't think I can do it, do you?"

"No. I don't, Den. You turn the channel on the TV every time the show you're watching has a car accident."

"I do not," he scoffs.

"You do," she says. "And it's understandable. What happened to Mom and Dad was horrible. I just can't imagine you not thinking about them every time you saw an accident. Or had to witness someone dying."

Denver looks like he's going to argue.

I clap my hands together. "Anyway, whatever you decide, I'll help you however I can. I'm in need of a new project now that I've sworn off women."

"You've what?" Denver asks.

"I don't have the best track record with the ladies," I say.

Aspen touches my arm. "You haven't heard from her?"

I shake my head. "It was her birthday last week. She turned twenty-five."

"Did you try to contact her?" she asks.

"No. But I sent flowers. I didn't send a card, but she had to know they were from me."

"Maybe she didn't."

"She knew. Besides, nobody else she knows would have gone through a competitor. And nobody sends daisies to a woman for their birthday. Roses and that other romantic shit, but not daisies."

"Why did you send daisies?"

"They were her daughter's favorite flower."

"Really?" Aspen looks at me thoughtfully. "Well, maybe she didn't like the reminder."

"No. That's not it. She was fine with daisies. She just doesn't want anything to do with me. I sent her a few texts over the past month, but she never responded. The flowers were a last ditch effort."

"I'm sorry," she says.

The door flies open. Sawyer walks through followed by Caden Kessler and Brady Taylor with their wives in tow.

We make our greetings and everyone settles in with a drink.

"So, how is it playing for opposing teams?" I ask the guys.

"It's not so bad," Caden says. "We all have friends in the league who are on other teams."

"Yeah, but it sucks that we all can't celebrate our win together," Brady says, clinking his glass to Caden's. "Well, it sucks for Mills anyway."

Sawyer laughs. "You two go ahead and celebrate. We'll see who's celebrating in two months when we make the playoffs and you jerkoffs go home and cry in your beers."

"Game on, Mills," Caden says.

"Oh my gosh, they are adorable!" Aspen squeals. "Bass, Denver, you have to see these pictures of their twins."

Murphy passes her phone to Denver. He does some obligatory fawning over them before handing the phone to me. But all I see as I look at the two babies in the picture are the two children Ivy lost. One boy. One girl. I hope Caden and Murphy know how lucky they are to have two healthy children.

I stand up and hand the phone back to Murphy. Then I go in the kitchen, open another beer, and lean back against the counter.

Aspen follows me in. "Are you okay?"

I nod.

She looks out at the crowd and then back at me. "Those pictures made you think of Ivy, didn't they? And the children she lost."

I nod again.

"You really love her, don't you?"

I take a swig of my beer. "You'd think I'd be over it by now. Hell, I've been apart from her longer than we were together. Why do I have a habit of falling for the wrong women?"

She rubs her forehead, looking at me sympathetically. She knows *she* was one of those wrong women.

"I'm sorry," I say. "I didn't mean anything by it."

"You can't help who you fall in love with, Bass. Things will get better. And then one day, when you least expect it, your whole world will change."

She looks back at Sawyer and I know she's thinking of the day she almost got hit by that bus. The day she met Sawyer. But she's a chick. Chicks always believe there will be some knight in shining armor. Some happily ever after. That's not the way life works. Life gets your hopes up and then tramples on you by ripping those you love out of your arms. Just ask Ivy Greene.

Yet in some odd way, I hope Aspen is right. But I don't wish it for me. I hope that one day, things will get better for Ivy. If I had one wish, it would be that Ivy has that day—that one day where her whole world changes, only this time it would be for the better.

I chug the rest of my beer and reach for another, knowing I won't be the one there to witness it.

CHAPTER TWENTY-EIGHT

IVY

"I can't believe I let you guys talk me into this," I say, looking around the bar. "I mean, I can't even drink."

"Your virgin daiquiri," the bartender says, pushing my fruity drink across the bar.

"Cheers," Alder says.

Christina, Holly, Eli, and I raise our drinks and toast each other.

"I'm sorry Monica couldn't make it," Alder tells Eli. "I'm happy for you."

"I can't wait to see the rock," Holly says. "You got her a big one, right?"

"As big as this school teacher can afford, yes."

"You don't think three months is rushing it?" I ask.

He shrugs. "I guess when you know, you know."

Eli and I share a look. We both know we never truly felt that way about each other. We blamed it on circumstances, but I'm sure it's why we never pulled the trigger. We were each other's first love. But young love is different. It's different than the all-encompassing love that takes your breath away.

I look down into my drink, remembering the fruity drinks Bass bought me in Hawaii.

"She's very lucky to have you," I say.

It's true. Eli is a great guy. He's loyal, faithful, and funny. And even though he's getting married, I know he'll be by my side through the pregnancy and after.

Monica seems unfazed by our circumstance. I tried to warn her what she could be in for. But she said it's all worth it to be with Eli. She wants to have kids right away and he seems okay with it. I can't even imagine agreeing to something like that. Especially when we don't know what could happen with this baby. I suppose it's different when you're the father. Eli was involved, but I was the one who raised Dahlia. He couldn't even stand to be by her side when she died. And although he was devastated, he was able to move on.

I wish I could be as trusting of the future. I wish I could say it's all worth it to be with Sebastian. But it wouldn't be fair of me to put him through it. Eli still gets to live his life, no matter what happens. If we have another sick child, he gets to visit him in the hospital and go home to Monica at the end of every day. I'm the one who will be sleeping on a cot in the corner. I'm the one who will spoon feed him. I'm the one who will hold him when he cries after they put a feeding tube in his stomach because he's too sick to eat. I'm the one who will hold him until he takes his last breath. I'm the one who will be incapable of loving anyone but the child in the hospital bed.

I know all of that because it's already happened. Eli says we drifted apart. He claims it was him as much as it was me. But the truth is I just didn't have it in me to love Dahlia with everything I had and still have any leftover for Eli. It was my fault that we broke up. And I'm not about to let history repeat itself. I'm not about to let Bass fall in love with my child only to have him lose both of us.

"Ivy?"

I look up to see Holly trying to get my attention. She nods toward the other side of the bar. I look over and see Bass staring at me. My eyes immediately fall upon the two seats flanking his. One is occupied by a woman who is clearly with the man on the other side of her. The other seat holds a guy who's even bigger than Bass. He looks like he could be a firefighter, but I don't recall meeting him at the firehouse. Then again, I wasn't interested in anything other than being in Bass's arms when I was there that day.

I know I have no right to feel relieved that he's not here with a woman. But I am.

"Are you okay?" Alder asks. "Who is that?"

"It's Bass."

"No shit?" He looks over at him, appraising him like any big brother would. "He can't take his eyes off you, Ivy. Maybe you should go talk to him."

The guy to Bass's right is trying to get his attention, but Bass keeps waving him away.

I can't help but gaze back at him. He doesn't talk to his friend. He doesn't take a sip of his beer. He just stares at me. And I stare at him. It's been well over a month since I've seen him. I swear he's gotten even more handsome. His hair is slightly longer, and he must have had the past few days off because he has heavy scruff growing on his face.

I remember in Hawaii, he liked to let his facial hair grow because he said he always shaved for work. I loved the feeling of his scruff beneath my fingertips. Against my lips. Between my legs. I close my eyes briefly, savoring the memory. When I open my eyes again, I see Bass staring at Eli. But his demeanor has changed. He's not looking at him with a sad longing—he's looking at him like he wants to kill him.

Then Bass finally takes a drink. He quickly swallows his half-full beer and slams the empty glass back down onto the bar.

"Holy shit," Alder says. "If looks could kill."

"Yeah," Eli says. "And seeing as I'm the one who's likely to get killed, can you please tell the guy the truth already, Ivy?"

"Stay out of it," I turn around and tell all of them. "I mean it."

When I look at Bass again, their backs are turned to us and he and his friend are talking to a few women. The woman in front of Bass puts her hand on his chest and laughs like what he said is the funniest thing she's ever heard. I feel sick watching it.

I get up off my barstool. "I need to use the ladies' room."

"Want company?" Christina asks.

I shake my head.

When I get to the bathroom, I wet a paper towel and blot it on my cheeks. Then I turn to the side and stare at myself in the mirror. At fourteen weeks, I'm looking plumper, but I'm not yet showing. Good, because I'm not prepared to have that conversation with Bass. If I'm lucky, I can avoid him for the next five months. Or maybe forever. Because I hate feeling the way I'm feeling after seeing him.

Everything inside me wants to ask him to take me back.

But I can't be that selfish.

I take a deep breath before I go back out to the bar. I vow to turn my stool the other way and not look at him for the rest of the night. Perhaps I can convince my group to go elsewhere. Because just knowing he's here is hard. And knowing he may be going home with another woman would be pure torture.

I get two steps out of the bathroom when I all but run into Bass's chest. I have to put my hand up against him to keep myself from colliding with him. And when his smell permeates my senses, I almost fall to my knees.

"Hello, Ivy," he says callously. "Having a good time tonight?"

"Hi."

He laughs bitterly. "I haven't seen you in almost two months and that's all you have to say?"

"What do you want me to say, Bass?"

"I don't know. How about, *'How are you, Sebastian? I hope you're doing well after I led you on and then kicked you to the curb.'* Or maybe *'Thanks for the flowers'*."

I look up and lock eyes with him.

"Don't look so surprised," he says. "I know you knew I sent them."

I nod. "I guess I did. But I couldn't … I'm sorry."

"Everything okay back here?" Alder says, coming up behind me. He holds his hand out to Bass. "Alder Greene."

"Bass Briggs," he says, shaking Alder's hand. "I was just saying hello to Ivy. I was about to wish her and … Eli, is it? I was just about to wish them well."

Alder shakes his head. "Eli's with Mon—"

"Alder." I put a forceful hand on his arm. "Would you please wait back at the table?"

"Ivy." He stares me down with that brotherly look of his.

"Alder. Please."

Alder looks from Bass to me. "Fine."

Bass watches him walk away. "He seems nice. And protective of you. I wish I could have gotten to know him."

"Don't you have some girls waiting for you back at the bar?" I ask, a little too curtly.

He narrows his eyes at me. "Do I detect a hint of jealousy? Funny thing, coming from the girl who dumped me."

"Bass, don't make this harder than it already is."

"Oh, I can see how *hard* this is for you," he says, motioning out to the bar. "You out with your friends and your—what is he now, boyfriend? Fiancé?"

"Stop it."

"A word to the wise. Next time you want to play the grieving mother card, do it with someone who doesn't give a flying fuck, okay?"

Tears prickle the backs of my eyes. "That's not fair, Bass. I told you from the beginning that I didn't want it to go beyond Hawaii."

"Yeah, well, that's not what you were saying in the end, was it? What was it you were saying then? Oh, right, you were saying how much you loved me. What a load of crap."

"It was true," I say, using all my willpower to keep the tears from falling.

He snorts. "Goodbye, Ivy."

I sink back against the wall as I watch him go into the bathroom. Then I go find Holly and have her walk me home.

~ ~ ~

"Push, Ivy," the nurse says. "Just a few more minutes and your daughter will be here."

Something is different. Something smells *different. It doesn't smell clinical, like a hospital. It smells like flowers. It smells like daisies.*

I open my eyes, and the 'nurse' is wearing a fireman's uniform. I look around to see firemen all around me.

Someone squeezes my hand. "It's okay. Everything's going to be okay. Push."

I look up and expect to see Eli, but it's not him. It's Bass. Bass is holding my hand, urging me to push.

He kisses my hand and when I look at it, I have a ring on my finger. I'm married.

This is all wrong. He can't marry me. "Bass, no."

"It's okay, Ivy. Daisies gonna make everything better."

I stare at Bass, wondering how he knows about Dahlia's dying words. I didn't tell him, did I? *Then I sit up, remembering my daughter and everything we went through, and I squeeze my legs together to try and keep the baby inside me.*

I look over at the table to see vase after vase of Dahlia's favorite flower. I'm overwhelmed by the earthy smell of them.

"The baby is coming," Bass says.

I see him push my legs apart and then I watch as he pulls a pale, lifeless baby out of me. He holds the limp baby in his hands and looks down on me a broken man. "Why did you let me fall in love with you?" he screams. "With her? You did this to me. How could you?"

He holds the lifeless baby out to me, placing her on my chest. The weight of her crushes my heart and causes me to lose my breath. I want to cry, but I can't. I can't because I knew this was going to happen. Nobody believed me, but I knew.

"I'm sorry," I chant over and over, holding the blue baby to me while I stare at a sobbing Bass. "I'm so sorry."

Truer words have never been spoken. Because I know exactly what he's going through. And I put him there. I brought him into my hell and now he's paying the price.

The nurse tries to take the baby from me, but I don't let her. "No!" I scream, holding my daughter against the belly from which she was just born.

A bright light comes on, startling me. I open my eyes and look around. Holly is sitting on my bed and I'm protectively holding my stomach.

"Ivy, are you okay?"

Hot tears are flowing from my eyes as I frantically look around my room. "I have to … I need …"

Holly grabs the fetal Doppler from my dresser and brings it over. She lifts up the shirt I'm sleeping in and runs it over my lower belly until we hear it. *Whoosh whoosh whoosh.*

I finally take a breath and sink back into my pillow. "I'm okay. Bad dream. You can go back to bed."

After Holly leaves, I keep listening to the baby's heartbeat. I listen for so long, my hand goes numb holding the wand to my belly. But it's soothing.

Finally, when my need to pee overtakes my desire to keep lying here, I get off the bed. On my way to the bathroom, I catch a glimpse of myself in the mirror. The T-shirt I'm wearing is far too large for me. The short sleeves fall to my elbows and the hem almost touches my knees. I look like a waif of a woman wearing it. But somehow, I know it's the only shirt I'll ever sleep in.

And as I walk away from the mirror, I look behind me to catch a glimpse of the back of the shirt with Bass's last name printed on it, knowing this is the only piece of him I'll ever be able to have.

CHAPTER TWENTY-NINE

SEBASTIAN

It's a conundrum sometimes, being a firefighter. When you are in the middle of a life-and-death situation, you can't let emotions overtake you, so you try to shut them out and do your job. But at the same time, it's those emotions that make us work so hard to make the rescue. It's those emotions that have us wading through smoke and flames to find a missing child. And it's those emotions that have us risking our lives to save the drug dealer who got high and passed out, allowing his cigarette to start a fire. Because that idiot is someone's father, son, or brother. And no matter what happened before we got there, it's a life. And that life needs our help. And we're there to give it, no questions asked.

But it's days like today that really test my resolve to do the job. It's days like today, when I have to hold back a frantic mother because her child is trapped in the back seat of her overturned car.

"Jacob!" she screams, as I tighten my grip on her.

We both watch helplessly as Squad uses the jaws of life to extricate her toddler from the mangled vehicle.

The woman's leg is likely broken, and she has a scalp lac that's bleeding. But adrenaline is keeping her from feeling much pain and she's refusing treatment until her son is freed. I pulled her out of the front seat rather easily, cutting through her seatbelt after we stabilized her neck. But as I was working on getting her out, I saw her child, and based on what I saw, Lt. Cash and his team are doing a recovery, not a rescue.

As I hold the woman who is clearly in agony, not because of her injuries, but because of her child, I can't help but think of Ivy. And it makes me wonder which is worse—losing a child abruptly and without warning or knowing that your child will die and you only have a certain amount of time with her.

Either option seems unimaginably daunting.

Then I think about Denver and how he would have reacted to this scene. I'm glad I didn't try harder to talk him into applying to FDNY. In fact, Aspen pulled me aside after that night and told me to please not encourage him. Apparently, his fear of car accidents is even worse than she led me to believe. This, today, was hard for even a seasoned firefighter to watch, let alone someone who tragically lost both parents in an accident.

Everyone on Engine 319 is quiet as we make our way back to the station. I contemplate placing a call to the QA officer who will be able to contact the hospital and give us an update on the child. After all, Debbe did say they found a faint pulse after Squad got him out. But I remember Cash's face when he looked over at me as I held the mother. He shook his head in a way that let me know there was little hope.

In the end, I don't make the call. You learn early on in this job to leave it alone. We don't always get to hear the outcomes of our rescues. We don't get to follow the progress of our saves. Sometimes, after particularly tough runs, we do request information. But those cases are few and far between. And in this case, I prefer to think that Jacob was revived after they got him to the hospital. I prefer to think that his mother wouldn't have to make a trip to Hawaii months or years from now because she was simply unable to move on.

As soon as we pull back into the station and exit the truck, the alarm sounds.

"Engine 319, respond to a commercial structure fire at 547 Parker Drive," the dispatcher says.

"Shit," I say aloud as I pull my bunker pants back on. "That's Ivy's flower shop."

"Ivy? As in the girl who dumped you?" Noah asks.

"Just get your ass back in the rig, Probie," I say in irritation.

The flower shop is only seven blocks away, but I ask Duck to drive faster all the same. As we pull up, I'm relieved that I don't see any flames. But I do see smoke coming up over the backside of the building. White smoke, not black. And when I exit the truck, I smell something heavenly.

As protocol dictates for a structure fire, we all get a piece of gear from the rig. I grab the pike pole and head inside the building.

I see Ivy behind the counter and as we lock eyes, she goes completely ashen.

"Somebody call the fire department?" J.D. asks.

"Uh …" Ivy looks confused.

"I did," Holly says, coming out from the back. "There was smoke coming in from the rear door. I thought it might be a dumpster fire."

Ivy shoots Holly a look of death. "You *what?*"

"You stay up front, miss, and we'll go check it out," Duck says.

As we pass by the women, I glance over at Ivy. She looks embarrassed. She looks pissed.

In the back room, we see that the rear door is cracked open and smoke is wafting inside. And again, that smell has my mouth watering. Upon opening the back door, we see the culprit. The restaurant adjacent to their shop has a smoker going.

Noah shakes his head in irritation. "All this for a damn brisket?"

The cook looks up at the four of us, searching for words. "Uh, you guys want some?"

I pat Noah on the back after tucking my helmet under my arm. "Get used to it, bro. You should know by now that a lot of our calls end up being false alarms." I walk over to the smoker and grab a piece of meat the cook ripped from the carcass. "And some of them come with perks."

We head back inside, the three guys behind me all discussing how we should plan an outing to the restaurant next door. "Shhh," I say to quiet them when I hear shouting coming from the front of the store.

"Come on, Ivy. It's not that big a deal."

"Not that big a deal?" Ivy says. "You called nine-one-one, Hol. Just to get him here. Did you think that somehow we would see each other again and ride off into the sunset?"

"I don't know," Holly says. "But somebody needs to do *something*."

J.D. clears his throat as we walk into the front of the store. "It's all good," he says. "It was the smoker at the place next door. I suggest you leave your back door shut the next time he's cooking outside. In fact, you should leave it shut *all* the time. You never know who might come in."

"We *do* keep it shut," Ivy says, giving Holly a scolding stare.

Holly shrugs. "Sorry. I guess I just forgot. And when I saw the smoke, I didn't even think, I just called."

Duck walks over to Holly, clearly taken with her. "It's okay, miss. Better safe than sorry." He gives her a second look. "Do I know you from somewhere?"

"I was at the station once," she says, glancing between Ivy and me.

"She goes out with Justin sometimes," I tell him.

"Oh, yeah. That's it," he says.

"I'm Holly," she says, offering Duck her hand along with a seductive smile.

His eyebrows shoot up in appreciation of her flirting. "Steve Hanson."

"Holly," Ivy scolds. "Is one of them not enough for you?"

Holly giggles. "I like to keep my options open."

I look over and see Ivy watching me. I notice what I didn't at the bar the other night. It looks like she's put on some weight, which is good since she was so thin when I met her. I remember picking her up and carrying her thinking how light she was. Her gaining weight probably means she's healing. She is healing without me. She's healing with Eli.

Then I think about the call earlier and the child who most likely died and the mother who was in for a world of hurt. Maybe Ivy can only heal with Eli because they share a common past. I have no idea what she went through. I can't even begin to comprehend the depths of her pain. But *he* can. I can comfort her. I can sympathize. But deep down, I can't really understand.

And in the end, all I provided was an escape. She all but told me that in the beginning. She never wanted it to be more than a fling. Maybe she knew all along that I could never be the one for her.

I try to make my way to the door, but Ivy cuts me off. "Are you going to leave without saying hello?"

"Oh, now you want me to say hello?" I bite at her. "Hello, Ivy. How are you? It looks like you're doing well. The store looks good. You look healthy. How's Eli, by the way?"

"Bass …"

She looks like she wants to say something, but I guess she doesn't want to in front of an audience.

J.D. and Noah head out the door to the rig while Duck chats with Holly.

"What is it, Ivy?"

She shakes her head. "It's nothing. It's just nice to see you, that's all."

I pull on her arm and tug her to the side of the shop, out of earshot of the others. "I'd like to say the same thing, but I'd be lying. It's *not* nice to see you, Ivy. It wasn't nice seeing you at the bar and it's not nice seeing you now. It hurts to see you. And call me selfish, but it kills me to see you doing so well. I mean, I'm glad you are. You deserve to be happy. But I thought you were going to be happy with me, not him."

Her eyes get glassy, just like they did in the bar. And her arm—it reaches out to me before she pulls it back. She bites her lip as her eyes briefly close. I could swear she wants to tell me something. Her reaction confuses me. It's been months since Hawaii. She's with Eli again. Why is she still having this visceral reaction when she sees me?

I pinch the bridge of my nose. "Is he … good to you?"

She dabs the corner of her eye with a finger. "Eli is a great guy."

"I'm sure he is. But that isn't what I asked."

She nods. "He's g-good to me."

"Then why are you acting like you don't want me to walk out this door?"

My radio goes off. J.D. must have put us back in service. We're being sent on another call.

"Coming right out, Cap," I tell J.D over the radio. "Duck, time to go." I look over at Ivy. "See you around, Ivy."

"It's Ivy Greene," she says sadly. "That's what you always called me."

"Funny how quickly things can change, isn't it?"

I open the door and Duck and I run out to the rig. As I climb in, I look back to see Ivy staring at me through the front window of her shop. She's got her arms wrapped around herself and she's crying. She's shaking. She's looking at me like a woman who just lost the man she loves.

I look away. I've never felt so goddamned frustrated in my life.

CHAPTER THIRTY

IVY

I used to love this time of year. Right before Thanksgiving when people would start to put up their Christmas trees. But now, all it does is remind me of how long I've been without my daughter. The anniversary of her death is in four weeks. I've been trying not to think about it, but it's hard not to with this baby pressing down on my bladder every minute of the day.

Holly walks out from the back. "I'll go pick up lunch. What sounds good today?"

I shrug. "Sushi?"

She glares at me. "What is it with you and sushi? You know you aren't supposed to eat it, but you keep asking for it."

"Weird craving, I guess. I don't care what you get. Surprise me."

It's a lie. I don't crave sushi. I don't even like it that much. But it's the only food that doesn't remind me of Bass. Every time I eat steak, it reminds me of Kalapaki Joe's. Sandwiches make me think of the picnics we used to have on our hikes. Chicken, seafood, burgers, fries—they all remind me of him in some way. And pizza—that's the worst—all I can see is Bass naked in bed if I even smell pizza.

Hell, I can't even eat at the restaurant next door anymore. The owner's name is Erma.

It's been four and a half months since I got back from Hawaii. That's one hundred and thirty-seven days since I've been in his arms. And it still hurts just as much today as it did back then.

I often wonder how being with someone for such a short time could have evoked such feelings. But then I remember one of the movies I watched early this year when I did nothing but hole up in my apartment and watch TV.

It was *The Bridges of Madison County.* It was about a stranger who showed up on the doorstep of a married woman whose family was out of town for the weekend. The woman never meant to fall for the man, but in just a period of days, hours even, the two of them fell in love. They had a lifetime of experiences in a single weekend. And in the end, she could have chosen him over her husband. Over her family. It seemed like such an easy choice based on what they had shared. But she didn't. She did the right thing even though it killed her. Then decades later, a delivery shows up on her doorstep. It's a package from the man she never stopped loving. He had died, and the way she reacted—it was like they had just parted the day before, not twenty-five years earlier.

That woman is me. I'm Meryl Streep and Bass is Clint Eastwood.

I love Bass to the ends of my soul. And just like Clint was Meryl's soul mate, I know Bass is mine. And I know that no matter who I end up with in life, nobody could ever take his place.

Sometimes I fantasize about ending up with Bass. After everything else happens. Maybe the baby ends up healthy and Bass is okay being a stepdad. Or maybe the baby is sick like Dahlia and I have a few precious years with him, after which, I end up in Hawaii again only to have Bass follow me there. And then we live out our happily ever after.

But I know I'm just kidding myself. I've pushed him away and I've pushed hard. I can't expect him to sit around and wait for me. Not when he thinks I'm with another man. I've wanted so many times to tell him that I'm not. But I don't. I can't. I love him too much to let him experience the kind of pain Eli and I could be in for.

I try to suppress my tears when I look over at the wall with Dahlia's art. One picture hanging there still confuses me. It's a picture of Dahlia with a daisy in her hair. She's between two adults who are swinging her by her arms. One of the adults has long hair, like me, but the other has dark hair, so it can't be Eli. I used to think it was Alder, but why would she leave Holly out of the picture?

Is it possible that she knew even before she died that I would fall in love with someone? With Bass?

The bells over the door jingle and cold air wafts in when an old woman walks through.

"Good afternoon," I say.

She eyes my swollen belly. "Well, look at you, dear. Aren't you vibrant and full of life?"

I give her my best smile. "What can I help you with?"

"I need to order some flowers for the reception after my sister's funeral."

"Oh, my. Please accept my condolences."

"Thank you, dear. It was time. She was old. Older than me even. Ninety-seven. She lived a good life and now she's dancing with her husband in heaven."

And once again, I find myself swallowing tears. Every time someone makes a comment like that, I think of when I'll get to see Dahlia and Jonah again.

I get out a picture book of funeral flower arrangements. There are a lot of lilies—those are usually the flowers of choice. But the woman waves the book away. "Daisies," she says. "Minnie loved them. I know a lot of people don't care for the smell, but the old geezers will just have to put up with it." Then she laughs. "Our friends and family might be older than dirt, and we may not be able to see all that well, but we can smell. Oh, it'll be a hoot. Minnie would love it. I think I'll need about twelve dozen. Just arrange them however you want."

"I love daisies, too," I say, glancing over at Dahlia's art wall.

The woman studies my belly. "You must be having a girl," she says. "You're carrying high. That's a sure sign of a girl. My mama had ten children. Minnie and I were the oldest. Got to watch our mother go through ten more pregnancies because she lost two of them. We got good at figuring it all out. The boys carry low, like they can't wait to get out and get away from their mamas."

I try not to roll my eyes at her. I've had other people swear up and down that it's a boy since I'm carrying most of the weight in my belly.

"Uh … I'm not sure what I'm having. I haven't let them tell me."

She puts her hand on my arm. "Oh, dear. I'm afraid I've gone and ruined the surprise then."

"It's okay," I say.

She scribbles down her address for the delivery and hands me her credit card. Then she looks at Dahlia's wall. "The lucky papa must be so happy," she says, pointing to the picture of Dahlia with me and … whoever.

"Oh, he's not the … and that's not the … er, forget it. Thank you."

"No, thank *you*, dear." She walks to the door, but before she goes through, she turns around. "It's nice to meet someone who loves daisies as much as Minnie did. What was it the old bat used to say? Oh, yes. *'Daisies make everything better.'* Goodbye now."

I stare out the window long after she's gone, wondering if she really said that or if I was just hearing things. Then, my heart races when I think I see Bass outside. I know he walks by sometimes. Holly tells me she sees him occasionally. He does live and work in Brooklyn, so it makes sense. But somehow, we've managed to avoid each other for the past two months.

But as I see him walk by a second time, I wonder if he often comes by to catch a glimpse of me. And part of me hopes he does. I look down at my not-so-small baby bump and wonder if he's seen it yet.

When I look back up and see him in the window, staring at me with a gaping mouth, I have my answer.

He throws the door open. "You're pregnant? What the hell, Ivy?" He looks me up and down. "Is it mine?"

I put my hands on my belly protectively as I shake my head. "I didn't know how to tell you, Bass. I was"—I clear the viscous knot in my throat—"I was already pregnant when I went to Hawaii."

"You were *what?*" he screams across the shop.

I walk behind the counter to put more separation between us. He looks more than hurt. He looks mad.

"It's Eli's. I didn't know."

"How could you not know? You lied to me in Hawaii? The whole time I thought we were falling in love, you were still with your ex?"

"No. I didn't lie to you. It was a big mistake," I say. "I hadn't been with him in years. Not since we split up. But she was gone. And it was her birthday. And we just … we just …"

He shakes his head and paces around the shop. I watch him as he goes through a myriad of emotions. His hands run through his hair. He pinches the bridge of his nose. He looks over at me and then at Dahlia's wall.

"This wasn't how this was supposed to happen," he says.

My shoulders drop. "I know. I'm sorry."

"Do you love Eli? Or are you just with him for the baby?"

I can't answer without giving myself away. So I just cover my mouth with my hand and shake my head.

"What the fuck, Ivy? You went and *married* the guy?" he asks, his voice choking with tears.

It's now that I realize he saw the ring on my finger.

He turns around and heads for the door.

"It's not what you think, Bass."

He pushes the door open, and on his way out, he says, "I think I just let you rip my heart out for the last time. Goodbye, Ivy."

My body crumples onto the ground behind the counter and I break down in sobs. That was it. That was the last time I'm going to see him. I know it for sure now. But then the door chimes jingle and I rise up on my knees, hoping he changed his mind. When I see Holly come through with our lunch bags, however, I collapse back down onto the floor.

"Was that Bass leaving the shop?" Then she sees me. "Oh, God, Ivy."

She drops our lunch and quickly locks the front door, then she sits next to me on the floor, cradling me in her arms as I cry into her shoulder.

CHAPTER THIRTY-ONE

SEBASTIAN

"Call her," Aspen says, as we finish up our cool down on the treadmills.

"I don't know. It's been so long since we've talked. Maybe there's just too much water under the bridge."

"I ran into her last week, you know," she says.

My eyebrows shoot up. "You did?"

"Yeah. And your name may have come up once or twice."

I laugh. "Once or twice, huh?"

"It's time, Bass. I'm tired of seeing you mope around."

"I'm not moping."

She rolls her eyes at me. "Denver pretty much tells me everything. I know you have a 'bro code' and all that, but twins trump bros. And he says you go home early from every outing. *Alone.*"

"Not every guy wants to have a girlfriend, you know."

"And he says you practically live here at the gym. He tells me you work out with him a lot."

"He needs someone to hang out with," I say.

She laughs. "He does not. I happen to know that *he* doesn't always go home alone. He does live in our place, in case you forgot."

"Did I mention how nice it is to have you back for the holidays, Aspen?" I say sarcastically. "I mean, it's been years since I've had so much mother henning."

The truth is, it *has* been nice having Aspen back in town for the past week. They moved back into the townhouse after her fall finals and they'll be here for a month until spring semester starts—well, except when they take their honeymoon. And even though they have a home gym in their basement, she's here spending time with me.

Aspen is getting her master's degree in music back in Kansas City. Obviously, with Sawyer being one of the most skilled MLB players of our time, she won't ever have to work if she doesn't want to. But music has been her passion since she was a little girl. And I'm willing to bet big money she'll never give it up. Just like I still play my guitar every day, the piano will always be her first love.

"Have you given any thought to what you want to do when you graduate?" I ask.

"Every day."

"And?"

"Well, Sawyer's job is demanding. I like to be home for him in the off-season. And it would be nice to be able to come back here whenever we wanted to. But doing what he does keeps him on the road a lot and I need something for *me* when he's gone. Something to give my life purpose."

"So?"

She widens her eyes and shrugs a shoulder. "So, I have a year to think about it. Right now, I'm just trying to make sure all the wedding plans are in order."

Then she looks sad.

"What it is?" I ask.

"I don't know. It's just with the holidays coming and all the wedding planning, I guess I just miss my parents. When I was little, I dreamed of my dad walking me down the aisle."

"I'm sorry, Penny. I know that will be hard for you."

"Denver will be there for me. And I love him. But we both know it won't be the same."

"Speaking of Denver, what's he been up to lately? I haven't seen him this week."

She shakes her head and sighs. "Your guess is as good as mine. He's living off the restitution money while he figures it out. He spends all his time downstairs in Sawyer's weight room. Oh, shit," she says, turning off her treadmill. "You don't think he's working out so much so he can apply to FDNY, do you?"

"No. That ship sailed a few months ago. As I told you before, they only offer the test once every four years."

She blows out a relieved breath. "Good. I'm not sure I'd be able to watch him fail. He's been through so much already."

"Why are you so sure he would have failed?" I ask. "You really think he can't overcome what happened to your parents?"

"You have no idea, Bass. When I went home for the summer right after they died, he wouldn't even drive a car. I'm sure I told you this before. If he couldn't walk or get a friend to drive him somewhere, he would just stay home. He took a lame job at the mall a few miles down the road just so he could ride his bike. When I visited him the next summer, at least he was driving, but only when he absolutely had to. His girlfriend at the time drove him everywhere. I'm not sure why he thought it was okay to get in a car with someone else behind the wheel, but he did."

"Most fears are irrational," I say. "And he obviously overcame his fear of driving in order to become a cop. Maybe he can overcome his fear of accidents as well."

"How do you suggest he do that, stand on street corners, waiting for crashes to happen so he can desensitize himself?"

I see her point. "Well, maybe he doesn't have to get over it. I mean, living in the city, he doesn't even need a car."

"That's true. One more reason he should live here," she says sadly.

"Are you sorry that he's not back in Kansas City?"

"No. I know it's bad for him there. And having him here just makes me excited to come visit."

"What am I, chopped liver?" I ask, laughing.

"Never," she says.

I turn off my treadmill and wipe my face with a towel. "Well, Denver doesn't need to be in a hurry to get a job," I say. "It sounds like he's set for money, and I'm not sure anyone is hiring now anyway. He can enjoy holidays and your wedding and then see what's out there. Plus, he wouldn't want to miss the bachelor party because of a new job."

She raises her eyebrows. "I wasn't aware they had planned a bachelor party yet."

"Yeah. Brady and Caden told me to keep a few days open the week after Christmas."

She nods. "That's when we're doing my bachelorette party as well. Are you going to come?"

I laugh. "To your bachelorette party? I don't think so."

"But you're my 'man of honor'," she says, pouting.

"Penny, I'm not going to go to a strip joint with you and your friends to watch you tuck dollar bills in some guy's banana hammock."

"We're not going to a strip joint. Wait, are *you*? What are you guys planning? Are you getting him a stripper?" She puts her head in her hands. "Oh, God, he's going to get a lap dance, isn't he? It'll probably be all over the Internet, too."

"We're not getting him a stripper. The plan is to go to Atlantic City."

"Really? You promise?"

I step off the treadmill and put my arm around her. "Aspen, you have nothing to worry about."

"Says the guy who was left at the altar."

"You don't really think Sawyer would do that to you, do you?" I ask. "Not after all you've been through."

She shakes her head. "No. I know he wouldn't."

As we pass the front desk on the way to the shower, I see Caden's wife talking with a tall redhead and someone else who looks vaguely familiar. Penny grabs my arm, pulling me over to them.

"Didn't Murphy just have twins?" I ask Aspen in a whisper. "She still works here?"

"Caroline and CayJay are almost a year old now. She still helps manage the gym, but not on a full-time basis."

"Hey, guys," Murphy says in greeting.

Aspen pulls the familiar-looking woman in for a hug. "Oh, sorry," she says. "I'm all sweaty, but it's been a while since I've seen you." Penny turns to me. "Bass, do you remember Piper Lawrence?"

"From the Knicks game last year. Yeah." I hold out my hand. "How are you?"

I remember meeting her and her famous husband who plays football for the Giants. If I recall, he's also part-owner of this gym. Last summer was a surreal time in my life. Aspen had just started

… well, for lack of a better word—*dating*—Sawyer, and because of it, we were introduced to a lot of famous people.

"I'm good, thanks," Piper says. "Nice to see you again."

"And this is Charlie Stone," Aspen says, introducing me to the tall redhead.

"Ah, the wife of the private investigator," I say.

She smiles. "That I am."

"Would the two of you like to join us for lunch in the café?" Murphy asks. "We can talk about the wedding plans."

"I'd love to," Aspen says. "But Bass has a phone call to make."

"I do?"

"Yes, you do. Now go get on with it. And I want details later."

I don't know if I should be irritated with her persistence, or grateful for it. "Fine." I turn to the others. "I'll leave you girls to your lunch then."

After I say goodbye and walk away, I hear Charlie say to them, "I've only got an hour before I have to pick Eli up from school."

"That boy is adorable," Murphy tells her.

I stop in my tracks and look back at them.

Eli.

Aspen looks at me as if she knows exactly what I overheard and exactly what I'm thinking. She gives me a soft smile. Then she puts her hand to her ear with her thumb and pinky out to the side, signaling a phone.

"I'm going," I mouth to her.

Back in the locker room, I sit on the bench and look at my phone, wondering if it's the right time to make this move. My finger hovers over her name for a few seconds before I make the call.

"Hello?" she answers after two rings.

"Hey, uh … it's Bass."

She laughs. "I can see that. Your face popped up on the screen."

"Oh, right. Listen, I was wondering if you'd like to get a cup of coffee."

I don't hear anything, so I look at the phone to see if we've lost our connection.

"Are you still there?"

"I'm here," she says. "I guess coffee would be nice. When?"

"How about now?"

"Right now?"

"Sure. Unless you're busy? Are you at work?"

"No. Not busy and not at work."

"Great. I'm just finishing up at the gym. How about you meet me at the Starbucks on Forty-first in an hour?"

"I suppose I could do that."

I hear the hesitation in her voice.

"Okay. See you then. I'm looking forward to it, Brooke."

~ ~ ~

"I'm surprised you called," Brooke says after we find a table.

"Why would you be surprised?" I ask. "We talk sometimes."

She wrinkles her nose. "We don't talk, Bass. We text. And it's not like we ever really say anything. In fact, I'm pretty sure they have all been obligatory birthday texts or some other well-wishing pleasantries."

I nod. "I guess you're right. I'm sorry. I should have reached out to you a long time ago. I've wondered how you are and what you've been up to."

"Have you?"

"Of course I have. We didn't exactly break up because we didn't like each other, you know."

"No, I guess not," she says. "So, how's your job going? Every time I hear a siren, I think of you."

"It's great. I love it. Best decision I ever made. The guys, and girl, there are like family to me. How about you? Are you still working with the children's symphony?"

She smiles. "I am. But I'm also thinking about going back to school for my master's."

"Juilliard?"

"If they'll have me."

"I'm sure they'll accept you. You play the meanest cello around."

"Thanks, but seriously, you should hear some of these kids. They are so young but so incredibly talented. No way was I that good when I was their age."

"I'm sure you were. You just don't look at it that way."

"So, I saw Aspen a few weeks ago," she says hesitantly.

"She told me."

"She's getting married next month, huh?"

"She is."

Brooke eyes me speculatively. "Are you okay with that? I mean after everything?"

I nod. "I'm fine. I'm over her. That's old news, Brooke."

"But you're still friends?"

"I'm her best man, or 'man of honor' as she likes to call me."

"That's nice," she says. "And speaking of weddings and stuff, did you ever go on our honeymoon?"

I chuckle. "Yeah, I did."

"How was it?"

"Hawaii is incredible. Just like your parents said it would be. Did you ever make it there yourself?"

"Not yet. Someday." She picks at a spot on the table. "Did you … did you take anyone with you? Aspen maybe?"

"No. I'm not sure Sawyer would have appreciated that, however platonic it would have been."

"So you went solo?"

"Yup."

I find it hard to make eye contact with her when all I'm doing is thinking about Ivy. I came here to forget her, and Brooke had to go and bring up Hawaii. *Fuck*.

She takes a long sip of her coffee, studying me over the rim of her cup. "But you met someone there."

It's not a question. It's a statement.

"Am I that transparent?" I ask.

She laughs. "You always have been, Bass."

"I did meet someone. But I'm not with her. We never dated after Hawaii."

"I'm sorry. Does she live too far away?"

I shake my head. "No. She lives in New York. It just didn't work out, that's all. Some things aren't meant to be."

"And maybe other things are," she says, flashing me a toothy smile.

I laugh. "Yeah. Maybe."

"So, what keeps you busy when you aren't working?"

"I play guitar, even at the station. Although I'm usually relegated to the garage. And during baseball season, I go to a lot of games. Hey, maybe you could go with me sometime, you know, when the season starts up again."

"Sure. I think that would be fun." She puts a hand on my arm and leaves it there. "I'm glad to see you haven't given up the guitar."

"Never. I still play every day."

"I used to love to listen to you play."

I try to look embarrassed. "Aw, that's what all the ladies say."

She wrinkles her nose. "Playing the cello is not quite as sexy."

"What are you talking about? It's sexy as hell. I guarantee every heterosexual guy who watches you play wants to *be* the cello and have you stroking him between your legs."

She almost spits out her sip of coffee when she laughs. Then she raises her brows. "*Every* heterosexual guy?"

I shrug.

I shrug because I can't honestly say yes. I mean, Brooke is very attractive. Hot even. And I want to want her. And because of the promise I made to Aspen, I'm going to try. But the truth is, there is only one woman's legs I ever want to be between.

Brooke and I spend an hour chatting and laughing and I realize I'm having a good time with her.

Then I hear it. The barista calls out, "Ivy!"

My back stiffens as I look over at the counter. I see a woman going up to get her drink, but all I can see is the back of her coat and the wool hat on her head. It might not be her. It could be anybody. Then she turns around and I see her. Her cheeks are rosy red from the cold. Her coat is open, and her large baby bump protrudes out of the front of it.

She starts to walk toward the door, which means passing by our table, but then she sees me. She startles, almost dropping her coffee. She locks eyes with me and time stops.

My heart falls into my stomach and twists over and over. It's been a month since I saw her at the flower shop. A month since I decided to stop letting my feelings for her rule my life. But as I sit here and stare at her, I know what a fool I am.

But the thing is, she's staring back at me. She's staring at me like she doesn't have a ring on her finger. A husband at home. A baby in her belly. *His* baby.

Why is she looking at me like that? Like how she was at the bar and in the flower shop. Like she's seeing her long-lost love.

"Bass?" Brooke says, rubbing my arm to try and get my attention.

Ivy's gaze shifts to the woman sitting across from me. I watch as Ivy's lips press together and form a thin line. She looks at Brooke, taking in her oval face and auburn hair. She stares at her hand on my arm. She closes her eyes and nods. And when she opens her beautifully sad eyes, they are full of tears.

Then she starts walking again, passing me without making any more eye contact on her way out the door. I turn around and watch her until she's out of sight.

When I come back to my senses and realize what just happened here and how this must have looked to Brooke, I open my mouth to try and explain.

She holds up her hand to stop me. "Don't tell me. That was her, wasn't it? The Hawaii lady. Oh my God, Bass, is that *your* baby she's carrying?"

I shake my head. "No."

Her arms cross in front of her chest. "Based on the look on your face, my bet is you wish it was."

All I can do is stare at her. I have no words. There is nothing I can say to change what just happened.

"Shit." She laughs maniacally, shaking her head as she gets up from the table. "I knew I shouldn't have come here. When are you going to stop falling for unavailable women, Bass? Are you so scared of a real relationship that the only women you will truly love are those who can't love you in return?"

"I—"

"I'm not going to do this again," she says with a bitter smile. "Goodbye, Bass. I hope you get everything you want."

I stare at my cup of coffee long after Brooke leaves, knowing that everything I'll ever want walked out that door right before she did.

CHAPTER THIRTY-TWO

IVY

"Just call us if you need us, honey," Mom says. "Your father and I are here for you. Anything you need."

"I think I just need to be alone today, if that's okay."

She nods and hugs me. "I understand. But if you change your mind …"

"Thanks, Mom. Daddy." I hug my father and then they walk out the door.

Everyone has come to the apartment today. Alder brought me breakfast. Christina delivered me lunch. Neither of them brought Ricky with them. I think they knew that even though I now have a good relationship with my nephew, today was not the day I needed to see him.

Holly wanted to stay home from work and baby me today. She said Janie could cover us at the shop. But the last thing I needed was someone hovering over me when I just want to curl up in Dahlia's blanket and look at all my favorite pictures of her.

The doorbell rings and I wonder who's decided to be on *Ivy watch* now.

But it's a delivery. It's a huge bouquet of daisies. I search inside for a card, but there isn't one. Still, I know who sent it. The arrangement is not from one of our shops, so there is only one person it could be from.

It's funny, everyone else brought food. They all know that daisies were Dahlia's favorite flower. But not one of them brought me any. Maybe they thought it would make me sad. But in some strange way, as impossible as it seems, I think Bass knows me better than my family knows me.

He knows that today is the one day I *have* to think about her. I have to think about all the good times. I even have to think about the bad times. Because thinking about it has helped me heal. Talking about it has helped me heal. And no one knows that better than the man who sent me the flowers.

On my way to put them in my room, the doorbell rings again. I close my eyes, hoping it's him. Hoping he wasn't really with that woman at the coffee shop the other day. The one who was touching him. And a part of me hopes he won't take no for an answer this time. That he will say he will love me no matter what. Even if I'm married to someone else. Even if I have another man's child. Even if that child will rip his heart out. Part of me wants him to claim me in a way that makes it impossible for me to fight him.

I rip open the door and then step to the side with a heavy sigh. "Hi, Eli."

He walks in and wraps me in a hug. "Are you okay?"

I put the vase on the table. "I'm managing. How about you?"

"I'm okay." He eyes the flowers. "Daisies? Who would send you daisies today of all days?"

"*He* would."

"Who, Bass?"

I nod.

"Want me to get rid of them?"

I grab the vase protectively. "No," I say, walking them back to my room.

"Why would you want a reminder?"

I put the vase on my dresser and sit on the end of my bed, pulling Dahlia's blanket onto my lap. "See, that's what you all don't seem to get. All of you do everything you can to take my mind off the fact that she's gone. You want me to get out and party. Make new memories. Have new experiences. But Bass"—I start to choke up—"Bass orders flower pancakes for me. And he kisses me under waterfalls. And he … he sends me her favorite flower."

Eli looks at me in confusion, studying my puffy face and red-rimmed eyes. "And that helps?"

"Yes, it helps," I cry. "I'd never felt closer to Dahlia than when I was in Hawaii with Bass. He made me remember. He didn't try to get me to forget. He's the only one who didn't."

I see tears pool in Eli's eyes. "God, Ivy. Then why won't you tell the man the truth? You still love him. Everyone can see that. And he still loves you."

I shake my head. "He doesn't. He thinks I'm married."

"What?"

I hold up my hand. "A while back he saw the ring."

"And you didn't tell him?"

"Of course not. Anyway, he's with someone now."

"Are you sure?"

"I saw him at the coffee shop the other day. And the woman sitting across from him was touching him."

"Did he see you?"

I nod.

"What did he do?" he asks.

"He just stared at me."

"He stared at you when he was with another woman?"

I shrug.

He sits next to me and holds me by my shoulders. "Ivy, why are you doing this to yourself? You are the smartest woman I know, but these last few months, you've just been so stupid."

I laugh. "Gee, thanks."

He puts a hand on my large belly. "I'm going to keep telling you this until it sinks in. This baby might not be like them."

"I know, and I hope that it's not. But if it is, I – I just can't put him through that."

"Maybe that's not for you to decide. Look at Monica."

I stare at him through my tears. "That's different and you know it, Eli. You're a great father, I've never thought anything different. But you know as well as I do that you get to go home at the end of every day."

"Yeah." He nods his head. "Yeah, I guess I do. I'm sorry for making you shoulder more of the burden."

I wipe my tears with the sleeve of my robe. "I wouldn't have it any other way. I wouldn't give up one single moment I had with her."

He wraps his arms around me and holds me through my tears. It wasn't so long ago that Eli and I would end up in bed at a time like this. It was the way we comforted one another. And even though I could use a few moments of peace right now, I know he's not the one who could give them to me. I glance at the flowers on my dresser knowing there is only one person who could do that.

He pulls away, both of us crying now. He looks at me like he did when it was Dahlia's birthday. He looks at me like the way he did right before we had sex.

He leans in, looking at my mouth as he does.

"Eli, no."

He hops off the bed, running his hands through his hair. "What the fuck was I thinking?"

I grab his hand. "You were thinking that we are both hurting. It's okay, Eli. Old habits are hard to break. And it's a normal response to what we're going through. It crossed my mind for a second, too. But we both know it won't solve anything." I look down at my belly. "Case in point."

Then we both share a laugh, a laugh that turns into more tears. And we hold each other for a few more minutes before I ask him to leave.

"Eli, you should be with Monica right now. She should be the one comforting you."

"And you should be with Bass."

I hold up Dahlia's blanket and then pick up her scrapbook. "It's okay, I have Dahlia."

He leans down and kisses my cheek before he walks out. "I'll always love you, Ivy. I hope you know that."

"I'll always love you, too."

But what I don't tell him is that I didn't even understand what love was until I had those years with Dahlia. Those weeks with Bass. And I wonder if I'll ever have the chance to experience that kind of love again.

I walk over and bury my nose in the daisies. Then I wrap myself in the blanket and page through Dahlia's scrapbook until I cry myself to sleep.

~ ~ ~

"Ivy, we think it's time," the doctor says, putting a hand on my shoulder.

I look over at my precious daughter, small and curled up on the hospital bed. The doctor and nurses are crying, just as the rest of us in the room are.

They've all worked so hard to try and make her better. To get her another transplant. To prolong her life. But it's all been in vain. We've known for days, weeks even, that the end was coming.

I run to her side, climb on the bed with her and pull her to me. No way is she going through this alone.

Eli walks to the other side of the bed and grabs her little hand. "I love you, princess," he says, tears streaming down his cheeks.

Her chest rises and falls in a big sigh as the heart monitor slows even more.

"I can't," he says, leaning down to embrace Dahlia for the last time.

I nod at him. "It's okay. I'll be here with her. It's okay, Eli."

He looks guilty as he steps away, glancing back one last time before he walks through the door. I can hear him break down after he leaves the room, his deep sobs echoing off the hallway walls.

Alder and Christina cross the room and give Dahlia one last kiss. They won't stay either. I can't blame them. They have a toddler of their own. No way can they watch a child die.

Even Dad breaks down and has to be escorted from the room, leaving only Mom and Holly in here with us. They both say their goodbyes to her and then stand back, giving me the last moments with my daughter.

As her breaths come farther and farther apart, I talk to her. "Baby girl, it's okay. It's okay to let go. You've been so brave. You have always been so strong. But it's okay to give in now. Jonah is waiting for you. He's waiting for his sister to teach him how to run and play and jump rope. You'll teach him how to draw. You'll tell him everything there is to know about flowers, especially daisies. And where you're going, daisies will be everywhere. You can sleep on a bed of them. And they won't ever wilt. They won't ever die. Just like you, my sweet girl. You are going to live forever. Just like Jonah. And Mommy will be with you again one day. And the three of us will go to Hawaii. We'll dance under a waterfall and squish our toes in the sand."

I hear Holly and my mother sobbing behind me. But I can't cry. Not yet. I'll never get a second chance at this moment. I'll never again get to see my baby transition from this world to the next. I'm her mother and she needs to know that I'm okay.

Her breathing slows even more. I can feel it happening as I hold her.

"Dahlia, you are the best thing that's ever happened to me. I'm going to be alright. Everyone will be. You go, baby."

Her little fingers squirm underneath mine. She turns her head and opens her eyes. "Mommy," she says, in barely a whisper. "Daisies gonna make everything better."

Then her eyes close and I feel her take her last breath.

"Yes, baby," I say, still holding back my tears. "Daisies are going to make everything better."

The nurse comes in and turns off Dahlia's machines. Then I collapse onto my daughter's body and sob. I pull her lifeless form to me as if I can somehow merge her body with mine and carry her with me so we can live as one. I've never wanted to trade places with another person more than I do now. It should be me who's leaving this world. Not her. Children aren't meant to die before their parents. Daughters aren't supposed to go to heaven before their mothers.

The doctor comes in and listens to Dahlia's heart before pronouncing her dead. But he might as well pronounce me *dead. Because there is no reason to live. Not anymore.*

I startle awake, drenched in sweat. I look over at the flowers. I look at them somehow knowing Bass would have been the only man to stay in the hospital room that day. He's the strongest man I've ever known.

I take off the damp clothes I'm wearing and reach in my dresser for a shirt. I study myself in the mirror after putting it on.

Bass's T-shirt still fits me even though it's now tight around the middle.

And as I stare at myself, I wonder if I made the biggest mistake of my life by pushing him away.

CHAPTER THIRTY-THREE

SEBASTIAN

"You *what?*" Aspen shrieks across the table at her brother.

"I got in!" Denver shouts, handing her the letter. "FDNY invited me to become a candidate. My training starts next month."

She studies the letter before dropping it on the table. Then she turns to me in disgust. "Did you know about this?"

"Of course I didn't." I look down at the same letter that was sent to me a few years ago. "You took the exam?" I ask him. "You never said anything."

"Well, you guys didn't seem to think I could get in, so I kept it to myself."

"It's not that I didn't think you *could* get in, Den," Aspen says. "It's that I didn't think you *should* get in."

Brett looks between all of us, clearly confused. "You don't want him to be a firefighter?" he asks Aspen.

She shakes her head. "Our parents died in a car accident when we were nineteen. Denver can't stand to look at car crashes ever since."

"You know a lot of our calls have to do with MVAs, don't you?" Brett asks.

"Yeah," Denver says. "I get it. I've got it covered, guys."

I look at Aspen, who's clearly concerned about her brother. Sawyer is whispering in her ear, but she's not happy about whatever it is he's saying. I know she has huge reservations about this and I feel horrible that I'm the one who brought it up several months ago.

I reach over and squeeze her shoulder. "I'll look out for him, Penny."

"What am I, five years old?" Denver says. "Will you guys quit babying me and just let me have a minute to fucking celebrate?"

"To you, Denver!" I say, raising my glass. "If I weren't already a smoke eater myself, I'd be damn jealous that you got a call after only a few months."

"To Denver," Sawyer and Brett say.

"Enjoy these last few weeks of drinking," Brett says. "You'll want to make sure to detox before training. You need to be in the best shape you can be, and every advantage you can give yourself will make it that much better."

"Take the lieutenant's advice," I tell Denver. "Toughest months of my life. But it's all worth it, man."

"Why do you think Denver got accepted so soon?" Aspen asks. "You said it could be years before applicants get invited to fire school."

"It usually is," Brett says. "The candidate list is longer than my wife's book of complaints."

I laugh, but I know he's not joking about his wife. He says Amanda has become a different person since having their son earlier this year. I'm glad he could come out with us tonight. He's usually stuck at home with Leo since his wife is always at work. And even though they have a nanny, he tries to be there as much as he can. Brett going out on the town is a rare occasion these days.

"Are you sure you didn't call in a favor or something, Bass?" Aspen asks.

"I just told you I didn't know about it, Penny. And it's not as if I have that kind of pull. My guess is they like that he used to be a cop. That and he probably killed it on the exam, the physical test, and the interview."

"Any idea where you want to get stationed?" Brett asks.

"Please don't pick Manhattan," Aspen says.

"Somebody has to do it," Denver says.

"Somebody who's not you," she says. "Can you pick a more benign station like Bass and Lt. Cash's?"

"Yeah, because we just sit around and twiddle our thumbs all day," I say.

"That's not what I meant," she says. "I'm sorry it came out that way."

I wink at her. "I'm just messing with you. If he can prove himself in training, we'd love to have Denver at our house. In fact, we may have an opening next year if Steve gets the transfer he's been trying to get. And *that* we might have a say in, right Cash?"

Brett raises his eyebrows at me. I know what he's thinking. He's having doubts about Denver based on what Aspen said. Hell, *I'm* having doubts about him.

"It would be great to have you watching over him," Aspen says. "I mean if he insists on doing this."

"You think I need a babysitter, Pen?" Denver says.

"Absolutely," she says. "At least until you get your feet wet. I'd feel so much better knowing you were with Bass and his company."

I smile at how much confidence Aspen has in my abilities.

"Hey, Sawyer, sorry to talk so much shop," I say, wondering if he's feeling left out. "You getting nervous about the wedding?" I ask.

He pulls Aspen close to him. "Hell, no. Believe me, you're the only one at this table who's getting left at the altar."

The four of them share a laugh. "Thanks a lot," I say, raising my glass in a sarcastic toast.

"Briggs, that woman across the bar is staring at you," Brett says, elbowing me.

I look across the room and see Ivy's sister, Holly, sitting by herself. She smiles at me and I wave her over to our table.

"It's Ivy's sister," I tell everyone before she comes up to us. "Be cool, please."

I get off my barstool and give her a hug. "Hi, Holly."

"Hi, Bass. I was just waiting for my friends to arrive."

"Just your friends?" I ask, before introducing her to everyone.

"She's not coming if that's what you're wondering."

"Well, you can wait with us if you want," I say.

"That won't be weird?"

"Not if we don't let it."

I motion for her to sit on my barstool and I stand up next to her. "You meeting Justin? He didn't say anything."

She wrinkles her nose. "No. Not Justin."

"It's all good. I won't say anything."

"It's not a big deal. Justin and I hang out occasionally. We date other people. Neither of us wants to be tied down."

"It's nice you can both feel the same way," I say.

Holly gives me a sad, guilty smile. We both know what the other is thinking.

"Holly, maybe you should go on a date with Denver," Aspen says. "He doesn't want to be tied down either."

Holly laughs, looking at Denver. "This baby?" she says. "He looks wet behind the ears. What are you, twenty-two?"

"I'm twenty-four," he says. "And I'm hardly wet behind the ears. In fact, I'm a hardened criminal."

Aspen spits out her drink all over the table. "Really, Den?"

"Okay, so not technically," he says to Holly. "But I did spend some time in prison."

"Prison?" Holly asks, intrigued.

"Well, maybe not *prison.* It was three nights in jail, but still."

Holly laughs. "I'm not about to be labeled a cougar."

"Just how old are you?" he asks.

"Twenty-nine."

"Nice," Denver says, nodding. "But that hardly makes you a cougar."

"Don't even think about it," I whisper to him. "It's bad enough having her date someone from the station."

I order everyone another round and then head to the bathroom. When I return, I see someone I didn't expect to see walking up to Holly. I see Eli. As in Eli—Ivy's husband. And I see him with his goddamned arm around a woman who is not his wife.

"What the fuck?" I say, walking over to remove his arm from the woman before I push him in the chest. "Are you cheating on her, you asshole?"

The woman looks at me and Eli, confused. "Cheating on me?" she asks.

"He's cheating on Ivy," I say. "His *wife.*"

"What is he talking about, Eli?" she asks.

My jaw tightens and I know my face is getting red. "This asshole is married to his pregnant wife, yet he's at a bar with *you.*"

Holly gets up and tries to stand between me and Eli. She probably thinks I'm about to hit him. And she'd be right. I am.

"Get out of the way, Holly."

"There's been a big misunderstanding," she says.

"Somebody needs to start talking," the woman with Eli says. She holds her left hand up, flashing her ring in front of Eli's face. Her *engagement* ring. "Is this for real, Eli? Please tell me you're not really married to Ivy."

"I'm not married to her, babe," Eli says. Then he turns to me. "I'm not fucking married to her. I told Ivy to tell you. I told her it was ridiculous to keep things from you."

I'm trying very hard to keep my cool, but Brett is having to hold me back. "Will somebody please tell me what the fuck is going on?"

"Ivy's not married," Holly says.

"But I saw the ring!" I yell. "What's she keeping from me? Oh my God. Is the baby mine? Is that what she's keeping from me? And why the hell would she do that?"

"Calm down, Briggs," Brett says, offering me his barstool and a drink. "It looks like maybe the rest of us need to give you and Ivy's sister some room to talk."

Everyone goes over to the next table and Holly sits down beside me. "The baby is Eli's," she says. "I was there when she first went to the doctor. Ivy wears the ring because she was tired of getting dirty looks and inconsiderate comments about being a single mother."

"Why didn't she tell me?" I ask. "Back when I first saw her wearing the ring at your shop, why didn't she say anything?"

"The way she tells it, she tried to tell you it wasn't what you thought, but you just walked out."

"Of course I walked out. What was I supposed to do when I saw a wedding ring on her finger? And if she wanted me to know she wasn't married, all she had to do was pick up the damn phone."

"She's hurting," Holly says. "She's convinced this baby will be like Jonah or Dahlia."

"Anyone can understand why she's scared. But, what the hell, Holly. From the looks of it, Eli is engaged to another woman. Ivy had me believing all along that she was getting back together with him. Why the hell did she lie to me from the beginning? Why didn't she just tell me back then that she was pregnant with Eli's baby?"

Holly puts her hand on my shoulder. "These are all very good questions, but maybe they are ones you should be asking Ivy."

"She won't talk to me. She never answered my calls or texts. She never acknowledged my flowers. She doesn't want me, Holly. And quite frankly, at this point, I'm not sure I want her either."

She studies me. "Really? Because from the way you were about to disembowel Eli, I'd say you still have feelings for her."

"Sure I still have feelings for her, but there is a lot of water under the bridge. She's tried very hard for a long time to keep me out of her life. I'm not sure I can look past that."

"She has her reasons, Bass. Talk to her."

I shake my head. "No. I promised myself I wouldn't go back down that road."

She closes her eyes and blows out a deep breath. "I'm not like my little sister," she says. "Hell, I'm not sure I will ever settle down and have kids. But do you know that all Ivy ever wanted was to be a mom? When we were little and played with Barbies, I would always play with Barbie *and* Ken. I would make them go on dates and kiss and even have sex. But not Ivy. She would pretend Barbie had a baby. And then one Christmas, she got one of those dolls that eats and wets and cries. It was her favorite present ever. She took that doll everywhere. My little sister was born to be a mother.

But that dream has been taken away from her. *Twice*. And she lives in fear it will happen again. That has to mess with a person, Bass. So maybe you could cut her a slight break."

"Why didn't you tell me?" I ask. "Back in July, when I came to the flower shop and you said something was wrong but that I had to talk to her, why didn't you tell me then? Hell, why didn't *anyone* tell me? It's been almost six months and you were all okay going along with this? Even when you knew I loved her? I know she still has feelings for me. I could see it in her face at the coffee shop the other day."

"I'm sorry," she says. She motions over to Eli. "We all are. But she's my sister. I have to follow her wishes. But the jig is up now. So go talk to her."

"No. She can talk to me if she wants. But she won't. I know she won't. She's gone through too much trouble pushing me away."

"Bass, don't close the book on this. Everyone wants her with you. The question is, do you? Do you want her if she's carrying another man's baby?"

I laugh halfheartedly. "I think I've asked myself that a thousand times over the past two months."

"So, what's the answer?"

I toss back a shot that one of the guys left on the table. Then I get up. "It's been nice seeing you again, Holly. I hope you all enjoy your evening."

CHAPTER THIRTY-FOUR

IVY

I sit and stare at the guitar in the corner of my bedroom. I still play sometimes, just to feel closer to Dahlia. But every time I do, I can't help but think of Bass. I think of him playing his guitar and then of him holding me in his arms as we strum chords together. I wonder if he ever thinks of me when he's playing.

I will myself to get out of bed, knowing I can't lie here forever. The anniversary of her death has come and gone. And the world didn't end. I'm still here. I didn't jump off a bridge.

The baby kicks me in the ribs. I love it when he kicks. It lets me know he's alive. I still use the fetal Doppler a lot. It comforts me to hear his heartbeat when he's sleeping. Still, the nagging feeling I get tells me something is wrong. My doctor says I worry too much. She's done a half-dozen ultrasounds to check for kidney abnormalities. And although she hasn't found any, she won't come out and say the baby will be healthy. Because nobody knows for sure that he will be.

I remember being pregnant with Jonah. I remember being so happy every time he kicked. Eli and I would sit for hours, poking my stomach and then laughing when Jonah would poke back. We made a game of it, trying to guess which body part he was using to poke us. I remember naming him and making all kinds of plans. And then one morning, he just never kicked again.

That was the second worst day of my life. I've been through eight anniversaries of the day Jonah died. But unlike Dahlia's death, I have no favorite blanket to comfort me. No scrapbook of drawings. No pictures.

I was young and naïve when I was eighteen. The chaplain at the hospital urged me to allow the hospital photographer to take a picture of Eli and me with Jonah. With a *dead* Jonah. I refused, thinking it was morbid and unnecessary.

Oh, how I wish I had that picture now. All I have of Jonah is the framed hospital document of his tiny footprints. And although the vision of his little, lifeless body is burned into my memory forever, it's getting harder to remember what his face looked like. Did he look like me? Eli? Dahlia? I remember him being this perfectly-formed tiny human with ten fingers and ten toes. They let me hold him before taking him away. But Eli never did. I think I remember him touching Jonah's face, but he refused to take him into his arms. Just like he refused to watch Dahlia die.

A tear runs down my face as I cradle my belly thinking that I might have to go through losing a third child.

I finally get up, catching a glimpse of myself in the mirror on the way to the bathroom. I still wear Bass's shirt to bed every night. It's far too tight in the belly and will probably never regain its shape, but just like Dahlia's blanket, it's how I hold onto that little piece of him.

After my shower, Holly tells me what a comfortable, sunny day it is outside. She says she's going for a run. I check the temperature and see just how nice it is, so I put on my boots and grab my coat and head out the door.

I walk down the block, inhaling the cool December air as I enjoy the warm sun on my face. I look at all the Christmas decorations lining the streets and in the storefront windows. I had promised myself I would do better at Christmas this year, but I've yet to make a single purchase.

I decide to change that right now and walk into the nearest store. I pick out some sweaters for Holly and Christina, a collection of cookbooks for Mom and Dad, and a Nighthawks jersey for Alder.

Then I take a deep breath and go into the kids' section.

"Can I help you?" a young lady asks.

"I need a present for a two-year-old boy. My nephew."

She smiles as she looks at my belly. "Oh, then this must be your first."

I don't acknowledge her statement and I know she must think I'm a class-A bitch.

"Well, does he like cars? Trucks? Disney characters?"

I shrug. "I'm not sure what he likes."

"In my experience, you can't go wrong with machinery. I've got lots of choices right over here."

I try to get my legs to move, but they won't. I'm stuck looking around at thousands of toys and I feel my throat swell up. I haven't been in a toy department in well over a year. I unbutton my coat because it's getting hot in here. The air has become thick and is weighing down on my chest. I feel like I'm suffocating.

"Can you please just pick something for me?" I hand her three twenty-dollar bills. "Anything will do."

"Of course." She nods to my belly. "Would you like to pick out something for the baby as well?"

I shake my head as a wave of nausea courses through me. "I should probably go. I'm not feeling well."

She eyes the bags in my hands. "I'd be happy to have all your purchases sent to your residence so you don't have to carry them."

I nod. "Thank you. That would be great."

I hand over my bags, scribble my address on a piece of paper, and then bolt out of the store.

I walk around the corner and lean against the side of the building, catching my breath. I think I'm having a panic attack.

"Miss, are you okay?" a man asks.

His companion looks at my large belly. "Oh my gosh, are you in labor? Should we call nine-one-one?"

"No!" I shout. "Please don't. I'm okay, I just lost my breath for a second."

The man escorts me to a nearby bench where I sit down and try to calm myself. The couple stays with me until they are sure I'm not going to pop the baby out right here on the street corner.

I shake my head at my stupidity. What if they'd called 911? Would it be Bass's company who was called to the scene? Of course it would, his station is just a few blocks away.

After sitting on the bench for another few minutes, I find myself getting up and walking in the direction of said station. It's in a residential area with row houses across the street. I stand behind a tree next to the sidewalk and stare at the firehouse. The garage doors are open, making me wonder if they are always open as they were when Holly and I visited earlier this year, or if they are just trying to get some fresh air on this unseasonably mild December day.

I see the two large trucks. What was it Bass called them? Engine and Squad? And I see an empty bay where I assume the ambulance must go when it's not out on a call.

And then I see him. I see Bass near the back of the garage, off to the side of the trucks. He's sitting on a chair playing guitar.

Someone walks by him and he stops temporarily to have a conversation, laughing with one of his colleagues before resuming his playing.

I wonder if he plays outside so he doesn't bother anyone in the house. As I recall, it was all fairly open and maybe the guitar would echo throughout. Do they know what they're missing out on? His music is incredible. My body is begging for me to get closer so I can hear what he's playing, but there isn't any way for me to do so without being seen. So I stand here, leaning against a tree, pretending I can hear him play. And I like to think he's playing the song he composed for me in Hawaii. The one he called *'Greene Eyes.'*

"You can go over there, you know," a woman says, startling me from behind. "They love to have visitors. They'll give you a tour if you want."

"Oh, no. That's okay." I turn around to face her, nodding to my belly. "I was just stopping to rest for a second."

"I'd say it was more than a second," she says. "I've been watching you from my window for twenty minutes. It's why I came out here."

"Sorry."

I'm not sure what else to say. Does she think I'm stalking her house or something?

She looks at my belly speculatively, then back over at the firehouse. Then her lips pucker and her face falls into a frown. "Six babies have been left at this station this year. I suppose it's more honorable than a dumpster." She shakes her head in disapproval. "Just don't leave it out in the cold, okay, miss?"

I gasp at her insinuation. "I'm not leaving my baby there. I'm not even sure why I'm here."

"Oh." She nods in understanding. "I see. The baby daddy is a fireman."

I shake my head sadly. "No, that's not it. I'm sorry. I should go."

"Good luck, miss. Whatever you decide."

As I walk away, I look back at the station one last time. That's when I see Bass standing in the driveway in front of the trucks, staring at me. We lock eyes for a second. Or maybe a minute. Or an hour. I'm not sure how long it is because time stands still.

He looks at me differently this time. I can't put my finger on it, but it's almost the same way he used to look at me when we first met—like he feels sorry for me, but at the same time, like he wants something from me. Something more.

I surmise that I'm just imagining things. He said he's done with me. He thinks I'm married. And it's for the best really. He's better off being as far away from me as he can be.

I can't stand here any longer without wanting to go over to him. So I do the only thing I can. The thing I've excelled at for the past five and a half months. I walk away.

~ ~ ~

"I'm proud of you, little sister," Holly says on her way to the shower.

I stare at all the Christmas presents I wrapped that are now stacked high on our kitchen table. I stopped at five more stores on my way back from the firehouse. I had to do something—anything to get my mind off the man who was staring into my soul.

I think I'll tell Holly that we should get a tree. I know she hasn't brought it up because she's afraid it will upset me. But what nobody seems to understand is that remembering Dahlia and Jonah isn't the problem—it hasn't been for a while—not since Hawaii. It's the fear of history repeating itself that keeps me up at night. And causes panic attacks in toy departments.

I stand back and look at the mess I've made in the room. Pieces of wrapping paper are all over the floor. Bows, tags, tape, string—they litter the room in colors of silver, red, and green. Dahlia would be happy. She loved Christmas. In fact, she'd probably sit in the middle of the mess and wrap herself in the scraps of paper. And then I'd unwrap her and pretend to be surprised and tell her she was the best gift I'd ever gotten. And it would be true.

Then the oddest thing occurs to me. I wonder what happened to Dahlia's stocking. We didn't hang stockings last year—at least *I* didn't. I never bothered to ask my family what they did. I spent the entire day in my apartment dreading Mom, Dad, Alder, and Holly coming over to dole out the obligatory presents before they left and I could go back to being a zombie.

Holly said they put all Dahlia's stuff in storage. Maybe it's time for me to go through her things. Because standing here, thinking about Christmas—it just feels wrong without having her stocking here. In fact, I think I'll make one for Jonah, too.

There's a knock on my door. I look around at the messy room, knowing that with my huge belly, there is no way I can tidy things up quickly. But I doubt the kid delivering my dinner will mind too much.

When I open the door and see Bass, I freeze. Immediately, dread washes over me. I glance down at what I'm wearing. *His* T-shirt and a pair of yoga pants.

When I look back up at him, I see that he's doing the very same thing. His eyes are glued to the T-shirt he gave me in Hawaii.

"I, uh … was wrapping presents," I say, as if that explains why I'm wearing his shirt.

I roll my eyes at my stupidity.

"Can I come in?"

My stomach flips over at the sound of his voice. The low, sultry timbre of his words that I'd forgotten just how much I loved to hear. Of course, maybe it wasn't my stomach flipping. It could have just been the baby kicking.

I back up and move to the side, not finding any words to say that won't make me sound even more awkward.

He walks in, paces around the room, and then nods to my left hand. "I know you're not married, Ivy. In fact, I know Eli is engaged to another woman."

"What? How?"

Holly walks into the room, ready for her night out. Bass motions to her. "Because I ran into them on Friday."

My jaw drops when I look at Holly. She doesn't even have the decency to look guilty. "Why didn't you tell me, Hol?"

She grabs her purse off the table. "You two need to work your shit out," she says. "I'm leaving."

"Holly." I stare her down.

"Ivy, I'm tired of it. Aren't you? Isn't lying to him exhausting? Now sit your asses down and talk."

She walks out the door. But Bass doesn't sit down. He paces around again, running his hands through his hair.

"Make me understand," he says.

I rub my hands over my belly. "There's nothing to understand, Sebastian. I'm having someone else's baby."

"You came to the firehouse, Ivy. And the way you looked at me there, and at the coffee shop. Hell, the way you've looked at me since I've known you. How can you look at me like that and push me away?"

"What is it you don't understand about me having Eli's baby?" I say.

"But you don't love Eli. You love *me*."

I shake my head as if what he said isn't true.

"Ivy, I know you do." He gestures to my shirt. "Look at you, you're wearing my goddamn T-shirt even after all this time." He rubs his forehead in frustration. "Listen, I know it's not your fault that you were pregnant in Hawaii. You said you didn't know and I believe you. Why are you letting that keep us apart? Do you think I can't love another man's child?"

My eyes become moist and my throat tightens as I shake my head again. "It's not that," I whisper.

"Then what is it? Why the hell won't you let me in?"

I sit down on the couch, my legs too shaky to hold me. "You can't understand, Bass. No one can."

"Why don't you try me? I might surprise you."

I look over at a picture of Dahlia hanging on the living room wall. "I think losing a child might just be the hardest thing anyone could ever go through. I wasn't about to put you through that."

"Put *me* through that?" he asks.

I nod, picking at a piece of lint on the sofa. "I knew you'd still want to be with me," I say. "Even if you knew I was carrying Eli's child." I look up at him. "Am I wrong?"

"No. You're not wrong. I loved you, Ivy," he says, his voice cracking. "I still love you."

"Don't you understand what would have happened?" I ask. "You would have gone through this pregnancy with me. You would have put your hands on my belly every night, feeling him kick, and squirm, and get the hiccups. You would have talked to him and bonded with him even before he was here. You would have tried to name him and make plans."

"Him?" he asks. "It's a boy?"

I shrug. "I'm not sure. I didn't want to know."

"All those things you said I'd do sound like pretty normal things, Ivy."

"Nothing about this is normal, Bass. I've had two babies. Two babies who are dead now. Two babies who made me fall in love with them before my heart got ripped out. And it's about to happen all over again. I'm not about to take you down with me. It's not fair."

His face falls into a sympathetic frown. "Oh, God. Does the baby have it? Does he have ARPKD?"

I shake my head. "I don't know yet. There is nothing definitive on the ultrasounds. But that doesn't mean anything. They didn't see anything abnormal with Dahlia, either."

"So he or she could be perfectly normal," he says. "In fact, odds are that he will be."

"I don't look at odds anymore," I tell him. "I don't have the best track record at beating them."

He stares at me, trying to get a handle on the situation. Then he huffs in anger. "So, what the fuck, Ivy? You just unilaterally decided to cut me out of your life? You took away *my* choice in the matter? You didn't even talk to me about it. You just made up lies to push me away? What gives you the right to mess with my life like that?"

"You don't understand," I say, a warm tear rolling down my cheek.

"No, *you* don't understand." He strides over and pulls me off the couch.

He takes me into his arms and kisses me. He kisses me hard. So hard it's almost painful. But I think it's painful because his kiss hurts my soul. It hurts because I love him so much. It hurts because I think about him every day and dream about him at night. It hurts because it makes me remember the good times we had in Hawaii.

His kisses become softer. They become the words he's trying to tell me. They become the pleas I've been refusing to hear. I get lost in his kiss. In his silent appeal. I get lost in *him*. The only thing in the world that is real in this moment is this kiss. And for a second, I remember what it's like to be happy.

Then the baby jabs me in the ribs.

I pull away, shaking my head. "Bass, I can't."

"Why, Ivy? Why can't you?"

Tears are streaming down my face. I wipe them with the collar of my shirt.

"Tell me!" he yells.

"Because I love you too much. That's why."

He lets out a deep breath, reaching out for me. "Sweetheart, it's okay. It's going to be okay. We can do this together."

I step out of his reach. "It won't be okay," I say. "You know what happened to Eli and me. I'm not capable of having a relationship when I have a special-needs child. And as hard as it will be to lose another child. It will be even harder to lose you both."

"But you've already lost me. We're not together."

"It's for the best, Bass. We haven't been together for almost six months. Surely you're getting over me by now. You're moving on. I saw it myself at the coffee shop. It doesn't hurt that much anymore, does it? But if we were together and lost this baby, and then lost each other, I … I wouldn't be able to take it. *We* wouldn't be able to take it."

He laughs sadly. "So all of this is to protect me? That's bullshit, Ivy. And you think it doesn't hurt that much anymore? Tell me what you did on the twelfth—on the anniversary of Dahlia's death. Did you go out and party because it *didn't hurt that much anymore*?"

"Of course not."

"I don't care if we were together for two weeks or two years, and it doesn't matter if we've been apart for six months or six days, it still fucking hurts. And if you don't think it does, then you're not the woman I thought you were."

"You're right," I say through my tears. "I'm not."

I'm screaming at myself on the inside. *He's here and he wants you!* But so many things race through my mind. Jonah's stillbirth. Eli moving out when Dahlia wasn't even a year old. Eli refusing to be with us when Dahlia died.

The doorbell rings and I pick up the money on the counter.

"I'd like you to leave," I say.

He stares at me blankly. "So that's it?"

I nod. "I'm sorry."

"Then I guess this is goodbye, Ivy Greene."

I open the door and pay for my dinner, watching Bass walk down the hallway as I trade my heart for a bowl of Kung Pau chicken.

CHAPTER THIRTY-FIVE

SEBASTIAN

"I asked everyone to step out because I wanted a minute alone with you," Aspen says, adjusting her veil. "I wanted to say thank you. Thank you for not giving up on our friendship and walking away back when I didn't share your feelings. You are like a second brother to me, Bass, and I love you more than you know."

I pull her into a hug, careful not to wrinkle anything she's wearing. "I love you, too, Penny."

"I know this must be hard for you," she says.

I nod. "Yeah, but not for the reason you might think."

She flashes me an arduous stare. "Bass, you're my best friend. I know you better than anyone. I know you got over me a long time ago. This is hard for you because you want the woman in the veil to be Ivy."

My eyes snap up to hers. "You think I wanted to *marry* her?"

"Want," she says. "There's nothing past tense about it."

I shake my head. "It doesn't really matter what I wanted. Or want. She's made her choice."

"But you told me she was wearing your shirt."

"That doesn't mean anything," I say.

She cocks her head to the side, raising her brows at me. "Do you really believe that?"

I've asked myself that same question for two weeks. And I can't get the image of Ivy wearing my shirt out of my head. She looked beautiful. The shirt was still far too big for her with the exception of her middle. Her baby bump stressed the fabric, showing every curve of her growing belly. It made me want to reach out and touch her. Touch the baby—the baby that isn't even mine.

I sit down on the couch and toss back a swig of brown liquor, remembering another wedding when I was in a similar room in the back of a church, drinking a similar drink, thinking similar things. Thinking that I *did* want it to be someone else wearing a veil. Back then I wanted it to be Aspen. But now, as I stare at my best friend who's about to marry the love of her life, I know I'll never get to marry mine.

"She said she loves me too much to be with me. Can you believe that? She said she was protecting me by pushing me away. Who does that?"

Aspen smiles sympathetically before she sits down next to me and takes my hand. "You bet I can believe it. Have you forgotten who I'm marrying today?" she says. "Listen, Bass. We tend to hurt those we love the most when we are hurting. Maybe you just need to give it time. Who knows, maybe she'll come around after the baby arrives. If the baby is healthy, she might change her mind."

I pinch the bridge of my nose. "Don't you get it? I want to be there for her *now*, not after she has a healthy baby. I don't care if the baby is healthy or not—I mean, of course I care, but I want her and the baby regardless. And I don't give a rat's ass that the baby isn't mine. It's a part of her and I want *every* part of her."

She squeezes my hand. "I know how hard it is to be in love with someone knowing they love you but can't be with you. I also know that until she realizes what she's giving up by pushing you away, there's nothing you can do."

"What if she never realizes it?"

"She's a woman, Bass. Trust me, she will."

I close my eyes and sigh. "Shit, Penny. I'm sorry. This day should be all about you and here I am being a huge downer."

"I'll always be here for you," she says. "I don't care if it's my wedding day or if I'm back in Kansas City or Timbuktu. If you need me, I'm here."

"Same goes for me," I tell her. Then I get off the couch and help her up. "Come on, let's go get you married."

"Eeeeeek!" she screams. "I'm marrying Sawyer Mills today."

"That you are," I say, offering her a genuine smile. "Thank you for letting me be your best man."

"Man of honor," she corrects me, laughing. She knows I hate that term. "There is nobody else in the world I'd want up there standing next to me."

There's a knock on the door and then Denver pokes his head through. "It's almost time. Are you ready?"

Aspen nods, so Denver comes in the room followed by Murphy and Rylee, who are her bridesmaids. I give her a final hug and head out to the sanctuary. The one concession she made was to let me stand at the altar along with Sawyer and his attendants rather than walk down the aisle with the girls.

As I wait up front for the ceremony to start, I look around the massive room. There are more sports stars in here than I can count. There are TV personalities. Celebrities. Politicians, even.

And photographers. There are lots of photographers. Aspen and Sawyer agreed to sell their wedding photos to a popular magazine and donate all the proceeds to shelters for battered women.

I look over at Sawyer, standing proudly next to his three groomsmen. He doesn't look the least bit nervous. Maybe it's because he's used to being in front of large crowds. Maybe it's because he's getting everything he ever wanted.

Brady and Caden stand next to him, rounded out by Danny.

Danny and his mother flew up from Arizona to be at the wedding. Aspen said that just as she wouldn't get married without Denver here, Sawyer wouldn't do it without Danny. They have a special relationship, those two. Danny is all smiles. He enjoys being the center of attention. Lucy, his mom, stands at the ready to help out should Danny have any issues during the ceremony.

The organist starts playing and all eyes turn to the sanctuary doors. When they open, three children walk through. Caden's nieces are the flower girls and Brady's son is the ring bearer. Everyone laughs when little Beth runs up to her uncle at the altar. Her father, Kyle Stone, rushes up to grab her so the procession can continue.

Rylee and Murphy come down the aisle looking gorgeous in their sequined silver dresses. And then Aspen appears in the doorway on Denver's arm. I've only ever seen one woman more beautiful than her. And that woman wasn't wearing a wedding dress. She was wearing a FDNY T-shirt.

Aspen was right. I wish I were standing five feet to my left and that it was Ivy coming down that aisle. I've never wanted something so badly in my life. Not Juilliard. Not FDNY. Not anything.

I glance at Sawyer, looking austere in his black tux and silver cummerbund. At no time since I've known him have I seen him look happier than he does at this moment. Lord, how I envy him.

When Denver and Aspen reach the altar, Denver kisses her.

"Mom and Dad would be so proud," he says.

They lock eyes and share a moment of sadness. I know they both wish their parents were here. That it was their father walking her down the aisle, and that it was their mother sitting in the first pew.

Denver hands her off to Sawyer and then I watch my best friend marry the only man she's ever truly loved. The man who pushed her away. The guy who went through all kinds of hell and came out stronger. And as they say their vows to each other, I wonder what my vows would be if I were ever to be standing at an altar with Ivy.

And I realize I could write an entire goddamn book of vows. After only weeks with her, I could recite a thousand reasons why she is the woman for me. Some of those reasons, I texted to her after seeing her at her apartment a few weeks ago. But like Aspen said, none of that matters if Ivy doesn't believe those reasons.

The sanctuary erupts in cheers as they are pronounced husband and wife. Sawyer kisses Aspen and then he picks her up and spins her around. He doesn't put her back down. He carries her back up the aisle, six-foot train and all.

Brady looks at me awkwardly. I guess we didn't really talk about the fact that we're supposed to walk up the aisle together. He jokingly holds out his elbow to me.

I shrug. "Oh, what the hell," I say, before threading my arm through his. "If nothing else, it will make for some great pictures."

Caden bellows out a laugh and takes Murphy's hand behind us. And then Rylee walks Danny up the aisle.

Aspen puts a hand to her mouth to cover her giggles when she sees Brady and me skipping through the main doors. I pull her into a hug. "Congratulations!"

She smiles brightly. "Sometimes dreams do come true, Bass."

"I hope you're right, Mrs. Mills. I hope you're right."

A woman comes bursting through the doors at the front of the church. The security team holds the jogger back as she belts out, "Someone call nine-one-one. I don't have a phone."

I run over to her. "What happened?"

She points outside. "Car accident. Looks like two or three cars got mangled up. I saw it happen. One tried to stop, but the street is icy and—"

"Call it in," I tell security. "We may need multiple ambulances. And please try to keep everyone in the church." I beckon to the guys as I head out the door. "Denver, follow me. Brady and Caden, I may need your help too."

The four of us run to the corner and see one car T-boned by a telephone pole and another two cars smashed together on an embankment of snow. One of the cars is on its side. I rush to it first, seeing a man in the driver's seat.

"Sir, are you hurt?" I ask, not seeing any blood.

"I think I'm okay," he says. "I'm just stuck."

"Can you move your hands and feet?"

"Yes."

I see fuel dripping out onto the snow. "Brady!" I shout behind me. "See if you can help this guy out of his car."

I hear someone scream and go to the car covered in snow to investigate.

"My son!" a woman yells. "He's in the back."

I stick my head through the broken driver's window and see a child in a car seat. He's crying but doesn't look injured. The mother, on the other hand, wasn't so lucky. Her head is bleeding, and it looks like one if not both of her legs are broken. She needs to stay still.

"Ma'am, your son looks okay. Please stop trying to turn your head. You have a head injury."

I look behind me to see Denver staring at the pile-up. He's stoic. Frozen.

Then Caden calls to me from across the street. "Bass, you need to get over here," he says.

"Denver, I need you to keep this woman's head stable. She could have a neck injury."

"I, uh …"

"Denver, get over here. Now!"

Sawyer comes up behind me. "I'll do it. Tell me what you need."

"Keep her head steady. Don't let her turn around to look in the back seat. Don't move her and don't let her try to get out. We need to get a collar on her. Just put your hands on either side of her head and pin her head to the headrest."

"Got it," he says.

I look at Denver on my way across the street. He's staring at the two cars surrounded by snow on the embankment. "Snap out of it, man. This is going to be your job in a few months. Get over your shit or get the fuck out of the street."

"Damn it," I think he says under his breath. Then he follows me to the car wrapped around the pole. "I'm sorry."

"Don't be sorry. Just help me."

I hear sirens in the background, so I know help is on the way.

A dazed man with a piece of glass sticking out of his chest walks toward me.

"Sir, I need you to sit down."

I lead him to the sidewalk and sit him on a bench. Then I take off my tux jacket and wrap it around the glass.

"Denver, hold the glass in place with my jacket. Do not let it move, and whatever you do, don't pull it out. I have to go check on the other victim."

Denver doesn't do what I ask. He just stands and stares back at the snow-covered cars.

"Do it now, Andrews, or people could die!"

He finally puts his hands where mine are, taking the jacket covering the glass from me.

I run over to Caden and see him using his own tux jacket to stop the bleeding coming from the passenger's head.

"She's bleeding badly," he says. "I don't think the airbag deployed when they hit the pole."

An ambulance and an engine pull up behind me.

I quickly give the paramedics my assessment of who I think they should see first, and then I help them until the second and third ambulances show up.

After the victims are all transported, the guys and I walk back and stand on the frozen front steps of the church where Sawyer's security detail is holding back the large crowd of wedding guests.

"Do you think they'll be okay?" Aspen asks.

"Yeah," I say. "I think they got lucky." I turn to the guys. "Thanks for your help."

Denver shakes his head, clearly disgusted with himself. "A lot of fucking help I was."

"You helped someone," I say. "That man would have bled out if you hadn't been there. No way could I have helped all the victims myself."

"I froze," he says.

"You did. But then you helped."

"I can't fucking do this," he says, getting up and walking away.

I start to follow him, but Aspen puts her arm on me. "Don't," she says. "Give him a minute. Our parents died in the snow, trapped in a car."

"Right," I say, watching him walk away with his head hung low.

I look down at my shirt to see it smeared with blood. Then I look at Caden to see the cuffs of his shirt stained red. "Well, shit," I say to Sawyer. "There go the wedding pictures."

"Are you kidding?" he says. "The pictures will be epic. It'll be a great story to tell the grandkids."

I laugh. "That it will."

The four of us look at each other. "Let's go get a drink at the reception," Caden says. "I think we've earned it."

~ ~ ~

Since neither Aspen nor Sawyer have much in the way of family, they decided not to do the traditional family table at their reception. Everyone has been invited to sit wherever they want. Since I only know the wedding party, I sit at a table with Caden and Murphy.

Denver joins us, carrying a large plate of food. I laugh, knowing how many calories he'll be burning at the fire academy, which he starts in a just few days. I guess he's carb-loading now.

"You're not drinking?" I ask, nodding to his glass of ice water.

"No," he says, looking frustrated. "Other than the sip of champagne at the toast earlier, I haven't had a drink since Christmas eve. I was detoxing for training." He puts his plate down and rubs his forehead. "But now I'm thinking I might as well tie one on. Maybe Aspen was right all along. I shouldn't be a firefighter."

"Listen, Denver. I'm not going to blow smoke up your ass and tell you that what happened today didn't concern me. You have to be able to react. You can't freeze up like that. You can't avoid horrible situations. Running into horrible situations is what we do. Being a firefighter isn't just a job—it's a way of life. You have to want it, man. If this is just some job you thought you'd try on for size, keep looking. But if you really want to help people—if you think you can overcome your shit, then don't let anyone, including Aspen, hold you back."

He nods, taking in my words. "I've thought a lot about this since I applied," he says. "I couldn't do anything to save my parents. But maybe I could save someone else's parents."

I put a hand on his shoulder. "I like the way you think. And yes, you could, and you will. But you have to be one hundred percent committed."

He nods again in silence.

I try to lighten the mood. "Just don't give up on day three of training when every muscle in your body will hurt like you've been run over by a Mack truck."

"Sure," he says noncommittally.

"Anything you need, I'm here for you."

He lifts his glass of water to me. "Thanks, bro. I guess I have a lot to think about."

A redhead comes up and talks to Murphy for a minute. Then she turns to me. "We met last month at the gym, right?"

I hold my hand out. "Bass Briggs, nice to see you again."

"Charlie Stone," she says. "Mind if I crash your party and sit here? I'm without my better half this evening."

"Your husband away on PI business?" I ask, pulling out a chair for her.

"Yes and no," she says. "We have a few clients in California that we usually let our West Coast office handle, but Ethan's mom hasn't been well lately. They live in Malibu and he wanted to go for a visit."

"You didn't want to go to California, too?" I ask. "Get out of the cold maybe?"

"I'm not supposed to fly this close to my due date," she says, rubbing her hands on her belly.

I stare at her round stomach, just now realizing she's pregnant. From the front, she doesn't even look it, but when she turns sideways I think she's about as big as Ivy was when I saw her a few weeks ago. I'm surprised I didn't notice that Charlie was pregnant last month when I met her at the gym. Then again, I think she had a coat on.

"Congratulations."

"Thanks," she says, sitting down a bit awkwardly. "It's a girl. If you want to suggest any names, go right ahead. Ethan and I are having a time of it. We can't agree on anything."

I can't help myself. I'm staring at her pregnant belly like a creepy stalker. I wonder if Ivy has thought about names yet. I think she probably hasn't. I know she thinks naming the baby will jinx it somehow.

"Do you have any kids?" Charlie asks, catching me staring at her belly.

I shake my head. "No."

"Oh, I just thought with the way you were looking at my baby bump …"

"Sorry," I say. "I know someone who's pregnant and you look about as far along as she is."

"Really? When is she due?"

"I'm not exactly sure."

"I've got six more weeks to go. It can't come soon enough." She touches her stomach again. "Did you hear that, baby? If you want to come a few weeks early like your brother did, that's perfectly fine. I'm so over this."

"You look radiant," Murphy says.

"Thank you." Charlie shifts around in her chair. "I just wish she'd quit kicking me in the ribs."

"Is she kicking right now?" Murphy asks. "Can I feel? I miss that feeling so much."

"Sure," Charlie says, putting Murphy's hand on her belly.

I watch as Murphy's face lights up when the baby kicks.

Charlie looks at me to catch me staring. Again. "You can feel, too, if you want. I have to admit, it's pretty amazing."

"Uh …"

She grabs my hand and puts it on her bump.

"Six years ago, if you told me I'd enjoy being pregnant, I would've called you crazy. But then fate intervened and gave us Eli. I hated being pregnant with him. I didn't even want kids. And then there was the whole not knowing who the father was."

"You didn't know who the father was?" I ask. Then I realize what I said. "Sorry, I didn't mean to ask such a personal question."

"No, it's fine," she says. "I'm the one who blurted it out. Ethan and I weren't really dating back then. We were just hooking up occasionally. And there was this other guy one night. I still can't believe I was that stupid. But, hey, shit happens." She rolls her eyes and says to her bump, "Don't tell Daddy Mommy said *shit*." She looks back up at me. "But everything turned out okay. And now, here I am knocked up again."

I feel a kick under my hand and look up at Charlie.

"You feel that?" she asks.

"That's incredible," I say, looking at her stomach.

I know I should remove my hand. This woman is practically a stranger to me. But I feel compelled to keep it on her. To feel the life growing inside of her. I leave it there until I feel another kick, and then I pull it away, instantly mourning the loss of the feeling.

"Excuse me," I say to the four of them. "I need to go wash up before dinner."

In the bathroom, I stare at myself in the mirror, the pathetic man who is so hung up on a woman that he gropes a stranger's pregnant belly. "Either man up or get over it," I tell my reflection. "But cut this shit out."

I've spent the last two weeks willing myself to go back over to Ivy's. To tell her I won't take no for an answer. I even texted her a few times. Texts she didn't open. Aspen is probably right—there isn't anything I can do unless Ivy makes the decision to be with me. Maybe I need to let her go.

But I know as well as the guy in the mirror that it will never happen.

CHAPTER THIRTY-SIX

IVY

Eli rolls over in bed, spooning me from behind. I smile at the feel of him pressed against me. We don't get to sleep together much. After all, we just graduated high school and both still live with our parents. But this weekend, Mom and Dad are out of town, so we're playing house.

We spent all day yesterday making plans for the future. Even though our parents aren't exactly happy that we're eighteen and having a baby, they've agreed that we can live together after Jonah comes. But with Eli going to college for the next four years, it's not like we can afford a place of our own with just my salary from the flower shop.

Mom and Dad's house is a lot bigger than Eli's parents' house, so we'll live here. There is a large room over the garage that they're converting into an efficiency apartment for us.

Eli's arm is wrapped around me, rubbing my large belly. He loves to feel the baby move, so he's poking around, hoping Jonah will protest and kick him back. His rhythmic caress of my stomach is putting me back to sleep. When I wake up an hour or so later, I turn around to see Eli's concerned face.

"I can't get him to move," he says.

"Maybe he likes lazy Sunday mornings like I do," I say, giggling.

Eli sits up in bed. "No, really. I've been lying here for two hours with my hand on your belly and he hasn't moved. Not once."

"Babies sleep just like we do, Eli."

He rubs his forehead and I can see how upset he looks, so I sit up next to him and poke the baby. When Jonah doesn't respond, I push harder.

I look back at Eli, who's tapping around on his phone.

"Do you have any orange juice?" he asks.

"Orange juice? Why?"

He holds out his phone to me. "It says that a boost of sugar can get the baby moving. They recommend orange juice."

"I think we might have some."

Before the words are fully out of my mouth, Eli darts from the room, coming back a minute later with a large glass of juice. I drink all of it quickly, appeasing Eli, then I set the glass down and we stare at my belly.

"Does it say how long it takes for it to work?" I ask.

He shakes his head, putting his hands on me to do more pushing and poking.

"Something's wrong," he says. "We should take you to the hospital."

"Nothing is wrong, Eli. He was doing somersaults yesterday, and last night, he had the hiccups."

"Humor me," he says, worry etched into his brow.

I roll my eyes. "Fine. But I'm getting dressed first."

Eli calls a cab and has it waiting when I emerge from the bathroom. The cab driver looks at my protruding belly, then at the two of us. He shakes his head in disapproval just like everyone else does when they see me.

When we get to the hospital, they put me into a gown. Then someone in a short white coat comes into the room with an ultrasound machine and introduces himself as an intern. "You said you haven't felt the baby move since yesterday?" he asks.

"Last night," I tell him. "He had the hiccups. I'm sure it's nothing. He's just sleeping." I nod to Eli. "My overprotective boyfriend made me come here."

"Let's take a look, shall we?" He tries to squirt the gel on my stomach, but it ends up getting all over my hospital gown instead. "Sorry," he says, giving me some tissues to wipe it up. He tries again, hitting the target this time. Then he awkwardly moves the wand around my belly.

I get the idea this guy hasn't done this very much. He said he was an intern. Does that mean he's a new doctor? Maybe he's not even a doctor, just some guy who does ultrasounds.

He moves the wand around for a minute or so, all the while, glancing at me apprehensively. Then he puts the wand down.

"I have to get my superior," he says.

"Is something wrong?" Eli asks.

"I … I'm new here and, uh … I really should get my superior."

We watch him leave the room in a hurry.

"That guy doesn't have a clue about what he's doing, does he?" I say.

Eli just stares at the ultrasound monitor. "That or he saw something bad."

I look up at the monitor, seeing a blank screen because the intern turned it off before he left. I think of the ultrasound we had a few months ago—the one that showed us Jonah was a boy. You could actually see his fingers and toes. It was so cool seeing this little life that's inside me. I'm glad Eli made me come today, because I realize how excited I am to see the baby again.

A woman with a long white coat walks in with the intern guy trailing behind her. "I'm Dr. Marbaugh," she says. "Ben tells me you're concerned that the baby hasn't been moving?"

I point to Eli. "He's concerned." I rub my stomach. "It's actually nice not to have this one kicking me in the bladder every five minutes. He's taking a long nap. Probably because of the walk we took yesterday. I was exhausted afterward."

Dr. Marbaugh turns the monitor back on and squeezes more gel onto me. She moves the wand around far longer than Ben did. Her face is stoic as she studies the screen. Then she puts the wand away, wipes my belly, and takes my hand into hers.

"Ivy, I'm so very sorry, but there isn't a heartbeat."

"Because he's sleeping?" I ask.

Eli makes a noise beside me. It sounds like a sob.

Dr. Marbaugh sits on the bed, holding my hand in a motherly fashion. "There isn't a heartbeat because the baby isn't alive, Ivy. I'm so sorry."

"What? That's impossible. He was moving last night. Eli, tell her Jonah was moving last night."

I look at Eli, but I'm not sure he can see me through the tears in his eyes.

I hold my belly protectively. "Oh my God. The baby is dead?"

"I'm afraid so," the doctor says.

"I … I … how?" I say through my own tears. "Did I do something?"

She shakes her head. "No, Ivy, you didn't. Sometimes these things just happen."

Eli climbs on the bed, pulling me into a hug. We sob into each other.

We might not have planned for this baby. We might be too young to be raising a child. But that doesn't make this any easier. As the gravity of the situation sinks in, my sobs become heaves and I find it hard to catch my breath.

Dr. Marbaugh puts an oxygen mask over my mouth. "Breathe, Ivy."

"What now?" Eli asks the doctor.

She looks at us sympathetically. "You have a choice to make. You can go home and wait for labor to start naturally, which should happen in the next few days, or we can admit you now and induce labor here."

"Labor?" I cry, removing the mask so I can speak. "I have to go through labor?"

"You're well into your third trimester," she says sadly. "I'm afraid you do."

"Eli." I bury myself into his shoulder, knowing I'm not strong enough.

"It's okay," he says. "I'm here. I'm not going anywhere."

I look up at him. But it's not Eli, it's Bass. "I'm not going anywhere, Ivy. I'm with you no matter what."

~ ~ ~

I wake up, crying into my already wet pillow. I can't even count how many times I've relived Jonah's death in my dreams. And when I'm not dreaming about Jonah or Dahlia dying, I'm dreaming about *this* baby dying. Vivid dreams of him being born blue. Except that in my dreams, he's not a he, he's a she. And Bass is there. Bass is always there.

I grab the fetal Doppler and put it on my belly, relieved to hear the rapid whooshing sound of his heartbeat.

I look at the calendar on my wall. February 12. Three days past my due date. My doctor said she will induce me if I haven't gone into labor in a week. But I'd rather just keep him inside me. As long as he's inside me, we don't know. We don't know if he will have to live his life on dialysis, waiting for a transplant. We don't know if he will suffer from hypertension, anemia, liver disease, or breathing difficulties. And even if he's born seemingly healthy, ARPKD can present itself later in life. If he tests positive, we'll always be wondering when it's going to strike.

But as long as he's inside me, we don't have to worry about all those questions being answered. As long as he's inside me, I can still fantasize about him being a normal, healthy child. One who isn't tied to doctors and hospitals and machines. One who can run and jump and play without worrying that his cysts will rupture or that he'll catch a cold from another child that could turn into a life-threatening infection.

I try to go back to sleep, but it's too bright in my room. Besides, I'd probably just have another bad dream. I prefer the good dreams. The ones where I'm back in Hawaii. Oh, how I wish I were back there with him. I long for the days when the only decision I had to make was which bikini to wear.

I pick up my phone and page through the pictures of Bass and me. Then I open the text messages he sent me more than a month ago. The ones I didn't read.

December 23rd

Sebastian: Reason #1 why you should be with me: I love you and you love me.

December 24th

Sebastian: As if Reason #1 wasn't enough - Reason #2: I want you AND the baby. I will love him as if he were my own.

December 25th

Sebastian: I know this day must be hard for you. You always said how much Dahlia liked Christmas. Reason #3: I want to help you remember all the good things.

December 26th

Sebastian: Do you recall back in Hawaii, you asked me how long I would wait for you? Reason #4: I can't see myself with anyone but you.

December 31st

Sebastian: Happy New Year, Ivy. I wish I could celebrate it with you. Reason #5: Every

new year is a clean slate. A new beginning. I want to be your new beginning.

I put down my phone and curl up with my pillow, wishing it were Bass.

That was the last text I got from him. He hasn't sent any more. Maybe because two days later he met someone at Aspen's wedding. I've seen the pictures. There were several photos of him with a tall, gorgeous, plump redhead.

So much for Reason #4.

I wanted so desperately to call him after he showed up at my apartment. I *should* have called him. But now I've lost my chance. It's been too long. He's finally given up on me.

It's my own fault. I knew that what I was doing was going to alienate him. That was my intention. But, deep down inside, I guess I thought he really *would* wait for me. I thought he would keep trying. I thought he would wear me down.

And he did. Damn me for not reading his texts sooner. I'm such an idiot.

I take a handful of his shirt and lift it to my nose, wishing it smelled like him and not me.

I think about how he is the best man I've ever met. The best *person.* He didn't have to do what he did in Hawaii. Most men would have run the other way when I acted like I did. Most men wouldn't think twice about being with someone so obviously damaged. And what kind of guy still wants a woman when she's pregnant with another man's child?

I stare at a picture of Bass, tracing the outline of his face with my finger.

I guess the same kind of guy who risks his life day after day to help strangers. The kind of guy who orders flower pancakes and sends me daisies. The kind of guy who sends me texts with all the reasons I should be with him.

I close my eyes, squeezing the tears out of them. Because I realize just how much I want him. I want him no matter what happens. I want him whether or not this baby lives or dies. I want him to help me remember Jonah and Dahlia. I want him to be my shoulder to cry on. I want him to take me back to Hawaii if things go bad. I want to love him like he's my sunshine, my waterfall, my puddle in the rain. I want to love him forever.

The problem is, I might just be too late.

I get out of bed, halted by another Braxton Hicks contraction. This one makes me stop and hold on to the dresser. I sit back down, wondering if I'm in labor. I look at the clock and mark the time. But after fifteen minutes, when I don't have another one, I get up and get ready for work, knowing that Holly will have some good words of wisdom for me when I tell her what a fool I've been. Well, maybe not words of wisdom, but she *is* the queen of getting men to notice her. And maybe, just maybe, she can help me win him back. Because despite the fact that I feel fifty-two weeks pregnant and can no longer see my feet, I'm on a mission. And it might just be the most important mission of my life.

CHAPTER THIRTY-SEVEN

SEBASTIAN

I'm lying on my cot, staring at the ceiling, trying to get in a few more minutes of shut-eye since we were out on calls almost all night. But it's no use. I can't sleep. My mind is racing. Is Ivy okay? Did she have the baby? Is the baby sick?

I don't even know her due date, but I assume it's right around now based on how she said she got pregnant on Dahlia's birthday. I've done the math. She could be in the hospital right now giving birth. She could be at home with a healthy baby. She could be burying another child. The not knowing is killing me.

I still jog past the flower shop a few days a week, but I've kept myself from looking in the window. Every time I've wanted to, I remind myself what Aspen said about Ivy needing to come to me. That is what Aspen meant, isn't it? That I should wait it out and let Ivy come to me? Wait for her to have some epiphany or something?

Despite my better judgment, I pull out my phone and page through my Hawaii pictures again. Then, just to torture myself even more, I open up our texting thread so I can go back and read what we said to each other the week after I came home. But I notice something. I see that she finally read the texts I sent over the holidays. I can't remember the last time I checked—it must have been at least a week ago. And since then the indicator has changed from 'delivered' to 'read.'

She read them sometime this past week.

Does that mean anything?

Before I can think too much about it, dispatch comes over the speaker sending us out for a commercial structure fire. I pocket my phone and race down the stairs, pulling on my turnout gear before I hoist myself into the back seat of the truck.

"What does it look like, Duck?"

Steve is our driver. He knows every address, street, and building number, so he can usually tell us where we're going before we get there.

"Garment factory," he says. "Some local designer owns it. High-end stuff, if I recall. My sister loves the brand."

"Garment factory. Great," I say. "Lots of flammables. Do you happen to know what kind of clothes they make?"

"What does it matter what kind of clothes they make?" Noah asks.

"Some fabrics are more flammable than others," I tell him. "Cotton, linen, and silk will burn more readily than wool or polyester. Anything with a weave will burn slower. Most synthetic fabrics like nylon and acrylic tend to resist ignition. But with those, if they do ignite, they will melt, which can cause severe burning. The greatest risk is when natural fibers and synthetic ones are combined because you get a high rate of burning and melting at the same time. We also need to keep an eye out for fabric dyes and additives. Generally anything used to provide color will be highly flammable. They could have drums of those lying around that could become like cannons or bombs. And, of course, boxes and packing material will just be kindling, adding fuel to the fire."

Noah is glued to my words. I know he learned a lot of this in the fire academy, but it's hard to remember everything. I learned a lot when my company responded to a garment factory fire last spring. Luckily, it was on a Sunday and no workers were present. We're not as fortunate today. It's Tuesday. Everyone goes to work on Tuesday.

J.D. looks back at me like a proud father. He nods. "Good job, Briggs."

Getting kudos from J.D. is not an everyday occasion. I've found when he doles them out, it means he's impressed.

As we approach the four-story building, we see flames coming out of several windows.

"We got a job, people," J.D. says. "Get your air packs on."

When we exit the truck, I see two other engines and a ladder truck pulling up alongside us. Then Battalion Chief Mitzel drives up in his SUV.

"We've got a live one," he says when he gets out. He motions to Lt. Cash's unit. "Squad 13, you get up there and vent the roof. Engine 319, stretch a line to exposure two, bottom floor. Engine 77, give me a primary search in exposure four. Ladder 51, get Squad 13 on the roof and standby for my orders."

I lean in to Noah and whisper, "That's the left entrance he's sending us to, Probie."

He rolls his eyes at me.

"Where do you want us, Chief?" someone from another company asks.

He points to the people funneling out of the building. "Engine 98, I need a secondary in exposure two and perimeter control. Help get those folks to safety."

We grab our gear and head to the entrance on the left side of the building. Smoke is billowing out, so we mask up. J.D. goes in first, waving us in behind him. "Briggs, take the probie and go down that hallway. Duck and I will go this way."

"Okay, Cap. Follow me, Auggie."

We run into a half-dozen people who we help get outside. "Six coming out of exposure two," I say into my walkie.

Then Chief Mitzel comes over the radio. "Engine 319, 77 needs help moving their line in on the second floor, south stairwell, can you assist?"

J.D. comes into view with a woman over his shoulders. He hands me the thermal imaging camera. "Take this. You and Noah go to two and assist 77. Duck is coming behind me with another victim. We'll follow you up as soon as we can. I'll notify the chief."

Noah and I find the south stairwell and climb to the second floor where we see Engine Company 77. Jason Bortles looks at the Halligan in one of my hands, the axe in the other, and the water can extinguisher Auggie is holding.

"Shit, you don't have anything better than that?" Bortles says. "There are people behind that door."

"What were you expecting?" I ask.

"I dunno, a little C-4 maybe?" he jokes. "Look." He points to the second-floor stairwell door that appears to be cemented shut. "They're remodeling, and some idiot dropped two hundred pounds of wet fucking cement here." He uses his Halligan, demonstrating how solid it is. "Somebody's gonna be in a lot of fucking trouble."

"The south stairway is blocked," I report into my walkie. "Cemented shut. We need another way up."

"The north stairway is impassable," the chief says. "The elevator shaft is twenty feet to the left of the first-floor stairwell.

Find it and I'll have someone meet you there with a ladder. Looks like you're climbing."

"You heard the man. Let's go!"

Five minutes later, we're on the second floor, evacuating the last of the workers down the elevator shaft as the smoke plumes up from below. It's getting harder to see more than two feet in front of us.

"Floors three and four are clear," Chief Mitzel says over the radio. "We're going to hit it from above. You have two minutes to get out of there."

J.D. is carrying a woman in respiratory distress when we hear a scream. I look behind us, trying to gauge where it came from.

"Captain, there's one more," Noah says.

J.D. mouths a few choice words, clearly wanting to go himself, but as his mask is on the woman he's holding, there's no time. "Go," he says, nodding to Noah and me. "You have exactly ninety seconds. This building is going down."

"Got it," I say.

"Don't make me come after you!" he yells behind us. "Ninety seconds!"

I hand Noah the thermal imaging camera. "Find her," I say.

I look over his shoulder as he scans the walls with the camera. Damn, we're in a fucking hot box here. The whole goddamn building is on fire around us.

"We open any of these doors and it's going to flash," I say.

I hear an explosion behind us. "Fuck. I'll bet that was the elevator shaft. We might be trapped."

"There are some windows on the east side," Noah says. "If we can find her and make our way there."

Then something on fire darts in front of us. "There!" I say.

Noah falls on it, putting out the flames. Then he stands up, holding a cat.

"What the fuck, Briggs? We came back here for a goddamned cat?"

The cat squeals and jumps out of his arms. It's the same high-pitched sound we thought was a woman.

"Engine 319, report," J.D. says over the radio.

"It wasn't a victim, Captain. It was a cat. And I think our way out just collapsed."

The captain radios me, confirming my worst fear. We don't have any way out.

Noah tries to open the stairwell door, the one that's cemented shut on the other side. "We're fucking trapped, Briggs."

I take a quick peek at Noah's regulator and then my own. We both have about ten minutes of air left. "We're going to try for the east-side windows, Captain," I say, choosing my steps carefully as my glove runs along the wall. "Oh shit."

"What is it?" J.D. asks.

The walls are bubbling. "We've got to get out of here. Now!" I yell to Noah.

"There!" he says, pointing to a door at the end of the hallway. "No thermal feedback."

I try the knob, but it's locked. I turn around and brace myself against the sides of the doorframe and then kick it in with the sole of my boot. We just make it through the door when I hear the scariest sound a firefighter can hear. I hear the fire flashing in the hallway behind us.

Noah and I hold the door shut with our body weight. "Find whatever you can and shove it under the door," I say.

"There isn't anything!" he yells. He scans the room. "Oh, holy fuck, Briggs."

"What is it?" I ask, still holding the heavy steel door shut.

"Remember what you said in the rig about the fabric dyes?"

"Yeah?"

"Well"—he motions behind me—"I think we found them."

I turn and look around the room. The storage room with no windows. The room with a dozen drums labeled with various colors of fabric dye.

"Fuck!"

"Captain, we have a bit of a problem." I look over at Noah and then I say into the radio, "Mayday, Mayday, Mayday."

Most firefighters never have to call Mayday in their entire careers, and here I am, barely eighteen months in and with a probie. It's a situation we all train for. It's a situation we hope we'll never have to be in.

"Tell me, Briggs," J.D. says.

"This is Engine 319," I report. "We have two firefighters trapped in a storage room in the two/three corner of exposure two. End of the hallway. No windows. There's a dozen barrels of flammables in here. You'll have to come through the building wall about six feet from the corner."

"Shit," I hear J.D. say through the radio.

I laugh. I laugh because in this moment, there is nothing else I can do. "Yeah, that's what we said."

"Air?" he asks.

I look at my regulator. "About eight minutes."

"The rescue team is on their way. You hang in there."

"We'll do our best, Cap." I look around the room again. "Grab that chair, Probie."

Noah brings the chair over and we brace it against the door. I look around and see boxes piled against one wall. I open one of them and look inside. "Fabric adhesive," I say. "It's not flammable."

"But the boxes are," Noah says.

"We don't have much choice, do we? We need to keep the smoke out. We're running out of air." I motion to his water can extinguisher. "We can wet the boxes first."

Noah sprays the boxes and then we pile them as tightly as we can get them against the door. Then we back up into the far corner and sit on the floor.

Noah looks at me and I can see the fear in his eyes. "Ever been in a predicament like this?" he asks.

"You want the truth?"

"Always."

I shake my head. "This is about as tough a spot as I've ever gotten into."

He nods over and over.

The alarm goes off on my PASS device, letting me know I'm low on air. Usually when this happens, we stop what we're doing and leave the building.

I get up and move some drums to the side, hoping to find an air vent or a compromise in the outer wall. I start poking around with the axe. But after a few minutes, I realize I'm just using up more air by exerting myself. It's just my luck that we ended up in the most fortified fucking room in the building.

Then I hear Noah's PASS alarm go off. His air is getting low, too.

"How's it looking, Cap?" I ask into the radio.

"Rescue is coming for you, Briggs. They're going to break through the south wall, about six feet from the corner like you said. Hold tight."

"We're holding," I say. "But the door is getting hot, the smoke is getting thick, and the air is getting low."

J.D. forgets to take his thumb off the radio button when he yells, "Hurry the fuck up, people. We are not losing these firefighters."

Noah's eyes go wide and he starts to hyperventilate.

"Noah, you have to breathe slowly. You'll use up all the air. Look at me. Look into my eyes. That's it. Breathe with me. Slowly. Slowly. You've got it."

The lights in my mask start to flash. I look at my regulator and see that I'm almost completely out of air. I take my mask off and put it to the side.

"What are you doing?" Noah says, handing me my mask. "Put it back on."

I can see that he's starting to panic again. I put my hand on his. "Noah, I can't put it back on. If I run out of air, the mask will get sucked to my face and I won't be able to breathe at all. Remember?"

The lights in his mask start flashing now, so I remove it for him. He's not thinking straight and I'm afraid he'll suffocate himself.

"We're going to die," he says.

I scoot over next to him. "Do you know how many people are working to save us right now? Literally all of FDNY is out there figuring out how to get us out of here. And I'd bet my life they're going to succeed."

"If it's all the same to you, Briggs, I'm not going to bet against you. If I win, I won't get shit because we'll be dead."

"Nobody is dying today, Noah. They're coming for us."

I want to believe the words I just spoke. But deep down, I know I said them to keep myself from panicking like he is. But the truth is, it's smoky in here and more smoke is coming in under the door with every passing minute.

"Lie down on the floor," I tell him. "The air is cleaner down there. If things get worse, breathe shallow and cover your mouth and nose with your coat."

We lie next to each other on the floor. I grab the axe and hit it over and over on the outside wall, making noise to help them find us.

I look over at Noah and watch as a tear coming from his eye blazes a clean path through the soot on his face.

"I stole a hundred bucks from my sister two years ago," he says. "I was between jobs and there was this necklace that my girlfriend, Sophie, really wanted. One day, I just saw the money on Pam's dresser and I took it. My mom fired the cleaning lady, thinking it was her. But it wasn't, it was me. And last year, when I was—"

"Stop confessing shit to me, Auggie. I'm not your goddamned priest."

But then I start thinking about all the things *I* regret. But there's really only one thing. Ivy. She's my one regret. If I had to go back and do it all over again, I wouldn't take no for an answer. Aspen said I needed to wait. Wait until Ivy decided she wanted to be with me. Well, fuck that. I should have told her. I should have walked back into her apartment the day she said she loved me too much to put me through everything. I should have walked back in and made her believe that I was okay with however things turned out. I should have made her understand that anything we had to go through would be okay as long as we were doing it together.

I've wasted so much time. Time I could have spent with her. Time I could have loved her. I've been such a fool.

"How long do you think we have?" Noah asks, looking at the door.

I assess the smoke filling the room above us. "I don't know. Five minutes, maybe? Pull your hood over your mouth to filter the air. And keep your flashlight pointed toward the ceiling," I remind him.

I do everything that I instructed him to do. But then I radio my captain.

"Captain, I need you to do something for me," I say.

"You mean something other than rescue your sorry ass?" he says.

"I need you to contact Ivy Greene. Tell her …"

I stop talking. Because I know this is an unauthorized transmission. I need to keep the radio clear for the rescue team. But damn it if I don't want to tell him to find her and tell her that those two weeks were the best two weeks of my life. I want him to tell her I screwed up. To tell her I should have fought harder for her. That I'm a damn fool for letting her go.

Suddenly, the south wall of the room starts to crumble. Noah and I scoot back as bricks and drywall fall into the room and fresh air clears some of the smoke. Then Lt. Cash pops his head through the hole they just made.

"Tell her yourself, Briggs."

Noah and I run to the hole in the wall. I take in a deep breath. Deeper than any breath I've ever taken. Then I nod to Noah. "You go first, Auggie."

He laughs, tears streaming down his cheeks. "I've never been so happy to have someone call me that."

Once we're clear of the building, Debbe and Ryan check us out for smoke inhalation. Debbe looks at my throat and listens to my chest.

"You look good, Briggs. Based on your ramblings on the radio, I thought for sure you were half dead," she jokes.

"It was close, Deb. I'm not even sure we had a few minutes left." I shake my head, thinking I've never been nearer to death than I was today. "It was close."

Noah walks over to me as I button my shirt back up.

"You check out?" I ask him.

"Yeah. You?"

"Yeah."

We both smile and then laugh. Then I pull him into a hug. We're a brotherhood at FDNY. Family. But when you go through something like that with someone, it creates a bond even greater than before.

"You did good, brother," I tell him. "Next time you'll do even better."

He nods, finding it hard to come up with words. I know the feeling.

"Come on," I say, patting him on the back. "They still need our help. Let's go finish the job."

Noah and I help with the victims as the fire is attacked by both aerial suppression from Ladder 51 and by fireboat in the Upper Bay. The benefit of a structure fire being next to a body of water is that the fireboat never runs out of water and can pump tens of thousands of gallons of water per minute.

An hour later, with the fire out and most of the victims transported, Chief Mitzel finds our company.

"Engine 319, you can head out. We'll handle the overhauling." He grabs my shoulder. "I believe you've all earned your keep today."

"Pack it up, 319," J.D. says, shaking hands with the chief.

When we get into the rig, Noah says, "I'm going to call my mom when we get back to the station. Maybe she can find the cleaning lady's number so I can apologize."

"Sounds like a fine idea," I say.

"Anything you're gonna do?" he asks.

I nod. "Yeah. Yeah, there is."

I check the time to see how many hours we have left on shift, because as soon as it's over, I'm going to find Ivy. I'm going to find her and make her listen.

En route back to the house, a call comes over the radio. "Engine 319, EMS 64, respond to OB emergency, 547 Parker Drive."

My stomach turns. "Shit. That's Ivy's shop. Duck, get us there fast."

"On our way," he says, turning the rig around.

Debbe radios that they're stuck in traffic.

I radio back. "This is the real deal, Deb. I think someone might be having a baby. We need you there."

"It's gridlock at the hospital," she says. "We'll be there as soon as we can."

I take off my gear in the truck, ready to hop out as soon as we pull up. When we do, I'm out the door and into the shop in record time.

"Ivy!" I shout.

"Back here," someone calls.

I go into the back room where a very pregnant Ivy is lying down on some towels. Towels with too much blood on them.

My fucking heart sinks.

CHAPTER THIRTY-EIGHT

IVY

"Bass!" Holly runs over to him. "She's in labor. There's blood. It happened so fast. She said it hurts too much to move. Her water broke a few minutes ago."

The other firefighters walk in behind Bass as he gets down on the floor with me. When I look at him, my eyes go wide. He's covered with black soot.

"Oh my God. You came from a fire?" I ask, grunting through my contraction. I reach out to touch his face, getting soot on my fingers. "Are you okay?"

"I'm fine. When did your labor start and has there been bleeding other than what I see here?"

"I think it started this morning," I say. "I don't think there was any more blood."

"This morning? It's three o'clock, Ivy."

"I know. I thought it was just a stomach ache. But—" I stop talking and grit my teeth through another contraction.

Bass grabs my hand and lets me squeeze him until it's over.

"I feel pressure," I say. "I think the baby is coming right now. But it's different. This doesn't feel like last time. It hurts so much, Bass."

"Hold tight, Ivy. We're going to help you."

I hear one of the firefighters talking over the radio. A woman on the other end tells him they will be here in ten minutes.

"This may all be over in ten minutes!" Bass shouts at them over his shoulder.

Bass tries to stand up, but I don't let him go. "Don't leave me."

He brushes a stray hair behind my ear. "I'm not going anywhere, sweetheart. I just need to wash up so I can deliver your baby."

"You?" I ask, terrified about delivering here on the floor of the shop.

"If I have to," he says. "I'm a paramedic, remember? I've delivered sixteen healthy babies."

I nod, looking at him through my tears. "Okay."

Bass uses the bathroom to wash up as he tells Holly what he's going to need. By the time he's back at my side, the guys have set up as sterile an area as they can around me.

"You sure you want to do this?" someone asks Bass. "I'd be happy to step in."

"I'm doing it, Captain."

I scream in agony when it feels like something rips through me. I look up at Bass. "Something's wrong."

From where he's standing, he looks between my legs and his face goes ashen.

"What is it?" I ask, my whole body trembling.

"Just a little blood," he says, glancing at the other firefighters.

But I can tell by the look on his face—on all their faces—that there's more to it than that.

Bass gets down on his knees and gloves up. "Ivy, it's possible that you're experiencing placental abruption."

"Oh, my, God," Holly says behind me. "What's that?"

"The placenta could have a tear in it," he says. "Or it could be separating from the uterine wall."

I reach down and grab his gloved hand. "I'm scared."

"I'm here, Ivy. I'm going to do everything in my power to make sure you and the baby are all right. But right now, I need to check and see where the baby is, okay?"

I nod, beads of sweat running down the sides of my forehead.

He does a vaginal exam. "I can feel the top of the baby's head. Good. At least he's not breech."

When he pulls his hand out, I can see that it's covered in blood and clots. He turns around and tells his captain, "Call ahead to the hospital and have some O-neg waiting. They may need to do a transfusion."

I'm not sure if the sobs I hear are coming from me, or from Holly.

Bass leans over and grabs my hand when the next contraction comes.

"Ivy, you're fully dilated. I'm going to need you to push. Holly, sit down on the floor behind her and give her something to push against."

When the contraction is over, I'm exhausted.

I hear one of the firefighters whispering to Bass. "You have to get the baby out. And fast. If the abruption is as bad as I think it is, they are both in danger. Ivy could suffer from massive blood loss, and the baby will be deprived of oxygen."

"Oh my God! Bass," I cry.

"I'm going to get you through this, Ivy. Have you called Eli yet?" he asks Holly.

She nods. "He said he'd call everyone else and meet us at the hospital. I thought we had time."

"Sebastian," I say, feeling more terrified than I've ever been in my life. "I was wrong. I don't want to do this without you."

"I was wrong, too, sweetheart. In fact, I was going to come find you today and tell you that very thing. I've been a fool to stay away."

I feel a gush, but my water already broke. "Was that blood?" I ask in horror.

"Ivy, you have to push hard. I know you're tired and hurting. But your baby needs you right now."

I can hear sirens getting closer.

"Do you hear that?" he asks. "They're coming to take both of you to the hospital. But we need to get the baby out so we can help him."

I push so hard I think I might pass out. And I scream. I scream loud.

"That's it. I can see his hair," Bass says.

"What color is it?" Holly asks.

"I, uh … can't tell," he says, looking at me sadly.

"Why?" I ask, gasping for air. "Why can't you tell? What's wrong?"

"There's just a little too much blood on his head and the hair is all matted."

I collapse back onto Holly. "I can't do this."

"Sit her up straighter," he says to my sister. "Look at me, Ivy. You are the strongest person I've ever met, and you are the only one who can save your baby right now. He's not getting enough oxygen. You need to push him out. You need to push him out right now. You can do this."

I scream once more as I squeeze my eyes tightly shut and give it everything I have with one final push. Then I watch as Bass pulls a small, lifeless baby out of me.

Two paramedics run into the room. One tends to me while the other falls to her knees, taking the baby from Bass. She clears the baby's mouth and massages his chest.

I can feel my world ending for the third time. "He's not breathing?" I cry.

"Give it a second," Bass says.

When the baby starts to cry, I cry. And everyone in the room breathes an audible sigh of relief.

"Is he okay?" I ask in a panic.

Bass takes off his gloves and scoots over to my head, rubbing a gentle hand down my hair. "*She*," he says. "You have a baby girl."

"It's a *girl?*"

He nods, tears pooled in his eyes. "It's a girl."

"Is she okay? Did you check her kidneys? Are they firm?"

"All of that will be checked at the hospital," he says, looking more than a little concerned. "Right now, we need to get you both in the ambulance." He looks over his shoulder at the guy who must be in charge. "Captain?"

"Go," the guy says. "We've got you covered."

Bass turns to Holly. "If I go, there's no room for you."

"You go," she says. "Help them. I'll meet you there."

As they lift me onto a gurney, I catch a glimpse of the baby. She's so pale and her little lips are almost blue. "Oh, God." I use a hand to cover my sobs, right before everything goes black.

"Ivy? Ivy, can you hear me, sweetheart?"

I hear a siren. And I feel hands on my stomach. I open my eyes and see Bass's face above me. "What happened?" I ask from under an oxygen mask.

"You fainted," he says. "You've lost a lot of blood." He nods to my belly. "I'm doing something called fundal massage that will hopefully help your uterus contract and reduce the bleeding."

I look over at the paramedic holding my baby. I see her little hand moving, so I know she's alive.

"Ryan is giving her some oxygen," Bass explains. "He didn't have to intubate, but she might need an umbilical catheter to give saline and maybe blood."

"Blood?" I say, my heart racing. "She needs blood? Give her some of mine."

He shakes his head. "You've lost too much yourself. And you might not be a match. They'll type and cross her as soon as we pull up."

"Is she … is she going to be okay?"

He smiles at me. But it's not a happy smile. "It was a tough delivery, Ivy. But we're hoping for the best."

I close my eyes, clearing the tears that pooled in them. "It was just like my dreams," I say.

"Your dreams?"

"I dreamed of you being there, helping me have the baby. And I dreamed of the baby being blue when it came. And it was a girl. In my dreams, she was a girl. I *dreamed* this, Bass." My throat tightens. "And you were so mad at me because I made you love her and then she … she—"

"Shhhh," he whispers. "It was just a dream, Ivy. I'm not mad at you. I could never be mad at you for making me love her." He looks over at the baby then back at me. "And I do. I love her. Because she's a part of you. And I love you."

More tears fall down the sides of my face as I reach out to my daughter. The paramedic holds her closer to me so I can touch her hand. "I love her, too. And I love you, Sebastian. I never stopped. I'm so sorry."

"I know," he says. "I'm sorry, too. I should have fought harder. But none of that matters now. We need to focus on you and your daughter. Everything else can wait. Because I'm not going anywhere, Ivy Greene."

"Thank you," I say, just as the ambulance stops and the doors open.

"They're going to take her up to the NICU now," Bass tells me. "And you'll probably stay in the ER until the bleeding stops."

"Go with her," I beg. "Please."

One of the doctors in the ambulance bay hears my request. He starts to wheel the baby away but then turns to Bass. "Are you coming?"

"Are you sure, Ivy?" Bass asks. "Maybe Eli should be with her."

I can tell he's torn between staying with me and going with her. But I need him with her. "I need you to be with her. I know you'll protect her."

They wheel the baby away and Bass follows, looking at me as they walk through the ambulance bay doors.

"Tell her I love her," I call out after them.

And then I do something I haven't done since Dahlia died. I pray.

CHAPTER THIRTY-NINE

SEBASTIAN

I'm sitting outside the NICU, waiting for news when Eli walks around the corner. I stand up and shake his hand.

He looks at our clasped hands. "The last time I saw you, you wanted to kill me."

"Yeah, I'm sorry about that," I say. "I guess I didn't have all the facts."

"Well, you're here now. Holly gave me the rundown on what happened. Do you think the baby will be okay?"

"I hope so. It's hard to tell if she was deprived of oxygen or not. And I haven't heard anything on the ARPKD either. In fact, I'm pretty much in the dark right now. I've been pacing back and forth for ten minutes out here waiting for someone to tell me something."

"What happens if she didn't get enough oxygen?" he asks.

I shrug. "I'm not a doctor, Eli, but I know it's not good. There's a guy who works at a firehouse in Manhattan whose son has cerebral palsy because he was oxygen-deprived at birth."

"Oh, shit." He rubs his hand over the scruff on his jaw. "I'm not sure we could take any more bad news."

"Well, let's not jump the gun until we find out." Then I nod to the doctor I see coming toward the door. "And I think we might be about to find out."

"I'm Dr. Moran," he addresses me. "Her heel-stick hemoglobin shows that she's anemic. We've got her on saline through an umbilical I.V., but if her oxygen saturation doesn't improve quickly, we'd like to give her whole blood."

I motion to Eli. "Dr. Moran, this is Eli Snow, he's the baby's father."

"Oh. The mother wanted you to be with the baby, so I just assumed …"

"He's the boyfriend," Eli says. Then he turns to me. "Right?"

"Yeah. Of course. Yes."

"Well then, Mr. Snow, do I have your consent to give blood if needed?"

"Yes. Do it. Do you need my blood?"

"Possibly. If you're a match, that is," he says. "The hospital is short on O-neg, which is what we would normally give her, so we're waiting for the type and cross to come back. It should be any minute now."

"I'm a universal donor," I tell the doctor.

"You're O-negative?" he asks.

"Yes. And I'm on the registry. I donate several times a year."

"I'll keep that in mind," he says. "Don't go very far."

"I'm AB and Ivy is B," Eli says.

The doctor raises his brows, surprised Eli would know that.

"We're both ARPKD carriers, but we didn't know it until our second child got sick. We had a lot of genetic testing."

"That's tough," he says. "Are the children both sick?"

"They both died," Eli says.

"I'm sorry to hear that," Dr. Moran says. "I didn't see any kidney abnormalities in my examination, but I'll add that test to her bloodwork just to be sure."

"Thank you."

A nurse comes out of the NICU, handing Dr. Moran an iPad. "The type and cross results, Doctor."

He looks at the iPad and then he asks the nurse, "Are you sure this is for baby Jane Doe?"

"Baby Jane Doe?" Eli asks.

"Since they were brought in by ambulance, we didn't have time for an admit," he says, still studying the results.

"I'm sure, Doctor," the nurse says.

The doctor looks at Eli. "Mr. Snow, are you absolutely sure about the blood types of you and the mother?"

"I'm one hundred percent sure," he says. "We only had about a thousand tests back then. Why, is something wrong?"

"Well, according to the baby's blood typing, there is no way her parents could have AB and B blood types."

"What?" Eli asks.

"The baby's blood type is O-negative," the doctor says. "And because we know for sure who the mother is, assuming she really is type B as you said, there is no statistical chance a man with type AB could be the father."

I back up against the wall, feeling like I just got punched in the gut. "The baby is O-negative?" I ask.

"Yes," he says.

There are so many emotions going through me right now, I'm not sure which to express.

"Oh, shit," Eli says. "You just said *you're* O-negative." A smile crosses his face. "Well, damn. Congratulations, Dad."

I sit on the bench next to me and put my head between my knees.

"Wait, now *he's* the father?" the doctor asks.

Eli pats me on the back as I struggle to catch the breath that just got knocked out of me.

"I guess I am," I say, both elated and saddened at the same time.

I have a child? A child who needs blood and might have been deprived of oxygen. I stand up and hold out my arm. "Give her my blood. Do it now."

The doctor motions for the nurse to come back out. "Type Mr. …" He looks at me.

"Briggs," I say. "Sebastian Briggs."

"Type Mr. Briggs to be sure, then set up for a transfusion for Baby Jane Doe."

"Baby Briggs," I say.

"Right," the doctor says. "Please follow Gabby, she'll get things going."

"Wait," I say. "What about the oxygen? You said her saturation was low. And she wasn't breathing for a minute at birth. Can you tell me what we could be looking at?"

"The paramedic told me the baby cried shortly after delivery and had good reflexes," he says. "There are no guarantees, but based on my initial exam, she looks good. She's still crying and very responsive. She's a bit pale because of the anemia. But I think once we get that under control you'll be the father of a healthy, full-term baby girl."

My heart stops beating for a second.

I'm a father.

I have a daughter.

I'm in love with her mother.

We can be a family.

In the turn of two minutes, my entire world has changed, and I realize that this is the happiest moment of my life. Ivy's baby—*my* baby—isn't sick. There won't be dialysis machines or kidney transplants. No funerals with tiny caskets. No trips to Hawaii to forget.

Before I walk away, I shake Eli's hand again. "I'm sorry, man. I guess I don't know what this even means for you. I'm sure you already bonded with the baby when Ivy was pregnant."

"It's all good," he says. "It turned out the way it was meant to. I'm just glad she's going to be healthy."

"Thank you for everything. For supporting Ivy through this. You've been a great friend to her. And I'm sure you'll be a good uncle."

"Uncle." He laughs. "I like the sound of that."

"This way, please, Mr. Briggs," the nurse says, motioning for me to follow her.

I call back to Eli. "If you don't mind, I'd like to be the one to tell Ivy."

He nods. "No problem. I think I'll sneak out the back. Just be sure to let me know if I can help with anything. And I'd like to come back later and see both of them if that's okay with you."

I nod. "Yeah, it's okay with me."

"Good. Now get the hell out of here and go help your daughter."

The smile that overtakes my face is almost painful.

I have a daughter.

Even as they await my blood typing to make sure I'm a match, they are taking a pint of my blood in anticipation. As I'm tethered to the needle, I pull out my phone and call Holly.

"Bass, what's happening? Ivy's going crazy down here."

"How is she?"

"She's good. They are giving her fluids to help replenish her blood volume."

"Same for the baby," I say. "But she might need to be given some blood."

I hear her gasp. "She needs a blood transfusion? Oh, God. That doesn't sound good."

"Actually, all things considered, the news is pretty good," I say, not wanting to give too much away but at the same time needing Ivy to know the sky isn't falling. "The doctor didn't feel any kidney abnormalities."

"Really? Well, I guess that *is* good news."

"Yes, it is. They think she's going to be okay, Holly. Tell Ivy that."

"I will," she says. "How's Eli holding up?"

"He's … good, I guess."

"Briggs, what aren't you telling me?"

"Nothing. It's nothing."

Holly whispers forcefully into the phone. "Don't mess with me, Briggs. I'm not about to tell Ivy that things look good if they aren't. I won't get her hopes up just to have them dashed. I want more than anything to give her good news, but not if it's just temporary."

"I get that, Holly. And I'll explain more when I come to see Ivy. I'll be down as soon as I can. And I think I have more good news."

"You *think?*"

"I hope," I say, not revealing any more. "Listen, go ahead and tell her that the baby's oxygen saturation is lower than they'd like. But the doctor didn't make it seem like any kind of emergency.

He's giving her saline through her umbilical cord. He said she's crying and responsive and that those are both very good signs."

The nurse comes over and stares at me.

"I have to go, Holly. I'll be down soon."

The nurse removes the needle and holds cotton on my arm for a few seconds before wrapping gauze around it. "Here," she says, handing me a glass of orange juice. "Drink this before you try and stand up."

The baby's doctor comes in the room as I'm sipping my drink.

He nods to the bag of blood I just donated. "Looks like we won't be needing that after all."

"What? Why not?"

"Your daughter's O2 saturation levels have risen significantly. And I'm happy to say, she looks and acts like any other healthy newborn."

The relief that courses through my body brings tears to my eyes. I've only held her once, when she was pale and lifeless. I've never kissed her. I've never looked into her eyes. I've never held her tiny hands. But I love her so fiercely that it hurts.

All I can do is nod as tears of joy stream down my face.

The doctor pats me on the shoulder. "I'm heading down to Ms. Greene's room now to explain everything."

I swallow hard and find my words. "Doctor, would it be okay if *I* told her about me being the father?"

He looks at his watch. "I tell you what. Your daughter's saline I.V. should be coming out soon. We'll have to keep an eye on her hemoglobin and O2 levels, but I see no reason to keep her in the NICU. If you think Ms. Greene can wait another thirty minutes or so, we can all go down together."

"All?" I ask, wide-eyed. "As in the baby, too?"

"Like I said, she's looking good. So, yes, we can take her down."

I smile. "Ivy can wait. I just called her sister and gave her an update. I don't think she's panicking anymore."

"Good," he says. "Then you can wait for us in the NICU waiting area and I'll find you when we're ready."

I reach out to shake his hand. "Thank you, Dr. Moran. I can't tell you what all of this means to me."

He nods, handing me a tissue. "You don't need to, son. I can clearly see."

CHAPTER FORTY

IVY

The door to my hospital room opens and a bassinet gets wheeled through. My heart leaps when I see it. She must be well enough for them to bring her down here.

Then I see a doctor and Bass following behind. I wait for Eli to come in as well, but he doesn't.

"Where's Eli?" I ask.

"He left," Bass says.

"He left? Why would he do that?"

Bass looks around the room, seeing some familiar faces like Holly and Alder, but also a few people he's never met—my parents. But somehow, I feel that now is not exactly the time for introductions. I need to hold my baby. Everything else can wait.

"Ivy, can we have some privacy?" Bass asks.

I strain to sit up and look at the baby. "Why? What's happened? She's not okay?"

"She's okay," he tells me. Then he looks at the others in the room. "We just need a minute. Please."

Everyone looks at the doctor for verification. He nods, and I guess that's good enough for them because they all get up and file out of the room, taking peeks at the baby on the way out.

When the door is closed, the doctor steps back and motions to the baby. "Go ahead," he says to Bass. "Introduce them."

Bass carefully picks up my daughter and steps over to the bed, placing her in my arms. I look at her through thick balls of tears. "Oh my God," I say, taking her in. "Oh my God."

I move her little pink cap to the side and kiss her dark hair. I examine her fingers. I open the blanket and look at her toes. I lean down and inhale her intoxicating scent. And then I begin to shake, sobs bellowing out of me. Happy sobs.

"Is she … is she okay?" I ask the doctor.

"She appears to be," he says. "We haven't seen any effects of oxygen deprivation. We'll want to monitor her milestones for the first year, just to be sure, but I don't think you have any reason to worry."

"And the ARPKD, did you test her? Does she have it? Is she a carrier?"

I stare at the doctor, my eyes pleading with him for good news.

"It looks like we don't have to test her for it after all," he says.

"Why would you not test her?" I ask, appalled. "And where's Eli?"

He nods to Bass. "I think Mr. Briggs can best explain that."

I eye Bass in confusion. He sits down on the bed next to me and puts a hand on the baby's head. "They thought she might need a blood transfusion, so they had to get her blood type."

"But she didn't get one, right?" I ask. "I mean, she's here and there aren't any tubes or wires."

"No, she didn't. But when they were preparing for it, they made a discovery."

"Bass, what are you trying to tell me? And why are *you* telling me instead of the doctor?"

"Eli was upstairs with us earlier when we were talking about the baby possibly needing a blood transfusion," he says. "He told the doctor your blood types."

"I'm B and he's AB," I tell them. "We had lots of tests after Dahlia was born."

"That's exactly what Eli said. But, sweetheart, when the baby's blood-type results came back, it said she's O-negative."

"Okay. What does that mean? Is that bad?"

"Ivy, that means Eli can't possibly be the father. But *I* can. I'm O-negative, too, just like she is."

I look down at the baby, then up at Bass, then over at the doctor. I'm not exactly sure what's happening here. "But … but they said she was conceived on Dahlia's birthday. That was two weeks before Bass and I …"

"That's why we call it an *estimated* date of conception, Ms. Greene," Dr. Moran says. "We go off the date of your last period."

"Which was always screwy," I add.

"And even if there were minor variances in the growth of the fetus, if you didn't voice any concerns over the EDC, then your doctor wouldn't have either."

I look up at Bass, my mind absorbing what they are telling me. "Oh my God, Bass, this means—" My lips press together as I try to hold back more tears. My heart just swelled so much, I think it might burst open. It's like every dream I had has just come true all at once.

Bass leans in and presses his forehead to mine. "This means she's *our* daughter, Ivy. And there's no way she has ARPKD."

"She doesn't have ARPKD," I repeat as if saying it again will make it more real. "And she's yours."

"She's mine," he says. "You both are."

He leans down and places a kiss on our daughter's head. Then he kisses *me.* He kisses me like I've wanted him to kiss me for months. And with his kiss, he tells me everything I need to hear. That he's with me. With *us*. Through thick and thin. For better or worse. That he's not going anywhere. Not ever again.

The doctor clears his throat from across the room, reminding us of his presence.

Bass pulls his lips away, but he doesn't let me go. "I love you, Ivy Greene."

"I love you, too, Sebastian Briggs."

We revel in our daughter as the doctor explains everything to me in detail. Then he exits the room, leaving the three of us alone for the first time.

"She looks like Dahlia," I say. "Except she has your nose."

"She looks like you," Bass says. "She's beautiful."

We bond for a few more minutes before a nurse comes in asking me if I want to try breastfeeding.

"More than anything," I tell her.

I didn't get to nurse Dahlia. She was too sick at first, so I pumped. And by the time we got her home, she just never took to the breast. So while she got the benefit of my breast milk, I never got to feel her nurse.

"Can you go tell my family?" I ask Bass. "I'm sure they are out there wondering what's up."

"You want *me* to tell them?" he asks.

I smile. "I can't think of a better way for you to meet my parents."

"I'd be happy to," he says, pulling up a chair next to the bed. "Right after I watch you feed our daughter."

~ ~ ~

The past twenty-four hours have been life-changing. I know a lot of people throw around that term like it's nothing, but in this case, it's true. I have a baby with Bass. A healthy baby. One who we can watch grow up and teach to play sports and travel with and give away at her wedding.

A tear travels down my cheek as I look down at my baby girl. "You would have loved your big sister. She would have taught you how to draw. She was so good at it. Someday, I'll show you her drawings."

Suddenly, a strange feeling comes over me. I think of the drawing on the wall at the shop. The one Dahlia made of a child being swung between two adults. The man in the picture, could it have been Bass? The child, was it *this* child?

"Could Dahlia have known?" I ask the baby.

She doesn't respond. She's asleep and her little mouth is puckered like she's nursing.

"Who are you talking to?" Eli asks, coming into the room.

"Nobody," I say.

He puts a vase of daisies on the side table, adding to the other flowers that are already there. I smile. He knows it's okay now. He knows I'm not afraid of daisies anymore.

I look at Eli, not sure if he's happy or sad.

"Are you … okay with this?" I ask.

"It's not like I have a choice in the matter, Ivy. He's her dad and that's a fact."

"I know, but I just want to make sure you're all right."

He sits down on the bed and kisses my cheek. "Ivy, you need to quit worrying so much about other people and take care of yourself for once. You have every reason to sit back and enjoy life. You deserve this. You deserve Bass. And, yes, I'm okay with this. I'll always love you, but I'm happy with how this worked out. You have a healthy baby. And I'm about to get married. Maybe I'll have a healthy baby sometime soon, too."

I put my arm around him and squeeze. "Thank you, Eli."

"Where is everyone?" he asks.

"At work mostly," I say. "Holly was with me all morning while Bass went home to shower and get a few things. But she went in to relieve Janie after lunch." I look at the clock. "I thought Bass would be back by now. He's been gone a while."

"You want me to stay?" he asks. "I could have someone cover my classes this afternoon."

"No. That's okay. I'm sure he'll be back any minute. I could probably use the peace and quiet after all the jabbering Holly was doing this morning. She made me go online and order a ton of baby stuff. Then she was figuring out where to put everything in our apartment."

"You don't have any baby stuff?"

I give him a look. "Of course not. I didn't want to jinx it."

He laughs. "I'm glad she made you do it, Ivy. Someone needs to whip your ass in gear since I'm not around to do it. So, you're not going to move in with Bass?"

I shrug. "I don't know. I mean, we haven't really talked about it."

"But you would, right? If he asked you?"

"Of course I would. But this was all so sudden, I'm not sure he will. I pushed him away for so long and now this. I love him, and he says he loves me, but he's probably still trying to catch his breath. I don't expect him to move both of us in with him at the drop of a hat."

"I think you underestimate him. I'm pretty sure we all did." He checks his watch. "Can I get you anything before I leave?"

I nod to the table. "My purse. Can you get my wallet out and bring it to me?"

He does what I ask, leaving it sitting on the bed next to me. Then he kisses me and walks out the door.

The baby squirms in my arms and opens her little eyes. I pick up my wallet and pull out a picture, holding it up for her to see. "This is your sister, Dahlia," I say. "She was beautiful, like you. You have a brother, too. But I don't have a picture of him. His name is Jonah." I cock my head to the side and study her for a second. "What's *your* name, little one?"

There's a knock on the door and then Bass comes in carrying two very large vases of flowers.

"How are my girls?" he asks.

All I can do is smile. *I'm* his girl. *She's* his girl.

Bass puts the vases down on the table. He leans down and plants a careful kiss on the baby's head and then a not-so-careful one on my lips.

"We haven't had much of a chance to talk, have we?" he says.

"No. I guess not. I'm sorry I fell asleep on you last night."

"I'll let it slide this one time considering the day you had yesterday."

I laugh. "Gee, thanks."

"What did you do all morning?" he asks. "I hope you weren't alone all day."

"Holly was here for a few hours and Eli just left."

"Are you expecting anyone else?"

I shake my head. "Not until after they get off work, why?"

"Good. I was hoping we could have a minute alone." He nods to the flowers he brought. They're daisies of course. "I brought two dozen," he says. "One is from me and the other is from Dahlia. I know she would want you to have them."

My eyes mist up. "Thank you. I was just introducing her to the baby."

"Do you mind?" he says, reaching out for our sleeping daughter.

"Take her," I say. "She's yours."

"Say it again," he says, looking at her beautiful face.

"She's yours," I say.

He closes his eyes as he cradles her. Then he puts her in the bassinet and sits on the bed. "Are you mine, too, Ivy Greene?"

I nod. "Yes."

He pulls the table with the flowers closer to me. "Can you guess which one is from me?" he asks, motioning to the two vases of flowers.

I eye him skeptically.

"You have to look closely," he says.

I let my eyes wander over the daisies in the vase on the right, not noticing anything that would give me the slightest clue. I look up at Bass.

"Keep looking," he says.

I look at the ones on the left. And then it catches my eye. One of the stems has a sparkle on it. Stems don't sparkle. I pull the vase closer and see the diamond ring.

My heart races as I turn to him, speechless.

"You don't have to say anything now," he says. "I mean, we haven't been together for a long time. I know this is sudden. And maybe a little crazy considering we were only ever together for a few weeks. But I want this more than anything. I want you. I want her. I want us to be a family. And crazy or not, it feels right."

I didn't think I had any more happy tears to cry. As they fall down my cheeks, I ask him, "What if I *do* have something to say now?"

"You do?" he asks. "I mean, you will?"

"Well, that depends. I'm not sure I know exactly what the question is," I tease.

He smiles. It's a smile I haven't seen since the day I got back from Hawaii. Then he pulls the flowers out of the vase and gets the ring off the stem. "Marry me, Ivy Greene. Marry me and I promise I'll make the two of you the happiest girls in the world. I promise never to let you forget to jump into puddles. I promise to take you to every waterfall we can find. I promise to help teach her how to make flower pancakes with fruit in the middle." He looks over at our daughter. "Marry me and I promise never to let our daughter forget that it was her sister who brought us together."

I wipe my tears, wanting to see him clearly when I say the words I've only said to him in my dreams. "Yes, Sebastian Briggs, I'll marry you."

"Yes!" He pops up off the bed and does a fist pump. "Sorry," he says, sitting back down to slip the ring on my finger.

He kisses me passionately, letting our tongues taste each other while giving me small glimpses of the possibilities that lie ahead. Possibilities I never thought existed. Possibilities that wouldn't have existed without him.

We pull apart when the baby starts to cry. Bass picks her up and places her in my arms. Then he walks over to open a curtain to let in the afternoon sun. On his way back to the bed, he looks around the room, noticing the daisies Eli brought. "Damn, I see someone beat me to the punch."

I laugh, admiring my ring. "Nobody beat you to *this* punch," I say. "Plus, I can never have too many daisies." I look down at the picture of Dahlia that still sits next to me on the bed. "Did I ever tell you what Dahlia said about daisies?"

"No."

"She used to say that daisies would make everything better." I smile as I remember. "Actually, she would say *'Daisies gonna make everything better.'* I didn't have the heart to correct her grammar."

Suddenly, my breath catches and my heart soars. I look at the flowers. I look at the picture of my first daughter. I think about her drawing on the wall at the shop. I look down at my new baby. And I know. I just know.

"Oh my God," I say to Bass. "She was right."

"Who was?" he asks, looking confused. "Dahlia?"

I nod, swallowing more tears. "Yes. She was right. Daisy's gonna make everything better." I look down at our miracle baby as I finally give her a proper greeting.

"Hello, Daisy."

EPILOGUE

SEBASTIAN

I lie here watching my beautiful bride sleep. It's one of my favorite things to do. She's completely at peace. I remember the days when she wasn't. Even after Daisy was born, Ivy would still have nightmares about her dying. For the first year of our daughter's life, my wife would go into Daisy's room and check on her—actually put a hand to her nose to make sure she was breathing.

I never said a word about it. It was Ivy's way of working through her demons.

Every time Daisy hit a major milestone, Ivy lightened up a little more. When she rolled over, I instantly saw Ivy's stress level go down. When she sat up, Ivy looked five years younger. And when Daisy took her first steps, which was the very same week she called Ivy '*Mommy*' for the first time, I think that was when I saw it with my own eyes, the final stages of healing.

Healing, however, doesn't mean forgetting. Ivy will never forget her first two children. She talks to us about them often. Daisy refers to them as '*Mommy's heaven babies.*'

Dahlia's artwork still remains on the wall at the flower shop. Her scrapbook still has a place of pride on Ivy's dresser. Photos of her are interspersed throughout our house along with family pictures of the three of us.

I look at one such photo on Ivy's nightstand, thinking of just how much Daisy looks like Dahlia. Like Ivy. I once asked Ivy's mom for a baby picture of her. I was stunned when I saw it. Ivy, Daisy, and Dahlia could have passed for triplets had they been the same age at the same time.

"Are you watching me sleep again?" Ivy says, rolling onto her side.

"Old habits are hard to break, sweetheart."

I tuck my arm behind her when she puts her head on my chest.

Her hand accidentally brushes against my morning erection. She looks up at me with raised brows. "Well, good morning."

I laugh. "Just how good are we talking?"

She eyes the clock. "Daisy won't be up for thirty minutes or so. I'm thinking that could make for a pretty good morning."

"Thirty minutes?" I say, as I wink at her. "I think we could make *two* good mornings in that time."

I watch as she shimmies out of her panties and then climbs on top of me. I pull her shirt up and over her head to reveal her glorious breasts. I take them in my hands. "Have I told you lately how much I love these?"

"Only about a thousand times."

I pinch her left nipple, the more sensitive one, and she moans as she squirms on top of me.

"One of these days, I'm going to get you to come just by playing with these."

She puts her hands on either side of me and leans over until she's almost kissing me. "But not today," she whispers into my mouth. "Today I want to feel you inside me."

"Anything you say, Mrs. Briggs."

I lean up on my elbows so she doesn't have to stoop over so far. I kiss her as my erection dances between us. I need to feel her with my hands, so I sit us up, her still straddling me as I work my boxer briefs off underneath her.

I reach around her and caress her silky-smooth behind as she undulates on top of me until I'm hard as steel. Then she lifts herself up and sinks down onto me. She looks into my eyes as I fill her up completely. She braces herself on the headboard and works up and down in slow, controlled motions.

I love it when she's on top. When I can see every nuance of her face as she makes love to me. For three years now, every time we make love, we watch each other. That is, unless she's on all fours, which admittedly, we've done a lot more of lately.

I palm her breasts, kneading them, molding them to my hands before I attack her nipples again. That's all it takes to make her throw her head back and scream.

I cup my hand over her mouth the best I can so she doesn't wake up Daisy. But it's hard to make any purposeful movements when I'm in the throes of orgasm myself.

Her climax lasts longer than mine and I have the pleasure of watching every exquisite moment of it.

She collapses onto my chest with a satisfied sigh.

That's when I feel it.

"Every time," she says, giggling into my shoulder.

I feel another jab. This time, I jab back. Then I push Ivy off my lap and onto the bed next to me. I lean down and talk to her belly.

"Listen in there, whatever your name is—you better start learning now that Mommy and I need alone time. Lots and lots of alone time. How else do you think we'll be able to give you and Daisy three or four more siblings?"

"Three or four?" Ivy says with wide eyes.

I run my finger down the side of her nose. "All the girls will have freckles. Just like you and Daisy."

She rubs her hands across her belly. "How about we just get through *this* one first?"

"Fine," I say, handing Ivy her shirt before I pull on my boxer briefs. It's the FDNY shirt she's always worn ever since we met in Hawaii. I've offered her a new one, but she'll have nothing to do with it. I reach into my nightstand and pull out the long list of possible baby names we started right after the ultrasound. And damn, who knew there were so many friggin' flowers? "So can we finally give her a name, please?"

"You know I don't want to jinx it," she says.

"Sweetheart, you have nothing to worry about." I put my hand on her seven-month belly and feel another kick from our baby girl.

This pregnancy is different from any of Ivy's others. Different because we're in love and married. Different because we know the baby won't have ARPKD. Different because we have a healthy, happy, three-year-old daughter whose existence reminds Ivy every day that there are good things in the world, not just bad.

And we've enjoyed every second of it. We've made so many plans. Bought so many things. Laughed so many times. But the one thing we haven't done is choose a name.

I give Ivy the list. "Come on, let's pick one. Right now. Just close your eyes and point to a name, and that will be the one."

She hesitates, but finally closes her eyes. Then I grab her hand and stop her.

"Wait. Don't pick Petunia," I say. "Or Lavender. Or Marigold. Crap, give me the list back."

I grab a pencil from the drawer and start crossing off names.

"Are we ever going to agree on a name?" she asks.

I throw the list on the floor and cage her to the bed. "You know what? I don't really care what her name is. Name her Petunia if you want. It won't stop me from loving her as much as I love you and Daisy."

"You love all of us so well, babe," she says with glassy eyes. "How did we ever get so lucky?"

Lucky. It's not a word that was even in her vocabulary for a good eight years of her life. But I know how she feels. I feel like I hit the jackpot with her. With *them*.

I reach over and grab my guitar from beside the bed. I play a soft tune for Ivy and the baby. Ivy says the baby stops moving every time I play, like she's listening to the music. I play the first song I ever composed for Ivy. I've composed about a hundred since then, but the first one remains her favorite.

When I'm done, she lays her head on my shoulder.

I lean down and place a kiss on the top of her head. "I'm the one who's lucky, Ivy Briggs."

She runs a hand across my jaw. "I love you, Sebastian."

I close my eyes and revel in her declaration. It's a miracle every time she says it. And I love how she says my name. She hardly ever calls me Bass anymore. And I'm okay with that. This woman could call me anything and I'd still come to her. She owns me. She rules me. Well, she and the pint-sized mini-Ivy in the next room.

As if Daisy hears me thinking of her, she comes bursting through the door and up onto the bed. She has a drawing with her. Like Dahlia did, Daisy loves to learn about flowers and draw pictures of them.

"Hey, pumpkin," I say, lifting her high above me on the bed as she squeals in delight.

"Hi, Daddy. I made you and Mommy a picture." She turns to Ivy. "Can we hang it on the wall at the shop? Please, Mommy, can we?"

"Of course we can," Ivy says. She reaches her hand out for the drawing, but Daisy tries to play keep-away with it and Ivy ends up with a paper cut on her finger.

"Oh, shoot," Ivy says, putting her finger in her mouth to suck on it.

"I'm sorry, Mommy," Daisy says, giving her a hug.

"It's not your fault, baby. It's just a little paper cut." Ivy shows Daisy her finger. "See, it's not even bleeding."

Daisy holds out the drawing to her. "Here, Mommy. You can have this. Flowers gonna make it better. Flowers make everything better. Especially lilies. I like the stick thingies in the middle."

Ivy looks up at me, covering her mouth in surprise. Then she asks Daisy, "Baby, what did you just say?"

"The stick thingies," Daisy says, pointing at her picture. "Right there."

"No, what did you say before that?"

Daisy shrugs and goes back to mumbling about her drawing.

I scoot next to Ivy. "You heard her," I say, knowing we're thinking the very same thing. "She said flowers make everything better. Especially lilies."

Her eyes tear up and she grabs my hand. "Lily's gonna make everything better?" she asks.

Ivy looks at me. I look at her. We both look down at her belly. And then we smile.

Stay tuned for the next book in The Men On Fire Series.

SPARKING SARA

ACKNOWLEDGMENTS

Even as I write this, I'm thinking, *thirteen?* This is my *thirteenth* book – how did that happen? And yet I'm so excited for the day when I can say I've just written my thirtieth! Lucky for me, writing today is just as satisfying as it was five years ago. Even more so, because now I get to interact with so many new people around the world.

Igniting Ivy was a difficult book to write. There was so much loss involved. Loss that I know many of my readers have experienced firsthand. To compare my fictional character's lives to theirs is neither fair nor possible so I won't even try.

There are so many people to thank, I don't know where to begin.

I know so little about firefighting that it took a village to educate me. First and foremost, I must thank Thomas Butler, former FDNY firefighter. The information he provided me will help tremendously with all three books in this series. Thank you to Tina Lynn McCain, Rusty Henry, and Rick Martin for sharing your expertise as well.

Shout-outs to my medical guru, Dr. Brandon Crawford, and my legal expert, J.D. Steele, are also in order.

To my tireless editors, Ann Peters and Jeannie Hinkle, I appreciate you so very much. Thank you to Emily at Murphy Rae Solutions for your copy editing. To my beta readers, Tammy Dixon, Shauna Salley, Joelle Yates, and Laura Conley – your keen eyes and suggestions helped make this book ready for publication.

Finally, a big thank you to Elizabeth Harris, a member of my private reader group and former resident of Hawaii. Elizabeth told me all the wonderful things I needed to do during my visit to Kauai last year. Most of them made it into this book. Mahalo!

About the author

Samantha Christy's passion for writing started long before her first novel was published. Graduating from the University of Nebraska with a degree in Criminal Justice, she held the title of Computer Systems Analyst for The Supreme Court of Wisconsin and several major universities around the United States. Raised mainly in Indianapolis, she holds the Midwest and its homegrown values dear to her heart and upon the birth of her third child devoted herself to raising her family full time. While it took time to get from there to here, writing has remained her utmost passion and being a stay-at-home mom facilitated her ability to follow that dream. When she is not writing, she keeps busy cruising to every Caribbean island where ships sail. Samantha Christy currently resides in St. Augustine, Florida with her husband and four children.

You can reach Samantha Christy at any of these wonderful places:

Website: www.samanthachristy.com

Facebook: https://www.facebook.com/SamanthaChristyAuthor

Twitter: @SamLoves2Write

E-mail: samanthachristy@comcast.net

Made in the USA
Monee, IL
11 January 2025